THE

····················

CROSSING

····················

GUARD

THE

CROSSING

GUARD

DAVID RABE

Based on the Motion Picture

written by Sean Penn

MIRAMAX
B O O K S

HYPERION

NEW YORK

Library of Congress Cataloging-In-Publication Data
Rabe, David.
The crossing guard / by David Rabe; based on
a screenplay by Sean Penn.
p. cm.
ISBN 0-7868-6119-3
I. Penn, Sean, 1960– . II. Title.
PS3568.A23C76 1995
813'.54—dc20   94-35012
CIP

FIRST EDITION
10 9 8 7 6 5 4 3 2 1

For Jason, Lily, Michael, Dylan, and Hopper.

Thanks to Sean Penn for the script, the invitation, and the license. To Lily for her input in Chapter Nine. To Vane Lashua. To Deborah Schneider for assistance above and beyond. To Scott Greenstein, Francesca Gonshaw and Lesley Bryce for crucial help along the way. To the staff at Hyperion. To Jason for some lyrics and Michael for some stuff.

INTRODUCTION

Sometime between the contract signing and pre-production on the movie of my screenplay "The Crossing Guard," Miramax Films' chairman, Harvey Weinstein, asked me a question: "Who do you want to write the *novel*?" "Novelization?" I corrected him. "No", he said. "Novel. We're trying something new with Miramax Books. . . ." he went on. They wanted to put out books from screenplays that were a cut above those silly "take it off the screen and put a man with a gun on the cover" familiar market reads. It was a simple idea: Get a great writer and let him "rock" with the story, the characters, and a bit of the dialogue, but ultimately free him from the restrictions of the screenplay or the film. Needless to say, the "simple" part of this idea was not in finding the great writer. The short list would be strongly inhibited by the stigma of the source material and the old form "novelization." Immediately my parallel synapses of wicked egocentricity and a tiny portion of unorchestrated humility collided. To our tremendous fortune, it was orchestrated humility that won out. The words spilled like warm honey out of my mouth: "Well . . . He'd never do it . . . but in a dream . . . how about David Rabe?"

Rabe had been a long-time friend of mine, and I an even longer-time fan of Rabe, the playwright. We'd orginally known each other from the bars in New York, but later he directed me in three of his plays—*Goose* and *Tom-Tom* in New York, and *Hurly-Burly* in Los Angeles. "I'll call him," Weinstein said. I thought, you will? What insult had I appointed my old friend, collaborator, mentor? Would Weinstein say *novel* to him?

Weinstein would. I got "the Rabe call." "The Rabe call," for the unfamiliar reader, is usually received in the early morning, West Coast hours. It is sent however, from the East Coast, oh, about the time one would be dry from their after-breakfast shower. The mastery of "the Rabe call" is for the comfortable and well-slept *caller* to out-groan his sleepy counterpart immediately upon contact:

> PENN
> (groggy or hungover)
> Hell-o?

> RABE
> (rested, but like a dying cow)
> Ahh . . . (deep sigh) . . . Sean . . . ?

The King of Angst was calling.

> PENN
> David.

> RABE
> (Sigh)

> PENN
> David?

> RABE
> Hi . . .

It is at this point that the masterstroke occurs. It is now clear to the receiver of the call that it is upon him to begin the conversation . . . and I did:

> PENN
> Did those Miramax guys call you?

A Beat.

RABE

They did.

PENN

I can't believe these guys.
They asked me who I'd like to do it
and I said, you know . . . In a dream?
You know . . . you.

RABE

I think it'll be fun.

PENN

Who is this?!

It was Rabe. I've not yet asked if he had fun, but he's written an astonishing novel.

Thank you, David,

Sean Penn

THE

....

CROSSING

....

GUARD

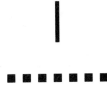

Misery, Mary thought. Mrs. Tennov was a hazy figure, a smear of ochre Kmart slacks, the product of synthetic fabrics and cheap labor topped by a yellow sweater strewn with embroidered roses like bruises across the collapse of her somewhat asymmetrical breasts. The bulge of her middle stretched the seams on her hips and crotch, the outline of the pockets stressed into scars threatening to open up. Mary could imagine Mrs. Tennov in a sudden disintegrating melee, a disruption of parts. They were all barely intact, having been repaired, having been sutured and clamped. But the stitches didn't always hold.

Her thoughts, along with her glance, expanded to take in the room of more than a hundred people seated on tiers of benches like spectators at an entertainment. The central event was a long table where the newest arrivals were packed around the evening's moderator, Dr. Glazier. Closing her eyes, Mary felt she could hear their functioning bodies, their shifting thoughts, the whir of organs beneath their actual speech.

Three years ago, Tommy Tennov ran around the front of his halted school bus. The onrushing LTD, speeding at an estimated sixty miles per hour on the little back road, plucked Tommy out of both shoes and left shreds of his jeans, along with blood and skin, imprinted into the grill. Thirteen years old, the boy had been escaping from a game of punching—last punch wins. The game had been going on for most of the bus ride home, and so the competitive level was high. Normally responsible when stepping into the street, Tommy knew to look both ways. But given the flashing red stop lights whose alternation he could hear clicking, given the conspicuous STOP sign sticking out from the side of the bus, he must have felt safe. He did this every day. The traffic was always obedient, cars and trucks lining up dutifully at either end of the bus. So he let the game take him over, punching a friend and ducking the outstretched paw of a pursuer.

Glass from the headlight splattered into his belly like shrapnel. The frame that buttressed the fender mangled his hip and buttocks. But it was the impact against the stone wall bounding the road that ended his thirty-foot airborne wail. Brain matter and bone fragments littered the roadside. One of the stones turned pinkish like the interior of a melon. The driver, a twenty-nine-year-old former Radio Shack salesman, had been fired that morning for drinking on the job. With a blood alcohol count twice the legal limit, he'd been curled on his side across the front seat as he groped the floor for a mishandled Bruce Springsteen tape, *Tunnel of Love*. A sensation of impact was his only clue. "I looked away for just the littlest second," he told the first police officer to arrive on the scene. "I stopped to help. That's why I stopped. I didn't even know I was involved."

Misery, thought Mary. That was what they had in common. Misery and bewilderment and coming here. Mr. Hammond, dapper and reasonable, sat a few rows in front of her. She was familiar with his pain just as she knew her own and that of Mr. Hazen, a large African American who occupied the seat beside her.

Mr. Hazen's fleshy cheeks began a pattern that the rest of his body followed in waves to his robust belly. He was a garbage collector, who came to each meeting freshly showered, emitting a halo of deodorant and wearing one of a pair of suits, their cut identical, one a blue verging on black, the other gray. Tonight he wore the gray. He seemed to have four ties. Tonight's was the more subdued of the quartet. His sixteen-year-old son, Oxford, had been picked up by a man fleeing arrest for failure to pay child support in Nevada. It was not Oxford Hazen's practice to hitchhike, but he was late for school. In fact, he was just jogging along the roadside in order to get to school as quickly as possible when the Jeep Cherokee, driven by Dwayne Values, pulled over and Dwayne asked if he could help. Once in the vehicle, Oxford knew he was in trouble. Dwayne jumped them up to seventy in a forty-mile zone, and he was talking just as fast.

Mr. Hazen had learned of these events from Oxford as the boy managed a half day of lucidity in the hospital bed in which he died the following morning. Sometimes Mr. Hazen obsessively described the electronic beeping on a screen above the bed where the angular line full of jumps and squiggles leveled out and fled with his son's life.

For Oxford, it had been important to make clear the fact that he had not been disobeying his father's orders against hitchhiking. When the Cherokee started to take corners on two wheels, he had demanded that he be let out. He'd shouted that they'd missed his stop. Dwayne Values, chugging Heaven Hill bourbon from a nearly empty quart bottle, had declared that he would turn around then and back up. He wanted to be of help. He wanted to do right. He bellowed about a need to make recompense for sins committed against Oxford and his kind all over the states of Texas, Oklahoma, and Nevada. He declared himself a former racist who, through the travails of divorce and its subsequent misery, had been made human. Tilting with the overwhelming sincerity that this declaration aroused in him, he tried to pat Oxford's cheek and rub his hair. When Oxford ducked, Values lunged and dropped the bottle. "Pick it up now," he screamed. "It's gonna spill!"

The road turned, but Values was too busy rescuing the bourbon. They smashed into a stand of palm trees and ricochetted broadside into an Impala parked in a driveway. The Impala skidded, then flipped over and ended up wedged against the garage. Values, spraying blood and spilling organs, died in the area compressed to nothing between the dislodged engine and the collapsing chest of Oxford Hazen.

Every once in a while, Mr. Hazen retold the story, laying out the details from start to finish. Each time was oddly verbatim, as if he were delivering a memorized speech in a tone that suggested thoughtful research. Earlier tonight, when he'd stood to take the floor at the start of the evening, Mary had attended him closely, meeting his eyes with a sympathetic interest, not wanting to be rude, but her mind wandered. Every now and then she returned to him, visiting one sad point or another. As always, he ended with a puzzled sigh and a waggle of his head as he found himself unable to alter the bitter facts and ironies of his loss.

Richard Hammond was tall and groomed. He liked trendy suits tailored to his well-exercised physique. His taste in ties was exquisite, while his attraction to tasseled loafers made Mary want to take him aside and give him advice. He was a venture capitalist, whose wife had died in a head-on collision with a pickup truck exiting a San Diego Freeway entrance ramp. The driver, a recently retired Army sergeant with rifles in the rack, dead birds in bags in the rear, and six packs of Pabst strewn all over the cab, had wept when he testified that he was just trying to get home fast; he was alone and he had to pee.

As she scanned the tiers of seats around her, she decided that the fate of the dark-haired girl with the pouty lips who'd lost her mother was simple. Soon, almost against her will, she would recover. The distracted Mexican woman was probably praying. Mrs. Tennov was still talking. An array of arthritic knots and tangled emotions, she was telling how the sight of a boy who resembled Tommy in a shopping mall had left her sleepless for the last three nights. Mary sighed and closed her eyes, listening the way she might to the rushing of a creek. The Styrofoam cup in her grasp gave up rhythmic squeals in response to the scraping of the nail of her forefinger. It was the only flaw in her otherwise perfect stillness, her willed stoicism. A downward glance showed her the chemical white of the cup through the last quarter inch of cold black coffee.

Everyone in this room had lost someone to a drunk driver. The second African American, a sturdy square of a man whose name she couldn't remember, sat glaring in a blue athletic jacket. She couldn't tell for sure, but it appeared that he was fixated on the slightly overweight woman wearing the dark suit and the necklace of pearls, her short-cropped hair combining with the vaguely unfinished cast of her mouth to create an impression of prissy condescension. She was a recent arrival, having lost her husband just a few weeks ago. She was probably still in shock.

They were a tidepool of suffering, a coffee-klatch talking over mayhem. Sometimes Mr. Hazen took refuge in religious platitudes. He would rise and clear his throat and then ramble on for a while, making do with volume and vocal resonance until he found a phrase that rang in him. Then he would grow impassioned, seeking to share the power and comfort he had found by stirring a similar chord in the hearts of his listeners. In such moments, Mary imagined he was imitating the preacher she was sure he listened to each Sunday.

By now Mrs. Tennov had concluded, and Mr. Hammond was raising his lean length. He snugged up his tie, then brushed the wings of his suit coat straight. He shoved one hand in his pocket and, after a practiced pause, he reported on the value he'd found in pouring every spare minute into the political, legislative aspect of the problem. He wanted them all to know how much it helped to feel you were doing something about the scum on the roads by organizing and lobbying for tougher, more punitive laws to deal with drunk drivers. Especially the repeat offenders. He had a grass-roots organization with secretaries in his offices volunteering time. Anyone who wanted to participate in what he was doing was welcome. There were fliers by the door.

Mary never said much anymore. Long ago, she had talked a lot. Now she often had a hard time listening. But she continued to attend for reasons she couldn't state. Not that an explanation was required. She always left home on the spur of the moment, telling herself that she might not come next time. That she might get up and leave at any moment, though she arrived early and stayed until the end. They comforted her somehow. That was the sad part. They were a kind of lullaby, these tales of drunks and the way they managed, with a brutal and amazing inventiveness, to end up behind the wheels of an ever-expanding horde of cars poured off assembly lines, or raced out of used car lots. All glamorously christened with sexy names like Lumina, Monte Carlo, Corolla, Seville, Eldorado, Fleetwood. There were Legends, Lexes, Impalas, Mustangs, Saturns, Thunderbirds, Supremes, Jaguars. At enormous speeds, drunks careened about sowing disasters, each one a dreary repetition of all its predecessors at the same time that it left behind a fresh and peerless grief.

"I miss me," someone said. Mary hadn't spoken, yet she felt exposed. Her aroused interest focused on a blondish man in Levis, a white T-shirt, and suede jacket. He was seated at the table. His hair lay in wavy clumps, the original brown touched with a spattering of gray. While seated more or less straight, he managed to convey a hobbled impression. His voice arose from a confounded place, each word weighted with incomprehension, as if he had just discovered it in his mouth. Each breath and gesture reflected the existence of something hidden breaking apart, leaving only these random shards to go by, an inchoate ache beginning to fill the room.

"It's five years now, see? I look in the mirror—Where's Bobby? I don't know. I guess Bobby couldn't take it. No way. Just no way. I went on, I thought. Just went on. Until I realized I wasn't what I used to be anymore—what I was before, I mean. I was gone. Or something. So here I am—the same face—but no Bobby. The rest of my family are driving me up the fucking wall. I guess to them I am still the same guy, the very same me—the very same Bobby I always was. I don't mean that they haven't noticed that I changed. That's not what I mean."

He laughed. Before the sound emerged, a kind of spasm pushed his head back with a sense that something was hurting him, and then he laughed. He took a sampling of the faces around him. To Mary, he appeared worried about violating a protocol he didn't believe in, but lacked the will to assault. "They joke about it. It's a joke to them somehow," he said. "My brothers call me 'sibling number three.' Some kind of nickname for what I have become— which in their eyes is 'Bobby Depressed.' That's what I finally realized. Fuck them. Do I call them names? The thing is, I am sibling number four, see. It was my oldest brother Danny—he's the one we lost. All boys. Four of us. Four boys. In the family. He was number one. I was four. First and last. I'm still four. I'm not three. They shouldn't call me 'three,' I don't think. Maybe I'll bring one of them here. I should have brought one of them here. With me. To ask them. Did they forget that? Did they forget about number one? I don't know. That's what I'm saying. I don't know.

"So I'm here. And what I am doing is—I think I am looking for the pain. Or so I am told—that's what this therapist said, and he's smart, I guess, and it seems to be what some of you here are saying. That if I find the pain, I will find me. Does that mean . . . what? I mean, it sounds like it means I have become pain and I have fled. I sort of feel good riddance if that's the case. But I'm here. Because of something, and I don't know why exactly—I don't even really want to ask why. Why is like a question with no real answer, even though we ask it. We ask it even when we know we shouldn't, when we know there is no answer. Why? See. See how it works? See? Why?

"But still I'm here. I got in my car and I sat there and then I drove over. Is that good? Is that brave? See? That's what I'm asking. Who's to say? Now what?"

His head jerked back again, only this time he stood without a sound. Mary was staring at him. Around him was an aura she couldn't identify, though she felt it, and then she thought she recognized it: Expectation. But she didn't know whose. Was it his or her own? His tilted head angled the oval softness of his face toward the ceiling. "So who's running the show?" he said.

She blinked, waiting, and this time the expectation was clearly her own. When he started to look around, his gaze scanning the crowd, she worried that he had felt her interest and he was searching for her. She couldn't tell for sure because he was thirty or forty feet away, but he appeared to stare at her, and his expression flickered with a questioning awareness that could have resulted from contact between them. She recoiled. She saw the Mexican woman, her lips moving in prayer. Watching that fishlike fidget of soundless words, Mary lifted the cup to her mouth and drained the last of her cold coffee. Her finger, with a jagged squeak, knifed through the Styrofoam.

Driving home, she veered off course, entering a poor neighborhood of adobe houses and apartment buildings set on paltry plots giving way to frame and brick residences with manicured lawns in geometrical rows. She continued on through their calmness and civility, until she came to the corner where her daughter had been run down. She eased to the curb and shut off the engine.

Before her lay the intersection. Nearby she saw the schoolyard. Though the hour was late and the moon only half full, she could hear the *splat-splat* of a basketball on the outdoor court adjacent to the low brick building. The player was a solitary flash of white T-shirt and pattering feet interrupted by periodic silences as he left the ground to shoot.

With only a little effort, the surrounding scene could be imagined as a memorial, the stillness reverential, the lace of palm fronds and their fragmented shadows transformed into a flowery but spectral tribute. Classical music, a muffled complexity of stringed instruments, emerged through the walls of a nearby house. She hadn't been back here for nearly a year. The spot where the auto had roared out of the afternoon to collide with Emily was nondescript. Nothing identified it as distinct in any way from the rest of the concrete whose gray-bellied surface rolled between the curbs.

Suddenly, the music swelled, identifying its source as the house immediately to her right. Either the volume had been turned up or a window opened. Whatever the cause, the result was that the thoughtful richness of those notes was forced to contend with the contamination of television sitcom babble. She hadn't really absorbed it before, but every twenty or thirty seconds there was the jarring pulse of artificial laughter, suggesting that a number of the houses were tuned to the same channel. The high-pitched cackle made her think of Freddy, her ex-husband. She wondered what show these people were all watching and was Freddy off somewhere watching it, too? Her taste for classical music had been at war with his television habits when they lived in a small apartment during the first years of their marriage. Once they managed to move into a house, the additional space allowed for the conflict to recede somewhat, though Mary was dictatorial about limiting Emily's access to shows and tapes.

At the sound of a door slamming, she looked around but couldn't tell where the noise had come from. Feeling edgy, she decided to leave, starting the engine. She didn't want to arrive home late and have to explain to Roger, her new husband of three years, where she had been.

Slipping the gearshift into drive, she checked the road behind her and pressed the gas. The advance of the car brought her a sensation of violence, its moving tonnage seeming to crush something invisible in the air, and she felt an icy chill. With her heart in a clamor, she jammed on the brakes.

Her throat straining, she looked out, but there was nothing there. In the nearest of the houses, the figure of a man passed the window and then returned to lower the blinds. Above her, the moon was a mercurial clot buried in the larger surrounding leaden haze. Along the sidewalk, the basketball player approached, a pale lanky shape in shorts and T-shirt, the sphere of the ball bulging out from his hip where he held it in the arc of his arm. The delicate music still played. Then the sitcom laughter leaped at her. She saw a flash of electric light as the door to one of the houses opened.

She felt compelled to look at the area where her wheels had stopped. She was climbing out as the basketball player strode past, barely glancing at her. With one hand on the fender, she leaned over the front of the car and surveyed the curb and pavement. There were twigs, a scrap of newspaper. Weeds sprouted through several large cracks.

"Car trouble?" said the man who had come down the walkway from the house. He was trailed by a small dog on a leash, a breed of spaniel edging up to sniff Mary's leg. The man tugged the dog back. "You having car trouble?"

"No," she said.

He was in his fifties, a mass of pinkish skin, and she could see his wide, civil eyes trying to suppress the suspicion her being in front of his house had aroused. "You don't live around here, do you?"

She wanted to help him out of the discomfort he felt over not being fully hospitable. "No," she said, searching for a simple lie. "No, no. We're just—I mean, we're thinking of moving—my husband and I, and the kids. I was just sort of checking out different neighborhoods. Driving around."

"Oh."

"I just drive around looking. Like a scout. You know." She smiled.

"Oh. Well, we like it here," said the man, as the dog flopped at his feet. "We've been here almost thirty years."

"Really." She could see how her lie appealed to him, how it flattered him.

"Raised four kids," he told her. "Every one of them a winner. They're gone now. All of them. Two away in college in the Midwest. The older two are married. Going to be a grandpa soon."

"Congratulations," she said, noticing how the dog was preoccupied with something down the street.

"I don't know what I did to be congratulated," the man said, "but I'll accept. Not much coming my way these days."

She wondered how he would respond to the truth about the loss that lay behind her visit. He probably knew about the accident, living here that long. Why didn't he tell the stranger he took her for that a little girl died on this exact corner in his precious neighborhood? What would he say if she told him? If she said, "My daughter was killed right over there." Most people had a stock portrayal of compassion they served up when faced with the unhappiness of strangers.

"It's a great little area," he said. The dog was snorting and rising.

"I just thought I'd stop, you know." She smiled again.

"Well, it's certainly a pleasant evening." The agitated dog was straining at the leash. "I better let Mac here have his walk," the man shrugged, drifting a step to his left before striding off.

The moon slipped some inhibition, sharpening the outline of the nearest live oak. She returned to her car, entering carefully, as if wary of making a loud noise. She reached to the ignition and gave the key a turn. With the engine humming, she started forward, and, like a drafty old house, the car filled with a wintry chill.

No, no, she thought, keeping her foot to the gas, her heart locked in a harsh contraction. There was nothing there. Emily was gone. She couldn't run over Emily. Emily was dead.

2

■ ■ ■ ■ ■ ■ ■

For the longest time I awaited rescue, said Emily to her sleeping father, whispering at a point deep and hidden inside him. *I listened to the water falling past and imagined it would end. I thought that you would come to get me. Or if not you then someone—one of the many who loved me would come. The dark never changed; it had a texture, a color, a mood. Still I convinced myself that it wasn't something unfamiliar—not really all that different from the dark of my room when I was at home in bed, my clean sheets printed with daisies, my bedspread of Disney characters—Goofy playing baseball, Goofy on a scooter, the Donald Duck family cavorting in a red jalopy. On the wall were my posters of WHERE'S WALDO? along with CINDERELLA framed and hung near the pictures of the swans and the puppies and Mommy and Daddy and Grandpa and Grandma in matching frames on my bookcase. Even then I would still get scared sometimes, laying with Jasmine and Lucinda and Samantha, my dolls, and Roscoe the stuffed monkey, and Puzzle the giraffe. Alone at night in the dark, my ears would get as alert as the ears of the puppy-dog-I-wanted-but-didn't-have listening to a spooky noise. Even the shadows could breathe and fill with mean desires. Scary things hid in the walls, in the closet, the monster waiting for me to go to sleep. Because in sleep I wouldn't be able to protect myself or even to scream if I wanted.*

Every story of danger I'd ever been told, or had read to me, every movie or TV show I'd ever seen—all of them ended in rescue. And so for the longest time I kept remembering them. I played and replayed all the tales I knew of little girls, of dogs, of bears, of grown men and women saved from the path of onrushing trains or arrows—stories of broken falls, of leaping cowboys, firemen, soldiers, police—stories of resuscitation and release, of the last-second arrival of goodness.

But now with so many minutes like hours, and days like weeks, and months like years, and years like centuries gathering and thickening upon me, I am afraid that there is no advance in this night, no end to this dark, that there is no exit, no antidote, no nemesis. I have begun to fear, Daddy, that once death has you it holds on. I have begun to fear, Daddy, Poppa, Honey-man, that you will not come for me, that I will not escape, that death is forever.

"You're snoring," she said.

Freddy heard her and felt bad. Peering up through a bubbly, staticky blur, he tried to reach out to her. The effort was daunting, but he kept at it, parting a barrier stinking of bourbon and cigarettes, as he rose through the rubbish of his own consciousness until he saw the sad oval of her face inches from his own.

"What?" he said.

"You were snoring. Real loud."

He felt miserable, as if he had agreed to save her and then failed to do it. He wanted to make amends, and he patted her arm. "I'm sorry," he said.

"If you roll over, sometimes it helps."

"Was it loud?"

"Yeah. And you made these other noises, too."

"God, did I? Jeez, I'm sorry."

"It's okay."

His sense of being at fault worsened as he realized he couldn't remember her name. "God," he groaned.

"It's okay."

"No, no," he said.

"It wasn't that bad. You were dreaming, I think."

"No, I don't think so. Was I?"

"Mmmmmhhmmmmmm."

His hands fell over his eyes. It was the gesture of a man whose thoughts had reached an unmanageable density. "What the hell is wrong with me?" he said.

"Yeah," she said, giggling. "Dreaming and snoring. What a terrible guy."

It was just then, as he leaned and met her eyes, a whiff of meatballs or something escaping the slight part of her lips, that he realized what day it was. Or what day it would be when morning arrived. The thought catapulted him out of the room. For a second, he didn't know where he was.

"Should I brush my teeth?" she asked, and when he didn't answer, she nudged him and said, "What's up?"

He was staring, as if the ceiling were of sudden startling interest. He wasn't really thinking about her. Still he spoke aloud, asking, "What time is it?"

"I don't know. But it's too dark to get up. See how dark it is. The window is all dark. There's time to sleep. I'm still very sleepy, okay, Freddy."

She patted his leg, a feathery stroking that ended with her fingers falling one by one near his knee. As she rotated onto her side, turning her face toward him, he felt the heat of her snuggling nearer, her breasts cradling his arm, her pubic hair a mist against his thigh.

"Sure," he said.

"You're fun," she told him.

He chuckled, trying to remember her name. Fun, he thought. He doubted it. "Well, maybe."

"Sure."

"Sometimes."

"That's what I mean."

He decided not to say anything more and seconds later she was asleep.

Alone, Freddy lay in a whirlwind, wondering if he might find a way to neutralize the more disturbing of his impulses and ideas, so that he could manage just a little more sleep. This was what he'd had to do last night, too, and then, apparently, it had worked. He'd brought her along to help him get to sleep. Wanting to escape from the shadows of what this morning would bring, he had tried to dive into her, grabbing and squeezing and sucking and humping away.

But for the most part he'd been unable to really think about her. Not that she seemed to notice. Habit and his body had taken care of things. She'd slipped from orgasm to sleep with hardly a hint of the difference. Just as she had a moment ago, talking on one breath and leaving the conversation on the next.

It was quite a job, this effort at sorting. He kept seeing John Booth. Over and over. John Booth. The time had come, but Freddy wasn't quite ready. He was a little hungover, his head like a plane of cracked glass. He needed a few minutes more sleep. But his thoughts didn't give a shit about his needs at the moment. They were insistent about their own priorities, and struggling against them was not a calming experience. And now on top of everything else, he had to pee.

Starting to rise, he was reminded of Mia's presence by her enveloping warmth. That was her name. Mia. He'd known it all along. He got to his feet, determined not to disturb her. Halfway across the room, he looked back. The peace of her slumber struck him as something he could take credit for, as if the trust that allowed her to sleep so deeply in this shadowy room was a result of his proximity. He went back and looked down at her, wanting to guarantee that she would be able to sleep peacefully, trustingly, as long as she wanted.

In the bathroom, he raised the lid before starting to pee. The mirror threw him a sidelong flash of his own pale nakedness as he flushed and turned to leave. The image tugged at him, delaying him for a second. When he moved on, something seemed to tear loose.

By the time he climbed back in bed, his eyes were big and the possibility of sleep had sailed off for good. Looking at the window, he saw sunrise edging the drawn shades, light seeping into the room. He started running a preview of the coming day, as if it were his to arrange: he saw the bustling traffic, the first few cars growing into a belligerent herd that jammed the streets. He imagined the city rising and entering this day, just as he was about to do, all kinds of people climbing from their beds and walking around, derelicts in rags mixing with the more responsible and more fortunate citizens getting on and off buses and in and out of cars, as they clutched their cellular phones or lunch buckets and sipped their coffee from cardboard containers and hustled about, making plans, calculating, anticipating what they were going to buy, who they were going meet and convince, or trick. Who they were going to align with. Or defeat. Or kill. It was an odd, intriguing thought, but it had to be true. He wasn't the only one who, by the end of the day, would have killed someone.

Now the escalating light revealed the telephone on a nearby table. Some magazines by the window came into view, followed by the glitzy blue vinyl material that hung on the wall in a huge rectangle above his bed. The light moved over the floor and across the ceiling, and even though he knew what was coming, because after all it was his apartment, he found himself watching in a state of genuine suspense as a blur beside the refrigerator began to evolve, turning into a colorful calendar. The image of a woman spilled into view. Naked from the waist up, her butt cheeks overflowed the frayed ends of her cutoff jeans. With her back to Freddy, the definition of her spine pushed through the gloss of her skin, a nub of breast available around the edge of her ribs, as she arched to peek over her shoulder, a band of hair caught in her mouth. Large block letters identified the month as October. Blots of black Magic Marker obliterated the numbers of the days from the first through the seventeenth. The eighteenth was outlined in an emphatic red.

When he'd started his tally, there had been thousands of days to contend with. Calendar after calendar purchased and marked and stored in the closet along with a growing pile of legal documents and newspaper clippings, as he attempted to possess the multitude of days that stood between where he waited and that one day, that single day that lay somewhere ahead. At first, there had been uncertainty about the amount of time he was dealing with. But then after the legal bullshit had run its course, the hearings and trial and sentencing and appeals, it had become clear that John Booth would spend in the vicinity of eight years in prison for having run down and killed Freddy's daughter. A few months ago, as was his right through the victim's notification provision, Freddy had learned the exact release date. He could remember a day when the intervening years had appeared a barrier as gigantic and formidable as a mountain. But now the crags and cliffs had disappeared. Of that seemingly limitless bulwark, there remained nothing. John Booth, the drunk who had run his daughter down, was getting out of prison today.

He sat up. His hand fell to Mia, and he shook her. She responded, blinking, rubbing her eyes. "Hi."

"You oughta go."

"Huh?"

"You should go." The motion of his hand on her shoulder was gentle but insistent, "Go. You should go."

"Go?" Pawing at the mattress in order to rise, she sank back as if the bed were mud.

"You oughta go," he said again.

Sleep seemed to have turned English into a foreign language she didn't understand. "What, Freddy?"

"Mia, c'mon."

"You want me to go?"

"Yes."

He could feel her gaze registering the facts of the morning, his apparent rejection of her the most perplexing among them. "Go on, Mia, okay?" Filling with a bleary sadness, her eyes persisted to press him with a mute version of the same question she had already asked. "I'm serious," he said. "It's time to go."

"Can I use your shower?"

"Help yourself."

"Glass of water?"

"What?"

"Can I have a glass of water?"

"What are you asking me? Why are you asking me that?"

"Because I'm thirsty, Freddy."

"Of course you can have a glass of water. What do you think I would say? 'No. No, you can't have a glass of water.' Of course, you can have a glass of water. There's a glass by the sink."

"You told me I should go."

"There's a glass by the sink."

"I thought maybe you were mad at me. So you were being a prick. Telling me I should go."

When she arrived at the bathroom door, she stopped and turned to look at him. Daylight washed over her from the side. The soft swell of her hips curved away into the fall of her legs. She threw the bathroom wall switch and a flickering halo arose behind her. It was unexpected, the desire he felt, the charge of emotion almost electric in the way that it hooked him to her. This was not what he wanted right now; it was not at all what he needed.

"Hurry up," he said to her, feeling that her presence was going to make him foul up when he could least afford it. He was pacing at the edge of uncharted territory full of high-voltage demands.

"What?"

"You gotta get goin', Mia."

"You were lookin' at me. You were lookin' at me, Freddy."

"Yeah," he said. "I know." He turned away and lit up a cigarette from the pack on the bedside table. As he inhaled, he heard the bathroom door shut behind him. She must have stood there waiting. He padded over to where his underwear and trousers lay on the floor and pulled them on. Anxiety was a coldness in his guts, like tiny ice cubes filling him. Faced with the arrival of a moment he'd been waiting for, he couldn't quite recognize the fact that it was here. Nothing in the quality of the light, or the way he had to take another piss, nothing in the tousled bed sheets or the familiar rug under his feet betrayed any evidence of the fact that today was the day John Booth was going to die.

Freddy was staring at the calendar with its orderly parade of X's blotting out the days and waiting for Mia to come out of the bathroom so he could go in and take a piss at the same time that he was thinking of using the handgun he had purchased to protect his jewelry store to go and kill a man. He was seated on the black leather couch, a cigarette poised at his lips, the fingers of his free hand toying with the gold chain around his neck. Squeezing through the louvered blinds behind him, the morning brushed him with a fan of warmth. He glanced over his shoulder as if the light had just asked him if he wanted to change in a new and dangerous way. He swooped his fingers through his hair.

When Mia emerged from the bathroom, she was tiered in towels, a blue one swaddling her body, a red one around her sopping hair. Freddy went to the refrigerator and took out a carton of orange juice. She offered him a smile that was more than a simple greeting and stepped up to him. Though he had slipped into his underwear and trousers, he didn't have his shirt on. At the end of her smile, her expectations unsettled, she reached out to trace the dangling gold chain from his neck to his chest. She paused to peek up at him before turning a finger on his nipple. "I'm very fresh and clean now," she said.

The moment was weird, because her interest in him made him angry at her. "Here's some juice," he said. "It's better than water." He turned his back and filled two glasses. Then he walked to the bathroom because he still had to piss, and the stab of her miffed annoyance followed him.

"God," she said.

"Go ahead. Drink up," he called to her.

When he stepped out, she had dropped the towels. Naked, she gulped the rest of her juice, gave him a mean look, and wheeled away. Returning to sip his own drink, he watched the bewildered little fit that developed as she tugged on her panties, skirt, and blouse.

There was no way he could explain to her. She didn't even know that he'd been married, or that he ever had a daughter. That he had other children. Nearly a decade ago, a chunk of his life had been hidden away, a legion of eerie impulses not so much discarded as sequestered. They waited in a sanctuary lost inside him. And the figure governing this place was not exactly Freddy. It was Freddy, and yet it wasn't, because everything had to be handled furtively, via codes and shadowy communications. And now the buried Freddy, the banished one, was emerging after years of exile to empower the ordinary Freddy standing in the room sipping orange juice and watching Mia dress.

"Unpredictability has its appeal, Freddy. I admit it," she said, pulling up the zipper on the side of her skirt and stepping into her shoes. "But as you maybe know, it's limited."

"What isn't?" he asked.

She looked at him as if he'd pressed a burning match to her skin and then she rushed for the door, carrying what clothing she hadn't managed to get on. He walked to the window and opened the blinds, waiting for her to appear on the sidewalk below. The streets were crowded, the traffic stymied by an eighteen-wheeler backing into a loading dock. When Mia popped into view, she stormed along with her head down, her purse slung over her shoulder. He leaned forward, his hand cupped against the glass to chase away a reflection.

Her blue Toyota waited in the corner of the parking lot adjacent to his building. Several years old, a rusty dent in the right fender, it was alone in that wedge of pavement at this early hour. The red brick mass of the next-door building was an overpowering, austere block except for a huge frosted window at street level in the front. Over this conspicuous pane of glass, flowery blue swirls depicted naked girls in dancing silhouette. The nearby door looked like a sheet of ice. Above the decorative female shapes, the words THE CALYPSO CLUB hung in a neon fuzz dull in the daylight. Beyond that window, inside that door was Freddy's hangout, the local strip club, where Mia worked as one of the new breed of up market, super-glossy, liberated, money-minded strippers.

She was almost to her car and he watched as she plunged in. Gunning the engine, she fired dark fumes out the exhaust. In reverse, she sent gravel flying and honked to clear a path in the street. She probably hoped he was watching, so she was putting on a little show to leave no doubt about the fact that she was still in a huff.

Sensitive, he thought. What the hell had she expected?

3

■ ■ ■ ■ ■ ■ ■

Freddy put on a pot of coffee and took his time in the shower, letting the water coddle him. He soaped up several times, as if to scale away a crud, and washed his hair. In the end, he gradually reduced the flow of cold water until the rising temperature started to hurt. Leaving his forearm and hand exposed, he stepped back and stood watching the skin flush. He felt a scarlet throb shoot into his chest. Then he got out, shut the water off, and toweled down, pampering himself. He shaved meticulously. He pressed after-shave lotion into his cheeks, before brushing and flossing his teeth.

With a cup of coffee, he faced his closet and selected a white dress shirt fresh from the cleaners, a black blazer, black slacks, and black shoes. Leaving the top buttons of his shirt open so the gold chain would show, he slipped on the jacket, then transferred his keys, change, and money clip from yesterday's trousers. At the mirror, he checked himself and went for one more cup of coffee.

Minutes later he was moving at a brisk pace along 7th Street. After a block or two, he stepped off the curb, angling for the other side. The bluish-gray of the pavement was coated with dirt and oil in large patches which he sought to skirt in order to protect his shoes. He was crossing against the lights, as were a number of other people jockeying for an advantage. Everybody was in a rush toward wherever the hell it was they were all going. Big fucking deal, he thought. Almost absently, he continued to play with the idea of an ordinary Freddy and a new emerging Freddy. Clearly, Mia had sensed his shifting priorities and had been thrown by the change. Getting her pissed off and confused was a good sign, really. It meant that something he hadn't exactly intended was starting to happen. Eight years ago his hunger for vengeance had been born. Now it had been restrained for so long that the return of the past this morning was like strange sounds in a dark room where he lay trying to awaken. He knew they pertained to him but wasn't sure what was required of him.

Impulsively, he tried to challenge the glance of an approaching stranger in a gray Nike running suit. But the man ignored him, or failed to notice, which was just as well, since Freddy didn't really know what he was doing. To every one of the people streaming past him, he was a total stranger, so what could they tell him about who he was, or who he was becoming?

When he arrived at the entrance to his jewelry store with the flashing three-dimensional figure of a diamond above the door, habit turned a proprietorial eye to the windows. Behind the gold lettering of GALE's FINE JEWELRY dancing across the glass on both sides of the doorway, there was nothing on display. Incredibly, the windows were empty; they were barren, containing unoccupied shelves and pedestals of naked gray felt like the store was closed or going out of business.

"What the hell!" he shouted, pulling open the door, his voice drowning out the little ringing bell above the entrance. "Jeffrey! Jeffrey!"

Effete and dapper, Jeffrey sprang through the curtains partitioning the store proper off from the storage areas, the vault, the stairway to the second-floor office. A youthful Japanese, Jeffrey wore several earrings in each ear, an ivory cardigan shirt under an open vest, and baggy chocolate-colored trousers with a single, asymmetrical pleat. His haircut was like a mushroom, thick black waves blooming from buzz-cut sides. "Mr. Gale, good morning," he beamed.

"Wait a minute, wait a minute! You're my store manager, right!"

Looking puzzled, Jeffrey managed a playful smile. "Excuse me, sir."

"Jeffrey, it's five after ten. Look at your watch. I got a display window of nothing but gray felt out there. What are you doing? I pay you to put the display out the minute you arrive."

"Mr. Gale. You took all the vault keys home last night."

"What?"

"What could I do?"

"I took all the vault keys home?" His hand was already pawing the jangle in his pocket and, of course, Jeffrey was right. Freddy shook his head and strode past, heading toward the back of the store and the vault. "Oh, for fucksake . . . !"

"Mr. Gale, Mr. Gale," said Jeffrey, trailing along, "I've been day-dreaming all day, all of yesterday—I can't get it out of my mind." He was in his stylish bullshit mode, one that Freddy had told him more than once to save for the customers. "Emeralds," Jeffrey said, as they passed through the back room. "I think it would be wonderful to put the emerald pieces in front of the diamonds. I don't know if it's true for everyone, but for me—it's my experience, Mr. Gale, that nothing grabs the eye like an emerald. They are like no other element."

Freddy thrust the key into the vault and said, "What's your point?"

"That is my point. I've just said it."

"Listen, I trust your preference in stones, but do me a fucking favor. I'm very busy, you know what I mean? All the time. I'm very busy." The door clicked open, revealing the drawers of diamonds, emeralds, and other precious stones.

"I know that, Mr. Gale."

"So think ahead for me, could you do that? Just a little bit. I'm walking out the front door at night, you're closing up—you're there—we're both there, and you don't have the vault keys in your pocket. Then either they're lost, right? Or I have them. Stop me. Find out if I have them! You see what I'm saying? Think ahead."

"Yes. Yes. I will."

"Why don't I believe you?"

"No, no, I will do it. I will stop you."

"Fine. That's all I ask. Emeralds in the front. Wonderful."

Slipping away, Freddy climbed the stairs to his office while be-hind him, Jeffrey lifted the diamonds, the emeralds from the vault, conveying them toward the front window. He would perform this task with great care, Freddy knew. The thing about Jeffrey was that he really loved the jewelry, the gems, the designs. Freddy didn't love them, and he wasn't sure he ever had. But Jeffrey worked with an acolyte's devotion. The blank expression that overtook his face as he handled the stones was a kind of trance mixed with a touch of carnal delight. Diamonds, Freddy thought. Crushing pressure and towering heat labored in complex, mysterious harmonies to squeeze and scorch carbon until it transformed, like a bug in a cocoon. They were old. More than three billion years sometimes. Nobody knew exactly how they traveled, but they did. They journeyed up from the depths of the earth. Studding the deep interior, they bubbled up in a swirl of foam rising hundreds of miles. Volcanic activity was involved, and in the end they settled near the surface, far from where they had been generated. There men came to gather them up, digging and sweating. And then they filled store windows like Freddy's, and people bought them and gave them as gifts to commemorate events of significance. Anniversaries. Birthdays. Important encounters between people. Engagements. Rendezvous.

Maybe I'll take one to John Booth, thought Freddy, having arrived in his office where he stood dialing the phone. On his desk sat a black and white TV monitor, a part of the store's surveillance system, and he could see Jeffrey moving around on it. Maybe I'll give John Booth one when I pop him, he thought. He could see the flesh split open like a fish's mouth, oozing its sad pink interior through the hole that his bullet would slam and slice into John Booth. As he stood listening to the buzz of the ringing phone, waiting for Mary to answer, he filled the wound with diamonds, with gems. He put them on John Booth's dead eyes. Fuck him, he thought, as someone picked up on the other end.

"Hello?" said the voice of his ex-wife Mary. He didn't answer and again she said, "Hello."

The breath he took began as one intended to fuel what he had to say but it ended up being held. Instead of speaking, he stood there thinking, You know who this is. I can hear your suspicion, your guess, your goddamn female intuition, telling you, It's him, it's him. It's Freddy. Do it. Do it, Freddy! I can hear you, Mary. Take a chance. Say hello Freddy.

"Do you want the Manning residence?" she said.

Say hello to me. Just do it. Tell Freddy hello.

"This is Mary Manning. Who are you trying to reach?"

Today's the day. He's out. Do you remember? Tell me that you do. Take a chance. Just blurt it out. Without a cue from me. I don't want to help you. I'm going to kill him for us, you stupid bitch. You chickenshit whore. I'm going to do it.

"This is ridiculous," she said.

He had believed he would speak, but now he saw the pointlessness of words. Especially with her. The value of remaining unknown. Suddenly, all the words he had imagined he would deliver fled, and the little that was left came out as a sigh.

Then she hung up and so did he, settling into the chair behind his desk and plucking his pack of cigarettes from his jacket pocket. With a sense of developing significance he turned a cigarette in his fingers, then placed it in his lips. The image he was contemplating, as he touched the match flame to the tip of the cigarette, was that of Mary in her home. He drew the smoke in, watching her puzzled expression as she placed the phone back in its cradle. Or maybe it was a wall phone, and she was in the kitchen. He smiled, his conviction that she knew it was him pushing away all doubt. It pleased him that she was unable to escape him, that he could reach out to her with the phone and with his thoughts, and she couldn't escape. Like he was haunting her.

Inhaling, he clenched his lungs so he could feel the smoke, its seeping effects melding with his satisfaction at the fact that he and Mary were still connected on this matter. Emily spanned the gap between them with an airy web, a delicate, durable bondage, as hard and complex as diamonds, he thought. Fucking eternal.

4

■ ■ ■ ■ ■ ■ ■

Through its first few beeps, the telephone was a mild nuisance ruf-
fling only the background of Mary's thoughts. She was halfway out
the door, rushing to set the lock and fretting that she was going to be
late for work. But then one particular ring detached from the others.
She felt a stabbing sensation, and she faced the recollection of a
dream. It was not the details so much as the mood that washed over
her, a desolate ache bringing with it a barren vista, jagged blood red
rocks. Maybe Joshua trees? A wandering figure.

Though the pull to return to the house was strong, the demands
of her morning kept her going. Even as she argued with herself, she
set the locks. Her heels clicked down the sidewalk in an effort to put
some space between herself and the house, her eyes fixed on the
waiting Ford Tiempo. The morning had been a series of misadven-
tures already: a run in her stockings, a misplaced earring, a coffee
spill. She had to get going.

But as the ringing telephone grew more muffled, it seemed to
gain in importance. When she pulled open the car door, a scolding
set of chimes informed her that she had neglected to remove the
keys from the ignition last night. Once more she heard the phone.

She slammed the door and bolted toward the house, surrendering to a conspiracy of small, bullying castigations. The forgotten
key was a reminder of her tendency to make minor mistakes that

somehow led to calamities. Only blind luck had kept her car from being stolen. The cumulative effect of all this nagging was to force her to admit that the phone call could be an emergency. That it might pertain to her twin sons. Now she had to answer if she wanted to be reassured that it wasn't their school calling. That it wasn't the police. Someone trying to alert her to a disaster involving Anthony or Andrew, or both.

She burst into the house, racing for the nearest extension. When she said, "Hello?" and no one responded, she feared that she had delayed too long and they were gone. Still, she waited, hoping she was wrong, wondering if there was trouble on the line, a little distracted by the anxiety that the dream had left behind. Had it been last night? Was that when it occurred? Or was it longer ago? With so few details, it was hard to determine anything about it.

"Hello?" she said again, listening intently, because something—a sound, a breath—had made it clear that there was someone on the other end and they were waiting; they were refusing to speak to her. It could be a wrong number, but wrong numbers asked for someone and then apologized or got annoyed at their mistake. It was weird, considering the rush she was in, that she didn't just hang up. Given the fact that she'd raced to the phone worrying about her children, the idea of a crank caller touched an unsettling nerve. "Do you want the Manning residence?" she said.

Still she received no response, though she could feel the presence on the other end, a dark blot pulling at her, crowding her with a silent demand that began to annoy her with its refusal to reveal itself.

"This is Mary Manning. Who are you trying to reach?"

She felt taunted by the way this person had intruded on her, only to withhold their identity out of a kind of perversity, a kind of cruelty. It struck her as arrogance, all this secrecy. Goddamnit, she thought.

"This is ridiculous," she'd said and hung up. Now she really had to run. The locks on the house were reset and the leap into her car accomplished in a state of rising irritation that she'd gone back in the first place, because now she was going to be late for sure.

She backed down the driveway and veered onto the street. Only as the jade and jacaranda trees in the yard at the end of the block fired their colors at her did she realize who it was on the other end. The radio was playing a high sad voice riding the pop rhythms of loss, and she saw Bobby. It was Bobby from the meeting last night. She saw his tousled blond hair, his anguished eyes, the awkward twist of his torso. Why had he been calling? What did he want?

5

■ ■ ■ ■ ■ ■ ■

Girders, blocks, concrete. Plastic, steel, clanging. A turmoil of the unnatural. Prison. It was all blast and clamor without a trace of the rich alternative world from which this mirage of steel and stone had been segregated.

And the stink of the anonymous men who preceded him was bred into his cell, secreted into the walls, the air they exhaled and breathed in again, their shit and piss in the toilet, the residue of their bodies, the flakes of skin they shed, the hair their scalps surrendered to the pillow at night, to the comb or the brush in the morning, the refuse of their days and hours and years sucked out of them into this enclosure and swallowed and somehow impounded in the walls that closed him in. Murderers, madmen, arsonists, thieves—fuck it. Even rock and steel consisted of particles, and the oils of their skin coiled in the molecules of the bars their fingers had stroked, a legacy as personal and hidden as the lives they had lived before they walked into this hellhole.

That had been John Booth's idea at the moment of his incarceration, and it persisted to some degree through every day that followed. It started with the cell door slamming behind him, the electronically triggered cylinders sealing out the world that knew him as he really was. The lock shut with a falling clank as loud as a hammer blow on the top of his head. The misery of his predecessors awaited him. He could feel it, smell it.

Disbelief at what had happened to him had to give way. Continued denial of where he was and how long he would be there demanded a fanaticism he could no longer sustain. But even thinking of giving up left him wobbly. He had to settle down, but he didn't know if he could. That was the problem. He didn't know anything anymore. He didn't know how to think. He wasn't sure he knew what thoughts were. How to use them, how to deal with them. Or what time was. Not in here.

The accompanying anxiety turned his chest to a stone he could barely budge to breathe, his asshole shriveling, his scrotum pulling up. Alarm, launched in his gut, fired out in all directions till it filled his fingers, ignited the roots of his hair. When it retreated, he felt his life was leaving him. The fact that he trembled made him worry that he would end up shaking violently, like a man in an arctic cold instead of in a small room from which he could not walk out.

When he raised his hand to check, he found the fingers wavering no more than a leaf in a mild breeze. Then the fear went through him again, so that he cried out and had to muffle his own mouth with the pressure of both hands, the way you might struggle to hold back the eruptions of a broken water pipe. He sank into a crouch, trying to make himself small. The rest of the transition to his hands and knees happened without his even knowing. He knelt there, taking thin breaths and trying to shut out the whining sound of his own thoughts. It had seemed an eternity, that first minute. And now four million two hundred thousand more had passed. Four million two hundred thousand minutes. Roughly. And in several hundred more it was over; he was leaving. At least that's what they told him.

The electric razor with which he was shaving buzzed. He fingered the smooth surface of his cheeks and chin and throat. For a second he savored the length and thickness of the Fu Manchu mustache he'd nurtured over the last few years. His eyebrows needed trimming. The scar above his right eye went on for more than two pale, hook-shaped inches, but it could have been worse. Souvenir, he thought. To the right of his mouth was a spot of beard that he'd missed. He lifted the razor, placed it, and felt the tug of the hairs being sliced from his face.

That he would be out by the end of the day seemed almost as impossible as the fact that he had come here to begin with. That he hadn't been able to go out for dinner, or to a movie, or anywhere at all—that he couldn't eat or telephone a friend when he wanted. On more than one occasion, he had awoken in the night, raised up from sleep full of childish belief in an approaching exemption. It was a state beyond forgiveness. It wasn't that he was absolved for what he had done, but rather he was granted a literal elimination of his circumstances. It hadn't happened. She wasn't dead. Or if she was, he hadn't been involved.

He was always about to explode with relief when the facts reclaimed him, striking with the impact of a hurled concrete block. The breath went out of him, and one night he started crying. It wasn't good to be heard crying, but every night somebody was. That was the night he'd ended up with the scar. He'd been the one wailing and he couldn't stop. Some nearby con told him to hit his head on the wall. Then everyone was yelling at him. So he did it. He just slammed his head, and lay there working on what he had to work on. Trying to learn what he had to learn. And the block, the idea of the block was the key. That was what he had come to understand. In its design, the prison was a block. It was gigantic and complex. And its complexity contained other blocks. It was a block built of blocks. Cell Block A. Cell Block B. Cell Block C and D and E and F. And every Cell Block consisted of cells, each one a block hollowed out into a cubicle. That was what you had to understand. It was huge and piled around you. His cell was the block he lived in, and on either side were other blocks and in them other men, and beside them there were other cells with still other men.

The solution to living in this place was the same as living anywhere—he had to become something that could cope with the laws in operation here. Waves of paranoia sometimes washed through the corridors with a taste like a garbage stench entering your mouth. He felt small and pulpy and unprotected against it, but everywhere around him, the prison was instructing him on what he had to do. One more block was needed—that was all—one final block had to be added to the prison's construction, and it was up to him to build it. This was the block he must make of himself, the island fortress he had to become if he wanted to survive.

And it wasn't just the hours in the gym that would provide the means. Not just the squats and thrusts and lifts. Repetitions and routines. Bars and various combinations of iron disks heaved through a mind-dulling crucible of muscle torn into new muscle. An inner steeling had also to be acquired to hold back the pressures of the prison itself, coiled around him, like some python of granite and time that had caught him, and every time he breathed, it grew heavier, and the capacity of his lungs diminished, making it harder to try again.

When it was time to clean the shaver, he pushed the release button and the head fell open. He dumped the gathered fuzz of tiny hairs into the sink, took the cleaning brush and inserted it, laboring meticulously to rid the interior of every last tidbit of beard. The silver of the floating heads grew distinct. He pressed the Remington closed, and started splashing water on his face. He liked to soak his hair, then comb it flat and straight back, breathing slowly as he performed each gesture.

Behind him, Thomas "Two Tommy" Duetmeyer, his cell mate for the last three years, lay on the bottom bunk of their rack. John knew that Two Tommys was watching him; he could feel the steady gaze of those feline eyes floating in bloodshot pools.

"I hope you're not counting on shavin' clean and washin' up to punch your ticket in the outside world," said Two Tommys. "To put you back among the certified."

John, gazing at the head of the razor, said nothing.

"Tell me you are not that kind of dipshit."

Moving to the small canvas gym bag in which he'd already collected most of his possessions, John inserted the razor in its case and then the case in the bag. Only his alarm clock and the photo of himself as a small boy in short pants with his parents, the three of them wearing straw hats, remained to be packed.

"I know what you think. It's common, in fact, a man like you full of denial and disbelief. What's going to happen today, John?"

"I'm gettin' out."

"See. Denial and disbelief."

Mind games, thought John, as he walked back to his bunk. He scaled over the sprawled hulk of Two Tommys, climbing to the second level, being careful to avoid Two Tommys' huge leg dangling off the side of the bunk to make room for his massive body. He was nearly three hundred pounds on a six-foot four-inch frame. His pants leg was tugged up several inches so a strip of fish-white skin showed through a fuzz of dark hair. That leg was about all John noticed, that and the colorful splash of the paperback book lying face down on the gray denim of Two Tommys' shirt. Two Tommys read more than anyone John had ever met. When he'd walked into John's cell that first day, he'd come carrying books, and he'd sat down and started reading. Claiming to have learned to read in prison, he spent hours every day scowling over the pages of science fiction novels and philosophy texts.

"You going to breakfast, John?"

For some reason, he didn't feel like speaking.

"Sometimes cons, on the day they are to walk out these gates, they are too hyper; they don't think they should leave their cell. They don't need to eat. They think the best thing is just to hole up. Avoid all risks of any kind. Some accident, you know—they are very concerned by every little thing. Paranoid. You know."

"I think I'll eat."

"You're not like that. You're not nervous."

John took a breath and placed the palm of his right hand over his brow. He hoped the faint discomfort recessed in the left side of his head would not turn into a headache.

"I'll eat, too," said Two Tommys. "I think I will. If I can find the time."

The sensation of movement that arose through the bed told John that Two Tommys had started reading again. John was over six foot three, and he was hard and pumped from his work with the weights. Two Tommys was powerful but soft. A junkie on the street, he'd been in and out of the prison system since he was thirteen. In his thirties now, he'd taken his last fall for armed robbery. That was a mistake that was going to keep him dropping a long time. His nickname had come shortly after he was born, when his older brother told their mother that she'd gotten two babies for the price of one, because that's how big and fat he was. Say hello to your brother Tommy, she said. He's Two Tommys, Momma. He's Two Tommys.

With a mammoth shifting accompanied by a grumble, as if he found the silence undesirable, Two Tommys sat up. "I've just been having some very interesting thoughts here, John. You interested in knowing what I'm thinking about? How would you like to guess what I'm thinking about?"

"Not right now."

"When? When, John?"

"I don't know." You never knew what was in store for you with Two Tommys. Besides, John's headache had started. He was feeling brittle and anxious. Like the board game Two Tommys had invented called "Prison." It was modeled on Monopoly. He'd taken an old Monopoly board and carefully relabeled it. If you settled on a certain square, you could buy the Cigarette Trade. Another put you in the Drug Trade. There were unlucky squares that sent you to Solitary, or added years to your sentence. Among the Chance cards, there was one that let you bribe the warden. Another gained you a Successful Parole, or A Day in the Infirmary. Your records could be lost. Some beefs you won. You could end up knifed. Land on a certain square and your skin pigmentation was changed: you went from white to black or black to white. There were gangs and turf. Trapped in the shower, a throw of the dice determined if you escaped or were fucked. In the Visitors' Room, if you tossed a six and a three, which were code in Two Tommys mind for "69," it didn't matter who was visiting—your wife, your girlfriend, your brother, your father, your mother, your priest, or your lawyer—you got a blow job.

"I don't understand this reluctance on your part, John. Here we are, the two of us, more or less isolated—how can you not be interested in what I'm thinking?" said Two Tommys. "Especially when I've been layin' here thinkin' about Descartes. Mr. René Descartes. How can you not be interested in that? Maybe you could tell me—"

"Well, you know, I got a headache—I'm a little preoccupied by everything today, you know."

"Sure. But I've been trying to imagine what would happen if certain creatures on a certain unknown planet read some of his writings—the writings of René Descartes—and what if, after they read 'em, they decided to make their government right out of his thinking, right out of those ideas? So if you came to that planet, what happened to you was that they took you and they put you in this room. This sealed-up room. Or maybe if you didn't even want to go there, they kidnapped you and put you in that room. Extraterrestrial kidnapping. There are reports. You know that? Witnesses; sworn accounts. So what if they took you to this planet and put you in this room and locked the door? Sound familiar? Then imagine that they taped up the windows, pulled down the blinds. No light. Just you and the truth. According to Mr. Descartes. That's what I've been thinking.

"And furthermore, I've been wondering if maybe that's where we are. On that unknown planet. That the state already took care of the preparations without me knowing it. Like maybe that's the idea of this place—the prison idea. To have us sealed up better than anything Mr. Descartes could have done. Yes, there's light but it's not natural. Anyway, I can just close my eyes. Do you want to try it with me, John? Try my idea as an experiment? How am I ever to know alone? I would be an inadequate sampling. But the two of us could do it. Just close our eyes, you and me, and see what's true—see what we can say is true. See if we end up at his conclusion, 'I think, therefore, I am.' "

Bullshit, thought John, looking at his alarm clock on the shelf near the sink and feeling a wan amazement at the fact that only nine minutes had passed since he finished shaving.

Two Tommys hurled himself backward onto the bunk, and it felt like the whole room was about to capsize. "You are really behaving like a troublesome asshole today, John. What the hell is the matter with you? Shut your eyes!"

The last thing he wanted was a beef. It had happened once, the two of them exploding, a fire out of nowhere hurling them at one another. "All right," he said.

"What?"

"I've closed my eyes."

The imposed dark was an altered world of flickering impressions that threw into prominence the morning sounds from other cells along the tier, a traffic jam of radios blaring different stations, the yammer of human voices amid a hivelike buzz of electric razors.

"Can I doubt that I am here?" said Two Tommys.

John lay in the dark with nothing to say.

"Can I doubt that I am in fact real?" said Two Tommys.

John waited, listening, as a minute or so passed with nothing more signaled from the man below except the heave of his breathing. Then Two Tommys said, "You there, John?"

John had started going over the list of the things he'd packed, as if it were such a varied assortment that he might have forgotten something.

"Are you real?"

It wasn't that his possessions were valuable. It was just that they were all he had.

"Are you real, John?"

John sat up. It was like his middle ear was faulty, the unbalanced way he felt. He was shaking his head to rattle loose a jammed thought. Below him, the upheaval of Two Tommys hurling his feet out onto the floor shook John like he was on a small boat in high seas. John jumped past Two Tommys, and then he hurried to his bag where he started unloading everything. He felt spooked, believing somehow that if he left behind anything that belonged to him, he would be brought back.

"No, no, you are right, John. You are right," said Two Tommys.

John had taken every article from the bag and they were laid out on the shelf before him. As he returned them, he examined each piece, then studied the order of the objects already in the bag, trying to determine the best place to fit each addition.

"I don't know how to handle such questions any better than you do," Two Tommys said. "They are a mean, vicious bunch of questions. They are terrible, hard-assed questions. If they were people who could walk in here and want to sit down, I would not be able to sit down with them. Not without some smack in me to guide me, to nourish me. Maybe for a little comfort. Maybe if I was high. Maybe then I would have the strength for these kinds of questions. Because they are devils; they are too much monster for me alone. I don't have the supplies. Not at this present moment, anyway. I mean, I have had certain experiences out there in the world of junk and in them were things that. . . . Do you know what a visionary is? Do you know what love is?"

"No."

"When I do junk, God visits. It is not *like* He visits—that's not what I'm referring to here. I'm saying, He is there. He comes right in, fills me up, runs in my blood. Runs right through me. Shows up in my brain. It is not that He ceases to be mysterious and unknowable, but He is somehow proven. He is somehow actual and proven beyond any power of disbelief I can raise against Him. And He's not what I expected, or anything like what I have heard about. Now if I had some heroin, maybe me and God together, we could sit down in the company of these questions."

Two Tommys walked to the sink and turned on the faucet. Scrubbing and turning his hands under the gushing water, he studied John, who stood only a few feet away brushing the blades of his electric razor.

"You already cleaned that razor, John. You cleaned it before. You cleaned it thoroughly. I saw you."

"I'm doin' it again."

"You think you will come back to prison again?"

"No."

"That's one hell of a clean razor you got there, John. Stop it. Just stop it."

John stood contemplating the silver shimmer of the basketlike interior, the tiny screws of the blades.

"There's a lot of ways back," said Two Tommys. "I'll be back on one of them. If I ever get out. Every time I get out, I find a new way back, so I don't realize exactly what I'm doing right away. I get going that way, get a head start on myself, so to speak. Then I go to the junk. I do methadone for a while. I do it. I try. But it's not—methadone just isn't God or godlike even. So how am I ever going to give it up?"

"I don't know."

"Methadone is a TV show with Billy Graham or some other fussy, glassy-eyed asshole talking. Talking *about* God. Words, but just this begging man's voice. This lost man, if you listen close. Words *about* God, but no God. It don't do anything at all except serve to aggravate the situation, to demonstrate the absolute emptiness of the facsimile."

The clang at the door turned them both toward the summons of a passing hack demanding that they call out their names and their state-assigned numbers as he conducted the second Lock and Count of the morning.

"John Booth," said John Booth. "Six seven three three two six."

"Thomas Deutmeyer," said Two Tommys. "Nine five two zero

two eight." He was wiping his hands now, his huge palms and fingers squirming in the towel.

John had moved to the door to identify himself. His arms fell laxly through the bars, the progress of the count past the succeeding cells drawing his thoughts along, as if he were accompanying the guard, as if he were uniformed and walking along, banging doors, making demands.

"You ever given any thought to the occult, John?"

Two Tommys clearly wanted an answer, but it was difficult for John to pull back from the corridor and situate himself in his body in the cell.

"I thought you were interested in me, John."

"What?"

"I hope you've been listening to me. I mean, I've taken you for a trustworthy man. I really have. What is it, John, I asked you?"

He didn't know what Two Tommys was talking about and he looked at him with puzzlement in his eyes.

"I asked you about the occult—what you know about it."

"When?"

"Sometimes I think you haven't paid any real attention to me. I hope you haven't been pretending all these years just to survive in here. Giving me this lie of attention. It's a lie if you have just tolerated me. You have just placated me. Letting me waste my breath."

John walked to the sink and started washing his own hands.

"You ever think about all the air we have breathed together? Outa you and into me. Outa me and back into you. Outa you and back into me. In this book I'm reading, it's called *The Planet of the Infinite Return*—do you know what that is? There is a planet where every day is a day that could become the day you have to live over and over for ever. What you are living on any one day could become the life you have to live forever. That one day. Only you don't know which day it is. It could be any day—they don't tell you until it happens. This is a young writer, a new guy—Edward Brees Baxter. In the class of Philip K. Dick. Superior to Asimov. Superior to Silverberg. Well beyond anything that—"

The mechanical roar that overwhelmed his voice was the storm of every gate in E Block leaping sideways on its frame at the command of an electrical current. The cumulative impact sent a shiver through the walls and floor. Two Tommys and John Booth stepped into the corridor. They traveled along the balcony to the metal stairs, where they descended in a long line of inmates streaming toward the mess hall for breakfast.

With his tray full of powdered eggs and toast and cereal, John settled down to eat. Two Tommys had gone off on his own, and John was glad to be rid of him. He hoped eating would end his headache. He and Two Tommys spent little time together outside of the cell. Two Tommys claimed to need the company of people who were "indoctrinated. The high and righteous." By which he meant other junkies.

John was sipping his coffee when he realized that one of the two men to his left was talking about someone he'd killed or seen killed. John didn't want to eavesdrop, but he couldn't avoid it. If he moved away he would call attention to himself. So he adopted this glazed, daydreamy look, staring off at nothing as he ate, his motions slow.

"So he's on the curb, you know," the guy was saying. "So he's pissin' and squealin'. What else? Right. This jerkoff. He shoulda just died. It was pathetic. So I put it here." The man's head of black curly hair scrunched into the crooked wedge of his shoulders, and John could not help but follow as the man set two fingers behind his own right ear. "Pop, pop, pop. Goodbye."

On the way back to his cell, John kept hearing the killer's voice drilling a space for itself in a hard little niche in his head. The guy had sort of sung the word, "Goodbye," degrading the dead guy, mocking him.

Not that this was the first time John had heard such an icy tone. He'd even used it. At least to himself. Like when he thought about the little bald guy he'd come upon slumped on the prison stairs, a pinkish worm slipping out with the blood his fingers could not press back into his slashed stomach. Or the howls of that middle-aged guy, the embezzler, in the storeroom where they took him to rape him, yelling out their numbers so that, since he was an accountant, he could keep an accurate tally. Or that time he'd rounded the corner and seen that huge naked back and buttocks, the trousers dropped to the ankles, the acres of skin white as paper and flecked with pimples, and beyond it that kid's fear-filled eyes looking up at the face over him. The psychotic mood expelled from that conjunction of half-lit bodies had affected John like a force field repulsing and shoving him on.

Still, what he'd heard moments ago as he ate his eggs smothered in salt and pepper had left him wondering. Some people just did it and didn't care. Others felt pleasure. He almost envied them. But then the shooter in the mess hall probably hated whoever it was he killed. He probably knew the guy and had a reason to take him out. Whereas John had just been out having fun, driving fast, drinking and feeling good and then he'd run down a child he didn't know. A little girl.

Maybe that was what made all the difference—if you did what you wanted—if you hated and wanted to kill who you killed. Like the little girl's father. Vowing vengeance, swearing it. Maybe he would be like that—like the guy at the table, he thought. Like that. Cold.

When Two Tommys returned to their cell, he went straight to the sink and started brushing his teeth. He was a hubbub of gargling and spitting noises that stopped abruptly as he turned to John, pink foam on his lips.

"John Booth?"

"Yes."

"Do you think you could smuggle some heroin in to me? Don't rush your answer. Take a minute to consider. It's a complex matter. I mean, when you are out. Would you be willing to do that for me? Smuggle in some junk?"

"No."

"Wait, wait. You didn't think it over."

"No," said John. "I can't. No."

Two Tommys spit into the sink, turned on the faucet, and swirled his hand around the basin. "Would you lay there like that, John—would you just lay there if you knew that by doing it, you would have to do it forever? If you had to do what you are doing right now for the rest of your cocksucking life, would you do it right now? Is this how you would spend these minutes if you knew that by doing the things you would have to keep on doing them for ever and ever? Is it, John?"

As Two Tommys sagged into his bunk, John wanted to take a breath and hold it until the morning ended and he was processed out. They'd have to come for him soon. He was afraid Two Tommys was going to climb up onto his bunk and try to kill him. Lay on him, cover him up, imprison him so no one knew he was there. He folded his arms, telling himself that it was not a good idea to rise up and bang his head against the wall. The feeling that this would soothe him, that it would help him was wrong. He'd proved that when he did it. Though he could recall an upshot of pain zigzagging through his mind like stitching holding him together.

Then Two Tommys started to read aloud, his voice tense with restrained anger and volatility: " 'Can I doubt that I am sitting here by a fire in a dressing gown, these documents in my hands? Yes, for some time I have dreamt that I was here when in fact I was naked in bed. Moreover, madmen sometimes have hallucinations, so it is possible that I may be in like case.' "

The voice halted. They lay still for a while, each in their own uneasy place. When Two Tommys started up again, it sounded like he was weary from struggling against some surging emotion: " 'Dreams, however, like paintings, present us with copies of real things, at least as regards their elements. Therefore corporeal nature. . . .' "

This time the silence had a quality that suggested finality. He seemed to have given up, and as the quiet lengthened, John began to believe it would last and he let himself swim far into his own thoughts.

"There's something I got to tell you," said Two Tommys.

He didn't care, didn't want to know, but he said, "What?"

"I don't care if you don't want to know. What kind of tone is that to use on me? I don't give a goddamn about what you want or don't want. I know what's important. I know what my responsibilities are."

"What?" said John again.

"That little girl you ran over—you were drunk, sure. That's both a cause and an excuse, isn't it? I want you to think about what we have talked about—not all of it, but some of it—the right parts—just the right parts—and when you feel some pull to do yourself harm—I'm talking about when you're out there, and I'm talking real harm and it's pulling at you—you see what I am saying?—because she is going to be after you."

"What?"

"That's what I am telling you."

"Who?"

"You know who. And she is a witch."

"Bullshit!"

"Everybody gets out. Don't think you're so goddamn sanctified and pious and accomplished because you have managed it. Because I have heard what happens in your sleep—how she is after you. I have heard you fighting her at night. Trying to fight her off. Begging and bartering in your sleep. I hope you don't think you're going to deny it. How are you going to deny it? You were asleep! I heard you. I was awake. I woke up with the sound of it. I heard you struggling. I felt you shaking. I felt the frame of the bed shaking. I'll help you. Just bring me some smack."

"No."

"She's after you. You have to watch out for her!"

"What are you talking about? What the hell are you—"

"You got to! Just do it, just smuggle it in."

"I can't!"

"You're sure?"

"Yes."

"Because then I can't help you with her either. And I want to."

John thought it might be better to say nothing.

"Is that your answer, then? Is that your final answer?"

John took a breath and looked at his alarm clock, the single item he had left unpacked. Only twelve minutes had passed since they'd returned from breakfast.

6

■ ■ ■ ■ ■ ■ ■

Stuart and Helen Booth weren't bickering, but they could have been. A lot less than a day like this one had served to set them off over the years. But Helen had to admit they were getting along just fine. Each silent, each settled into something to keep them busy. Stuart with his newspaper, and she with her thoughts, as they waited in their Volvo station wagon parked in the desert outside Madison State Prison.

A harsh dry wind came rattling over the wastelands and slammed against the car with a heave strong enough to force the chassis to raise up. Blades of air wormed in, finding tatters to enter and scrape against them. Stuart looked old now. In his fifties, sure, but the way he looked was worse. More worn out, his paunch, this layered loaf of fat straining the fabric of the short-sleeved print shirt he wore.

Another car had just pulled up, a garish Pontiac Bonneville. Stuart gave it a narrowing glance, then went back to his newspaper. The way the fenders and hood flashed with their bright red curves in spite of being dusty made Helen think it was brand new. Two black men sat inside. She thought she'd watch them for a while, but then, just before the nearest one actually moved, she sensed that he was going to look at her. So she ducked her eyes, her fingers rising up to stroke her brow.

That made three cars waiting. The other was a vintage Chevrolet with a young blond woman in sunglasses behind the wheel. She'd arrived maybe thirty minutes after the Booths. Up she'd come, squealing to a halt and then looking around, her mouth pursed and perplexed, as if she was uncertain she'd found the right spot. For a while, the heavy throb of her engine had continued even though the car was stationary, as she let her car radio keep her company, the country and western music setting sadness loose in the wide open desert afternoon.

It was such a relief the way she and Stuart weren't bickering that she felt almost justified in taking it as a good omen. She didn't know if they deserved any luck, but they could use it. She'd almost got them fighting, that was for damn sure. She'd managed to light the fuse, the way she usually did, by leaving behind the thermos of coffee when they'd set out from the house in the morning.

Their son was getting out of jail, and so naturally, they wanted everything to go well, and then, when they'd gone about twenty minutes from the house, they'd turned a corner near a 7-Eleven and a teenager striding out of the front door with a cardboard container of coffee had sent her reaching for the thermos in anticipation of Stuart's request for a cup.

But the thermos wasn't on the floor, or in the back seat. Stuart loved coffee. But mainly he loved his own homemade coffee brewed from the beans he ground himself. And she'd left the thermos behind. Only it was his fault, really, sending her back into the house on a wild goose chase at the last minute. They'd been ready to go, the car running in the driveway, the thermos cradled on her lap, when suddenly he'd grown anxious that they'd left the bedroom windows open.

She knew they were fine. But she didn't argue. At the front door, she warned herself to make certain that she locked back up on the way out. As a reminder, she left the key in the lock. Because of this, she entered the bedroom at least partially preoccupied with her fear that she would end up driving off with the keys left behind in the door. Making a mental checklist, she placed the thermos on the dresser, and then unlocked, raised, slammed, and relocked the bedroom windows. He was honking by this time, so she ran.

As she scurried into the car, he hit the gas before she even had her seat belt fastened. They didn't want to be late, he told her. They didn't want John standing around the desert wondering where his parents were now, did they? He wouldn't be the only prisoner getting out today. There'd be thieves, murderers, rapists, burglars. Did she want John riding off with one of them?

She didn't say anything, because she hated the way he drove when he was upset. They were racing already. And besides, she knew they had hours to spare. After a few blocks, he slowed down just as she knew he would, if she didn't try to justify herself.

They went on quite happily until she saw that boy at the 7-Eleven and realized her mistake. Less than five minutes later, Stuart asked for a cup of coffee. By then she'd worked herself into such a frenzy that when his extended hand came toward her, she was close to tears and her bladder was in such a knot she couldn't tell if she was weepy because of guilt or out of worry that she was going to pee her pants.

He shivered once when he understood what had happened, shaking his head, as if to remind himself how he should have known he couldn't count on her. His fingers flexed on the wheel, his eyelids sagging shut.

As she waited for him to say something, she realized that his eyes were completely closed and that, as far as she was concerned, he was keeping them that way much too long for someone driving a car. But she didn't dare tell him, even though she was getting scared, her own gaze darting back and forth from his sightless countenance to the gray of the interstate humming by in a sixty-five miles per hour fuzz.

She started making a scratchy little coughing noise high in her throat to sort of pull at him. Ahead, the road was entering the first part of a curve that grew, as it went on, increasingly sharp. Staring at him, she said his name real loud in her head: *Stuart!* But he didn't respond, and she thought she was going to be forced to grab him or yell. Her tongue and breath were scrambling to come up with a warning, when he wheeled toward her and then back to the road. To her amazement, his gaze was forgiving.

"Oh, well," he sighed.

It left her blinking. He settled back into a proper, alert relationship to the demands of the gray two-lane and the oncoming semi that boomed past like a storm.

"We can stop along the way and get some," he said. "I guess. If we pick the right place, we'll do just fine. Some of these diners have some good java. Yes they do."

A mile or so on, he pulled into the stew of gravel and mud alongside a diner, an aluminum trailer on a foundation of cinder blocks, all windows and metal flare. He bought coffee for them both and for her he purchased a peach danish. As he came down the front steps, he waved the napkin-wrapped treat, crusted and golden, toward where she waited in the car.

"I'm really sorry," she told him once they were back on the road.

He nodded, sipping the coffee. "That's all right. This stuff is good."

"I could just kick myself."

"That wouldn't help much."

"I left it inside when I went back in, you know. When I went to check the windows."

"Did you?"

"I'm sure of it." She was chewing the danish, which she held daintily in the tips of her fingers.

"Well, we're both in a dither, I guess. That's how I'm lookin' at it. We're both just in one hell of a dither and why shouldn't we be?"

He peeked at her, and the wistfulness he showed wasn't everything he was feeling. Not that she needed much to remind her of the way trouble had walked into their lives when their son ran over that little girl, knocking them right out their ordinary world of thirty-four years and straight into one fit for a tabloid TV show. She was all of a sudden one of those people with a caption under her face that said: MOTHER OF DRUNK DRIVER WHO KILLED CHILD. Policemen. Bail hearings. Visiting hours. And the other parents, the mother and father of the little girl, with their hateful glances. But what could you say to them? Your words were lies, as far as they were concerned, your love of your son a kind of crime. They hated you, as if you had driven the car. And in a way you had. Sometimes she felt that in fact she had been the one behind the wheel, while her little Johnny was elsewhere, playing in his crib, safe at home, or scampering about with his daddy in some game, or a little boy in blue shorts racing a toy metal car propelled by pedals around the driveway in their first home in Seattle. That had been a lovely neighborhood, the Meyers and the Wilsons for neighbors. Oh, if only they hadn't moved.

Stuart raised his wristwatch to the window as if there wasn't enough light in the car for him to make out the dials accurately. But the sun was still high. It was just his way of making clear the importance of the gesture.

Helen glanced off through the gusty winds kicking in all directions. Around them stretched the Mojave Desert, strips of stone and weird light and golden dirt. Inhaling the Winston which she had nursed down to the bitter nub, she exhaled, blending smoke and worry in a sigh.

Stuart turned a page in the newspaper he was pretending to read. She could tell by the fixed position of his head that he was daydreaming, staring through his new bifocals into some reverie with blurred newsprint for a background.

"Are those new prescription lenses right, do you think?" she asked him.

"What's that?"

"Because you can return them you know, just take them back if you want. They're still in the trial period."

"I know that."

Stubbing out the cigarette and reaching to light another, Helen was caught by movement off to her left. The release gate had opened. A flat, empty yard was suddenly visible through the doorway where a cluster of uniformed inmates were on the move, crossing the yard at a forced pace and in a direction that took them parallel to the gate, not toward it. Mostly they were black men.

"What does that mean?" she said. "The gate opening."

"I don't know."

She glanced at the Bonneville and the two passengers. It wasn't the first time she'd had to fight such thoughts, but she hoped she would never have to think of South Central L.A. and gangs again. Of Crips and Bloods, and her son in cages with them. It was frightful to consider such a life—if it could be called that. She felt like she was peering into an alien, brutish planet, and in the end, she couldn't face it. She wanted to blink it away and when it wouldn't go, she stared at Stuart, who was trying to herd a buzzing insect of some kind out the window of the car. She didn't know what she was doing, and then she realized she was attempting to reach him by means of a telepathic silence empowered by their years together. She was full of miserable ideas that she didn't even want to admit were her own. But sometimes she feared that the person they were waiting for, the man about to walk out of this place, was not going to be their son anymore. He would look the same and talk the same, but he would have changed, the way people do in spite of themselves sometimes. Like if they have private shameful thoughts they can't share with anyone. Or if they're suffering from an incurable disease. Somehow, she imagined that her husband knew about this kind of thing. She imagined that, while the questions were all hers, he had the answers. He was rolling up the window, having finalized his evacuation of the bug with a flick of his forefinger and a retreat so hasty it looked like he feared being bitten. The bug was a tiny gleam absorbed in the desert glare, as Stuart settled back with his newspaper.

"Well, whatever this place is, it's better than that Folsom," she said.

"That was a rough one, that's for sure." He glanced at her.

"I was so glad when they moved him out of there. I was just so thankful. Do you remember?" She smiled at him, but he was serious, his big head of silvery hair offering a nod of solemn assurance.

"Your prayers'll be answered," he said. "Pretty soon, he'll be out of this place, too."

Was that his answer to her earlier questions? The best he could give her? she wondered. The unlit cigarette in her fingers caught her eye and she turned it, thoughtfully, as if it were something she'd never seen before.

"It's twenty minutes after," he said. "About. I think." He gave his watch a quick pass.

She was gazing off toward the prison yard beyond the gate, and as the fuzz of her thoughts cleared, she was intrigued by the way certain details previously unnoticed came into focus. It amazed her that every door she could see was painted blue. It was so weird the way a person could look at things but not see them. That's what her art teacher, Mr. Russell, kept saying at the YWCA, where she'd been going for the last year.

"Look at that, Stuart. See how all those doors are painted blue? 'You look at red, through blue, and yellow looks at you,' " she told him, quoting an axiom she had picked up, trying hard to be a good student.

Stuart was staring past her. "What you mean?"

"It's one of the little sayings from class. A little teaching. Inside red is blue and yellow, too."

"I don't understand."

"It's just a little saying. I wonder if they paint them like that to give the men inside the feeling that they can see out. So it's not so oppressive."

"Probably just an accident."

"An accident?" She looked again. "All of them? You think they could have painted all those doors the same pretty blue by accident?"

"If they knew, they probably would have painted them black. I mean, Helen, I doubt the warden here—the warden from this prison—or whoever makes such decisions as door colors—I doubt very much the prison interior decorator went to your art class."

"I wasn't saying that. I can't believe you think I was saying that. What I was saying was just that these are generally known as more or less common, I would think, artistic principles."

"Oh," he said. He nodded, but he wasn't agreeing. His eyes were hardening, the pupils almost wrinkling the way they did when he was going off with a thought he would never say aloud to her, not if he lived to be a hundred.

Just then a yellow van appeared in the frame of the gate. Helen's heart did a funny spin. "That's him," she said. "Didn't he say it would be a yellow van?"

Stuart brushed his hand through the air, as if to clear his vision.

When a door slammed beside her, Helen looked at the Bonneville. The driver was out, his companion emerging to join him. They stood there, two lean dark streaks of bodies in gaudy shirts and baggy trousers and Nike sneakers, sinewy muscles winding through blue-black skin topped by baseball hats on backwards.

In the Chevrolet, the blonde started her engine.

Stuart was opening his door and edging out, struggling through the stiffness their long wait had engendered in his joints.

One of the black men sprang off, galloping a short distance into the desert, where he kicked at a desolate bush. His companion was watching, hooting these loud noises that were scary even though he was smiling. About to arrive back where he had started, the runner jumped up in the air and came down sideways, digging in his heels, throwing up sand. Then the two of them celebrated their reunion with a bizarre and complicated handshake full of slaps, bumps, and all these snapping fingers. She wondered if maybe this was some kind of practice for whoever it was they were meeting.

The blonde flounced from her car. She leaned against the open door, her one hip tilted in a casual suggestive way, as she bent to tug the hem of her short skirt higher on one thigh than the other in an impression of dishevelment. Her blouse was open to the waist, her cleavage spilling through a lacy camisole.

What a dangerous world, Helen thought. And then she flung open the door and stepped out. She was a little surprised by the arid wind boiling in the spooky light. She took a breath and told herself to hide her apprehensions with a welcoming face. Clutching the top of the door, she raised up on her tiptoes to watch the van shimmering like a mirage, the body iridescent in the late afternoon light blotting out the windows behind which the mystery of her son was being conveyed toward her.

7

■ ■ ■ ■ ■ ■ ■

Gushing from the state-of-the-art amplifiers, the guitars were ransacking a batch of chords, knocking them around and wringing out of them shrillness, license, an inducement to luxury, a daydream of tits poured through the hard, simple-minded thud of the drums. Humping. Boom boom. Freddy could see right through to its raunchy core. He kept his gag of scorn to himself. This dopy, dreamy set of standardized, more or less inane sentiments that made up the lyrics to every single song—what were they? Humping! Boom boom.

The strippers kept appearing one after the other, phantoms on an assembly line, summoned into the sea swells of light by the music. He'd been here for how long he didn't really know. Some time in the shop, some phone calls, then over here. Up to the door and in through the white frost of the window with the silhouetted blue chorus girls raising their legs to kick. He put his hand on the ass of one and pushed into the music and noise.

At the table directly in front of him, some gray-haired, pastyfaced guy in a sport coat over a pin-striped shirt with the collar open was ogling the African American princess who had condescended to sit down beside him. Pathetic. The fat guy in the baggy gray polo shirt knew how to strike a confident pose and guzzle the brew, but he was hopeless. Dreams of tits, thought Freddy, enjoying a quick pop of bourbon before opening a fresh box of Marlboros, tapping one out, letting his Zippo do its work. Puff, puff. Mmmmmm.

He got a real kick out of the regal black guy in the brown sport coat with shoulders so bulked up he looked like he was wearing a hockey uniform under his clothes. The jerk-off looked like he thought that this entire event had been arranged just for him. Then there was the fat broad and the fat guy, the both of them peering out of thick glasses and wearing clothes that made you think they'd left home expecting to go to Burger King.

Sunny Ventura, the club owner and MC, was swimming through tides of smoke and blue jelled lights crashing into scarlet on his way up to the stage to start one of the pointless fucked-up raps he used to introduce the strippers and in which he took so much pride. There he was in his pink shirt and his pink skin, hair combed forward in this hopeless attempt to camouflage the glowing pink of his bald spot. *You're going bald, you asshole!* Freddy wanted to shout to Sunny, who was up there now, riffing away, his face this wad of misery packed in a lumpy wrinkled sack like a scrotum with a mouth. But the sad part was the way he imagined himself entertaining. He saw himself as some kind of cutting-edge wit. God, thought Freddy. Lemme take the next bus to Pasadena if this guy is funny. Lemme move to fucking Iowa if this guy knows how to tell a joke.

Freddy was watching with his cronies at his favorite table, his home away from home. Or maybe it was the other way around and his apartment was his home away from home. Maybe his real home was this corner, this wedge of black leather. The blue tablecloth was strewn with crumpled cigarette packs and ashtrays spilling butts, a menagerie of glasses, the full, the half-full, the empty. Drink up, he thought. Accompanying these words was a snarl deep in the back of his head, as he imagined John Booth staggering with impact, blood flowering out of his chest, gore taking over the space that used to be his fucking head.

Coop and Silas and Buddy and Manny were arranged to the left, his buddies, his chums, yammering away. And as always the subject was women.

"Their feelings," said somebody. "Their feelings this, their feelings that. Whata they talkin' about? Is this some space-age discovery? Their fucking feelings! Have they never heard of logic?"

"You know what the difference is between your ex-wife and my trampy girlfriend, Manny?" said Coop to Manny.

"No."

"Who she's with!"

"Right. Exactly!" piped in Silas.

"I don't get it."

"Whadya mean? How could you not get it?" Coop was twisting his face into this exaggerated mask of scorn.

"I don't get it!" said Manny.

"Jesus Christ—your ex-wife *is* my trampy girlfriend. When she's with you, she's your ex-wife—put her with me and she's my trampy girlfriend."

"I gotta pay her the fucking support, though, no matter who she's with—the fucking alimony is mine to—"

"And I get to fuck her!" Clearly, this was the line Coop had been working toward, and he slapped the table for emphasis, then toasted Manny and drank.

"Why are women like dog shit?" said Silas.

"What?"

"I think I heard this one," said Manny.

Freddy leaned toward Silas and said, "Why *are* women like dog shit, Silas?"

"That's what I'm asking."

"I don't know," said Freddy.

"Anybody know?"

"I don't," said Coop.

"I think I heard this one—but I can't remember it!" said Manny. With one hand on either side of his head, he was squeezing as if to pop the idea up from his brain like pus from a pimple.

"Nobody knows?"

"Wait, wait! I know this one!"

"Women are like dog shit because of how the older they get, the easier they are to pick up."

"That's it! That's it!"

As their laughter swelled, the crowd around them exploded at something Sunny had said. He was rocking back and forth in a celebration of his own crass accomplishment, when the audience poured on another load of applause that he acknowledged by waving his hands and giving them this condescending little bow. Though Freddy's table didn't have a clue regarding the content of Sunny's triumph, they all joined in, glancing from one to another with a connoisseur's appreciation.

Sunny tilted the ice cream cone microphone up to his mouth and blew. The crash he produced bred something oceanlike with an electrical explosion. It all but ripped holes in the speakers. His fans went mad, amplifying their pounding palms with hoots of pleasure, and the shrill praise of whistles.

"That fuckhead thinks he's Jay Leno," said Coop.

"Bobcat!" Freddy shouted.

"Sam Kennison he ain't. That's for sure."

"She says, 'Are we gonna go for breakfast?' " said Silas. He was talking to Manny but Manny wasn't listening. Nobody was listening. "I said: 'What breakfast? I came already!' " Silas yelled.

With a wave of his hand, Sunny cried out the name, "Joy!" It was a cymbal-smash of a word, and everyone at the table, like they were all parts of one startled, multiheaded beast, wheeled in the direction of the stage. Just then a momentary foul-up in the lighting threw Sunny into silhouette. Wide at the base and narrow at the head, his shadow looked like a pile of old tires under a tarp, as he cried, "Straight from the saga of History! Direct to our stage—that fabled tease!" The lights were bouncing around, searching for something on the pleated curtains behind him. Suddenly, the fabric shuddered with a current of movement to guide the lights. "Good Lord, it looks like Marie Antoinette!" Sunny cried, grabbing his crotch with one hand while the other swung back toward the curtains. Cued by his fingers, the pleated sheath opened, just as the lights reasserted themselves, turning the blue to a lurid pink. "Let them eat cake! Off with their heads!" shouted Sunny.

Out stepped Joy, her expression aloof in spite of the synthetic, neon glare of the blue satin ballroom gown she wore, this big pink bow across her breasts. At her hips, the dress ballooned out with the period style and fell to the floor to chastely conceal her feet. A white wig disguised her hair in a cotton candy crown spilling aristocratic ringlets to her shoulders. If not contemptuous, her steely eyes and tight little mouth suggested a haughty belief about herself. The front of the gown opened in a wedge of glitzy layers and folds that revealed a petticoat but no skin. The only visible flesh was her throat above the sweetheart neckline, where several strings of pearls looped before dropping into her cleavage. White lace cuffs billowed around her wrists and her long fingers were closed on a pearl-colored fan, which she snapped open with a hot little flick of her wrist and a bump of her hip, as the music started to move her around.

Freddy and Coop and the rest of the crowd clapped, chattering to one another like sightseers glimpsing the Grand Canyon for the first time. A natural wonder at their disposal, she circled the stage, her eyes downcast one moment, then brazen the next. Here a bit, there a bit, she shed her clothing. It didn't take long and her historical pose was undone. The last item to go was the wig, her back turned to tease them, her hands lifting away the fuzzy white, and out swam the dark luster of her natural hair. She was a titillating length highlighted by scraps of lace, the film of a push-up bra and bikini panties, a garter belt afloat above transparent hose. But then, even these thin items were on their way to the floor, leaving her with nothing but her shoes, as she grabbed the golden pole at the edge of the stage, one long leg on either side, this fantastic fucking motion. The lights went nuts, melting the backdrop, turning it liquid so that it seemed to drip and then to gush in a rainstorm of pink and blue streaks.

"Not bad," said Coop.

"What happened to that bitch? I mean, the real one—they decapitated her, right?" said Silas.

Freddy glanced at his watch. He took a sip of bourbon. It was barely past six. Hours remained before he could leave. The glow of the front windows confirmed that it was still daylight outside. Maybe he'd eat, have a sandwich. He had a drinker's famished appetite. A burger, some fries and chips. Fucking right, he thought, and took another sip. He didn't really want to think about what lay ahead. He just wanted to do it in a blur, the deed rising up to envelope him from the night, passing over him like a storm. He was relying on an instinct that wanted him to trust it the way a blind man had to trust. Just walking ahead. Let it come. From the unknown. Just find the motherfucking guy—that's all he had to do— wait till a late enough hour. Walk the midnight dark. The A.M. hours. Get himself to the house and let the fucking storm do the rest. Rain, wind, and blam, blam.

Sunny was introducing the next stripper. *"Mia!"* he cried. It was Freddy's Mia, so he looked, but she wasn't on stage yet. *"Little Bo Peep!"* said Sunny. *"Bo Peep!"* He gave the name a lewd twist as it spilled from his worming lips to the mike before erupting from the speakers. Coop groaned and shot Freddy a sarcastic dig using nothing but his eyes.

Freddy smirked. This was barely a challenge, something he could handle with ease, his own expression indulging in a large dose of bragging, token humility, and pure condescension. "I am the stick man, Coop," he said.

Coop snorted, grinding out his cigarette and muttering something Freddy couldn't hear. Everyone knew Mia had the hots for Freddy, that he could more or less take her home when he wanted and that he had in fact taken her with him last night. A chance to fuck Mia was something Coop wanted. He whined about it, plotted and calculated, but never managed to get near her except in his dreams.

"What's up, Coop?" said Freddy.

"You know what you can do, Freddy."

Just then Mia peeked out from the curtains, presenting them with the tease of her eyes and brown bangs under a childish pink bow. The scorn in Coop's expression dissolved, leaving behind sadness and envy. Clad in a frilly white little girl's dress that stopped at her thighs, Mia entered into a red blaze of stage lights and stood there sucking a gigantic swirl of a lollypop.

Coop said, "You asshole, Freddy. I don't get it."

"That's right," said Freddy.

Mia's theme song was "On the Good Ship Lollipop." At the start, she portrayed innocence, or as much as she could manage given the length of her bare legs extending into spike-heeled pumps. Her routine was a variety of exuberant gestures, her hands flung up, then pressed to her cheeks, a bunch of twirls followed by this dainty little curtsy, and every now and then a hapless misadventure with her clothing that left her confused and a little more nude.

"What could she possibly see in Freddy?" asked Coop.

"You gotta remember," said Silas to Coop, "they are as helplessly driven by instinct as we are. You gotta remember that."

"That is not the reason. You cannot tell me you think that's a good reason. I don't accept that."

"Well, then there's a wide variety of other possibilities. For example, she could have been scared by something terrible when she was little."

"So this turns her to Freddy?"

"This could be a reaction to that."

"I don't get it."

"Then there's hormones. There's always hormones."

"That's true."

"You can't forget about hormones."

"But why Freddy? Why, why, why?"

"Freddy's cute."

"I suppose."

Mia was working her way through a sequence of steps that appeared derived either from cheerleading, or the panic of someone about to miss their plane at an airport Abruptly, she gave up all hope and fell to her knees. Bereft, she knelt beside the golden pole at the edge of the footlights. Sadly, she pressed her cheek to the gleam of the tubing. In seconds this intimacy transformed into a lingering kiss. Glassy-eyed, she ran her tongue along the length of it.

"She's unbelievable."

"The Japs sure love her."

Revived, Mia regained her feet, but she was having more trouble with her clothes. Two Japanese businessmen in conservative suits at a front-row table gazed up with impartiality that failed, as far as Freddy was concerned, to conceal their hearts' fond wish for a glimpse of some colossal American snatch. Mia was passing right above them, and her troubles had worsened. Her shoulder was out of her dress, her shoes were gone, and sadly, she'd lost her lollipop, too.

Then suddenly, in the midst of a step, she appeared stricken, as if she had just realized that her lollipop was missing. She kept looking around, until her gaze fell on Freddy. She smiled at him, wiggled her fingers in a babyish wave, and gave him a wink.

"What's going on here?" said Coop.

"I think she was waving at Freddy," said Manny.

Though back to dancing, she was still working hard to make contact, trying to let Freddy know he was special. She was performing for him. The whole thing. Every step. It was all shamelessly for him. And with this thought, he had to ask Coop's question: What the hell was going on here? What the hell had he done to get her to look at him like that, except to fuck her without hardly thinking about her? Was he in reality, not just in bullshit, some kind of sexual fireball? So that even a lazy, throwaway fuck was enough to have her up there waving at him like this, winking and calling for more? He'd taken her back to his apartment like she was a goddamn sleeping pill to divert him. That's all she'd been, a goddamn TV game show.

He remembered goofing in the elevator, where she'd slipped into his arms. The way they'd come through the door in a dance, the dizzying embrace begun in the hall. From its place in the corner, the bed exerted a magnetic pull, and its wide waiting softness reached out and caught them, their hands occupied with the discarding of clothing, the management of arousal. The last of their garments, her panties, his shorts and one sock, floated away like bubbles. He ate her for a while till she came; then she sucked him. When he entered her, he felt she enfolded him, her hot tugging cunt the center of the sensation, but encirclement was repeated in the overlaying of her arms on his shoulders, and the hug of her legs, her heels polishing little circles at the base of his spine, while her mouth drew his tongue in.

He was a little amazed, sitting there, taking a drink. This morning, he hadn't remembered any of this. The fogbank of his hangover had muffled everything, giving him only a detached, tepid appreciation. But now he saw clearly the way she pulled back to look at him. There was no way for him to avoid her searching eyes except by closing his own. So he pretended to give up sight in order to indulge his other senses. But she shut her teeth on his tongue, nipping and calling him back, and he obeyed. The hazel expanse around her pupils was flecked with yellow as she came again, her hips in a seizure of blood and chemicals and delight out of which she looked at him.

Freddy finished his drink, sucked the dregs, and chewed some ice chips in a famished way. He lit up a cigarette. Maybe you had to have a few drinks before you could remember what you did when you were smashed. Maybe there was like this booze sector in your brain—this alcohol compartment—and your drunken life was stored there and it was off limits when you were sober. You had to have a few pops. Booze punched your ticket, so you remembered.

Meeting eyes with a tall brunette waitress who appeared to be aimed in his direction, he gestured for another drink. She shot toward him, a blur of skin and sleeveless, sequined black bodysuit, bearing her round, cork-topped tray.

"Got something for you," she said, surprising him.

"Whadya mean?"

She was handing him this weird cardboard crown with little plastic diamonds glued onto it. Sticking out of one of the decorative holes in the crown was a piece of paper rolled into a tube. "Bet you can't guess who it's from?" she said.

"What is that?" said Coop. "Whata you got there?"

Unrolling the sheet showed him a pencil sketch of a girlish figure dancing in a harem costume, her arms upraised. Bold angular printing asked the question: WANT TO HOOK UP TONIGHT? The signature was one word: ME.

"Lemme see that," said Coop.

Freddy looked to the stage, where Mia swayed and crossed her arms, each hand descending to the opposite hip. She started fingering the hem of her dress, her expression befuddled, as if she were wrestling with a confusing impulse to disrobe.

At the same time, Coop was sliding the note off past the empty glasses and ashtrays. Freddy's attention was drawn to the movement. "What the hell you doing, Coop?"

"I want to see what this is," said Coop.

The waitress moved to leave and Freddy signaled to her with his empty glass: "Bring me another!"

"Sure," she said. "Jack Daniel's and rocks, right?"

"And a cheeseburger, okay, with some fries. I'm starving here."

"Sure."

"Double cheeseburger, double fries. Okay?"

"Sure."

Through the glare of the stage lights shaping the cigarette smoke above the intervening heads of the crowd, he was trying to reach Mia, to meet her eyes so he could be sure she saw him. In pinkish light, she was still poised to lift the dress over her head, her brow furrowed with indecision, like she was facing this new, unexpected problem. Almost positive that he had her attention, he shrugged in a way he hoped would suggest gigantic forces beyond his control and then he mouthed the words: *Not tonight!*

She stepped to the edge of the stage and bent to show him her cleavage. *Are you sure?* she asked, her lips forming these big sound-less words.

"What the hell is this?" said Coop. "I can't stand this."

Mia flexed her shoulders, first one and then the other, while her eyes managed to preview some erotic innovation at which she was expert.

Lifting his palms in a gesture he hoped would convey the existence of issues whose stakes were beyond anything he could possibly explain, Freddy moved his mouth through exaggerated shapes to tell her with a sort of wince: *I can't.*

Mia's arms arose in a blur of fluff that stripped off her dress and left her standing in a décolleté bra and bikini panties. "Then dance with me!" she cried out loud.

What? he thought, caught off guard. It felt like a command; it felt like a threat. Her thin arms were asking for him, the palms open, her hips moving to sweeten the invitation. When he scanned the ban-quette of cronies to his left, he found their faces in an uneven row, like shrunken heads strung on a rope, their eyes and lips stitched into slits by their snide attitudes.

"I think she wants you to dance with her," said Manny.

They were smirking, like he was caught in an embarrassing predicament. Like he was going to turn into a joke right in front of them.

"She's waiting," said Manny.

"Better get going."

"Just remember, you gotta take your clothes off, too."

Because Mia was the focus of the crowd's attention, her interest in Freddy had people turning in his direction. A few rows ahead a muscular, dark-haired young guy in a leather jacket was elbowing his beefy companion, the pair of them sneering. Freddy met their contempt with a snotty smile. He pushed on the table and got to his feet. Why the hell not? Wasn't this what he wanted? Like that black guy in *Newsweek* who said the phone book burst into flames as he read the address of the man he was going to kill. At his victim's door, the murderer's thoughts began to surface in a weird irresistible voice. Like the new Freddy, the henchman, the hireling, whose arrival was due but not predictable. To be totally out of fucking control.

Just then the waitress arrived with his drink and the cheeseburger and fries. He threw down the bourbon and grabbed a handful of fries. His buddies were sniggering. So he shrugged and said to them what he'd said to himself seconds ago: "Why the hell not?"

He set off for the stage, stuffing the fries into his mouth, munching away. Left behind, the gang barraged him with catcalls and mockery. Though Mia clapped when she saw he was coming, most of his zigzag course through the staggered tables was accompanied by wisecracks: "What an asshole!" "Who is this jerkoff?" "He takes his clothes off, I'm gonna puke!"

Mia reached to welcome him, her hips lost in some pelvic initiative, ceaseless and instinctual. The volume of the music went up half a dozen decibels. He felt like he was at the center of a horde of bats. She dipped, so he dipped. She pranced, pirouetted and kicked, then reached out to him. They held hands and kicked. Face to face, she did that shoulder thing. He twirled away and when he came back, she was bending forward at the waist, her hands wedged in between her legs, her fingertips pushing her thighs out as if to pry them open, while her arms squeezed the sides of her breasts so her cleavage swelled from the bra. He just put one hand behind his back, pointed the other to the ground, and bounced around a lot. He was blasted by the lights dangling on a grid above the audience. Blinking, he whirled back to Mia.

The fingers of one hand were inserted in the hem of her panties, while the other moved to cradle her own crotch. Her hips were still going. He threw up his hands. Giving him an angry, dangerous scowl, she released the clasp of her bra. She tossed it upstage, simultaneously turning her back on him so she could torment him with one last denial. She peeked over her shoulder with a promising glance. She waved her ass at him and crouching down, slipped out of the panties, like a child. And he saw his dead daughter on the mortuary slab. The way he had found her that day. He felt himself walking down the emptiness of that institutional corridor, his legs hollow, the distance unnatural, the beige paint flawless except for tiny bubbles high up where water pipes must have done damage. The waiting double doors of the hospital morgue parted, pushed open he guessed by the attendant with him. Ahead he saw the table strangely isolated in the middle of the room. The form beneath the sheet filled only half the table and then fell slack. It was an excruciating sight. At his side Mary faltered, her quavering presence leaving him as she stopped, and he went on. Disbelief was still alive in him, though besieged and unreasoning, and then he saw Emily's bloody clothes in a plastic bag on the floor. The print jumper and little black sandals she had worn to breakfast that morning. The tiny cloth underpants. When the sheet was lifted, he saw her frail limbs scraped and crooked, bruises all over her legs, and a discoloring on the left side of her face. Her bright black hair was caked with dirt. The tiny nubs of her breasts. Her crotch, the little crease in the hairless skin. She was still warm to the touch. But he could feel the cold moving in. It was like the last of her life was still leaving her.

The music was loud and he was continuing to dance, the allure of Mia's gaze disappearing in a rising sadness. She did a bump and grind, and hit her hip against him. But he was barely paying attention. Her hurt eyes cried out at him her question: What did she have to do?

The gang at his table was delirious. His cronies were calling to him like they were partners in what he was doing. When they knew nothing. Gawking and screeching. They didn't have a clue. This is a war dance, he thought. I'm on war footing, you fuckheads, his heart still and cold in his chest, like stone around stone.

ठ

■ ■ ■ ■ ■ ■ ■

Helen's mind was full of pot roast and a nasty, sort of rumored sense of being at fault that clung to her no matter what she did, like certain smells, especially chemical ones. Not that the whole question was really a question anymore, because it wasn't. Dinner was going to be beef stew, and it was too late to change it. She'd crossed the Rubicon, as that goofy kid used to say in Johnny's school. He'd been Johnny then, not John; not too big to let his mother call him Johnny if she wanted. Little Doubleday Robbins, talking about Rubicons, and outer space monsters. What a goof he'd been, poor jinxed little thing, following Johnny around everywhere, the way dogs did when a person had food they thought they had a chance at.

Grabbing a Winston, she tilted cautiously to the burner to light up, then crossed to the back door so she could blow the smoke out into the open air. That was back in Seattle, on Dorrie Street with the mist-topped mountains in view and Johnny just a little boy. I think we've crossed the Rubicon, Johnny, that crazy little Doubleday would say.

She loved smoking, she thought, peering out at the dainty fruit on the flowering crabapple in the neighbor's yard. Of course it was addictive. That's why it was good. Before her, the smoke tainted the air, like a cold weather breath. Or those mists in Seattle.

Back at the sink, she dropped the butt down the garbage disposal, and went back to work. She'd pretty much gone sleepless last night, tossing and fretting as she tried to decide whether to make pot roast or beef stew with dumplings. She wanted John's first home-cooked meal to be perfect. But it was hard in the middle of the night to know what perfect was. At some point, staggering to the bathroom, pork chops got into the running. They pushed beef right out. Smothered or stuffed—both sounded good. But then she must have woke up a little more, so she was thinking more clearly as she made the return trip to bed. Because by the time her head hit the pillow, she was back to beef. Beef was just more basic and straightforward. She kept seeing John across from her at the table in their brightly lit kitchen, and he was making the kind of steady, satisfied chomps men used when they were enjoying a well-cooked hunk of beef. It was near dawn by this point, morning leaking in around the edges of the lowered blinds. She'd decided to put off all decisions about the rest of the meal until she got back from driving out to pick John up from that terrible, miserable, depressing place.

And then that yellow van with John inside had snaked to a halt outside the gate, and she and Stuart piled from their car, like fans racing to a locker-room door where some famous athlete was going to exit. Of the six men who got out, John was the last, blinking against the glare of the sun, something funny about him, though she didn't have time to say what. She just felt herself take a quick breath like the oxygen was running out, and she had to snatch it before it was all gone. It was like she'd forgotten what every baby knew except when they screamed because they couldn't get what they wanted, and screaming got to be more important than breathing.

By now, John was on the ground, his palm over his eyes. That's when the problem of the beef came back. She wondered if she had time yet to switch. John was recoiling, tilting away like this animal who might flee back to where he'd come from. She shot a glance at Stuart, asking if he was worried, but as usual in regard to anything important, he was keeping his thoughts locked up in a place that, even after thirty-four years, she couldn't enter.

"Stuart," she said.

He looked at her in a way that made her feel she had just violated a very important rule. "What?" he said.

Just then the other men from the van started capering around, like the sand and scrub brush were all set up for a party. Three of them were, anyway. The fourth black man was marching all by himself down the road, a skinny, forlorn figure with nobody to meet him. The only white person aside from John was swaggering up to the blonde, and the second he got within reach, she fell on him. They started licking and bumping each other, like a couple of doozies who didn't have the sense they were born with.

By now the blacks were in their car, popping beer cans, the radio/ tape deck player strafing the air like this automatic weapon shooting rap music, sounding like somebody falling down the stairs and blaming somebody else every step of the way. The blonde, who was backing toward her car with the guy all over her, made a groaning kind of noise like they were going to finish their hanky-panky right there.

She looked at Stuart to share her disgust at the things going on around them. But he wasn't even where she expected to find him. He was marching up to John, who stood in the spiraling dust left by the van, holding his little canvas bag and a box, and staring at his father. She couldn't see Stuart's face, but the way he was stomping along, it looked like when he got there, he might just reach back and punch John. She felt hurt that they were leaving her out of this precious moment, but she defied the impulse to run over.

When the Bonneville sped off, spilling carbon monoxide and trailing their rap-crap jabbering racket, Helen shook her head at their departing dust. Off to her right, the blonde fell into the front seat of the Chevy with her moron on top of her. It was scary how not a one of them had a regretful or rehabilitated bone in their body. They might as well have been coming home from Club Med.

Stuart and John were talking, but in these short poverty-stricken bursts, like they were worried their supply of words was about to run out. When they finally shook hands, it was in a way that made her feel one of them had sold the other a used car in a deal neither was comfortable with. There was more damn intimacy between a bunch of movie stars giving awards, than you got with these two. Her smile felt like a dry swatch of paste somebody had slapped onto her face. And then John stepped toward her. It was weird the way it startled and scared her. It took him forever to arrive. When his arms closed around her, he felt huge. The tip of her head barely hit his sternum. She couldn't keep back the tears. He'd always been tall, but he felt covered over in bulky sheets of flesh like he was wearing too many clothes. Her arms couldn't get all the way around him. She had to settle for patting. He kissed the top of her head. She patted the curve of his back, and then stroked in tiny circles, wondering when his shirt had last been washed, and who had done it. She took hold of his arms just above the elbows, the way she would with a little boy she might lift up, though he was more like a tree she would have to climb. Ready to celebrate, she met his eyes and it felt like she was looking off a cliff. His gaze was like his body, layered over. He seemed hidden, buried right in front of her, and above his eye there was a scar.

"Hi, Mom."

"Johnny, honey. How are you?"

"Fine. Good."

"Good."

"Are you okay, Mom?"

"Oh, yes," she said.

Stuart's big hands were a surprise clapping down on them. "Let's put some miles between us and this damn place, okay?"

They climbed into their car, and she was amazed to see that they were the last to leave. The scar on John's brow was a stem of dead skin angling to his hairline, like somebody had tried to open him up with a can opener. He was sprawled in the back seat, where they'd told him he would have more leg room. The first words out of Stuart's mouth were to tell the story of the coffee, and the main points were his tolerance and her negligence. They passed some road kills, a dog or coyote whose identity they could argue about, a snake, and several small creatures mashed beyond recognition.

In the silences, she wanted to ask John about the scar. But she restrained herself. Instead, she sought to divert them all by talking about her art classes and her painting. She was careful to warn herself against going on too long. In order to make certain no one thought she was bragging or that her hopes were exaggerated, she started with the comment, "I know this is silly, but guess what? I've been taking an art class." Periodically, she reissued the phrase, using it as a kind of regulatory device that gave her a chance to look around and see whether or not it might be best if she shut up. "I know it's silly, but my teacher, Mr. Russell, thinks I'm talented." A mile or two later, she said, "I know it's silly, but Mr. Russell said the last one I did, which was of these blades of grass as big as a Monterey fir, was almost professional." The odd thing was the way this opportunity to carry on about her hobby relaxed her. It seemed to relax everybody. Even John acted interested.

Once they arrived at the house, though, none of that mattered, because she had to get back to reality and straight to work, melting meat fat in the frying pan and browning the beef cubes. Having crossed her Rubicon, that was for sure, as the meat, the bones, the drippings from the frying pan were all dumped in the kettle of boiling water. The recipe gave her a little break then, so she had a chance to catch up with John and Stuart, who were out in the backyard walking around the mobile home in which John was going to stay. She brought them two cold Cokes, and then had to run back to chop and dice the vegetables. A little later, she found Stuart napping in their bedroom, while John was sitting in front of the television. She had to wake Stuart and give him coffee and tell him not to leave John alone just now. She couldn't stay, because it was time to prepare the dumplings, rubbing in the shortening with a knife and adding the milk so they would be good dumplings, soft dumplings. Somewhere in the middle of this task, John and Stuart passed through the kitchen, heading down to the basement. She was about to add the chopped and diced vegetables that lay spread on the cutting board when she heard them returning a few minutes later, their heavy feet thumping up the stairs. Sweat speckled her brow. Their arms were wrapped around cardboard boxes, their shoulders almost touching. Talking to one another, they strode toward the back door without even looking at her.

"Wait! Where are you going?"

"Why?" Stuart was startled, or annoyed, she wasn't sure.

"I was wondering. I'm almost done here. It won't be long now." With the cutting board over the pot, she edged a landslide of vegetable particles into the steam. "I want to come with you."

"We're just moving some of John's things out to the trailer."

"I'll meet you there," she said.

She gave the stew a stir, and thought of baked Virginia ham, with brown sugar and pineapples, and she felt as if somebody was saying awful things about her somewhere in the neighborhood. When she stepped out the back door, the silver wall of the mobile home crowded her, like a spaceship had landed in their little yard. Inside, Stuart and John were conferring over the open mouth of one of the cardboard boxes.

"Don't you think it's a good idea, you sleeping in the trailer like this?" she said to John as she joined them.

"I do," he nodded, plucking up several pair of shoes from the box.

"Those shoes need polishing."

"I can do it."

She hovered near John as he placed the shoes on the floor of the closet. "We thought you'd want privacy, so this seemed perfect," she told him.

She opened a nearby drawer of crisp, neatly stacked bedding. The neighboring drawer was stuffed with towels and washcloths. "You can change these whenever you want to. The washing machine's right in the basement. Or I'll do it."

"I can do it, Mom."

"Well of course you can do it. But it might be nice to have somebody do it for you."

He was back at the box, rooting around like he couldn't find something. She hurried over and peered in.

"All your things from in your apartment are either here in these boxes," she said, "or in those that are still in the basement."

"I was showing him," said Stuart, as if someone had accused him of failing at something.

"I mean, we didn't throw away a thing. Not even those filthy magazines. Not a scrap."

"I appreciate it, Mom."

"Are you missing something?"

"No."

"Oh, God," she said. They both looked at her, but she didn't have time to explain, racing to the kitchen and arriving just in time to add the potatoes. Studying the frothy brew, she thought of painting the steam. She wondered if John was ever going to ask to see her paintings. She wondered if he'd really been as interested as he seemed in the car.

When the back door opened, Stuart led the way in, his brow all craggy with concern. "Everything all right?"

"Fine. Almost ready. About a half hour, and then we can eat."

"Great," said Stuart, as he went off trailed by John into the television room.

Just beyond the window, leaves stirred with a mild breeze, the light of the sinking sun touching her face. Well, Johnny, I think we've crossed the Rubicon, she wanted to say, as if she were that little Doubleday Robbins himself.

Wouldn't it be nice if he came up to the door right now, that funny little boy with the spiral notebook he always carried under his arm. If he just came up and knocked like he used to, and when she went to answer, there he was looking at her through the screen, asking her, Where's Johnny? Is he home? And then she'd call Johnny, and Johnny would come out, blond and handsome as always, no taller than her waist, looking up at her with those straightforward eyes.

She wanted to go in and ask him right now about that little Doubleday—see if he knew anything about him, whatever had happened to him, he had been such an odd little thing in most every way, but John had been good to him, always so kind and patient, finding time for little Doubleday with those thick glasses that he seemed to have been born looking out of, and his brain full of baseball statistics while John always played the games—baseball, football, basketball. It had always touched her about her own son, the tenderness he showed, the generosity toward somebody he could have shunned or teased.

When she called John and Stuart, they came rolling into the kitchen, their voices bringing to an end some conversation that had excited them. She put the stew before them and they praised her. First Stuart, then John. It bothered her a little, the way John seemed to just parrot his father, and she started thinking about her after-dinner smoke.

"I almost made ham," she said, as John lifted a spoonful of beef and gravy up to his mouth.

"Ham would have been good," he said.

"I thought about pork chops, too."

"But beef stew's my favorite," Stuart said.

She tried to meet John's eyes, but he avoided her, and she knew he was pretending to be hungry, pretending to like the stew.

"Remember little Doubleday Robbins?" she said.

"Who?"

"Doubleday Ro—"

"Oh, sure."

"Do you know what happened to him?"

"Did something happen to him?"

"No, no, I mean where is he? Where he is now? What did he do with his life?"

"I don't know."

She took a drink of water, watching John, feeling like she'd come into her kitchen at midnight and found the table surrounded by ghosts. He lifted a spoonful of stew to his mouth and started chewing. When his father asked him to pass the salt and pepper, he didn't do it. The containers, one black and the other white, floated through the air. But it wasn't John handing them. John wasn't there.

9

Dear Mom,
    wrote Emily to Mary, who lay on her stomach, her arms wrapped around her pillow.

> *I feel dizzy. I am so confused. Where am I? Tired. I am going to try to sleep, so maybe this horrible confusion and nightmare will disappear.*

Mary sank through the night, fighting to hang on, while Emily scribbled letters on three-holed, blue-lined paper and sent them off:

> *I can see more clearly now, and my hand isn't shaking as much as I write. I am starting to remember. I remember a man. He was tall. He grabbed me, picked me up, threw me. He took me somewhere, pulled me away. Away from Mom and Dad. He had a car. A big car. Where are they? Why am I here? Must sleep. . . . Sorry. . . .*
>   *. . . I think I slept for a long time. But I'm not sure. I think it was a long time because I am very sweaty. It is hard to*

write to you, because it is almost totally dark. I am very hungry. My limbs feel sore, and my hair is sticky. I tasted it, blood. The sticky is blood I think. My head hurts. I miss you, Mom, and Dad. Too confused to cry. Too confused to think, or to write any more. Sorry. Sorry.

Sorry

Dear Mom,

Some time has gone by. I don't know how much, and it's scary to have no idea about the time that is passing, but I found some food. A bag was at the end of the room when I woke up. I guess someone brought it while I was asleep. I reached inside and felt some wrappers. A sandwich maybe. For now I ate some bread. I also discovered, I think, where I am. I think it's maybe a boat. There's a splashing noise. They are waves, I think. I'm sailing somewhere. Going away. Away, over the ocean. But what ocean? How far? Where?

Trying

Dear Mom,

Why don't you ever write me? I want to hear from you. Can't you answer? Please!

Scared

Mom,

I ate some more bread. I finally cried. No, sobbed. Once I started, it was endless. I am lost. I feel completely empty. All the time I think, why am I here? I've tried to think about all the possibilities of what could have happened. Who could have done this to me? All I can come up with is that it's some kind of awful mix-up. My family doesn't have much money, if this is a kidnapping. I've never committed a crime. As far as I know, the only person who really hates me is Christopher Abott from school. But he wouldn't/COULDN'T have *done this. Maybe it's a joke or something. But if it is a joke, then it is getting really old.*

Guilty

Mommy, Mommy,

I am so angry. Angry at everything. I hate, I hate every-one! I hate everyone, because they let this happen. Why me! I have to stop writing, I am so angry my pen is shaking, I am sweating like crazy. . . .

. . . I took a break, I feel a little better now. I ran back and forth, and rammed into the walls, screaming. Why! WWHHHYYYY!!!!!

I haven't told you about the bathroom situation. There is none, that's the problem. Finally I couldn't hold it anymore so I did it in the corner. Later when it was light, I looked, just a stain. I'm so glad I have my pen, so grateful for my pen with its pretty gold rings that you gave me—that you and Daddy gave me on my birthday. Without it what would I do!

Miserable

Mommy,

I'm sorry, but I had another banging rampage. I fell while I was running. My knee is sticky, it hurts. Not as much as everything else. But it hurts bad. Why can't I sleep!

Hurt

Dear Mommy,

More tears. I miss you and Dad so much. I miss Andrew and I miss Anthony. I miss the lemon tree in the backyard and the eldergrass in the rocks. I miss the sky and the wind and the gulls and kingfishers and plovers, especially the snowy kind. I miss TV, and Roscoe, my monkey, and Puzzle, even if his stuffing is coming out. And my dollies, Jasmine and Lucinda and Samantha. My bed—my own pillows and sheets, and my desk, candy, pie, noodles, FRUIT! Friends, teachers, even school, PEOPLE!

Another stain. I want to go home! I want to get out.

Crying

Mommy,

What would I do if I couldn't write, if I didn't have my beautiful new pen to write? It makes me feel like you're here, that you're close by. Without it, I would probably go crazy. I mean, really really insane.

Who knows, I might be dead.

I hope not.

But I'm tired. So very tired.

If I don't write anymore, it just means that I'm giving up.

Sorry

Mary had to go to the bathroom. Minutes passed in a halflight of resentment and irritation as she tried to find an option that would let her pee without forcing her up from bed. Shadows were coming in the open window. Her mind had a kaleidoscopic quality, shapes that broke apart and then returned as something less compelling but more familiar.

There was no choice. It was going to happen somewhere. Her kidneys ached. She sat up and made her way to the bathroom, noting that the digital clock was rolling from 1:16 to 1:17 A.M. Struck by a feeling as vigorous as if Roger, who lay behind her, had called her name, she paused at the door. However, her focus was not on Roger's sprawled form, but on the sheets she had just vacated. She imagined herself lying there, her mind narrowing toward a fleeing idea, the way a detective might chase an elusive clue.

When she left the bathroom a few minutes later, she was still feeling puzzled and she was also thirsty. She started toward the kitchen refrigerator for some Pellegrino. At the bottom of the stairs, she paused in the hall to root through the mail that lay in a basket on the antique table. It was bills and catalogues and junk mail. She never heard from anybody she cared about, she thought; only people who wanted something. Opportunists trying to sell her things or to collect for what they'd already talked her into buying. But there was somebody she was waiting to hear from. Somebody with whom she longed for contact. She wanted to know what they were up to. How they felt about things.

She was in the kitchen pouring Pellegrino into a blue plastic tumbler when it occurred to her that the communication she yearned for had been stolen. Or maybe just left in the mailbox, she thought. Was it her mother? She should call her tomorrow.

She opened the front-door locks, and stepped out onto the wide concrete porch with its descending stairs and black iron railings. The lawn rolled through the quiet moonlight to the street. At the bottom of the driveway, the mailbox was built into the first of the two matching brick mounds that flanked the entrance. On her way to it, she passed through moonlight and a mild breeze that cooled her skin beneath the cotton of her nightgown. Pulling the horseshoe-shaped metal door down, she reached in and touched an envelope.

Though it was what she'd come looking for, she had not really expected to find anything. The surprise immobilized her, and she saw Emily seated at a school desk, her brow furrowed with the strain of composition, as she nibbled the thumbnail of her hand holding the pen she'd been given for her birthday, an imitation Mont Blanc. Her need to express the complex secrets of her present circumstances held her mesmerized over the blank pages of a spiral notebook. Clearly, she was alive somewhere, having been kidnapped rather than killed, and the letter in Mary's fingers contained the explanation of what had happened, a description of the steps necessary for her return.

The envelope she was tearing open was stamped with the words PERSONAL and URGENT, but already she was back to reality. She must be still half asleep, she thought. Even in the moonlight, it was possible to see that what she had removed from the envelope was an elaborate four-page vitamin advertisement.

Back in the house, she dropped the crumpled mess into the trash and locked the door. Her Pellegrino was on the hallway table and she took a sip, then climbed the stairs.

Roger remained on his side, facing away, and she eased into bed carefully, trying not to disturb him. But as her head settled into the pillow, he asked, "Anything wrong?"

"I'm sorry I woke you."

"You were gone a long time."

"Thirsty."

"We should have a mini-fridge up here."

"We don't need that."

"We don't need it but it would be nice."

The silence that followed stretched on long enough to seem the beginning of sleep. "Roger?" she said.

"What?"

"You know that pen—Emily's pen—the imitation Mont Blanc pen that she had with her? Have you seen it?"

"I don't think I ever saw it."

"It must be in the basement. In the armoire."

"Didn't you and Freddy put all that stuff away in the armoire? I thought you did. I mean, if you kept it."

"Yes," she said.

"We better get some sleep," said Roger. "Morning will be here before we know it."

"It always is," she said, imagining the boys at breakfast, Anthony and Andrew yammering and chopping up fruit for their cereal, wanting to add chocolate syrup to their milk. She thought of their needs and pastimes, and the way everything changed so quickly. Trucks and then Ninja Warriors. Ninja Turtles. Baseball cards, and baseball uniforms. She tried to look into their eager, expectant eyes and that reminded her of Emily kissing them as babies, as she struggled to subdue her demon jealousy, patting their heads and looking up to Mary for approval.

"Good night, Roger," she said, patting his arm.

"See you in the morning."

Still, twenty minutes later, she remained wide awake, and shortly after that, she was sneaking down the basement stairs, padding across the concrete floor to the armoire in the corner draped in shadow like a shrine in a grotto. Carefully opened, the doors revealed four fancy dresses on hangers, their hems wavering. The drawers and shelves were filled with the toys and stuffed animals that she had been unable to discard or give to charity. Below the clothing three pairs of tiny shoes stood in a row, one dress-up, two sneakers. In the pocket of the backpack that had served as Emily's book bag, Mary found the pen, sleek and black with its gold clip. She took it out and closed her fingers around it, and the physical fact of its shape in her hand reassured her that Emily was not off somewhere writing furiously in an effort to reach her, waiting for her mother to respond.

10

■ ■ ■ ■ ■ ■ ■

"Are we boring you?" said Coop. "Freddy!"

Freddy looked up from his watch, registering the fact that it was almost 3:00 A.M. In the row of faces around him every eye was snotty and wise-assed, every mouth twisted with amused contempt.

"You with us? Have we hypnotized you?" asked Manny, using a singsong tone.

"He's probably thinking about his dancing. You thinking about your dancing, Freddy?"

"I hope not. It wasn't that good."

"You got guys here, Freddy," Coop said. "We're havin' fun, but you're not with us. You have dancing girls. Look at that. She's naked. What's her name again?"

Just the way he had discovered distance between himself and Mia this morning, Freddy felt removed from Coop and the rest of them. They were like a TV image with the volume very low and the TV itself in another room. "Do you know what?" he said. "Now I don't mean tonight. I'm not talking about tonight, but—"

"What? What'd you say, Freddy?"

"He said, 'Not tonight.' "

Freddy lifted his drink, and flicked his wrist, filling his mouth with bourbon. They were so smug and ignorant, he felt he could say anything to them. He could tell them exactly what was going on and they wouldn't know. "I'm talking about something that happened. It happened to me. And it could happen to you, too." He picked up the last crumbs of his second cheeseburger and ate them.

"But not tonight," said Silas.

"Of course not. Never tonight," Manny grumbled.

"What are we going to do here, play charades, Freddy?" said Coop. "You gonna do gestures and shit?"

Freddy pointed his finger at Coop, cocking his thumb like the hammer on a pistol. "It happened long ago."

"Great," said Coop. "Cowboys."

Freddy grinned with an exhilaration that all but ripped his face open. Wider and wider went his mouth, more and more teeth exposed as big as eggs, abandon lighting up his eyes.

"Look at him," said Silas, "the fuckin' cat that ate the canary."

"No, no, no, this ain't the cat that ate the canary," said Coop. "This is the guy that ate Mia's pussy. Am I right, Freddy?"

Freddy nodded.

"Answer like a man, Freddy. I want a real answer."

"Sure," he said. "I'm just trying to make a point. To let you in on something."

"Who cares?" said Coop.

"What I want to know," Freddy told them, "is have any of you guys ever heard a sound building in your head, building up over a period of many days—a strange sound, but it's like a vacuum cleaner?"

"A what?"

"A vacuum cleaner."

"Oh, sure," said Coop, rolling his eyes. "A vacuum cleaner sound in my head. Sure. Usually, of course, I find it most common when the maid is cleaning the rug on the hallway in the hotel."

"Or when you're jerking off with it."

"Or when I'm jerking off with it. Right. Exactly."

Freddy was nodding, his exaggerated, facetious grin splitting his face over his teeth like a hatchet. Somewhere in a back alley part of his brain, a clot of shadows was collecting and retreating around the wavering form of his handgun. Scarlet projections from the gelled stage lights swooped over the table, tainting his fingers nested on the glass of whiskey. He was trying to focus a version of John Booth's eyes, looking and seeing the handgun. But the image wouldn't come together. Things always raced ahead to the aftermath, the body sagging in a bloody narrow of crumpled sheets. Or else the fuckhead was a corpse in the kitchen, slumped at the table, one hand near a mug of spilled coffee. Eyes like puddles of mucus. Or maybe if Freddy found him in front of the TV, the asshole lay sprawled half off the couch, the volume still blaring, his gaze unentertained.

Suddenly, the music was as loud as a car wreck. The broad on stage was stripped down to the glare of her tits floating through icy blue underwater lighting tinged with blood, her pale sad nakedness swimming around, imploring the crowd and the night with her unprotected, sweet, perishable beauty that they hold her, watch her, protect her, love her, fuck her. At the same time she warned them to beware, because they could not have her, ever.

Coop stood up, violently. He raised his hands as if to slam them down on the table. But instead, he lowered them slowly, leaning forward to eyeball Freddy: "The vacuum cleaner, Freddy! The goddamn vacuum cleaner!"

"What?"

"What about it? You never told us, and you promised."

"It's the last time—the very last time you had an original thought," said Freddy. "Try and think when that was, Coop! Try and remember. Because then what happened was you got cocky and so you rode on it. Enjoyed it—savored it—until you started hearing that vacuum cleaner in your brain. And suddenly that thought was gone, and now you barely remember it."

"But you don't mean tonight?" said Silas.

"No. No, no, no. Not tonight," said Coop. "He said that."

Freddy flung his hands wide in a gesture that accepted their attack. He was totally immune to them. In the same breath, he managed to caricature a kind of world-weary disappointment. Then he opened his mouth and belched. He turned away, laughing, but it all felt pretend, like he was laughing at the fact that nothing was funny. Nothing anywhere. It was perfect. It was useless. Totally fucking useless. He lit a cigarette, and jerked his head back with the first drag, a move that brought him into eye contact with a new stripper. Verna. Dressed in combat fatigues, or what was left of them, she waved to him, adding a touch of hips, and running her hands under her breasts.

Another one, he thought. For fucksake. He waved back, smiling coldly, letting his fingers flutter and fall one at a time. It was hours since he'd left Mia on stage. He could see her at a nearby table trying to revenge herself by flirting with a couple of young, muscular guys. She laughed a lot, and kept squeezing the bigger guy's arm.

The siren of an LAPD squad car shot down the street outside. Freddy watched the blue of the front window break apart with a starburst of white and red, and he felt they were coming after him.

He shoved on the table and stood up. "I gotta take off," he said. "I'll see you guys later." He couldn't quite get his feet solidly under him, wooziness rampaging through him in search of a way to take him over. He stood there, watching Verna whip off the last article of her costume, except for two cardboard grenades hanging off her breasts.

"Where're you going?" asked Coop. "It's only three A.M."

"Commitments, commitments," said Freddy.

"But Mia's still working."

"Mia, schmia," said Coop. "He's got to go turn off his fucking vacuum cleaner. Ain't that right, Freddy? You got to turn off your vacuum cleaner."

"He left on his vacuum cleaner somewhere."

"I think I hear it."

"I think I hear it, too."

"But *do* you know what it is?" said Freddy. "Because do you really? Because what is happening is that it is sucking what was once your so-called brain right out of you and—"

"Yeah?" said Coop.

"Yeah?" said Manny.

"—and it is leaving it empty, because what I'm—"

"Sounds horny to me!"

He lunged the first few steps, trying to laugh, as he worked his way through the confusion of tables. He had to place his feet carefully because they were heavy and he was contending with a floor that kept shifting to unpredictable distances below him.

On the deserted street, he put the cigarette to his lips, dragging so hard he made a squeaky noise of effort and stress. He tossed what was left and set off alongside the mountainous gloom of the parking garage. He turned into the mouth, heading toward his eight-year-old white Cadillac Seville. The sight of it alone beneath the overhead lights trailing off through the expanse of empty stalls made him think of the day he bought it. He fit the key into the lock, and stood watching replicas of himself and Mary, a pair of youthful happy figures prowling the Cadillac showroom. As these distant shapes made their impulsive selection, giggling and a little giddy, he heard the buttons pop up on the car door. He looked off into the dimness, the banks of stone and steel girders. How different his life had been with Emily alive, the twins just born, his business thriving. He climbed into his car, lighting up another smoke. The Seville was a totem from that time. Sentimental, he thought, as he cruised onto the street.

Before entering the freeway, he pulled into a convenience store where he ordered a large container of black coffee. He was about to exit, when he realized that the flimsy cup would never protect his fingers from the scalding heat. He went back to the cashier, a chunky blond girl, who had just dialed a number on the phone. Above the cash register, there was a rack of plastic cups with handles, lids, and decals, and he asked to buy one, so he could drink the coffee comfortably. The girl could barely contain her annoyance with him for interrupting her phone call. She told whoever was on the other end that they should "Hang on just one stupid second." Then she handed Freddy a cup sporting a baseball bat and Dodger's decal, took his money, and stomped away, saying, "Okay?" to Freddy in a tone that would have been more appropriate if he had just made an obscene remark.

"Sure," he said. "Fine." I'm on my way to kill someone, you nasty little bitch. Maybe I ought to start with you. Huh? Why the hell not?

Something nervous flickered in her eyes, as she saw him studying her like he was measuring her for a piece of clothing he knew she would hate. Her mouth froze, and she started to lower the phone. So he smiled. "You're very rude," he said, and walked away.

"Sorry."

"You oughta be."

The freeway to Culver City was unusually empty. For a long time, no one passed in either direction. The tires hummed, pulling him along, some guy on talk radio ranting about a combination of corruption, deception, and ineptitude in the Democrats. Freddy started flicking the dial through a series of stations, until this shrill, officious voice caught him, and he listened to a different guy giving a commentary on the latest Laker loss.

Ahead, the first visible tail lights were more than a mile off, and beyond them floated a red speckling like a squadron of airplanes. Across the concrete divider, a truck and trailer, the side emblazoned with gigantic oranges, boomed past.

After a minute or two, he moved on from the sports, tapping the station button, until a classical broadcast brought him to a halt with a rain of delicate notes making him glance out the window to see if there were any stars visible. The instrument that seemed so unearthly was a harpsichord—if he remembered right. Not only did he associate it with the stars, but it made him think of Mary and Emily. Singing. Or running. Emily dropping a white porcelain bowl filled with floating flowers that broke into shards, sending water and petals all over the tile floor. She cried as he helped her clean up the mess, the two of them on their hands and knees.

Eight years ago, the last look he had into her eyes was one of happiness at breakfast. When later that day he learned she was dead, run down by a drunk driver, he thought, I'll kill him. His feelings possessed a cold authority. Like an overwhelming current, that would pull him along with it forever. He could remember the sunlight, the clear pure sky through which he was traveling along the San Diego Freeway. He was worried about business, that dealer Bobby Goleb who he believed was a crook planning to stiff him. He was sliding to the right for the exit that would take him to Emily's school. He'd been scheduled to pick her up earlier, and then the thing with Goleb had demanded additional attention, so he'd left word on the machine for Mary to help him out, if she could, he would be a little late. He'd called the school and left a message that Emily should wait for him or her mother. But somehow the information had gotten all screwed up. With Goleb, he'd closed a deal for earrings from Africa—they were ivory, with animal faces etched into them. On the jazz radio station Erroll Garner was reinventing

"These Foolish Things." Unsuspecting, blindly trusting in the guarantee of his ordinariness, his commonplace right to safety, cruised through the last seconds of his innocence. And then his car phone buzzed. He grabbed up the phone and said "Hello," but he couldn't understand what he was being told. Shock was a muffling element like an anesthetic which made him fearful that he was being cut open without feeling it. And he was right to be apprehensive, because moments later he felt like his skin was being ripped off.

The sign for the Buchanan Street exit flew toward him. The trip seemed only minutes long. He knew the route, having scouted it often. He took the exit, turning right onto Sumner, which brought him into a grid of residential streets. In less time than he was prepared for, he was slowing down, having arrived across the street from the home of Stuart and Helen Booth, lightless and cloaked in a greenish screen by the surrounding shrubs and Japanese maples.

He shut off the engine and sat waiting for a clear thought. When it came, he leaned to the right and opened the glove compartment. Inside lay the silver gleam of his nine-millimeter Glock coiled in the shadows, the barrel touching the brown paper bag with the pint bottle of bourbon inside.

He plucked up the cold heft of the weapon. Its sorcerous power passed through his palm to the bones of his wrist, and then went deeper, engendering a cold thrill.

With his left hand, he pumped the action, loading a round. Through the flash of the breech, he saw the rising cartridge jump into the chamber. The hammer was cocked so he lowered it, wanting to make certain everything was in working order. He used his thumb to release the magazine, then ejected the shell and pinched it back into the magazine, pushing down the other rounds. With the weapon empty, he set the magazine down on the passenger seat and worked the action, lifting an invisible shell into the chamber. Aiming at a street light, he squeezed. The hammer fell with a click. He tried it again, wristing the action, savoring the lethal machine sound of the bullet loading. He sighted on air, and squeezed. Click again. All right, he thought. He transferred the pint of bourbon to his pocket, pushed the glove compartment closed, and climbed from the car.

Across the quiet street a Volvo sat in the driveway. The house was small, a single floor with a tile roof and white clapboard siding dimmed and speckled by the play of the shifting leaves and their falling outlines. Billowing fuschia full of pinkish bulbs, and mondo grass like cradling knives, grew in beds along much of the house.

He crossed the lawn and went up to the front door. He took the knob in his fingers. Of course, it was locked. Well, maybe a window. It didn't matter. He'd kick the fucker in, if he had to.

He took a sip of bourbon. The driveway gleamed and made a sandy, scraping sound beneath his feet. He was checking each window, his gaze exploring the empty interior of the living room, the solitary chairs and couches, the glowing enamel of the kitchen, the waiting Formica of the chairs and table. On two windows, lowered blinds blotted his view, and he imagined the Booths asleep just out of sight, the parents behind one window, the asshole just beyond the other.

Gliding to the back of the house, he saw the rear entrance a few feet away. Across from it stood the silver frame of a mobile home unattached to any vehicle, and surreal in the moonlight, like something marooned, this gigantic discarded tin can. He took one final sip of bourbon and stepped toward the house, still stealthy, but with adrenaline firing his pulses. He had the screen door open and was closing his fist on the knob of the main door, when he noticed a thick orange electrical cord emerging from a back window to arc through the cool moonlight to the window of the trailer, where it entered.

He looked away and then he looked back, shocked that he had seen the fact but not the importance of the mobile home, as he came around the house. How tense he'd been—how uptight and fucking mechanical. The only reason for a cord to supply current to the trailer was that someone was living inside. The Booths' home was small and John Booth was a grown man. That's where they would put him, thinking he would like it, thinking they were giving him a present. That's where he would be and it was where Freddy would find him. In the trailer. And he'd be there alone.

II

Hello, John, said Emily to the tossing limbs and torso of John Booth. He pawed the bed, struggling to resist a colossal wind. *Hello, Hello,* she sang. When he tried to join the wind, flapping his arms as if to fly, her omnipotent voice intervened. *No, no,* she reminded him, deflating his hopes of escape. *Wait. Where are you going?*

He stopped. He lay there. It was pointless, and he knew it, his breathing tentative, as if it might cease, his bulk unfeeling.

John, she hummed, *John, so you're out. Out of that cell. Out of that sealed-up suffocating box. Out of that inhuman hole as miserable as my grave. They let you out. And so you went. Wondering how to live, expecting to live.*

But what about me? What about me, John? I want to live. Can't I live too? Or are you going to live without me, John? Is that what you think? Without me, John?

Rest was all he wanted. A kind of interlude of nothing. Just a pause. One he could come back from. Sleep. A little sleep. He had crossed into a world where mysterious laws beyond his influence ruled, and there she had waited. Now he was sinking further, alone and out of control, until he passed by the last particle of thought he would ever remember, like a rising bubble taking his last breath away, and then when he knew nothing, he found her again. Only now she wasn't alone. There were others. They were plentiful, the childish dead. Spilling up from their graves in a display of wide wet wounds and mortal fevers, bearing evidence of blows, and neglect, and starvation, they came to make their claims. They advanced with an anguished eloquence, filling the air like a horde of gnats. Infants in diapers. Newborns sucking pacifiers. Some were Emily's age. Others were younger, and still others were older. In Levis, in play clothes, in sarongs and saris, in sport outfits and academic uniforms, in rags and gay party dresses, wearing an assortment of T-shirts and baseball caps, or shamelessly naked. They hovered behind Emily in a flame of approval as she approached him.

No, no, John. No. It's not possible. It's really not. I can't allow it. Why should you live? I mean, can't you imagine how I feel?

I had so many exciting plans that day, such wonderful hopes, until you came along and ruined them. I'd been promised a new dress and Mom had said that when she arrived home and managed to get the twins settled down—because they were babies and needed all kinds of attention which I didn't have to have so much anymore because I was growing up. So we were making a date. And as much as I liked the twins because they were babies and cute and sort of stupid and everything, and as much as I was proud of how I was growing up, it was still really annoying sometimes, and kind of a little scary, too, the way everybody thought they deserved so much attention. That they just had to have it. But the good thing— the really, really lucky thing—was that Mom knew how this wasn't exactly fair—I mean, knew how I had more than one kind of feeling about all this, if I had a brain in my head. And so she made a point to do special things with me, to have Special Time just between the two of us.

And so on that particular day, John, we had one of those times planned. We were going to pick out a new dress for me. And then maybe we would go out and have dinner, together, just the two of us. Dad was supposed to pick me up from school and then he had agreed to baby-sit, as soon as Mom got Anthony and Andrew fed and changed and all that. It was a real promise he had made, and she had made, too, a solemn promise like in a fairy tale that we would sit down with our Storybook Heirlooms catalogue and decide on a new party dress for me, and then if there was time, we would go out to dinner. We had narrowed down the dress question to just two possibilities.

One was on page eight and it was a European length Renaissance print velvet and pink taffeta with a ruffle collar. There was a bow in the back, a fancy sash, and an attached petticoat. Sometimes I just felt I had to have it. Mom thought it was great, too, but another one was her favorite. It was on page twelve. A teal velvet portrait dress with a high romantic collar and a fitted waist. The bodice was lace and the sleeves had tucked stitching. I really didn't know how I was going to choose. At school, I had just started crying all of a sudden without being able to tell anybody why. When Mrs. Ambrose asked what was wrong, I couldn't tell her, "I don't know what dress to buy!" So I didn't say anything and she looked at me like she thought I was spoiled.

The other thing I was looking forward to was that, because Mom was going to be busy with the twins at first, it was almost for sure that I would be able to watch a tape on TV. I wanted to see The Little Mermaid again, even though I'd already seen it twice. Each time it left me with a funny sort of off-the-ground feeling I could not name. But part of it was scary and part of it was very, very sad. It had to do with the difficult choice the mermaid had to make, when she had to pick between her father, Lord of the Ocean, and the Prince, who walked in the air of the earth.

It hurt me to watch that story. To see her thrown into such a puzzle with no one to guide her but a crab who, though goodhearted, was certainly not wise. Because after all, he was a crab. So what could he really know about being a little girl in either the water or the world facing such questions? But this way that I felt, this funny hurt that I felt as I sat on the couch nestled in pillows, munching crackers and cheese from a plate, was a hurt that I wanted again. So my hope that day was to get home quick, check Mom with the twins, take the Heirloom catalogue to the TV room, put on the tape, and maybe with this viewing, figure it all out.

Now the more you hear about all this, I just bet you are starting to see why I'm so mad at you, John. And I know you're sorry, but that's nothing compared to what happened to me. Your feelings aren't even real things. My body was skin and delicate bones and lots and lots more weight every day. These are not equal, I don't think. I weighed sixty-eight pounds, and your car, John, was tons of metal coming at such a speed, heaving pistons and engines with the power of hundreds of horses. The speed multiplied the weight to generate a violence against which I could find no protection. My screams, my outstretched hands had no effect. Do you see? Because the point I am trying to make is about you, really, and the fact that you must understand that, as my body was crushed by the onslaught of your car, so are your feelings crushed by the onslaught of my death.

I was on my way home, John, but I arrived at the morgue. Dreaming of parading around in a new frilly dress, I was stripped of my skin. Instead of wrestling with the Little Mermaid's dilemma, I was laid out on a cold metal table whose surface was veined with channels and grooves. Two strangers approached wearing rubber gloves, carrying knives and clamps and saws, to find the cause of my death. One took up a short knife, while the other studied the forms they had to fill out. The first one worked to dig a semicircle across the top of my head from ear to ear, severing my hair as if he might scalp me. Inserting his gloved fingers, he started to struggle, pulling his hands in opposite directions. In minutes, he peeled my face down like some old Halloween mask, so I was a sheet of fat and veins in a glistening slime of wrinkles. With a saw he gouged a crevice in the top of my skull, and then, applying a circular clamp, he brought an increasing pressure until the skull cracked along the cut. The exposed brain appeared a spongy mosaic of ridges and folds whose color, visible through a pinkish film, was a dull white.

He opened my abdomen up with a scalpel, slicing down from below the base of my throat to a point just above my navel. With barely a pause, the blade sent a seam out to my right hip, then another to my left hip. My organs were clean and wholesome, as bright as the parts of a brand new puzzle whose freshness lay untouched behind its cellophane wrapper. My liver, my kidneys, my brain and my lungs, pink and virginal, were pilfered from the unprotesting thing I had become. All my organs were sectioned into specimens to be weighed, fingered, probed, and analyzed for my secrets. My disbanded parts cooperated helplessly, and the cause of death was announced:

Multiple fractures of the lower extremities, along with contusions of the spleen, liver, kidneys and lungs. Skull fracture and contusions of the brain. Death followed shock and massive internal bleeding.

But they were wrong. It wasn't the truth. That wasn't the real cause of death. Had they looked inside me forever, they would not have found it. Because it was you. You were the cause of death, John. The real cause of death was you.

Peering in the window, Freddy recoiled, fearing he had been seen. John Booth was surging into a sitting position. He swayed, unable to raise his arms. As he determinedly struggled, his expression evolved from stress to bewilderment. Slowly, his inability to control his own limbs depressed him. He sat there. Then he fell back, and a force that resembled a series of mild electrical jolts went through him. After several seconds, he was prone and motionless under the white sheet, his right foot sticking out from the wavy ridges.

Freddy took a breath and, with a cupped palm, worked the action of the handgun, so he'd have a round in the chamber. He lowered the hammer with his thumb and headed for the door.

When his left hand closed on the knob, his right started flexing on the grip of the automatic. The pressure needed to undo the catch and then to pry the door out from the frame inflamed nerve endings where his spine linked his body to his brain.

The interior of the trailer, visible in the gap of the opening door, was an oblong of synthetic wood paneling and tacky plaid upholstery overcast in shadows. He placed his weight carefully on the first step. As he slipped into the trailer, he could feel himself entering the strange and unknown dimension where his projections had always abandoned him, leaving him behind as they leaped ahead to show him the bloody aftermath.

The trailer ended with a window above the bed built into the wall. External light from the moon and several nearby street lights was saturating the brown and beige checkered curtains. John Booth lay as Freddy had last seen him, flat on his back in a tangle of sheets. Only now Freddy could hear him. He could hear him breathing. John Booth's upper body rose and fell at a staccato pace. His mouth was open and he seemed to gasp, a dry noise escaping with each little stab of air.

Freddy could feel the weight of the gun in his hand. He had never done anything like this before. But the way he felt, it was like no one had ever done such a thing before. It was like he had to invent it.

The first thing was to raise the gun. To align the barrel with the body on the bed. He knew that had to be done. So somebody did it. Freddy or somebody. Because he was looking down the silvery gleam of the barrel to the front sight as it intersected with the head of John Booth wedged into the crinkled texture of the pillow. Next he had to pull the hammer back, then realign the sights. His thumb started to do that, finding the circular tip of the hammer. It was his thumb drawing the hammer back. There was no one else there; he was cocking the gun in his hand, the nine millimeter that he had purchased years ago because he was a merchant.

Now he was passing over a threshold between the known and the unknown, peering into the uncharted moment, and there was a spooky allure to it, and an unexpected simplicity. All he had to do was decide whether or not he wanted John Booth awake and aware; and if he did, then he would have to say something and then squeeze. And if he didn't, all he had to do was squeeze.

For a split second, the question was a kind of screen disconnecting him from the present, fuzzing over the details of what actually lay in front of him. He saw only his question and his search for an answer; and then he realized that John Booth was moving. He was lifting his head from the pillow. The indented pillow lay behind John Booth, who was rising up on one elbow, and he was blinking.

"Do you see me?" said Freddy. "Do you see me?"

"What?"

John Booth's eyes were waking up with a wallop of recognition, and they were getting bigger, as if seeing better would help him. His mouth was opening, too, as if he hoped to drown out the muzzle blast with his own shout. As Freddy drew back on the trigger, adrenaline hit him so hard he yelped in anticipation of the explosion. But all he heard was a click. John Booth didn't reel backward with an anguished grunt. He just froze, his eyes narrow with amazement.

Freddy thumbed the hammer back in order to try again. Click, it went. What the hell, he thought, working the action. Click. It was almost as if he'd lost track of the purpose of what he was doing, and he was just trying to solve this embarrassing mechanical problem. Aiming. Squeezing. Click. John Booth was sitting up now.

The hammer slammed pointlessly again and Freddy looked at John Booth, as if for an explanation. He's going to kill me, he thought. The sonofabitch is going to get up and walk over here and kill me. The fucking thing is empty. It's empty. Or broken. He was staring at the gun, holding it flat in both palms and raising it up to his eyes, like it was a book with very small print.

"Did you test-fire it?" asked John Booth.

"What?"

John Booth swung his feet to the floor. "I'm not gettin' up here or anything. I'm not doin' anything."

"What?"

"I'm just sitting up."

"Whadya mean?"

"Nothing. I don't mean anything."

Stepping sideways to the nearest window, Freddy rotated the weapon in the light. With his left hand under the handle, he pressed the magazine release button so he could check whether there was something faulty in the magazine, but it didn't fall to his hand. The magazine didn't eject, and when he looked into the butt end of the handle, he saw that it was empty. The magazine must have fallen out somehow.

Sagging onto an angular little couch jutting from the wall, he scanned the carpet, his search jumping around on the striped pattern. For several seconds, he saw nothing but a haze of objects in which he had no interest, and then he saw the magazine. But it wasn't on the floor. It was back in the car. He wasn't going to find it here or outside on the driveway where he'd stood looking in the window. Because the magazine with all the shells was lying on the passenger side of the front seat of his car, where he'd placed it when he was testing the gun.

He groaned, looking at John Booth, as if he'd just realized something for which he must apologize. "I don't believe it," he said. "I don't fucking believe it."

"What?"

"Ohh, for Chrissake! Goddamnit! *Goddamnit!*" Freddy stomped his feet, and clutching his arms across his belly, rocked forward the way he might have with a terrible physical blow. "Ohhh, man. Ohhh, *goddamnit!*" He pulled the bourbon from his pocket and twisted the cap off. He lifted the bottle to his mouth for a swig, and then he waited, groaning and shaking his head, before he fed himself another shot to help him think, his shock and embarrassment leaving him oblivious to the fact that he was not alone.

"Listen," said John Booth.

Freddy felt intruded upon, as if this massive, half-naked figure was a new arrival. John Booth's upper body was pale but powerfully muscled. Thick waves of brown hair fed into scraggly sideburns, the back long and uneven. He had one of those Oriental-type mustaches, and a day's growth of beard darkened much of his face. In the narrow confines of the trailer, his natural bulk was magnified, and the layers of shadows packed around him made it seem he was peeking out of a cave.

"All right I get a cigarette?" John asked, gesturing to indicate a pack of Camels on the night table across the narrow aisle from his bed. A Zippo lighter lay beside them.

Freddy wasn't sure what was going on. "I don't care," he said.

John reached out, his big arm floating. The Camels and the Zippo vanished in the expanse of his palm. Carefully, he selected a cigarette, placed it between his lips. The Zippo clicked with a flame that flickered over his face. At the same time that he drew in, he lowered his eyelids and picked a fleck of tobacco from his tongue. Then he inhaled again, deeply this time, letting the smoke flood him. When he opened his eyes, smoke trailed from the corner of his mouth, and he tilted his chin to point in the direction of the door.

Freddy looked, wondering what was going to happen now.

"You know, would you mind shuttin' the door?" said John. "I don't wanna wake my parents. It'd be better, I think, if they didn't— if we didn't wake 'em."

Apparently, Freddy had left the door slightly ajar after coming in. Light was feathering the air around the frame. He had no quarrel with the notion that their business was something they should handle alone.

"I don't mind." Freddy trudged to the door and pulled it closed.

"You came to kill me."

The move had left him facing the blank wall of the trailer. Without turning back, he said, "I'm going."

"I don't blame you."

"Fuck you."

"Listen. When the thing happened, I wanted to be dead. That's what I wanted." Freddy pulled the door open. He had to get out of there. Standing there with his empty fucking gun, he felt like a jackass. He wanted to fucking shoot himself.

"What happened to the gun?" asked John Booth behind him. "I mean, did you figure out what went wrong?"

"Don't start this bullshit," Freddy said. "Just don't fucking start it."

"No, no, I know. You're right."

"It doesn't matter what happened to the gun."

"Sure," said John Booth. He took another drag and it surprised him to see that the cigarette had burned down so there was little left for him to hold. It didn't seem that long ago that he had lit it. Pinching the butt between thumb and forefinger, his other fingers daintily averting themselves, he forced in the last possible inhalation. When he sighed to unleash the smoke and started to grind out the stub, he was left with the rising presence of an unwanted thought. I want my life, it said, embarrassing him and making him feel petty and cowardly. Little more than a faint tapping, the words were just decipherable. But he loathed himself for hearing them at all. Whatever their original volume, he received them as a muffled scratching. It was like someone he couldn't see and didn't know wanted something, and it reminded him of sounds he'd heard in prison, an anonymous, unseen neighbor signaling from a far-off cell.

"I'll be back," said Freddy. "You understand what I mean?"

"I just want to get on with things," said John.

"What?"

John Booth was a little surprised by the nature of his own remark, but he thought it over quickly and saw that it was in fact what he meant. "I just want to get on with things."

"Do you? Is that right? You want to get on with things."

"Yes," said John. It was all so dreamy and strange. Only hours ago, it had been morning in prison. Now he was here with this stranger. He'd just been jarred awake in the middle of the night in this mobile home it felt like he'd never seen before.

"You want to get on with things, do you? What is it you want to get on with exactly?"

"Whatever I have to. Whatever it is that I have to do. I don't know what!" John sagged back on the bed, thinking of lighting another cigarette. When his shoulders hit the wall, he started wondering when they would come and take him back to prison. He asked himself when he would be shaken from the fable of this moment, the mirage rescinded. "It didn't seem there was anything to say before. It seemed that to speak at all was—that to speak in any way was wrong." It was almost like he was alone, talking to himself. There were just the two of them. The dark mobile home was scarcely larger than his cell. It was metal. It enclosed them. "But I wanted to apologize. I'm not saying I think I deserve forgiveness— that I want you—"

"You think I want your goddamn apologies? That I came here for that?"

"No."

"Because I don't! I don't, goddamnit! I don't wanna hear 'em!"

I don't wanna hear them either, John thought. Not to hear them, or fucking say them. He wanted to explain, but he didn't think it would do any good. To talk about how it made him sick to talk about these things. But he felt he had to. That was how he felt. Forced. The words squeezed out of him. Because compared to what happened to her, what were his words and feelings? They were bullshit. Compared to his car, that machine, crushing her. Bullshit. It wasn't that he wanted forgiveness. He really didn't know what he wanted. Just to say something, maybe. Just to speak, because they were here. They were in the weird dream of this moment together. "I don't have anything else to give you. I don't have anything else but my apology."

"I'm a jeweler. I've got a jewelry store. That's it. That's all I've got, and all I am. You know what I'm talking about?"

"I think I do."

Freddy lunged toward John, the Glock rising like it was a hammer. "You don't! No, you don't!" A yard or so short of contact, Freddy stopped. He stood there, glaring down at John, who tensed, his eyes narrowing.

"I'm not going anywhere," said John.

"What?"

"I guess you've been waiting for this day. You been waiting. I've only been out one day and you're here already. You must have been waiting all this time."

Freddy couldn't believe it. The guy actually thought he knew. Like everybody else. For eight fucking years, they all thought they knew what it was like to have a little girl, this sweet promise of a person, just disappear. Because they were humane or thoughtful, or they'd seen it on TV. Some movie of the week. Or they'd seen it on Oprah. A row of chairs displaying a row of assholes socially motivated to spill their guts in the spotlight, while the music played and Oprah cried, looking compassionate and noble. The Triumphantly Fucking Bereft seated on their little elevated island of self-importance, where they beamed with pride at the way they'd become role models. So everybody saw this kind of shit and thought they knew what it was like to love such a child and then be unable to find her one day. Unable to say: What's up, Emily-Pemmily? Or: Give me a hug. Or: Good morning. Or: Good night, sleep tight. Because they'd seen such shit on a TV, some talk show or some goddamn movie of the week, and they watched from their overstuffed chair, and they wallowed in their recliner sipping their beer, and they had to hold back the tears when the music played. He knew because he'd been one of them before it happened. He would just let the sadness come out, blowing his nose, dabbing his eyes. Especially when the child, looking just as jolly as ever, was brought back in these gauzy images, the gift of immortality through the shell game of editing, an option available to living actors playing the dead, but unavailable to the real dead. Or sometimes they even managed that, cutting in photos or slides. But now he knew the difference. Now he knew it was just electronics. You couldn't touch them. And somehow, no matter what the format, whether talk show or movie, whether drama or comedy, everybody always learned the same lesson. It was a triumph, this misery. It was a blessing, this theft, this loss. The music declared it, and there was no way to doubt the music.

"I'm not goin' anywhere," said John Booth. "Not callin' the cops or anything. I thought it over. But will you maybe just take, you know, a couple of days to think about not taking my life?"

"You don't think you paid? You're not saying you think you paid?"

"No, no. I'm not saying that. I'm saying, think about it—use some judgment here. For your own sake."

Freddy had to squint in disbelief at the insult of this remark, the fucking pathology. "For my sake?" he said, leaning and trying to see what kind of an asshole could have said such a thing. "Is that what you said? How's a day? Or two or three? How's that sound?"

"What do you mean?"

"Whadya you mean, what do I mean? You ask for a couple of days, I say how about two or three? Where's the mystery?"

John thought about ripping the handgun out of this jerkoff's grasp, and beating him over the head with it. It wouldn't be hard. It was just hanging there. Beating the shit out of him. Shutting him up.

"How many you want? Huh? How many days you think you want? For my fucking sake! Gimme a hint!"

Suddenly John wanted another cigarette and he scrounged up the pack from the mess of the sheets and covers. There were only four left, he noticed.

"Two? Two days? Three? Whadya say?" yelled Freddy.

The Zippo flared, and John bent to it, tilting his head like a dog listening to a noise beneath the floorboards.

"Five? Would five do? Or ten? How about that? Would you like ten?"

The flame shivered and shrunk as John inhaled. It was a second or two before he thumbed the lighter closed and, with a sense of having moved through a long complex pathway to a simple destination, exhaled. "It's up to you," he said.

"Fuck you. Fuck you!" At the door, Freddy put his hand on the frame to steady himself.

"Look, you oughta wipe your fingerprints—if you're planning to do this and get away with it," John told him.

"You asshole," Freddy said. The guy was mocking him. Still his sense of confusion was big enough that he lunged back, grabbing several sections of paper towel from a dispenser attached to the wall. He started swiping at the couch, anything he might have touched.

"Look, can I ask you one other thing?" said John.

"You know, you're digging yourself more of a hole—a bigger god-damn hole every time you open your mouth!"

"I'm just trying to understand a couple of things."

"Lotsa luck," Freddy said, and rattled down out of the trailer onto the driveway.

"I'm just thinking. What happened to the gun?"

"Don't worry about it."

Because he had to orient himself, Freddy stopped against the wall of the house, looking around, trying to remember the way he'd come.

"But it didn't work. Why didn't it work?"

"The gun is fine," he said, realizing that John Booth's voice had come from directly behind him. He turned, squinting up.

"But somethin' happened. Somethin' was wrong. That's what I'm trying to—"

"It didn't have any bullets. It's fine if it has bullets."

"Whadya mean, it didn't have any bullets?"

It was unbelievable, the way this guy could just stand there and say these things face to face. It was so fucking unbelievable, Freddy's brain felt like it was shrinking and knotting up. "The bullets are in the car. I had them. I left them. I was checking something."

"See! That's what I'm saying."

"What? What are you saying?"

"You left them in the car."

"I know that."

"Maybe you didn't want them. Maybe you didn't want them, so you left them."

"Fuck you."

"There's unconscious motivation. There is such a thing. It's a real thing, Mr. Gale. It's real. Have you heard of it? I mean, there was a shrink when I was inside, I had some sessions. I had some counseling. There's such a thing. And if it was part of what's going on here—if it came into play—then you came here to kill me, but you left the bullets. What does that mean?"

"It means tonight was your lucky night."

"Or maybe you don't want to do it."

"It means, I'm tired. I drank too much."

"Or maybe you don't want to kill me. Maybe it means that. So you left the bullets."

"Fuck you. You're dead." Freddy strode away.

"It could mean that," said John. "Couldn't it?"

Freddy waved the totem of the handgun in an arc above his head, a sheen of spooky promise in the moonlight, just before he went around the corner of the house.

12

■ ■ ■ ■ ■ ■

Standing in the doorway of the trailer, John monitored Freddy's departure in the gradual evaporation of his footsteps, as if his advance were carrying him up into the air. When the silence lasted for several seconds, John padded to the corner of the house. He leaned there, his head tilted out to peer along the driveway. It was a shimmering corridor overhung with a confusion of chunky eucalyptus leaves. Distorted shapes of foliage danced in the air, curtaining Freddy Gale, who stood in the wedge of an open car door parked across the street. He was motionless, almost rigid, like he was stunned by what he saw inside. John had to wonder if Freddy was going to return and try to finish the job.

Then he disappeared, sinking into the front seat so swiftly it seemed he'd collapsed. The door thudded shut, and the engine was startling on the otherwise soundless street. The big car cruised off to the corner, where it turned. The high-finned beacons of the tail lights flickered for a bit in and out of view through a row of curbside palm trees.

Clad only in his boxer shorts and a T-shirt, John was drawn forward by the departing car. He found himself standing at the curb studying the way Freddy had gone. Around John the neighboring houses faced one another on either side of the street, occupying the distance in mirrorlike rows. The sky was a harangue of stars, the moon a splinter dipping in and out of filmy clouds. Without actually looking at himself, he realized that he was a man in his underwear on a residential sidewalk, and the thought startled him. It sent him hurrying backwards, ducking along the driveway. He leaped into the trailer, pulling the door shut behind him with both hands, like a schoolboy fleeing the grasp of a nightmare he knew to be real.

Once inside, he looked around. He opened a drawer full of socks, and another full of towels, wanting to remind himself of where he was and what had happened. He sank onto the couch that Freddy had occupied.

It was night. It was the middle of the night: 2:30 A.M. Hack, he thought. Screw. Lock and Count. Cell block. Cell mate. Standing mainline. Snitches. Front gate. Contraband. The whole perverted world. John Booth—Six seven three three two six. E Block. Front gate. The box. Shops. Exercise yard. Crank. Smack. Wives. Nellies. He reached over to the bed, scooping up the pack of Camels and lighting another one. Cut your fuckin' ass, he thought. This ain't your business. Walk on by. Killed over in C. Scrip. Triple murderer. Tattoos. Seg. Syringes. HIV. Street Gangs. Crystal Meth. Infirmary.

He buckled over. His palms slapped the floor. He laughed, not with pleasure, but with recognition. He'd just spent eight years negotiating twenty-four hours a day through a population culled from the ranks of the semipsychotic, men who spent much of their waking hours trying to turn ordinary objects like toothbrushes, plastic spoons, and pencils into murderous instruments. And now he had this asshole swaggering around with an empty gun. I shouldha made him eat it. I shouldha stuck it down his fucking throat.

In the cigarette pack he snatched up, only three remained. One he lit up, that left two. He grabbed his shirt, his trousers, and an old pair of Nikes. He picked his billfold and coins from the drawer in the table across from the bed, heading for his parents' house.

The empty kitchen felt strange, the white of the refrigerator reflecting the street light in a pillowy haze, as if the enamel radiated. An open pack of his mother's Winstons lay on a shelf occupied by a rack of dishes drying in the night air. He eased over and pilfered four. With a knife on the cutting board, he sliced off the filters. Adding this modified batch to the two in the pack, he felt better. Sup-

plies, he thought. Taking one more, he stuffed the amputated filters
into his pocket and switched on the gas burner, a dancing hoop
which he approached, the cigarette in his mouth. When he stood up,
the sight of his silhouette playing over the white of the refrigerator
launched goose bumps over his ribs. Because it proved that he was
up and moving. It was night and he was up walking around.

He shut off the stove and went down the hall to his parents'
bedroom. The partly open door was easy to widen. Covered in the
ripples of a white sheet, his mother and father lay like huge bread
loaves nestled in shadows. The rapidity with which his mother
snatched each breath cut across the more methodical pace of his
father's sighing and snoring.

What would they think if he climbed in with them, he wondered, imagining his little body sharing their covers.

Looking down at his father, he asked himself, What little body?
His father's mouth was open, his eyes curtained. Acres of wrinkles
spread across cheeks under a bristle of gray whiskers.

Then his mother made a sudden move. But she was just scratching her forehead, the spray of blue veins on the back of her hand
flexing, as she sought to chase some irritation. Though he knew he
was doing nothing wrong, the idea that he might disturb them made
him nervous. If they woke up, it would scare them to see him standing here looking at them. He would have to answer questions—
questions they would have every right to ask—about what he was
doing. And he would have to try to tell them when he had no idea.

Once he left the bedroom, he just kept moving until he was out
of the house, another cigarette aglow in his mouth. He'd never sleep
if he went to bed now. He thought maybe he'd go out front. Make
sure Freddy Gale hadn't come back. But when he got there, he just
kept going, crossing the yard, heading for the street in spite of a mad
but inescapable warning that the trees contained watchtowers with
guards ready to shout that he stop or be shot at any second.

Reaching the curb, he paused. He peered to his left and then off
to the right. In both directions sidewalks trailed away skirted in
grass, periodically overseen by oaks. It was all identical, so that
choosing either way appeared arbitrary. But then he noticed that, far
down to the right, the clustered trees dissolved in a gleaming pond
of light where the narrow street joined with a large intersection.

That was what he wanted. The distance appeared to invite him.

Block after block of tranquil, suburban byways floated past. He smoked another cigarette. Except for an occasional night light or television screen, the houses were dark. His only counterparts were intermittent cars that glided by, the drivers busy with their own thoughts or engrossed in conversation with their passengers. Each intruder, a bubble of humming wheels and headlights, entered his silence and then left the silence behind.

When he arrived at the intersection, he stood for a moment contemplating a 7-Eleven, an island of color and focused light across the street. The road in between was wider than the one he had walked, more of a boulevard, with wall-to-wall business establishments receding in both directions, a fast-food franchise, some warehouse outlets, a dry cleaners, an electronics sale and repair shop, all shut down for the night. Halfway up the block was the illuminated shoal of an all-night self-service gas station. Somehow it felt he was facing a radical demarcation. To think of simply going over and walking in made him uneasy. Even to buy the Camels he needed, because the cannibalized Winstons were a poor substitute, and he would run out soon, anyway.

Still he went, pushing open the door. The chubby Asian boy behind the counter glanced up from the comic book he was reading. John stood in the doorway, waiting. He felt taxed by an aspect of the environment he couldn't specify. Something in the clerk's cordial manner made him feel unwelcome.

"Pack of Camels, okay?" he said. The young man smiled, hopped down from the stool. The store was a blaze of plastic and cellophane. To John's unaccustomed eyes, the gaudy bottles, bags, boxes, and tin cans awash in a fluorescent sea were an irritating blur.

"Anything else?" the young man asked, laying the Camels on the counter.

Beer nuts hung from a bush of wire to John's left, the limbs jammed with rows of stuffed packets like tantalizing fruit. "Some beer nuts," he said. "A couple of packs."

As the words left his lips, his glance was drawn into the corner where gigantic pretzels rotated like rare museum pieces behind the glass of a self-illuminated display case, each complex, twisted figure coated with pellets of salt. "And a pretzel. One of those pretzels."

"Sure. I love 'em myself."

He paced along to watch as the boy cheerfully plucked out the biggest of the three pretzels in the folds of a napkin and offered it to John.

"Mustard is right there on the counter, if you want it."

John walked to the mishmash of condiments, Styrofoam cups, plastic spoons. He painted the pretzel with a thick coat of mustard and started eating. His stroll back to the cash register took him through the panorama of the store. In every direction tier after tier offered him the spectacle of its abundance, the colors shocking, their sheer quantity somehow disturbing, a dizzying overload of sensation. He walked up to the clerk and stared for a moment.

"Yes?"

"Let me just look around, okay?" He waited, as if expecting to be denied.

"Sure," the young man shrugged.

"I'm thirsty."

"Soda is over there."

From the clean interior of the cooler, John drew out a six-pack of Coke. Nearby were bins of potato chips, and he selected a family-sized bag of Wise's. The next thing he had to have was a jumbo Cheetos. Standing before a collection of Planters Peanuts, he couldn't decide whether to buy the mixed nuts or the cashews, so he took a jar of each. Now he needed a cart. At the front of the store, he located several jammed together. With everything he had accumulated so far transferred into the wire enclosure, he wheeled off down an aisle. He grabbed four Slim Jims, a jumbo-sized bag of buttered popcorn, a big jar of salsa. He wanted a large bag of bean chips. Facing the shelves of beer, he decided to buy only one can of Pabst. He didn't want to risk drinking too much, but he had to have a taste. Just as he had to have a quart of Breyers' Vanilla, Strawberry, and Chocolate ice cream. From the shelves inlaid into the front of the counter where the clerk leaned slack-jawed over his comic, John plucked a bag of M&Ms, three Mounds bars, and two Reese's Peanut Butter Cups.

Though he paid in full, his heart was racing as he paused in the parking lot to open a packet of beer nuts. A block or so later, he popped the lid on a Coke and tore into a second beer nuts.

He intended to store everything in the cabinets and mini-fridge in the mobile home. But when he entered and looked at the narrow bed, he couldn't stay there, and he walked back out. The air and open space of the front yard drew him to the porch, where he settled on the steps.

The first thing he dug into was the chips. He drank another Coke and opened the Cheetos. He freed a Slim Jim and gnawed away, savoring the sweet mix of meat, honey, and chemicals. He popped the beer, drank it down. When he burped with the foam, he smiled, like he'd just heard a joke. Then he chugged a bag of M&Ms, and went after a peanut butter cup. There was still more than half a bag of Cheetos but it was time to get at the popcorn. He turned a mouthful of cheesy crunchy Cheetos into gruel, mashing it around. He took the popcorn in a violent series of handfuls, clamping his palm over his mouth. He sprang the lid on the cashews, then tipped the jar to his lips like the nuts were a liquid. He guzzled another Coke, and pulled the plastic tab on the peanuts. He ate what he could. He drank one more Coke and ate a Mounds bar, feeling sickened, as he pried apart the lid on the ice cream. Lacking a spoon, he formed his hand into a scooper and plunged into the cold, smooth surface. He sat there dredging up gobs of strawberry, chocolate, and vanilla ice cream and sucking his fingers.

Slowly, he slumped onto his back. His suffering gut ached, but he was ecstatic. His lungs felt constrained, forcing him to take panting breaths. The notion that if he budged he would puke somehow made him happy.

With his arms and his legs flung out, he gazed into the black heights filmed with clouds and a spill of stars whose retreating brilliance measured size and distance. He was the largest hunk of debris in a puddle of litter mussing his parents' front lawn, a mix of crumpled wrappers, a scattering of popcorn and peanuts, and a melting block of tricolored ice cream in a collapsing container.

He could feel the lawn beneath him, the contours and softness accepting the fit of his body. At the same time his excitement was not simple. His mood was haunted. There was an element of unease, a lurking, germinal fear, as if he were a child tiptoeing through a cemetery. Something threatened to jump out at him. Something he knew to be true but was not ready to accept was creeping up on him. The fact that he was out. It felt dangerous. Not being out. But the belief. Not being free. But the belief.

13

■ ■ ■ ■ ■ ■ ■

Remember when I hid my eyes that time? said Emily. *You were baby-sitting me, Daddy, remember, and watching this program on TV. Even though it was scaring me, you didn't want to quit. You were caught up in it, you were hooked, you said. So you told me to cover myself up in a blanket, to cover my head so I couldn't see, and I did. But even the music was scary. Remember? And I could still hear the woman screaming. I kept asking you to leave with me, to turn it off and leave, but you wouldn't. Just a minute more, you said. I want to see what happens, you said. It was awful how I felt. I kept thinking how the man with the knife who had the lady tied up on the couch had appeared like such a nice man, but he wasn't. His voice loved the way she was crying. He loved that he could hurt her.*

But I didn't have to worry, you said, She would be saved. Just cover myself in a blanket. So I did. And sat there. But the music and the screams were so terrible that I ran from the room. I just couldn't stand it. Because I didn't understand it, except for the hurt she was feeling and the fear. And even though you said someone would save her, I worried that you were wrong. I worried that if it were happening to me, if the man and the knives were happening to me, no one would come. And that's what I thought of at the very last second. That the man with the knives had got me, and that you

didn't care—that you weren't thinking about me, but were just off
somewhere doing something more important. Where were you?

Freddy awoke to TV mayhem and a headache like a screw working its way through his eyeball into the tender nerves just behind it.
With his hand covering one eye, he groaned. On the TV a woman in
a tattered ballgown was screaming. She was backing through a series of shots in a dark underground cavern, water foaming and grabbing at her ankles, the music unnerving, the light ominous, the des-
peration in her eyes growing wilder, as she recognized that her
retreat was not going to save her from the clutches of this onrushing
lizardlike guy.

Freddy groped for the remote control device. It lay on the coffee
table partially concealed behind the fifth of Jack Daniel's. His
searching thumb managed to pop the channel "advance" button and
the creature and his victim were replaced by a guy in a chef's hat
selling some kind of blender on one of those infomercials. His companion was a perky little blonde whose more or less robust figure
had been stuffed into a carrot costume.

Looking up at the burning track lights overhead drenching the
room, Freddy knew it was the middle of the night. He must have
passed out. He didn't remember getting the bourbon out, though it
was his good buddy Jack Daniel's.

The kitchen and bathroom were both ablaze. Through the window, he saw dark space, a trickle of stars, the spill of street lights, a
horizon like a melting iron bar. Night. He was still fully clothed,
even wearing the blazer. Having removed one shoe, he'd fallen
asleep with the place lit up like an all-night diner.

He had to pee, but as he stood up, nausea ballooned in a sickening parachute, his guts entangled in strings. He could feel bile backing up in his throat. He had to get to the bathroom. He pressed his
hands down on the coffee table. The infomercial chef guy was pointing to some graphs and illustrations on what appeared to be a series
of flip-top charts, and the carrot girl was toying with her zipper. The
chef guy flipped the card with tomatoes on it, bringing into view a
vegetable that looked like an amputated liver.

Freddy was on his hands and knees, making his way to the bathroom door. Somebody in the TV audience said something about the
importance of nutrients, and Freddy angled his arm out behind him,

pressing the "off" button like he was shooting a pursuer.

Clamping his hands on the rim of the toilet, he flexed for a secure grip. Though getting to his feet meant he might puke, he had to risk it or he was going to piss his pants. He pawed at his fly, fumbling his dick out. He hovered there, bent at the waist, like someone contemplating diving in. Pissing for what seemed like forever, he was exhausted by the time it was over. He fell to his knees, then settled onto his side, breathing in big gulps.

To distract himself, he signaled for the television to return. He couldn't stand the chef guy and hopped channels. Sprawled across the threshold of the bathroom, he ended up on CNN, where war footage of Bosnian savagery was on display. A woman whom the rescuers were raising from beneath a heap of fallen stone and shattered beams had her mouth open in a snarl of pain. The background was the wreckage of buildings shelled into ruins. Across an opaque border along the base of the screen flashed some names and numbers, the preceding day's baseball scores. Blood streamed down the woman's brow to her cheek. Her tattered dress exposed a mashed arm like a hacked tree branch that was held to her torso by the sleeve of her dress. According to the gray border, Boston had defeated the Yankees 9 to 3; Milwaukee had nudged Chicago 6 to 5.

When he arrived at the couch on his hands and knees, he heaved himself up and collapsed on his side. Images splashed across the screen, debris on a current. Cannon were firing, the barrels recoiling, the breeches spitting out shells. A man, begrimed and inconsolable, was battling the restraining arms of several soldiers. He was reaching toward a figure on a stretcher bundled in filthy blankets. In the National League, the Cubs had taken the Phillies 6 to 2, and the Mets had crushed the Pirates by a score of 8 to 1.

He needed to sleep. Tomorrow he would face facts. He would figure out how to go forward in a way that had a chance. In a way that had some fucking brains and balls. But he couldn't do it now. His head was killing him, his body a hive of open nerves.

He flicked the power button, and the crumbling walls of an apartment building, along with the dust cloud rising around it, vanished in a flash. Forcing himself upright, he scuttled across the room so he could douse the overhead track lights. But a misstep sent him reeling off course; he thought he might slam into the wall, and raised his arms. Thousands of shards of splintered glass were loose in his head, and all this running around had them twisting. But he persisted, finding and throwing each switch until at last the apartment was dark.

On the couch, he cupped his hands under his chin to stabilize his head the way a medical attendant might a patient who had suffered spinal injuries. Frightened that he was going to stay awake for the rest of the night, he flopped onto his side. Sleep and its oblivion were his only hope. He was begging that this new position would let him rest, because he was afraid that if he didn't find a way to dull his awareness, he might start crying or screaming. As a last resort, he took a chance on praying. He asked God to please help him sleep. Even though he was an atheist who never prayed for anything; a half-Jewish atheist, who felt he was imploring a vast and powerful indifference, a calloused and manipulative nothing. He kept praying and hoping, his fear that he would never get to sleep growing worse, until he saw that he was dreaming of dead children. Machines were annihilating them, huge wheels and gears careening into eight- and ten-year-old boys in baseball uniforms, and little girls in flowery dresses, some of whom fell trying to hang on to their school books.

When he sat up, the TV was blasting, and the lights were all on again. The bottle of Jack Daniel's was nearly empty. Cowboys were traversing a wide shot of barren buttes. He saw magazines and newspapers and news clippings all over the floor, coffee table and couch. He recognized these things as pieces he'd cut out and collected over the last eight years. But he had no idea what they were doing there. He kept them stored in the back of his closet. The large manila envelope, spilling sheets from its unclasped flap, was full of legal documents pertaining to John Booth's trial and his appeal. In the pile of newspaper articles, there were a few dealing with the accident, the drunk-driving charges and Emily's death. The rest were about the misfortunes of other children whose misery had engaged Freddy, as if they were somehow kindred to Emily.

He couldn't remember getting this stuff out of the closet, if that was what he'd done. But there it was. The first of the articles told of a three-month-old baby girl in Santa Barbara, who had been drenched with lighter fluid and then torched by the twenty-six-year-old au pair girl from Holland.

Moving on, he read how a twenty-two-year-old mother in West Hollywood, upon finding herself out of cigarettes, slipped to the corner Stop and Shop, intending to hurry back before her infant awoke in her crib. When the woman returned, five days and five nights later, the baby was dead. She'd needed a break, the woman said, and so she stopped off for a drink, and then she ended up having another drink and pretty soon she had had too much, and by then she was having some fun. She went home with this guy, so she lost track of things.

On the television, one cowboy in leather chaps and a faded workshirt wheeled to face another. They were alone on a street running through a ramshackle town. The second cowboy was young and smug-looking, while the first one was old and bedraggled. When the hand of the younger one snaked to his hip, the first cowboy raked his palm over the hammer of the long-barreled six-shooter. Smoke erupted. Impact, arriving in a sequence of at least five repetitions, would not let the loser fall. Every time he sagged, his arms limp and widespread, another bullet slammed him back until he collided with a fence. He bounced to the ground belly down, the dust flowering around him. The music, full of danger and mourning, shifted, growing receptive to a sprinkling of victorious notes whose sly infiltration began to alter the mood in a way that left no doubt about the value and virtue of the old guy's triumph. The craggy old face loomed in a screen-filling close-up. Freddy looked into the eyes full of pain and wisdom, and asked, Did he kill your daughter? Is that what happened? Did he kill your little girl?

A long shot jolted him, reducing the town to a pile of kindling in a wasteland. Still Freddy could hear the approach of an answer in the music. It was gathering itself and racing toward him, but it was erased by a silly little melody that brought with it a jubilant family on a picnic near a creek celebrating, as it turned out, peanut butter.

He stared at the commercial, and then he went back to the mess around him, picking up the envelope full of legal documents, several of which fell from his fingers as he pulled them into the light. They were Xeroxes, the borders clouded with a grainy field of ink. At the top of the page were the words *Per Curium*. He took a sip of whiskey, and while the television went from giggles to engine sounds, he read on:

Per Curium

Defendant appeals from an order of the Appellate Division affirming his conviction of one count of murder in the second degree (Penal Law {} 213.32 (4) (depraved mind murder)) and three counts of reckless endangerment in the first degree (Penal Law {} 122.32). The charges arose out of an incident in which the defendant drove his car several blocks on a Studio City, California, residential street and on the adjacent sidewalks, endangering the lives of several pedestrians and killing a child, Emily Gale. Defendant's only contention on this appeal is that the evidence was not sufficient to support the conviction of depraved mind murder. Inasmuch as the Appellate Division affirmed the jury's guilty verdict, we must view the evidence in the light most favorable to the People (see *People* v. *Robinson,* 62 LA 3 220, 227, cert denied). So viewed it established that at some time between 3:45 and 4:00 P.M. on May 12, 1988, defendant drove a car owned by the defendant out of the 7-Eleven at Brent and Belltower, where he had purchased a package of cigarettes. He entered Belltower at a speed of approx 40 mph. He then accelerated across Belltower, struck and bounced off a parked car, and continued traveling north, weaving from lane to lane until he reached the corner of Belltower and Wood. He turned west onto Wood, again accelerating according to two witnesses, William Gilchrist and Sheila Simon, who testified defendant appeared out of control as he sideswiped a parked van owned by Thomas T. Bernbaacher, scraping paint and denting the left rear side in the area of the sliding door. Mr. Bernbaacher had just exited the van and he saw the defendant bouncing off the van and braking furiously to stop with one front wheel up on the curb and the right front part of his bumper against a tree. The defendant exited his car and attempted to exchange insurance information with Mr. Bernbaacher, but defendant was so intoxicated that he could not remove his license or insurance card and had to be assisted by Mr. Bernbaacher. Mr. Bernbaacher testified that he advised defendant not to get back into his vehicle, that he informed defendant that he was too intoxicated to drive. The defendant declared that he

" . . . wasn't drunk . . . ," that he " . . . never got drunk . . . no matter how much I drink." Against the protests of Mr. Bernbaacher, defendant returned to his car, backed it off the curb and drove off down Wood at an accelerating speed. Two blocks later, at the corner of Wood and Wetlands, he ran a stop sign and nearly collided with a passing car. In his attempt to avoid colliding with the vehicle, a black sedan, defendant lost control of his vehicle, careened up onto the sidewalk, then back onto the roadway and up onto the opposite sidewalk, where he nearly ran down the Crossing Guard, Milton Mooney, who was at the neighborhood crossing holding his sign to safeguard Emily Gale, an eight-year-old girl, preparing to cross the street. The left front fender of defendant's vehicle collided with a stone wall and the impact and speed angled the defendant's vehicle back toward the street. The vehicle struck Emily Gale on its path back to the road. Emily Gale's body landed twenty-four feet southwest of where she had been standing reading a book and waiting near Mr. Mooney. A sneaker belonging to Emily Gale was found entangled in the grill of the defendant's vehicle where it came to a stop in the front yard of Edmond Peltz's home on the northwest corner of Wood and Wetlands. The cover and several pages of the paperback book Emily Gale had been reading were embedded in the tread of the right front tire of defendant's vehicle.

The first LAPD Officer on the scene was Lucinda Tillman. By the time of Officer Tillman's arrival, a number of people had gathered around the scene and the defendant was sitting on the curb near the body. Though several bystanders told Officer Tillman that victim Emily Gale was dead, Officer Tillman checked the victim's vital signs and confirmed that in her opinion the victim was dead. An Emergency Medical Service ambulance arrived only minutes after Officer Tillman and at this point Officer Tillman went to defendant, who was still sitting on the curb. With the permission of the defendant, Officer Tillman administered a Breathalyzer test. The test indicated that the defendant's blood alcohol percentage was .17. She testified that the defendant was "out of it," that his mood " . . . was sometimes almost hysterical, or else he just sat there." He was read his Miranda rights and kept asking Officer Tillman if she could tell him what had happened and could she take him somewhere because he had to go to the bathroom. Officer Tillman took the defendant into a nearby residence. By this time, Mr. Bernbaacher was present on the scene. When Officer Tillman returned, Mr. Bernbaacher reported the incident with his van. When asked about striking Bernbaacher's van, the defendant said that he " . . . didn't remember that, but that it could have happened." When Mr. Bernbaacher reminded defendant that he had warned him not to drive any more " . . . because he was too damn drunk, he was a menace . . . ," defendant answered that he " . . . didn't remember. But it could have happened." When asked by Officer Tillman what he did remember, defendant said that "Everything happened real fast. Some of it anyway had. . . . A lot of it. . . ." Defendant said that somewhere he bumped his head hard " . . . on something, maybe the side window and from then on I was nearly blacked out. . . ." Officer Tillman noted a laceration and mild bruise high on defendant's left cheek and requested that an EMS technician treat defendant.

After a jury trial, defendant was convicted and sentenced to one indeterminate term of imprisonment of 25 years to life on the murder count to run consecutively with three counts of reckless endangerment, one count of driving under the influence and one count of leaving the scene of an accident. This last referred to the van. On appeal, the Appellate Division modified the sentences by ordering that the terms imposed on all counts run concurrently to each other. It also upheld the jury's findings of guilt, stating that the proof was sufficient to establish that defendant acted with depraved indifference to life. Driving a speeding motor vehicle down a residential street and then onto a sidewalk more than once, after having damaged another vehicle, and most importantly, after having been warned of his intoxicated condition, satisfied the requirement that the defendant, John Booth, acted recklessly. In other words it was proved that he was aware of and consciously disregarded a substantial and unjustifiable risk. In addition, the People were required to satisfy the "depraved indifference" element of the law. The phrase "under circumstances evincing a depraved indifference to human life" is not a *mens rea* element focusing on the subjective intent of the defendant but rather involves "an objective assessment of the degree of risk presented by defendant's reckless conduct." It "refers to the wantonness of defendant's conduct and converts the substantial risk present in manslaughter into the very substantial risk present in murder, and on this basis justifies the conviction of murder in the second degree."

On the TV, an auto mechanic and a ballerina were transfixed by a sleek red car racing across a stretch of flat desert and leaving them behind. Sadness mixed with unfulfilled lust, as they reached for one another.

When Freddy looked down, intending to return to the trial documents, he found himself facing instead a newspaper clipping intermingled with the legal pile. The locale was Nezaba, Arizona, and the reported story detailed the fate of Sally Renne, a ten-year-old blonde wearing glasses with bifocal lenses, who had been abducted at knife point while enjoying a slumber party at a friend's home. Afraid all her life that a ghost or monster might get her in the dark, she slept with a night light on. Then a paroled child molester slipped into a room where she and several other girls slept while adults snored only inches away, and this monster took her off into the night to die at his hands. Some scumbag of a piece of dog shit ex-con monster named Bob Russel Smith out on parole after having been jailed for kidnapping. Would he die this time for what he did? Would he pay? Or would he cry and piss and moan and make excuses? You better fucking believe it. Count on it! What was the difference? Freddy wanted to know, taking a long swig of bourbon. Goddamn them all! Goddamn John Booth! How was he different? Careening down that street. Stealing her!

A snarling leopard was ripping to shreds the carcass of some kind of malleable antelope. Calamitous music accompanied a stentorian voice declaring that personal copies of these Time/Life tapes could be purchased by ordering from an 800 number. A gigantic snake opened its jaws and spit. A tarantula ensnared a squirming beetle, and then was itself dwarfed by the flames in which it was being cooked on a stick and raised toward a towering planetary mouth in the painted face of a human savage.

Dad! Daddy! Honey-man! Listen! I hate to tell you this, but John Booth is laughing at you. He thinks you are such a total jerk, the way you acted tonight. You know, coming to threaten him with an empty gun. It's like goofy. Really dufus. He just couldn't stop laughing when you left. So now he's so cocky about how he really fooled you with all that self-help therapy jargon at the end, like he was your friend, like he knew you, so he could almost laugh in your face. You have to admit it was stupid, what you did. I mean, going there like that—what did you think you were doing!

Because now he's starting to daydream about living the rest of his life. And why shouldn't he! He's alive, after all. Set free. Having paid his debt to society. But has he! Has he paid, Dad! Not like you. Not like me. With no hope except to see him join me in this agony.

Because otherwise he is going to live. If you don't do something. And then he'll start going around, and having fun, walking the beach or playing jacks, or Math Blaster or Loom on his computer. Going to funny movies and laughing, and having play dates and playing Dress Up and going shopping in the mall, eating chocolate cookies, going to dances and meeting a girl. Getting a girlfriend. That's what he'll do—he'll get a girlfriend and buy her a fancy dress. Then a ring. And he'll marry her, and after that he'll have children. He'll have lots of lovely children, a big lovely family, with a beautiful little daughter to hold and watch grow.

Or would you rather I burn in this misery alone! I want fairness. Justice! Retribution! Drinking this black scalding loss alone. Because without you, Daddy, I have no one. There's nothing here, Daddy. No angels, no devils. Just nothing. I hate him! Please, Daddy, please! Every breath he takes hurts me, mocking my untasted life.

Daddy, please. A little depraved mind murder, that's all. A little depraved indifference. Be a cowboy. Be a tarantula. Be a cheetah. I mean, what's the big deal, Dad! Just kill the fucker! Just fucking do it!

It was daylight. The room was filled with midmorning heat and glare. He was drenched in sweat, and the television, while still blaring, appeared smaller, its image faded by the brilliance of the daylight. The washed-out figure of a man wearing a striped shirt and suspenders was screeching and waving a long stick in a manic demonstration intended for the instruction of a puppet. Resembling a section of fire hose covered in ruddy fur, the puppet, with a gaping mouth, a red tongue, and big white eyes, was trying to follow the human's barrage of accents and mime. It was *Sesame Street*, Freddy realized, and the guy was a world-famous comic whose name Freddy couldn't come up with. The comic was talking to Grover, who Emily loved. Except it wasn't Grover. Because it was the wrong color. Grover was blue. Sometimes Freddy had imitated Grover's voice for Emily, and she'd giggled crazily. But it wasn't Grover that the world-famous comic was bewildering with an imitation of a band leader, waving the stick like a baton.

On the coffee table the silver Glock lay amid the debris of the night. The articles he'd been reading were neatly stacked to the left of the empty Jack Daniel's. An open container of Advil stood near a plastic quart container of club soda, and he grabbed it and almost emptied it, guzzling ounces. Had he gone down to the car to get the gun? He didn't remember doing it, if he had. He picked it up, and turned it so he could see the butt of the handle with the magazine inside. The world-famous comic was springing up and down like someone too uncoordinated to run in place, and the puppet was looking off screen in search of assistance.

Freddy took a couple more Advil and started moving the weapon from one hand to the other, like this was the best way to fathom its nature. He didn't even know if the damn thing worked! When was the last time he'd actually fired it? That was his first goddamn mistake. Going over there like he expected something to just take him over the way everybody was always talking about on TV. This big whispering voice, or this wind, or this animal figure, or this thunder no one else could hear wiping out your thoughts.

Did you test-fire it, John Booth had had the balls to ask him. Did you test-fire it?

No, he thought. But I will. He arose, his eyes darting around the room, corner to corner, through the archway into the kitchen. What he'd done was worry the damn gun to death, checking it over and over.

Hobbling, he pried off the one shoe he wore, then eased up furtively to a wall beside the door. He tapped with his knuckles, exploring several spots, listening for a solid point in the structure. His headache had receded to a vague fuzz coating his thoughts, a facade that sprung a leak of pain every few seconds.

Just beyond where he stood lay the hallway of the apartment building, where someone might pass by at any instant. Behind him the windows opened onto the sky eight stories up. That was a better idea. The brick that formed the outside of the building could serve as a backing.

Once he found a spot he liked, he started piling pillows against the wall, traveling back and forth from the couch. He drew the handgun from the waist of his trousers, jacking a round into the chamber. Stepping back from the pillows, he raised the weapon. At a distance of about seven feet, he took a breath and squeezed. The room burst with a cracking sound, a burning smell. His arm was cranked back at the elbow, the recoil a throb running into his shoulder. The empty apartment filled with a quickening strangeness, a wary excitement summoned by the gunshot. He placed the Glock on the arm of the couch, and went to search for the expended round. In each succeeding pillow the entrance hole was larger. The bullet, a crumpled lump of lead, was embedded partway in the wall. He pincered it out with his thumb and forefinger. He sniffed it, put it between his teeth, biting to feel its pliability.

He popped the magazine, and then the shell from the chamber so he could reinsert it before ramming it all back into the Glock with the heel of his hand. It was that fucking simple. Next time there'd be no questions. There'd been some bullshit about days. What a lotta bullshit. What had it been?

As he stepped to the window intending to let in some fresh air, he was struck by the feeling of being watched. But when he turned, he saw only the TV and the puppet show. The difference was that now Grover was there. Freddy knew the blue furrowed brow, the befuddled voice. He'd developed his own fondness for Grover, sitting with Emily on his lap. At the moment Grover was trying to maintain his dignity against a group of contentious, professorial-looking puppets, carrying books and wearing glasses. They were in the midst of a pedantic harangue, and he was trying to defend himself against their accusation that he was completely ignorant of the way clouds worked, the way they formed with rain and without rain. Emily loved him in such moments. She would gaze raptly, tittering with affection. If she was with Freddy now, they'd be having such a good time. Emily sitting on his lap. She'd be how old now?

Sixteen. Emily would be sixteen.

It seemed a simple enough question, but the answer was a knife slicing slowly so that every ounce of its jagged force was felt. Sixteen. A little woman. Not so little. Breasts. And she'd be having her period. A real woman. Almost. She'd be actually having her period. Emily.

A little depraved mind murder, he thought. A little depraved indifference to life. That was what was needed. He had to sober up. Stop drinking. He'd shower, get something to eat. Buy some vitamins. Get a decent meal. Have some coffee. Go over to the store. Put in some time at the store. Have a nice dinner. Get a good night's rest. He had to train himself. He had to tend to his anger like the precious thing it was, a delicate poisonous flower, not some rude weed he could take for granted. But something rare.

He was sitting on the couch. On the TV, Grover and another puppet were dancing to a forties big band pop tune, their stubby arms straining to wrap around the fuzzy blue and lavender merger of their bodies, their big buggy eyes staring skyward, their red tongues sticking out. Suddenly, the other puppet grabbed Grover and kissed him. Unable to ward off the loving but chaste smack on the top of his head, Grover responded by backing away shyly, groaning loudly and hiding his eyes. Freddy lifted the remote and turned off the TV.

14

■ ■ ■ ■ ■ ■ ■

Helen had climbed from bed at seven-thirty, and while still in her robe, brewed a pot of strong coffee. She was sure that prison would have turned John into an early riser. But then eight-thirty and nine o'clock rolled by without a sign of him, though by then she had to deal with Stuart. It was obvious he hadn't slept well, his eyes were so bloodshot. He wanted a ham and cheese omelet, so she made two, one for herself. Hoping John would walk in at any second, she prepared a jelly omelet, his childhood favorite.

Then ten o'clock came and went, and she and Stuart were stuffed and a little crazed from too much coffee. John's omelet had cooled and been reheated more times than was good for it, until it wasn't worth saving.

She and Stuart talked the situation over while they changed from their robes and pajamas. Stuart shaved and put on trousers and a shirt, but Helen just slipped on a house dress. Concluding that they had the right to spy if they were worried, they stole to the trailer, found a window, and peered in on John's sprawled form, his lowered lids and chest moving calmly.

Back in the kitchen, Stuart grabbed a blue windbreaker from a hook by the door. He was going to take the Volvo into the shop to have Eddie, the friendliest of the mechanics, see what they thought of a flutter he'd noticed in the brake pedal as he drove back from the prison.

"Is it serious, do you think?"

"It's the brakes, you know. You don't want to take any chances with the brakes."

She knew that he was talking about John's accident. The police had determined that, aside from his being guilty of drunk driving, his brakes had been in pretty bad shape.

She was at the front door watching Stuart drive off when she saw the crumbs and scraps littering the lawn. Startled, she bent down for a closer look. Maybe some homeless bum had camped there. It gave her the creeps. Then the phone rang, and she jumped like this intruder from the night had returned to yell at her.

"Hi, Mrs. Booth?" said the voice when she answered.

"Yes."

"This is Peter. John's friend."

"Oh, yes. Peter. John's home."

"Is he home?"

"Yes. And he's sleeping."

"Sleeping? Good for him."

"But do you know what, Peter? I'm going to wake him up. Call back in ten minutes, why don't you?"

"Maybe you shouldn't wake him, Mrs. Booth. Not on my account."

She hung up and marched out to the trailer. With her fingers flexing on the open door, she paused to let herself enjoy the way sleep drew an earlier, remembered innocence into his features. "Johnny," she said gently. "Johnny."

His eyes fluttered open, and he jolted into a sitting position. He saw her, and as he settled onto the pillows, the glaze on his eyes went away, just like the sun cooking the smog out of the morning to reveal a beautiful day. "Morning, Mom."

Goose bumps crept over her. "You've been sleeping a long time."

"I guess so." He was gazing at the alarm clock on the dresser.

"Would you like a jelly omelet?"

"Well," he said, entering into an amused silence.

She didn't like not getting an answer to such a simple question, but it pleased her to see him smile. "There's some coffee," she said. "But it's old. I'll make a fresh pot. And Peter called."

"Peter? Really?"

"He's going to call back in ten minutes. I said you'd be up by then."

She rigged the Mr. Coffee to make a strong pot, and went out onto the front lawn with a dust buster, a broom, and a dustpan. She was puttering away when John came out wearing the same gray trousers and wrinkled T-shirt as yesterday. She was startled anew by his size, but when his eyes questioned her amazement, she said, "Look at the mystery." Quickly, she went back to sweeping the crumbs jumping around in the blades of grass. "Somebody had a picnic."

"That was me, Mom."

"What?"

"I did it. But I thought I'd cleaned it all up. It was dark," he said, reaching for the broom. "Let me get it."

"You did this?"

"I went down to the Seven-Eleven last night. Then I bought a bunch of stuff and sat here eating it."

"I was worried it was some bum."

"Just *this* bum," he told her, chuckling with the memory of what he'd done, and with the fact that he was out there using a broom to sweep the lawn.

This time she was prepared when the phone rang. "That must be Peter," she said, and wrested the broom from his hands. As he headed inside, she called after him, "I'll make you that jelly omelet in just a few minutes."

Stuart and the Volvo were turning into the driveway and she waved, but he was preoccupied. A good fifteen feet short of where he normally parked, the car came to a jarring halt. Watching him start forward again, she knew he was testing the brakes. Suddenly, it looked like he hit a wall. He peered out at her through the window. "They made a quick adjustment. It's the right one, I think. But I'm gonna take another run around the block just to make sure."

"John's up."

"Good."

After a minute or two of watching John on the phone, she realized he was going to talk for some time. She took the opportunity to make him a fresh omelet, and had it waiting by the time he came to the kitchen. He dug in heartily and was sopping up a sheen of jelly and grease with a fragment of toast when Stuart traipsed in, a smudge on his nose, a big smile on his face. "So who's this stranger?" He looked at Helen, letting her in on the joke, and then he turned toward John, his manner almost a challenge. "Long time no see."

"You can say that again, Dad."

"Don't eat the plate, now." He was heading for the sink to wash up. "She's been waiting since sunrise to feed you. I think she figured you might enjoy a real meal without Chubby Mix."

"What's that?" Helen asked. "Without what?"

"Nothing, Mom," said John, eyeing his father.

"Could we get some?" Helen wanted to know.

"Chubby Mix?" said Stuart.

"What's Chubby Mix?" Helen was smiling, but she was growing suspicious of the way the two men were enjoying something secretive. "What is it? Some new cereal I've never heard of?" Stuart wagged his head and laughed, like he thought she'd made a joke. Or more exactly that she was a joke. The careless way he tossed the towel into the sink before moving to the table struck her as a celebration of the pleasure he got out of keeping her in the dark. "Or is it a crime that I've never heard of it?" she said. "Some kind of crime to have never heard of Chubby Mix?"

"They put it in prison food to keep men from getting erections, Mom," said John.

He was offering a kind of apology, but she didn't really care; it was too late, anyway. "Oh, sure. Saltpeter. I've heard of that. Does it work?"

"It helps. Well, it keeps you down. And it keeps you chubby."

"Is that what you've been eating, Stuart?" she asked.

She hadn't realized how bad they'd hurt her with their little conspiracy until she saw the sting in Stuart's eyes, because of how she was hurting him.

"Charming woman," he said. "Charming. Isn't she sensational?" Rising from the table, he strode toward the back door like he just might walk out on them.

"Well, you're the one who brought it up," she said.

"I thought you might want to know about it."

"You did not."

"I did too."

"You were teasing me."

"Were we teasing her, John? Were we?"

"Don't eat so fast," she said to John, who was sweeping a second piece of toast over the plate, collecting the last of the jelly. "You're gobbling."

"Say hello to your new warden, John."

"Meaning me, I suppose."

"If the shoe fits, Helen."

"All right," she said. "Stuart, I zinged you—you zinged me. So we're even. It's that ridiculous *Married with Children*—that TV show. They all treat one another so awful, everybody thinks that's how you communicate in a family. They're just all so mean and insulting to one another. I'm sorry, Stuart. I really am. I'll make you that hamburger."

"That's all right," he said, returning to his seat, as Helen moved to the stove. He picked up his coffee. "So what are you gonna do on your first day of freedom?"

"Peter's arranged a job for me down in Long Beach. That's what he called about. He wants me to go down there with Ray and meet the guy."

"Today?" said Helen from the stove. "You're supposed to meet him today?"

"What kind of job?" said Stuart. "Is it a good job?"

"Are you talking about today?" said Helen. "It's so soon."

"When did you talk to Peter?"

"Of course you have to work," said Helen. "But you just got home. You have to watch out for yourself. That's important, too."

"I will, Mom."

"Don't eat so fast."

"I have to. I have to go. And I should shower and shave. Peter said I should get down to the post office to meet Ray by two o'clock when his shift ends. Ray's going to take me to meet the guy in Long Beach. It's on the boats, a job on the fishing boats." He was pushing back from the table, rising to his feet.

"I just think it's silly to rush into it today," she said. "That's what I'm—"

The jangling telephone silenced them all, Stuart and Helen glaring suspiciously at one another, as if each was certain the other had arranged for this rude interruption.

"You expecting a call?" said Stuart.

"No." She was shaking her head and frowning, as the phone rang again. "Who could it be?"

"It's probably Peter," John said. She appeared besieged, her situation worsening, so he jumped to bring the suspense to an end. "Hello?"

"John?" said the voice.

"Yeah. Peter?"

"Who?" said the voice. "No. This is Freddy Gale."

"Oh. Hello." He scanned the room, wanting to check his routes of escape at the same time that he sought to assure himself there was no way his parents could hear the voice on the other end. With every trace of alarm removed from his eyes, he shrugged to his mother, holding up one finger to show that he would be quick.

"You with me?" said Freddy.

"Yeah."

"About last night. Don't misunderstand about it, all right? That would be a mistake."

"What would be a correct—I mean, the right understanding?"

"What happened last night will never happen again. Do you see?"

"I think so."

"I'm coming to get you. You should know that. It's important that you know."

"Why?"

"Why what? Why am I coming to get you? Or why is it important?"

"Both."

"We said something—there was something about days. Do you remember?"

"A lot of things got said."

"This was about days. A certain number of days you would have to live. Do you remember now? That's what I'm talking about."

"Right."

"You remember? That's what you're saying 'right' to? To the fact that you remember?"

"Yeah."

"There was some confusion. We got onto the subject of days and then this confusion developed. Maybe it's strictly my own confusion, but I don't want any confusion. Am I being clear here?"

"Pretty much."

"Good. Still, I'll try to hone in. A couple of numbers got thrown around—number of days, I'm talking about. You said some numbers. I said some. You remember?"

"Yeah, sure."

"Well, I want to establish the correct number. Is that all right with you?"

"Is that why you're calling?"

"I think it's important enough to merit a call. The number of days you have to live. I think that's important. Don't you?"

"I guess."

"You guess? Is that what you said?"

"Yeah."

"I would think that's something you would be sure about."

"I just think you should think this whole thing over. That's what I was saying then, when we talked. And it's what I'm saying now."

"The correct number is three. I've decided on three. And today is the second of the three. Last night counted. All right?"

"Yeah."

"All right. Good. A little depraved mind murder, John."

"What? Whadya mean?"

"That's my mantra, John. A little depraved mind murder. A little depraved indifference to human life. What's yours?"

"Think! Okay?"

"What?"

" 'Think,' I said. 'Think!' "

"That's all I do."

The click that signaled Freddy's disappearance left John to contemplate his own hand replacing the receiver.

"What did they want now?" asked Helen. She was serving Stuart his hamburger and freshening his coffee.

"Just arrangements, Mom. I better get going," he told her, but he didn't move. It was not only the aftershock of the call that he could not walk away from, but also a sudden apprehension of the delicate print of wildflowers on the light brown wallpaper on the dining-room wall visible through the doorway. White molding framed the ceiling. The baseboard was white. Everything was painted and cared for. Wicker baskets hung like pictures on the wall. A stained mahogany table shone. In a hutch, ceramic plates with fruity decals stood neatly in the shelves. Further away, another more distant doorway glowed with a fragment of brown paint that complimented the background of the wildflowers. It was the living-room wall, where taut squares of embroidery hung in wooden frames on either side of one of his mother's paintings, a large canvas portraying a man seated on a chair. Countless photographs occupied much of the rest of that room. He didn't have to see them to know they exhibited his life, showing him as a baby and then a toddler. In one he was an eight-year-old in a cowboy suit. In another, he wore a pirate hat. As a teenager in a baseball uniform—he could look out the window and see the spot in the front yard—he pretended to field a fly ball. There were also intermingled pictures of his parents. They started out young and then grew older, sometimes together, sometimes separately, the earliest showing them arm in arm, formally clothed and beaming on their wedding day—two eager people younger than John today.

It was all so simple and hard-earned in its normalcy, and it was more than rooms he was looking at. He was struck not by the familiarity of this house and its furnishing, which he could remember wanting to run from as a teenager, but its perishability, the amazing fact that such commonness existed at all. When he looked up, he saw two old people with coffee mugs in their hands. "I better shower," he said, turning and hurrying away.

But the mood this morning had brought him was not so easily slipped. It stayed with him as he rummaged clean clothes from the trailer. When he returned to the kitchen he found his parents gone. In the hall, he heard and followed their murmuring to the wall of their bedroom. He went on several steps to the bathroom, and then came back and stood listening, feeling driven and perplexed, like a man in the middle of a mystery, who believed that the walls were talking, or that he was hearing ghosts.

15

■ ■ ■ ■ ■ ■ ■

Freddy was on the phone with Robbie Perrin, a distributor of jewelry supplies, complaining about Robbie's "boring, monotonous, fucking, routine negligence." An order for modernized pedestals and velvet display cases had failed to arrive for the third week in a row. "That is exactly what I'm saying," said Freddy. "I know they were supposed to arrive. But they haven't, see! They're not here. That's what I'm trying to tell you."

Robbie defended himself by explaining that he had a new shipping manager, his tone shocked and harried. He seemed to think Freddy would have lost track of the fact that this excuse was little more than a reissue of last week's bullshit, which had centered on an inept foreman on the loading dock. Freddy couldn't remember the alibi for the first screw-up. Loudly, Robbie promised to make this particular problem his personal number-one priority. "Don't do me any favors, Robbie," said Freddy. Chugging his tenth cup of coffee of the day, he felt his stomach recoil, as if there was somewhere it might go to escape this acidic assault. "God," he said.

"I'm serious, though, Freddy. I'm serious."

Freddy was searching for the perfect trigger to launch a contemptuous tirade when the second line rang. Robbie was a low-rent asshole. You buy cheap, you get cheap, he thought.

"Wait here," he said, hitting the "hold" button and switching to the third line. "Yeah?"

"Freddy?" said a woman's voice.

"Yeah?"

The line went dead. No dial tone, no nothing. He said, "Hello," and as he waited, he knew it had been Mary on the other end. With one last angry gulp, he finished the coffee. He lit up a cigarette, leaned back in the chair. Robbie Perrin bobbed somewhere in the murk of telephone limbo, the blinking of line one marking his faint existence. Why would Mary call him? Right, he thought. Which one of a million reasons? Unless it wasn't her. He closed his eyes and took a deliberate drag on the cigarette, both gestures intended to feed his effort to recreate the voice exactly, and when he was certain he had succeeded, he knew without a doubt that it had been Mary. As the light on the first line went out, indicating that Robbie had given up, Freddy smiled and got to his feet, because he was beginning to feel that in addition to knowing irrefutably that Mary had called, he had a strong suspicion of what she wanted.

He drove through twenty-five minutes of sunny emptiness and glaring thoughtlessness. His lungs worked so shallowly, a chain might as well have been locked around his chest. The hangover and the clamor of caffeine marauding through his bloodstream had him worn out. When he realized that he was in fact pulling to a halt across the street from the pleasant house in which he had once lived, it was like waking up from a fevered nap in the middle of a hot afternoon.

Under the shade of the red maples, he made his way up the narrow sidewalk flanked by the manicured lawn on one side, and by banks of flowers on the other. It was almost like he was a guest invited to a party, the way he felt. Or a lover arriving for an assignation. He was eager to look into Mary's eyes, wondering how long it would take her to admit that she had called him.

Instead of the cheery, singsong chimes he had loved when he lived here, the doorbell gave a mechanized, impersonal buzz. He pressed it again, and again, and as it was sounding for the fourth time, he detected the whisper of footsteps, and then saw a distorted figure approaching on the other side of the thick glass door. He had just enough time to note a set of masculine traits to the image before Roger Manning, Mary's husband, faced him. The way Roger stood there with his mouth open, his expectations canceled, a cordless phone in his hand, it was obvious that he was far less prepared than Freddy for what he saw. He said into the phone, "Phil, hold on."

Freddy reached and grasped Roger's long, bony hand. "Hey, Roger. Good to see you."

"Freddy. How are you? What's up?"

"Is Mary around?"

"No."

"No?"

Stepping backward, though uncomfortable, Roger made room for Freddy to enter. "Do you want to come in?"

"Will she be back soon?" One stride brought Freddy into the wide alcove, his glance sweeping the simultaneously familiar and strange space. The floor had been redone with a dark tile. There was a new mirror on the wall to the right, and beneath it an antique table holding a large arrangement of flowers. A potted Banana plant bloomed, its assorted stalks rising from a large wicker basket in the corner. The vestibule walls, along with those he could glimpse through several visible doorways ahead, had all been repainted. Roger, his back turned, was huddled up with the flowers, as he murmured on the phone. The glance he threw Freddy was not one with which he actually saw Freddy, though he said, "Just a second, Freddy. I'll be right with you."

Freddy didn't care how long it took. He was lost in the dissonance of the years. He was savoring the intoxication of an almost psychic element surviving from his past, in spite of the disturbing way they had tried to wipe away every sign of the life he had lived here by changing so many details. In the first years after his divorce, he'd visited often, and none of this had been done. But since Mary's marriage three years ago, he had not stepped inside. So it was all new. On those occasions when he took the boys somewhere, he waited in the car.

"Place looks great, Roger," he said.

"What?" Roger waved, growing a touch exasperated with the caller, as he said into the phone, "I know, Phil. I know. But I'll get back. And if you go out, then you call me. What's so complicated?" He was looking at Freddy as he thumbed the "off" button. "What was that? What'd you say?"

"House looks great. You've done a lot of work."

"You know Mary. She's very specific about what she wants."

"I guess the boys are at school."

"Actually, they're not. They had school off for some reason, and Mary took them with her to the beauty parlor. Don't ask me why. They should be back at any minute. Can I get you something to drink?"

"No, I'm fine." He didn't want a drink. Certainly not from Roger, who was a tattletale if there ever was one and would use it against him with Mary. The whole thing was so amazing. It was like he was a sightseer in an exotic land, wandering about, comparing the detailed, polished present to the lurking past. Every now and then he happened upon a familiar item, and he paused to take it in. It was usually something immovable like a fireplace, which made him smile. Roger trailed him, the awkward mood between them growing more complex and less avoidable. With the air of a man overwhelmed by the unexpected nature of what he had seen, Freddy settled down on the couch in the living room, flinging his arms wide on the pillows. "You've changed damn near everything, Roger."

"Well, a lot. Yes."

"Not the fireplaces, though."

"No." Roger stood uncertainly in the center of the room, and then he dropped into the couch beside Freddy.

"So you expect them back any minute? Is that what you said?"

"Oh yeah, any minute."

"Good." His restless gaze left a watercolor painting of rarefied trees and a brown weave of mountains. He wasn't seeking anything in particular, but his appetite for the house was huge, so he just kept looking around. And then he caught sight of a ceramic statuette of a hobo standing on the mantel. This gnarled ruddy shape had been a marvel to Emily when she was three or four. Now the bronze-colored, bowed figure of an unshaven wanderer with a stick and bundle over his shoulder pulled Freddy toward it.

"Look," said Freddy. "God."

"What?"

"Em used to love this thing. I'm surprised it's still here. What's it doing here? We used to have it over there—it was on the counter. And she—Em—could barely reach it." The memory stole over him, the way he'd chanced upon Emily, who thought she was alone, sneaking up to the statue. There was a key in the bum's back that produced a sweet whistling tune when turned. "She'd stretch her whole body to the last joint in her fingers to turn that thing on," he said. "Does anybody listen to it anymore?"

"Not much."

A framed photo of Roger and Mary and Freddy's twin sons stood to the left of the statue, sunlight blurring the glass. He had to elevate it slightly to clear the image of his two boys, identically dressed in jackets and white shirts. Mary and Roger provided a background of adult convention, her left hand riding on Anthony's shoulder, while Roger pulled Andrew close. Freddy could feel Roger standing nervously behind him now. These were Freddy's boys, Freddy's sons. "You look like a natural family," Freddy said. "I mean, you could really be their father." As much as his words were conciliatory, his tone had treacherous undercurrents.

"Thank you, Freddy."

"She doesn't keep any of Emily around—any photos?"

"No. She . . . Not that I know of."

"You would know, I think."

As he put the photo back he seemed to have lost all interest in it. "Sensational-looking family. Really. You must be proud," he said, prowling away.

"What can I do for you, Freddy? Is there something I can—"

"Nothing. Nothing. I really came by to see Mary."

"Well, sure. I mean, I don't want to be nosy, but what about?"

"If you don't want to be nosy, Roger, the way to succeed is to not be nosy. Don't you think?"

"What is it, though?"

"I want to see Mary."

Roger seemed to refer to a set of remote principles in order to get through this moment. "Well, I suppose that would make sense," he said, producing a resigned smile.

Not to be outdone in the realm of complete insincerity, Freddy manufactured a phony grin that distorted his face like he wanted to take a bite out of Roger. He wiggled his eyebrows and said, "Well, sure. If I wanna talk to Mary, well then, I should just talk to Mary. That's the best way."

Roger shook his head in a way that suggested that encounters like this one were beyond his comprehension. He stood and paced away. "Well, I think maybe I'll have a drink," he said.

It sounded to Freddy like a car had just pulled up in the driveway, and he watched Roger, waiting for him to respond. Roger just poured himself a little glass of cognac, which he sipped. Why was he ignoring the growing sounds of arrival?

"I'm divorced, too, you know," said Roger. "My kids live with my ex-wife, too, Freddy."

"And my kids live with you," he said.

"That's right. And I take good care of them."

Now the front door was banging, the raucous voices of the boys changing the quality of the house itself as they came in. Roger whirled in apparent surprise. He downed the cognac and headed for the hallway. Freddy followed, but kept his distance. The boys were a robust pair in different-colored Nikes and cotton trousers distinct in cut and color. Andrew wore a Disneyland T-shirt while Tony sported a green shirt with the earth in orbit. They were calling "Daddy! Daddy!" to Roger, who snatched Andrew up into his arms. With the quick kiss he gave Mary, he made no effort to hide his conspiratorial intent as he whispered into her ear.

Anthony had wandered a few steps in Freddy's direction and he stared with an unnerving mix of curiosity and reserve. "Hi, Freddy!"

"How you doin'?"

Andrew edged up beside his brother. "Hi, Freddy," he said.

"Look at this, my own kids calling me Freddy."

Mary was moving toward the boys. "Why don't you go upstairs and see what's on TV?"

"Cartoons," said Anthony.

"Which ones?" Roger asked, herding them toward the stairway.

"Ninja Turtles."

They were gone quickly, their absence forcing Freddy to study the path they'd taken until the thud of a door took even their voices away. "You mind if I smoke?" he asked. He was looking around the room for an ashtray.

"No," Mary said, doing nothing to hide her annoyance.

"Okay, I won't." He smiled. Her fashion sense was simple but striking, as always, her black hair comfortable with the deep navy of her suit, the wide V of the jacket opening over a white blouse. He'd always liked to see her wearing a strand of pearls and pearl drop earrings, which she was, and it struck him as something other than an accident. "You know," said Freddy, "you look wonderful."

"Wonderful, I think, would be pushing it."

"No. You do. You look wonderful."

Carrying a bag of groceries, she walked past Freddy and he followed her into the kitchen. "How's your business going? Doing well?"

"So-so. It's a little jewelry store," he said. "What am I gonna do? A little store does a little business. What about you? You still doing real estate?"

"It's a tough market right now. I'm representing some good properties, though. And Roger's very active at the moment—it's uncanny really, considering the way Wall Street has been so erratic. But he's got such great instincts, and he's been so effective over the last year that I've been able to back off some and not worry too much. So I can spend more time with the boys."

"That's wonderful."

She didn't try to conceal her doubt of his sincerity, nor did she challenge him. She simply glanced at him and then went back to transferring eggs from a container into a slotted shelf in the open refrigerator door.

"No, no," he said. "Really. I think it's wonderful, Mary. I do."

"It's important. Everything considered."

"Yes. That's what I'm saying."

"I hope so."

Her task seemed to demand unusual care and thought. Her concentration mesmerized him for several seconds before he said, "I want to tell you something—I want you to know something. It's why I came over here."

"Freddy," she said, her voice putting up a kind of shield.

"What?" He shrugged, wondering why she would use such a tone, when she'd called him to come over. "Something I have to tell you, you know," he said.

"Freddy. You made me a promise. I hope you're going to keep it."

"I made you a promise. Sure, sure."

"And if it's more of the same, I want you to leave."

"No, no. It's two things. There are two distinct things. I made a promise. That's one. And I have great news. That's two. Now, are you going to let me speak or what?"

"You have great news?"

"Yes."

"So what is it?"

"It's great."

"So what's your great news? You're getting remarried?"

"No, no," he scoffed. "Great news, Mary. Really. Sensational news. Okay. You ready?" She was nodding, but clearly the elaborate form of his introduction made her nervous. Doubt was gnawing the edges of her smile, encouraging him to tease her. "You're sure? You're really ready?"

"Yes," she said.

"He's out. John Booth."

She glared at him. "I don't want to hear this, Freddy."

"Of course you do."

"I think you should go."

"Why did you call me, if you don't want to hear this, if you don't know he's out?"

"I don't know anything about him. I don't know where he is and I don't want to know."

"I'm going to kill him."

She closed the refrigerator and pressed her weight against the door, as if to restrain some dangerous force inside. "Call you? I didn't call you."

"The hell you didn't."

She whirled on him. "Get out! Now!"

"I'm not going anywhere until you tell the truth—until you—"

"What truth, Freddy?!"

Roger appeared on the stairs, moving briskly, leaning down as if to hasten his descent. "What's going on?"

"You promised you wouldn't, Freddy! You promised!"

"Wouldn't what? Wouldn't mention our child? Because you blackmailed me!"

"I never blackmailed you!"

"That if I want to speak to you, I must never talk about our daughter?"

Roger's breath came in little gulps, like a troubled goldfish, as he pointed toward the front door. "This can't be! Get out of our house!"

"This is my house," said Freddy. "By any natural law this is my house. If my children live here, then who's to tell me I can't come in here at any fucking hour—"

"You want me to call the police?" Mary shouted. She lunged one gigantic step in the direction of the phone, at which point she froze, as if the contest between them was charades and she was pantomiming a threat. "You want to tell the police about natural law? They'll be interested, I'm sure. Where the hell do you get off calling them your children? You haven't been a father to those kids. You stopped with our daughter."

"Emily!"

"That's right! Emily! And she's dead. But there are the boys, in case you've forgotten—I owe those two boys up there all the love I've got, so I'm giving it, but you can't stand that. It kills you that I can give it to them and you can't, because you—"

"Bullshit," said Freddy.

"You think—"

"Bullshit!"

"Bullshit yourself, Freddy. You're the bullshit! You're the—"

"Bullshit!" he shouted. *Bullshit!* He rushed her, his hands raised in a gesture begun from a need to grab her and shake her. But he could feel his desire mutating, some inner fury closing his hand into a fist so he could club her, so he could smash his knuckles into her lying, arrogant, bullshit cunt of a bitch nose. But he was stymied and unable to budge, because Roger had wrapped himself around Freddy from behind.

"I want you to leave our home now," said Roger.

Freddy wheeled, seizing Roger, who tried to retreat but ended up in a headlock that had him facing backwards off Freddy's hip, as Mary came forward slapping at Freddy. "Let go of him!"

Because of the awkwardness of the way they were grappling, Roger's buttocks were extended toward Mary, and Freddy was using him as a buffer to keep her off as he shouted, "Tell the truth, Mary. You want me to kill John Booth. Just like you want me to carry the burden of Emily's death. So you won't have to. That's my job, and yours is to go on like nothing ever happened."

"Go to hell."

"Freddy!" said Roger, tugging at Freddy's belt. "Freddy, let me go."

"You sonofabitch," said Mary.

"Why don't you let me go," said Roger, "and I'll make us some coffee, Freddy? I'll make us some coffee!"

It was all too ridiculous—Roger nattering at him and Mary's hate-filled accusing eyes. "Coffee!" said Freddy. "Good. I'd like some coffee." He released Roger and stepped back from the both of them, as Mary pivoted, glaring at him.

Roger straightened. He was retreating toward the kitchen, one hand raised to soothe the nape of his neck, the other patting the air, as if to calm a lurking turbulence. He was trying to make contact with Mary, but he couldn't find a way to break into her concentration on Freddy. "Why doesn't everybody just sit down. We'll have some coffee and talk civilly."

"You know what? Forget the coffee." Freddy couldn't bear another second of the wounded, judgmental vibes Mary was firing at him. "I don't like coffee at all. It makes my heart go nuts." With his fist against his chest, he pantomimed violent palpitations. His heart was in fact hovering between beats in a scary suspension which ended in a weird volley and a ping of pain. He felt like his legs had been taken from under him.

"You just said you wanted coffee, Freddy. That's what you said."

"I know, Roger. I'm hard to get along with these days." He was waiting for his legs to come back and then they did. "No coffee. I'm gonna go. I feel good." He wanted her to look away from him. He was trying to knife her, to slam her, to get her off him. "I mean, Mary, I feel good."

"Well, Freddy, that's a matter of the utmost importance to us all," she told him. "You know that. Perhaps to the whole world. Even to the universe. I would say certainly it's of the utmost importance to the universe."

"Let me just say this, damn you. I've done a lot of things for you. And I think it's cheap of you that you don't hear me out on things like this—things that matter more than—"

"You're an asshole, Freddy. You're a selfish—"

"Mary's upset, Freddy," said Roger. "Why don't you just go?"

"Yeah. You're right. I think I will," said Freddy.

"I'm not upset."

Freddy strode into the hallway, heading for the door, when suddenly Mary charged after him, like a barking dog pursuing a car.

"Because if you think I'm going to keep score with you over who's done what for who, you're very fucking wrong, Freddy!" she cried. "Do you hear me? And if you think that's cheap, fuck you! I don't know if you're serious about killing this man or not, but I know it's got nothing to do with our daughter. Our little girl is gone and she's not coming back, no matter what you do or don't do. As hard as that may be for you to believe. Is that hard for you to believe, Freddy?"

"Not if you tell me, Mary. Because I know I can trust you."

"Nobody is going to phone you, or write you a letter and take all this away!"

"Do you know, you sound like that satisfies you in some way?"

"You've never even been to her grave, you prick! You've never been to Emily's grave!"

"Of course I have."

"When? When, Freddy? I don't want to have misjudged you."

He felt that her hand had slipped inside him to seize a vulnerable tissue, and now she was going to pull it out of him. He had to stop her. "Why?" he said. "Why do you think that? Because I didn't come to your party. Your funeral? I went on my own time, Mary. In private."

"Really, Freddy?"

"Yes." How the hell did she dare disbelieve him? It was preposterous. "That's right," he said. It was none of her business that he'd never gone. Even now, the thought of entering the cemetery, of seeing the grave, lifted his pulse, his heart closing in a fist.

"Then you're a braver man than I thought. What is the inscription on the stone?"

He looked away, as if to ignore her was a cunning form of argument. But she knew the truth no matter what he did or said.

"What color is it?" she taunted him. "Is it on a hill, under a tree? Or didn't you notice? Were you to busy too notice?"

"Are you quizzing me?"

She eluded his maneuver and stunned him with the direct knowledge she stabbed into his eyes, her sarcasm ripping away his fabrications. "Does it lay flat, or does it stick up out of the ground?"

He tried to meet her challenge, but she just shook her head and wheeled away, leaving him with nothing to confront but the fact that his behavior was betraying something shameful about him, his frozen expression an image she found so repulsive that it disgusted her to continue to look at it. "That's what I thought," she said.

He watched her climb the stairs, vowing to defy her, hating her with every step she took. "Roger," he said. "Man to man—when you read in the paper about John Booth being shot to death, what you have to do is look into her face. You have the balls to look into her face and then you come to me and tell me—wherever I may be, if it's prison, you come there—and if you saw pride and relief on her face, then you tell me you saw it. You tell me the truth. And you will see it. Pride and relief."

"You're an asshole," Mary said from the landing, and then she was gone.

But he knew she was happy with his declaration, no matter how she acted. She might not want to admit it, but her grief, like his, could not stand to go unnoticed. She didn't want it mauling her while everybody else went on with their stupid business, like she was something extraneous, something marginal.

Ahead, the frosted glass of the door was a striated rectangle white with light, a sheet of frozen rain. The ribbed and wrinkled interior of some gigantic flower. Red and yellow bulbs and petals floated above a mist of ferns on the hallway table. Beside the door the sprawling green of the Banana plant filled the corner. The place was a funeral home, he thought, slamming the door, hoping it would shatter.

16

■ ■ ■ ■ ■ ■ ■

Once in the shower, John wanted to stay for hours, though he knew he couldn't. Time was no longer a vacuum with nothing but tedium to fill it, the way it was in prison. Already there were demands, he thought, pushing aside the curtain and stepping out. In the mirror, he charted the squiggle of the scar, as if it might lead somewhere he'd never seen before. Slowly, still staring, he lit up a cigarette. Everybody was after him. Come here. Go there. Do this. Peter. His parents. And Freddy fucking Gale.

The rapping at the bathroom door made him think that Freddy was out there with his gun again. Then his father's voice said, "It's me, John. Open up for a second."

Still dripping from the shower, he wrapped the towel around his waist and released the door. "What's up?"

"Listen," Stuart said, inching in. "We'll drive you to meet Ray, okay? That'll save you a little time."

"No, no, it's too far. You'd just have to turn around and come back." His father's neatly trimmed wavy hair was totally white. When John left for prison, there'd been numerous, strong, thick shocks of black.

"Your mother wants to," Stuart said.

"I can take the bus."

"She'd like to."

"I want to take the bus. I been locked up, Dad. You know?"

Stuart raised both hands with chagrin at having missed something he should have known, something so obvious. "We'll drive you to the bus stop, then, okay?" he offered.

"You wanna do that?"

"Yeah."

"Great. Sure."

Turning to leave, he faltered at the door. "But John, let me ask you one thing, okay?"

"Sure."

"It's a little thing."

"What?"

"When you come out and you're all ready to go, just take a minute to talk to your mother about her paintings."

"Her what?"

"Her paintings. You know, she talked to you in the car yesterday about her art class."

"Oh, yeah."

"You remember?"

"Yeah, yeah. Sure."

"She wants to talk to you about them. She's very involved in them, you know?"

"I don't have much time, Dad."

"It won't take long."

"She's been painting, huh?"

"I like the mustache," said Stuart, studying John's image in the mirror with a lingering curiosity that unexpectedly introduced him to the scar. "And the beard," he said. "It must have been hell in there." He was startled by the realization that he had missed the scar till now. "It must have been a sonofabitch," he said.

Splashing water on his face, John spread shaving cream. "It had its moments." He moved the razor in little skids from point to point.

"I mean, I was thinking maybe we could take the rifles and go out for the weekend. Get a cabin. Do some hunting. Give us a chance to bullshit."

"Sure."

"I'd like that," said Stuart, stepping from the bathroom and shutting the door. In the hallway, he looked around for Helen. Part of the reason he'd gone to the bathroom was to check how long John would be in there because Helen had to pee. He found her at the dining room table with a cup of coffee. "Won't be long until the bathroom's empty," he told her. She'd changed clothes while he was gone, slipping into a pair of dark slacks and a peach blouse under a long grey knit sweater. Stuart was still in yesterday's shirt and trousers; he carried his blue windbreaker. The cup of coffee she'd poured for him earlier had been kept warm with a saucer over the top, and she shoved the sugar to him as he sat. He stirred in a heaping spoonful and took a dainty sip, opening his mouth to let out a tactful belch. "Excuse me," he said. "Too much coffee."

John arrived in the archway, his bulk filling the frame, his hair and mustache damp. Helen rose quickly and hastened toward him. It seemed to her she'd been waiting for hours, and she was desperate to pee.

"You know, Mom, that painting in the living room is really good. How long have you been doing this stuff?"

"Which one?"

"The man," said John. "The man is the one I'm talking about."

"You like him? Did you see my painting of Grandma's house?"

"Where's that?"

"In the studio. That's your old room."

By now, they had arrived before the portrait of a dark-eyed man with black wavy hair and a mustache seated on a chair. John found himself wondering if the painting were in some way a depiction of his father. The tones were bold, the image flat and two-dimensional. Wearing an apron and holding a plate of food on his lap—maybe eggs—the man occupied a slant of light pouring in through a window behind him.

"It's acrylic," said Helen.

"Yeah?"

"I have to go to the bathroom." She was unable to wait another second. "I'll be right back."

"Truth is, it's time we got going," said Stuart.

"No, no, I'll be right back."

"But John's got a lot to do, didn't you hear him? We can't just stand around here all day. Isn't that right, John? We gotta go."

"Oh, well, okay," she said, squirming as she stood there.

The bus stop was ten blocks away at the corner of Diego and Weber. The midday sun forced them to climb out of the car. They leaned against the hood and fenders, reminding Helen of restless teenagers who were no longer certain how long they would be together.

"The thing is, you can learn it," she said, trying to rekindle the excitement and interest they'd been sharing in the living room just moments ago. Their attention had made her feel like she'd just drunk a big glass of champagne in a rush. "There are like these tricks that let you do things that you don't have to be born knowing. I used to worry it was all talent, and you could do it or you couldn't. But there's rules and people willing to teach them about how to mix every color. So if you make a mistake, you can correct it. Like Grandma's house in Seattle—I'm working on that now. There's this color I want to find, this green—"

She paused to light a cigarette, and John glanced at the bus halted a half dozen blocks away. As he brought one of his chopped-off cigarettes to his lips, his smile tried to show Helen the way her desire for a smoke had aroused his own. Then Stuart said, "Monkey see, monkey do," as he chuckled and lit up.

"You know that guy on the wall, Mom?" said John. "Who is he?"

"I've wondered, too. And he's eating what?" asked Stuart. "I know you told me."

"*Tsibla kuchen.* An onion roll."

"I thought it was you, Dad. For a second. Didn't you?"

"No, no," said Helen. She hated this kind of question. It made her feel funny and exposed, like all the buttons on her blouse were open. It made her wish she'd never done any paintings, if she could get interrogated like this.

"I was *afraid* it was me at first." Stuart chuckled.

"Well, he's not. So you don't have to worry." She pressed her sunglasses tighter to her eyes. "He's nobody. He's just out of my imagination." It was a complete lie, and she hoped she was the only one who knew.

"You have no idea the time she put in on that," said Stuart. "Worked on him for hours."

"Well, it's not easy, Stuart. That's what I'm telling you. Especially for a beginner like me, but somehow it's worth every second. It's so satisfying, somehow."

"You know who he looks a little bit like?" said Stuart. "Hitler."

"Hitler?" said John.

"He does not," said Helen.

"I'm not saying it is Hitler."

"For goodness sake, I wouldn't want to paint Hitler."

"Here comes the bus," said John. He was grateful to point it out.

"Here," said Stuart, offering his pack of Winstons to John. "I see you're almost empty. You can have mine. And you oughta use my sunglasses until you get your own—you'll need them if you go down near the water."

Helen was digging in her purse. "Here are some tokens—there's one for each way—I almost forgot."

John was reaching and taking from both of them.

"Should I cook dinner, or are you going to eat out?"

"I'll probably get something out. But I'll be back early." He was backing toward the bus, the muttering exhaust throwing up a distortion through which he had to run, as the hydraulics squealed and the door opened.

"You only get one chance at life. Remember that," called Helen.

"What?"

"Don't listen to her," yelled Stuart.

"What?"

"You better get on, John—they'll pull out without you, these days. They don't care if you're standing right on the curb in front of them."

"Thanks for the ride."

"Good luck, kid."

John scampered up the stairway, and deposited a token. The thin, sharp-featured black man behind the wheel wasn't interested in making eye contact. Without a glance up from the road, he pulled the door closed, and the bus lunged into motion.

John turned away. He crouched a little to get level with the window. His mother and father were on the curb, trying to see into the bus, their figures receding as he sailed away. They gazed after him, waving, and he thought of how just yesterday he'd watched them through a different window, the one in that van leaving the prison, and he'd filled with such an amazing emotion when he saw them floating toward him.

But now he was happy to leave them. He wasn't used to all this anymore. It was a relief to be away.

17

■ ■ ■ ■ ■ ■ ■

Still parked in front of Mary's house, Freddy was coiled over the steering wheel, thinking, Get up, get out. Walk back. From such ordinary acts, he felt promised huge results. But what? What were they? The promise was a shadowland in which everything would be learned later. All he had to do now was get out of the car and return to the house. Not even knock, just barge in and catch them at whatever they were doing. Talking about him behind his back. He would find them insulting him to his own sons. Or hugging one another. Kissing. Find them fucking.

He squeezed the wheel, and if resentment were a juice to be wrought in this way, it filled him. Mary and Roger were remodeling the house as a deliberate, malicious campaign to wipe out every sign of his own life. Of course Roger would want that. It was easy to understand in Roger. But Mary. What did it say about her? About her feelings? They were thin. They were ice. But why should he be surprised? With Emily's death, she had revealed her real nature. She'd let slip the sad secret of who she was. The way she wept and indulged in the preparations for the funeral, as if it was a show, an opportunity to demonstrate her fucking nobility. He'd watched her, a kind of spy for Emily, he felt. And what appeared to him, like the spectral outline of a malignancy brought to light in an X-ray, was the shape of her faithless soul. Out of sight, out of mind. That was the secret about her. She was double-dealing and dangerous. How dare she accuse him of neglecting Emily by not going to her funeral? What a load of shit to try to twist what he'd done into something shameful. He was proud of the decision he'd made. It was what Emily had wanted. For somebody to stand up against the unfairness. For somebody to rebel against the status quo that was trying, with its prescribed conduct, to anesthetize the truth, turning something obscene into something perfunctory, something acceptable.

His hand fell to the key in the ignition and he started the engine. There was no need to tell her anything. It wouldn't do any good. It wasn't even possible. He'd tried on the morning of the funeral, and she'd hated him for it. He'd tried today.

After a while he came to a corner where the street intersected with Sunset Boulevard. He took it all the way to the ocean. He cruised Venice looking at the hodgepodge of humanity sailing along on Rollerblades and jogging, all baking in the sun, half naked, girls with their asses bulging in bicycle shorts, their nipples like buttons in the latex. Guys with fashionably torn sweatshirts, displaying tattoos and rippling stomachs. All so madly in love with themselves. So crazed for their own pathetic flesh. What a waste, he thought. Life pumping through such an inane bunch, while Emily had none. A brainless stud in a red bodysuit was approaching on Rollerblades. His beady eyes were stupefied with testosterone overload, but he could breathe and pump his legs, while Emily was inert. With a flick of the steering wheel, however, Freddy could change the stud's mind. Slamming into the bumper of Freddy's Cadillac, flying out of control over the hood, would awaken him to a whole new world of dark alternatives, the hype and sham of his self-love.

At a restaurant with seaside tables, Freddy ordered a cheeseburger and fries. He watched the other tables, half-hearing the babble with which people occupied themselves. Trivia and bullshit. He wanted a drink, but knew it was better if he didn't have one. He'd made himself a promise, after all. He had things to take care off. The things he had to do would be best done sober. Then the cheeseburger, the catsup and pickle went from nectar on his tongue to a sickening metallic distaste in the same mouthful. He set the bun down. With the folds of his napkin, he caught the partly chewed glop and discarded it next to his plate. He finished his Coke and considered having a bourbon.

The waitress, a shapely woman with a birthmark on her neck, was passing, so he snatched at her. She looked down, her natural annoyance replaced by her job-description smile. She'd agreed to meet rudeness with charm, and she looked like she was swallowing vinegar.

"I'd like a cup of coffee," he said. "Black, no sugar. And bring it to me at the cashier, okay," he told her, rising. "Black. Okay."

She was already thumbing through her packet of bills. "Sure."

Returning to his store, Freddy hung around eyeing Jeffrey, who, when he wasn't exercising charm to dazzle a customer, fussed with the display cases. He nudged the ends of a necklace into a slightly softer curve. He fiddled with the order of a series of bracelets, tuning them to harmonies strictly his own.

Freddy found a pile of telephone messages on his desk, names and numbers of people who wanted to nag him about one thing or another, all written in Jeffrey's elegant hand. Jeffrey was still visible on the surveillance monitor. Freddy lit a cigarette and went through his messages, hoping to find one that might interest him. But he just didn't care. He counted them, thinking their total number might give them value. There were twenty-seven. He made two quick calls, and then he was back in his car.

The afternoon sun was low but violent as it cooked through palm leaves and reflected off the rooftops and windows of passing cars. He really didn't know where he was going, but mobility, even if it was pointless, kept him in a state of expectation, like late night channel hopping. He was lighting a cigarette when the Ford station wagon he was trailing halted abruptly, and he had to jump on the brakes. His front end seemed fated to slam into the waiting bumper with its NRA slogan. But then the Cadillac reared back and settled only inches away from impact. In the Ford the driver's head jerked up in a way that made it obvious he was glaring angrily at Freddy in the rearview mirror.

Freddy honked his horn and said, "Right, asshole, it's my fault." He rolled down his window and yelled, "You drive like a goddamn tourist." He was ready to get out if he had to.

But then the Ford started forward and Freddy followed it through an intersection where a little white-haired man in a short-sleeved polyester shirt and plaid Bermuda shorts came into view. He stepped up onto the curb near an aluminum lawn chair which stood in the grass. He carried a large traffic sign, a gaudy red octagon with the word STOP in big black letters atop a rod. It looked like a lollipop on a stick. He wore a quasi-military belt that consisted of two white straps, one around his belly, the other crossing his shoulder.

The Cadillac slowed and stopped. The angle at which Freddy parked forced him to twist in order to watch the man, who was in the lawn chair now, fiddling with a tiny black portable radio. In the next seconds, the man fit a buttonlike earphone into his ear. The stop sign lay beside him and he sat there, gazing off down the tranquil residential streets.

Freddy lit up and inhaled the cigarette he had been kept from by the bullshit with the Ford. Passenger cars went by at a regular rate, but the traffic was never heavy. Every now and then a delivery truck passed. The little old man didn't budge, and fifteen minutes later, Freddy lit another cigarette. His neck had stiffened from the awkwardness of how he was sitting. The cars kept going by and the old man sat there listening to his radio. When the second cigarette was finished, Freddy tossed it, and climbed to the street. He saw that the old man's complexion was ruddy, his nose collapsed and crooked from being broken too many times.

"How you doing?" said Freddy.

"What's that?" He disengaged the earphone.

"I just said hello."

"I didn't see you come up. Can I help you?"

"No."

"Sorry I didn't see you. Great day, huh?"

Freddy looked around. "Sure."

"What can I do for you?"

"Nothing. No, no."

"Just out for a walk, huh?"

"You do this every day?"

"What? Sit here like this? Kids gotta get across the street, you know."

"How long you been doing this?"

"I wasn't out here, I'd be watching the goddamn television, you know. In there fretting with Oprah and the rest of them about why the hell is this country going to hell in a handbasket? That's what

I'd be doing. Instead, I'm out in the sun. I like the outdoors. Always did. I listen to the Dodgers if they're playin', or the Lakers, or the Kings, or the Rams. I hate the goddamn Raiders, though. You a sports fan?"

"I was just wondering why you did this?"

"I thought I just told you."

"No, I mean, I was asking something different, I think."

"What?"

"Well . . . "

"Whoops!" said the old man, his eyes lighting up. "Wait a minute!" He was wrestling with the chair, fighting his way to his feet, his gaze locked on a trajectory shooting off past Freddy.

Two little girls were approaching, their bodies tilted by the drag of backpacks slung over their shoulders. One of them was dark-haired, the other blonde. They were maybe nine or ten years old. The blonde was dressed in a blouse printed with flowers and a plain beige skirt. The other, the brunette, wore a sun dress. The blonde ate a candy bar.

The crossing guard was already in the street. He walked fearlessly to his station, his sign and its command STOP borne forward like a shield. In the middle of the road, he planted himself. A sleek, regal Lincoln approaching from the opposite direction pulled up, as the old man lifted the sign. The two little girls, with barely a pause, entered the street, their cheery chatter uninterrupted. The blonde smiled up at the man as she passed. A FedEx truck had halted behind the Lincoln. In the other direction a row of three cars, a green Chevrolet sedan, a black Honda and a Poland Springs delivery truck all waited docilely. Freddy felt he was witnessing a miracle from whose grace he had been removed.

With the children across the street, the old man turned, and the cars started up, and it was clear from the eagerness with which he strode toward Freddy that he expected they would continue their conversation now.

But Freddy was shaking his head, and he wheeled away. The sensations filling him were unearthly, as if he'd been cursed by the old man's glance.

He jumped into his car and drove to the first mini-mall he found, prowling past a Korean market, a drugstore, a bicycle shop, until he came to the liquor store. He bought a pint of vodka and sat in the parking lot drinking to change the awful way he felt. He drank and waited, and what came was more numbness than relief, but it was a start. He took another big hit, closed the bottle, and sailed off toward one more afternoon in the Calypso Club.

18

∎ ∎ ∎ ∎ ∎ ∎ ∎

A woman wearing a tan coat was carrying a large checkered shopping bag down the aisle of the bus. She had to pass two or three empty seats before she reached John and he hoped she would take one of them. He had settled near the middle with a space between himself and a dark-haired girl. But the woman kept coming. He closed his eyes as she sighed into the vacancy beside him.

The doors shut with a squeal, gears shifting, and then the blazing California streets floated by once more. The idea of working on the ocean appealed to him. He was trying to imagine the kind of boat he might end up on. He hoped to let the rhythms of the bus and roadway lull him with a sensation like choppy seas. But then he found himself wondering what would Ray and Peter say, if he told them about Freddy Gale last night? If he told them about the phone call this morning?

"Do you know where the bus turns around?" said the woman beside him.

"Pardon?" He didn't look at her.

"Does this bus stay in Glendale?"

"What do you mean?"

"Glendale."

"I don't know."

"You mean you don't know if this bus stays in Glendale or not?"

"You mean, stays there? I don't think so. No."

"Does it turn around and come back to Marge Street?"

"I really don't know."

"Do you go back to Marge Street?"

"Me? You mean, me personally? No. I don't know anything about Marge Street."

"My sister has a car. A Valiant. Did you ever get a ride in a Valiant?"

She was pleasant enough, with light brown hair, her voice chatty, even a little shy. Her eyes were clear and the earrings she wore were white plastic buds. "No," he said.

"My sister has a green Valiant. I take the bus all day long."

"What do you mean?"

"What do *you* mean?" She appeared to think her response the epitome of a very special cunning she had perfected just for this moment.

"Well, you said you take the bus all day long," he said.

"Yes, I do. Do you?"

"No. I just get on and go somewhere."

"Where?"

"Wherever I'm going." He smiled. Already, he was finding a use for his prison experience. All that time wasn't a waste after all. This was the kind of conversation he'd spent most of his life involved in behind those walls. Negotiating breakfast with a psychotic. Getting along with a sociopath in the yard. A homicidal manic in the corridor.

"Did I tell you my sister's Valiant is green?" she wanted to know.

"Yes, you did."

"It's very nice."

"I like green cars," he told her. "I don't like anything else green, but I like green cars."

"I have a disability card, so I don't pay fare, but I don't know this bus driver. Do you know him?" She was leaning toward John. Her breath was peculiar, not exactly unpleasant but an odor he could not identify tainted the air between them. She was peeking around him the way she might if he were a boulder she was using to mask the fact that she was spying on the driver. "He might take us somewhere where we're not supposed to go," she said. "That's what I'm worried about."

"Why would he do that?"

"That's what I'm worried about. I don't know."

John turned toward the front and let her think he was evaluating the driver, as he watched the traffic, the pedestrians, and passing houses for a while before he said, "No, he's a nice bus driver. You don't have to worry."

"Because I am worried."

"He has a nice face. He has a nice face, I think," said John.

Her response was to engage in a direct exploration of John's eyes. For half a minute, she gazed at John. "He does have a nice face," she said. "I didn't think he had a nice face but he does. You're right."

He felt the tension leave her body, the seat they shared altered with her relief. Prison made you sensitive to so many things that the average person took for granted. You had to learn to read body language for moods and secrets. He liked this woman, but knew that she could in the next breath pull a knife from her bag and attempt to plunge it between his ribs, digging in search of his heart. When he got home, he thought maybe he'd check out his father's guns. It was unlikely they'd been changed since he left. So there would be two 30.30s and two twelve-gauge shotguns, a pump and a double barrel. Maybe he'd take one to the trailer. Maybe the next time the motherfucking sonofabitch came with his gun and his half-assed action, John would be waiting. I paid, he thought. Isn't eight fucking years enough?

"When you first left me, your sigh could break me in half," said the woman to John. When he looked at her, she was thinking about something very hard. He was sure the air of melancholy between them was hers. "I'm stronger now," she said. "But you have—it's true, I see it clearly—you have composed yourself better than I have."

"Who are you talking to?"

"Richard."

"I'm not Richard," said John, and then he shrank the space between them, their noses so close the hum of her body's aura tingled his nostrils, and he opened a veil in his eyes so she could see that he knew what it was to be crazy, too. "But I love you very much," he said.

"Thank you." Her breath was uneasy, as if the air had thinned. Though fearless, her expression was shadowed by a question. "But my heart still belongs to Richard," she said.

"I understand."

The bus braked with a jarring abruptness that slid her helplessly against him.

"What stop is this?" she asked.

"I don't know."

She was getting to her feet, patting her pockets. He kept his eyes peeled for the knife. At the front of the bus, the driver was aware of her, his uplifted head making it clear that he had her under surveillance in his rearview mirror. She was panting a little with the difficulty of gathering all her possessions, and the smell coming off her was chemical, he realized. Maybe medicinal. She didn't look at him. Carrying her many bags, she journeyed up the aisle to the exit.

A few blocks later, John got off the bus at the post office. He was on his way around the building to the loading dock in the back, where he was to meet Ray, when a side door swung open. Two uniformed postal workers pushed out. The first one, in his forties and pot-bellied, was in the midst of an anecdote. With a bark of unhappy laughter he made an exclamation point, and his companion, who was scrawny and pug-nosed, scowled and burst out laughing.

They were striding straight at John, who pivoted to avoid their eyes. He felt they were going to accuse him of breaking some rule he'd never even heard of. He took a breath and let them pass, reminding himself that he was out of jail and that these men, in spite of the fact that they wore uniforms, did not have the right to start screaming at him.

Numerous canvas mail baskets occupied the concrete platform of the dock. The big warehouse door was open. Slatted crates were stacked on top of one another, but what John saw were tiers of cells, the inmates bags, and large manila envelopes. He laughed and plucked one of his father's Winstons from the pack he'd been given. He popped the Zippo and inhaled, walking up a slanted concrete ramp. After a couple of puffs, he set the cigarette on the edge of the dock and did twenty rapid pushups, then swung onto his back and shut his eyes.

"Look at you. You're fuckin' huge," said Ray, crossing from the building. He was dressed in a leather motorcycle jacket and Levis, his black, short-cropped hair reminiscent of a tightly rolled stocking cap.

"Hello, Ray," said John.

"What'd they feed you, steroids?"

"Boredom," said John. "That's the main course. They got a lot of it."

"I bet," said Ray. "I bet they do. What else? What about bullshit? I bet they got a lot of bullshit."

"Yes, they do."

John was getting to his feet, and Ray merely hesitated and then went on toward the parking lot. "I'm sorry I never visited you. I wanted to."

"Well, I mean, maybe if you would have had more time you could have got out there." John fell into step alongside Ray. "I was only gone eight years."

"I'm going to tell you the truth, John. Places like that scare me."

"Do you know, I think that's because they *are* scary. That's the idea behind them."

"That's probably the deterrence factor they're always talking about. I mean, I started to drive over more than once, but before I would get there, I would turn around and come back. Sometimes I wouldn't even decide to turn around. I would come out of a gas station heading the wrong direction. It was very weird."

"I understand that. I would have done that, if I could."

"That's the way I felt. It seemed natural to me."

Ray opened the door on his car, an early seventies Riviera, with a maroon body and big sweeping windows. Darting around the back on his way to the passenger side, John noticed a cardboard FOR SALE sign taped into a window. "Is this thing for sale?"

"The sign? No. It's a style statement."

John laughed and moved into the front seat, slamming the door with a feeling that was both nostalgia and disbelief.

"You just gotta tell me one thing," said Ray. "Did you get buttfucked?" He worked his mouth like he'd bitten into something foultasting that he was getting ready to spit out.

You jackass, thought John. You fucking idiot. He put on his sunglasses. "I'd say I'd forgotten how unusual you are, Ray, but I didn't."

"Whadya mean?" Ray gunned the engine and cruised out of the driveway to Compton Boulevard, where he shot into the flow of traffic. "I mean, I don't think I'm unusual. But then, how would I know? I mean, strictly speaking I am with myself *all* of the time. So I am—I mean, to myself, usual."

Ray wheeled a corner, slid out into the left lane to pass a pickup with a large black dog perched in the back, and shot up the entrance-way and onto the Golden State Freeway.

"How's Peter?" said John.

"Did you know he got divorced?"

"I didn't know he got married," said John.

Bothered by a slow-moving Chevy station wagon, Ray jockeyed into the lane to his right, sped up like he was going to crash the gleaming chrome of a gray Mercedes, then slipped at an accelerating diagonal back into the original lane.

"So how's he doin' with the divorce—is he okay?" he said.

"When was Peter ever okay, John? But it's not the divorce. That's a couple years ago—and, if you want my opinion, he lets her come around too much, I think. The ex-wife. She sort of lurks; he sort of enjoys it. Like playing with sharp knives. But at the moment, he just broke up with his girlfriend. That's a fresh wound. It wasn't a long-term thing. But it was hot. You know, she's an artist type, and so tactile. Very in the moment. And Peter's strictly intellectual, even if he does play the guitar. That's just confusion, you know. He's the pop variety of intellectual. And she's visual—that's her orientation. Instinctual and sort of thoughtless. Though smart, very smart. But nonverbal. He keeps one of her paintings over his bed. So it didn't work, you know. Can you imagine being nonverbal and trying to cope with Peter?"

Breaking up with a girl appealed to John. It struck him as an enviable problem. He'd like to have that kind of trouble. First you had to have a girl. "But he's okay? He's doin' okay," he said, just to keep things going.

"The truth is, I think she gutted him. She's a fantastic piece of ass, you know. So he's like overly gregarious a lot of the time, and when he's not, he's black and blue and hard-assed. But is he okay? Sure."

Ray slid abruptly into the right-hand lane and shot past a rusting van that seemed confused about which way to go. John caught sight of a fluttering map in the bespectacled driver's hands. Ray looped a section of cloverleaf and entered the Glendale Freeway, heading toward Pasadena and picking up speed.

John looked over his shoulder at some signs on the opposite side of the road. This last maneuver had them headed away from Long Beach. He'd thought they were going straight out there to the pier. Hastily, he went over his memory of the arrangements. But it was hard to speak up. The regimen of the last eight years had been an array of absurd tasks fulfilled without question, and the residue muffled his tongue. Somehow it seemed wrong to worry about whether or not they were on the right road.

Ray smiled and said, "What's the matter?"

"Why?"

"You look worried."

"Whadya mean?"

"You look worried."

"I'm not worried."

"Good. I thought maybe you were."

Ray maneuvered them from the fast lane to the middle to the slow and all the way back again, leaving six cars in his wake. "I thought maybe the fact that we're not headed for Long Beach was causing you some concern," he said. "I thought maybe you'd noticed that we're headed in the wrong direction."

"What's going on?" said John.

"Change of plans."

"But I thought Peter said—"

"No, no, see, it's all gonna be easier than anybody thought. Peter and I both talked to the guy who owns the boat. And because you're a friend of mine and a friend of Peter's—and because this guy—his name is Ol' Hank, he's got emphysema but he's a great guy. Anyway, because he holds us both in this very high regard, he just said, 'It's a done deal. It's a solid.' So all you have to do is just show up and start tomorrow."

"Show up where?"

"In the morning. I'll drive you. Me or Peter. The boat leaves at six. He wants you down there by five-fifteen."

John's disappointment confused him for a second. Then he discovered that, at a less than conscious level, he'd been dreaming a fantastic image of surf crashing a stony fortification of shoreline. He'd been savoring the open vista of the sea. "I'd like to see the guy. Meet him," he said. "What's his name again?"

"Ol' Hank. He's a great guy."

"Why don't we go down to the ocean, anyway?"

"I think you'll be seeing enough of it, John. I thought we'd go see if Peter's home."

"You don't even know if he's home? I don't want to go all the way out there unless he's home."

"I think he is."

"Let's call him. Make sure he's there. Let's see if he wants to go with us. I just wanna see the ocean, man. And I should meet the guy, too. I don't want to just show up and go to work. What is the work? I mean, what kinda fish? How big is the boat?"

Ray took the next exit under a cluster of palm trees so polluted they could have passed for tobacco. Two blocks later a 7-Eleven appeared with a pay phone built into the white chipped wall. While John waited in the car, lighting up another cigarette, Ray threw in the coins and then talked animatedly for about thirty seconds. He kept waving at John, nodding his head. John was thinking about the boat he would be on tomorrow, trying to figure out its size.

Running back, Ray piled in to report. "He says, 'Great.' We should pick him up. He'll call the guy—the boat guy—and see if he can hang around down there till we get there."

"Do you know if it's net fishing, or do they troll?"

"I don't know that."

"What about the kind of fish? Do you know what kind of fish?"

"I'm a postman. I work in a post office, John. I don't know."

"Tuna probably. Maybe mackerel, though, or herring."

Peter lived just off the freeway in an apartment complex with a Mediterranean slant, a cobblestone walkway, abundant flowering plants, and a fountain near the front gate. The garage that came with the apartment was located down a narrow little alley of warped pavement, and Ray pulled right into the open doorway.

"Let's go," he said, when he stepped into the wavering fan of dust his arrival had spawned. "You ready?"

"I'll wait here."

"What? No! Peter's waiting—man, he wants to *see* you."

"Look, it's late. Just run in and get him. If we both go in, we'll get stuck bullshitting. Just go get him."

Ray started toward the building, but at the gate, a pinkish arrangement of bars with a flamingo head on the top, he stopped. He leaned there, looking suddenly exhausted.

"What'samatter?" John opened the door, but he didn't exit. "You look like there's something wrong."

Ray stalked back. "John," he said, and he seemed besieged, as if he was in the grasp of an adversary he couldn't fight anymore. "I have to tell you something. You have to come inside."

An alarm went off, a searching wariness in John, scanning everything he could see and think of for what had gone wrong. Who could have gotten to Ray? Who could have turned him into an enemy?

"You can't sit out here. You have to come inside," Ray said.

"What the hell's the problem, Ray? What is this bullshit?"

"You have to come inside, damnit! I'm not supposed to tell you—it's a surprise party. You know Peter—any fucking excuse, so he's arranged this goddamn party for you—only it's a surprise party."

John turned as if to leave, and then wheeled again, so he'd made a complete circle, on guard the way he would be if someone had thrown something at him and he expected it to happen again.

"Yeah. Right. So act surprised," said Ray, setting off through the gate.

The idea of people waiting for him made him nervous at first, then quickly ashamed. He wondered if they all would know he'd just gotten out of jail. If they would know what he'd done. "Do they all know me?"

"Some do, some don't. But you know Peter—it's wall-to-wall girls."

They climbed a set of stairs. John hoped the edginess he was feeling would go away and not become anger. A part of him was offended that he had been tricked like this. He'd been lied to by Peter and Ray since the morning. If he shouldn't have believed them before, could he now? Ahead, Ray stood in front of a large wooden door carved with a phony Indian design. In eight fucking years, the little prick hadn't visited once and the two letters he sent were each about four lines long.

"Just tell me," said John. "If this was all a set-up to get me here—

does that mean I don't have a job on a boat?"

"What?"

"I mean, is it all bullshit?"

"Oh, man, no. Are you worried about that?"

"Should I be?"

"I thought I made it clear. I'm sorry. You got a job."

"I mean, I don't want to be fucked with, all right? I got enough goin' on."

"No, no. It just got too late for us to get you down there and back and still have time to pull off the party the way Peter wanted. But I'll drive you in the morning. Or Peter will. Don't worry." Grinning, he reached for the doorbell, which barely chirped before Peter sprang out. He bulled past Ray to embrace John, tugging him forward while Ray slipped behind and shoved.

"I hope this is okay, man," said Peter, beaming. "It's just a little party, okay? I thought you might like to see some people, you know." He jerked his head back, like he wanted to perfect the focus in which he held John, and just that slight adjustment would do it. For a second, he savored what he saw. "Oh, man," he said, "you're *totally* surprised." Then he whirled to the waiting crowd strewn over the beige couches and chairs and he yelled, "He's totally surprised!"

"Surprise, surprise!" they yelled.

19

■ ■ ■ ■ ■ ■ ■

When Mary wheeled from the hallway landing into her bedroom, leaving Freddy behind, the whirl in her head was dizzying. She shut the door as much to cut herself off from the event as to rebuff him. Saying more threatened to carry her into areas where she sensed risks that outweighed any effect she might have on Freddy. So she slammed the door as a way of making a final statement. From the violence, he should understand that she was done with him. From the finality, he should know that she was not hysterical, but well under control. She was just walking away. It was an act of will, because she wanted nothing more to do with him. She had more important things to do. She was sick of him.

However, the truth was that the door didn't protect her so much as it sealed her up with the disruption he had brought into the house. His voice rose through the floor, a senseless rumble, as he berated Roger.

A basket of freshly dried laundry stood on the sunlit windowsill. She crossed, quickly, and transferred the clothing to the bed where she started sorting. Roger's boxer shorts mingled with her panties and several bras. His dress socks lay amid the white Thorlos she liked to wear with her tennis shoes. Her last opportunity had been the other evening when she played soccer with Roger and the boys in the backyard. Teamed with Andrew, she had scampered about feeling girlish and silly, giggling at the seriousness with which the boys threw themselves into the game. It amused her, the way they thought so much was at stake. Galloping around. Grunting, sweating. Reminding her of Freddy. Goddamn you, Freddy, she thought. His claims and the fever of their hold on him had spread to her, drugging her, making her lose her hold and slip back. The past waited, a field of poisonous flowers. She could feel its seductive intoxication, as it arose, or she sank, and it began to envelop her.

The frame of the house quivered with the crash of Freddy's exit below. His aggression was retaliatory, a counterpoint prompted by the door she had slammed. As usual, his response dwarfed her, leaving her feeling overwhelmed.

Her folded underwear belonged in the second drawer of the dresser she shared with Roger. She built a neat little stack, the bras beside them. The third drawer was reserved for his shorts and socks. They were boxers, mainly, pretty dull in their patterns, mostly cotton. Nothing funky or sexy like Freddy had. No bikinis. No silk. She tried to push the idea of Freddy from view, along with the actual items before her, hoping to shut away the sad insinuations from the past, as if her mind were a rack of drawers that could be segregated, the boundaries unbreachable.

In the boys' room the television was a dust of sound penetrating the walls with squawky animated voices and large melodramatic waves of music. She imagined the garish, muscular animal bodies swooping across the screen to execute impossible feats. She went to the wall and listened to the shouts and strange, motorized snarls filtered through the plaster and paint. It sounded like the cartoon animals were racing to escape some dark force. That's what they usually did. It pursued them through moody cartoon streets, over stormy vistas, through urban sterility and natural peril, and then it caught them, and then they escaped. At the moment, though, the tumultuous music accompanied the approach of a beast prowling Mary's mind with the belief that Freddy's shouts had contained a truth that she had willfully ignored. What was that thing he had said about carrying the burden so she could go on? That he had taken on the anger and guilt so she would be free of it, free to get on with her life? It sickened her to consider such a possibility. It placed her and Freddy on either side of a shadowy equals sign, left her with a sense of diminishment, an obscure dependence.

Just then she caught sight of her checkbook lying on a bedside table. At the beauty parlor she'd paid with one of several checks carried loose in her purse, a habit that both Freddy and Roger had condemned as careless, because it almost guaranteed a poorly kept record. She slid to the bed, grabbing the book and the pen beside it.

When Roger opened the door, she was working back through several other withdrawals she'd forgotten to note down in the last few days, jotting the figures, balancing her checkbook. He smiled sympathetically in response to the sheepish glance she gave him.

"He's gone," he said, joining her. "How you doing? Okay?"

"Sure."

His touch, as he patted her knee, felt intrusive. The supportive arm he looped around her shoulder was a violation. It seemed presumptuous of him. She was trying to remember why she'd married him, other than that he was orderly and available.

"That Freddy," he said. "He's so goddamn selfish and self-absorbed—just marching in here like this melodramatic adolescent and just walking all over our space without the slightest concern."

"I know," she said. But she didn't really. The truth was her heart was rallying behind a set of contradictory points. It was Roger who appeared shallow and thoughtless to her. If anybody was demonstrating selfishness, it was Roger with his petty analysis.

"I mean, I have to admit that his absolute, his complete obliviousness to other people is impressive. I've never seen anything quite like it. Don't you agree?"

"I do," she said, lying to Roger, and feeling an upsurge of virtue as a result. Something deeper and older and of far more value, an abiding allegiance with Freddy, was reclaiming its place in her.

"I'm sorry he upset you."

"It's all right."

"I thought about telling him, you know, 'No, thank you, Freddy,' the minute he arrived. 'Sorry, Freddy, but we are not in the market for your bullshit.' I thought about it, and in retrospect, I regret not acting on what I knew at the moment, but I just didn't quite think it was my place to tell him to leave. I mean, the balance in these things is so tricky."

"Yes," she said.

"I mean, what are my rights in these matters? What are they? When I go to Sally's to see my kids, her new husband is always lurking around. He's tactful, I'm tactful, that's the way you do it; but there's this area of complete unpredictability, and you just have to bear in mind that it's taxing for everybody."

"It's very difficult."

"So I bent over backwards. But the next time—I mean, God forbid that there ever is a next time—but if there is and I open the door and Mr. Freddy Gale is there with that smug, self-important twinkle in his eyes, I promise—"

"No, no," she said, "you did the right thing." She disliked him in a way that scared her and made her kiss him on the cheek, and then smile her fondest smile at him, as she told him, "Thanks for your help with this thing." He made a show of humility that declared that he had earned her gratitude, as far as he was concerned. Faced with her real feelings of contempt and resentment, Mary lifted herself from his embrace. It was this intimacy that she was fleeing, along with the sense of shameful betrayal it provoked.

Joining the boys, she watched a hawk-faced Superhero in a bloodred bodysuit storming through an urban landscape. Palatial angles and brooding colors engendered an atmosphere that was Gothic and coldly futuristic, and it left her wishing the boys were outside playing. When Roger arrived a few minutes later, the feeling of being pursued and suffocatingly contained increased. He sat beside her, and her distress grew so palpable that she patted him and strode toward the door.

"You're just going to let the kids enjoy this stuff today?" he asked, teasing her about her normal opposition to the television.

If this is the worst thing that ever happens to them, she thought, I'll be happy. A dark armored vehicle was plowing through a barrage of supersonic bullets, their pathways visible in streaks across the screen. "Gotta pee," she said, and went into the hall and then to the toilet in their bedroom, where she looked in the mirror and was startled by the almost serene image she found. "Look, can I tell you something? I have something to tell you, okay," she said aloud. "Sure what?" she said. Then she pulled down her panties and sat on the toilet, rubbing her temples, her gaze transfixed at the floor. Like the nearby television screen, and to the accompaniment of its ominous music, the tiles reflected her fear that the house might burst into flames tonight. Or that the gas jets on the stove in the kitchen were leaking. Or that they would start leaking tonight. Or that a wire somewhere in the walls was frayed, having been nicked by some indifferent workman during renovations, and now it was about to let current loose to ignite the wood along which it was strung.

In the kitchen, she found an open bottle of white wine in the refrigerator. She poured herself a glass and after a thoughtful sip, she telephoned Dr. Glazier. Along with moderating the group sessions, he was available for individual counseling. She'd seen him privately when she first started attending the group sessions. His recorded voice on his answering machine addressed her slowly, soothingly, as if his message had been conceived with hysterical, overwrought callers in mind.

"This is Mary Manning, Dr. Glazier," she said. "Could you please give me a call if you get a chance. I'm at home. I'm calling from home at about—it's the afternoon," she said, looking up at the wall clock, "late afternoon—"

"Hello," he said. "Mary?"

"Yes. Oh, hello, Dr. Glazier?"

"Yes."

"Look. Are you busy?"

"No, no. I have a minute."

"I mean, you don't have any time this afternoon, do you?"

"Is there something wrong? Is it an emergency?"

"Oh, no, no," she said.

"Actually, I do have some time in about half an hour. You couldn't get here by then, could you?"

"You're not that far. Sure."

"I have a patient out of town for the whole week."

"I'll come right over."

Roger was standing in the doorway when she hung up. "Who was that?"

"Dr. Glazier."

"Oh."

She nodded, affirming the worry in his eyes, as she strode up to him, gave him a little kiss on the cheek, and went into the hall. "I mean, who'm I kidding?"

As she headed west, she was faced by the late afternoon glare over the ocean and she plucked her sunglasses from her purse and put them on. It had been so conventional and stereotypical, the way she and Freddy had fallen apart after Emily's accident. She had thought herself more unique somehow, their union a creation whose vibrant strengths were like nothing she had ever seen before. Certainly not in her parents' marriage, which had managed to combine a tedious surface with an ultimately unreliable core as her father divorced her mother once Mary was out of the house. In the relationships of her friends she never saw values that struck her as anything equal to what she had with Freddy. For the most part the couples around her were conspicuously flawed. Their faults were always apparent to her, the stitch that would fail, the thread that would pull loose and leave the two of them unraveling. With Freddy she'd never felt so connected to anyone in her life. He'd always seemed capable and sturdy and resourceful. He could think his way through a complex, confusing situation and locate a path where she had believed none existed. If the problem were immediate and physical, he had a vocabulary of responses. He could be direct and confrontational as he had been that time with the guy who raced out of the parking lot and slammed right into them. He had jokes for all occasions, a capacity to shift almost any perspective with an unexpected remark. It might be silly, or it might be gallows humor, but its introduction would provide an altered understanding in whose protective circle she felt safe. Like that time on the plane. She'd tell Dr. Glazier, she thought, about the time they were flying to Vegas and she'd panicked, fearing they were going to crash and then Freddy saved her with a joke.

The pink single-story house containing Dr. Glazier's office had an orange tile roof and a walkway painted blue by the previous owners. She'd never been able to figure out why he didn't have it all changed to something more dignified. It was garish and trashy. His tolerance for a color scheme that Mary found offensive disturbed her, making her worry that he was frivolous and unobservant, that he was insensitive to physical details. It seemed the home of a silly man. Still she went in, and he was waiting. He led her to his consultation room and sat down in a sturdy brown leather armchair placed next to a matching couch with a pillow covered by a paper towel.

"I think I'd like to just sit and talk, if I could," she said. There was another chair facing him, an autumnal cloth patterned in leaves and dark trees upholstering its padded bulk.

"I think it might be better if you lie down. But it's up to you."

She sagged onto the couch, stretching out and sighing. Her right hand appeared above her, loose at the wrist and flopping as it lowered like a blinder to dim her eyes. "I feel like a lox," she complained. "Just lying here. God," she said, watching Freddy stalk her thoughts, prowling the rooms of her home, everything miniature in her mind.

"Freddy came by today." She watched him a moment, stomping around, pissing on everything, like an animal trying to leave his mark. "And when he left—I mean, he did this number on me, he did his Freddy routine. Like he used to, and I welcomed it. I mean, I know that now. When I was young and we first got together, and I loved him, it was because of how he could overwhelm me—just remove certain obligations from me. So there he was. Making this fucking announcement. Like it was something I wanted. Just like he did that morning—the morning of Emily's funeral, when he came and said—I mean, you remember this, don't you, you know what I mean?"

"Yes. Of course."

"That he wasn't going to go to the funeral, and I shouldn't either. God. Like it was this great, you know, this gigantic affront to something, this defiance that he was doing to the world. To the universe, probably. What did he think? Skip the funeral and what? I didn't understand it then, and I don't now. Except his anger. He was so angry. So he's going to kill this guy, he thinks. John Booth. The drunk driver. Coming to me with that—like it was this trophy. A good report card.

"I mean, I couldn't believe it that morning—that he would actually do that to me—try to make her funeral about himself. About his actions. You know, make us all look at Freddy. What is Freddy doing? See how special he is—he's not like the rest of us! Won't go to his daughter's funeral.

"But I didn't care about him. It was about her. Emily and people having feelings, and what do you do with them? And today? Didn't he know how it would make me feel, to come to me like that? I couldn't believe it that morning. That he was standing there saying those things. You know—and today was the same thing—that he didn't care what I was feeling. What it would do to me. He just didn't care. I was holding myself together that morning and I was counting on him to carry me through, to be there, to hold me up, you know. That's what he'd always done. He'd promised to do it and he'd done it, and by doing it he'd made more of a promise. And suddenly he wasn't even there. I hated him. I saw he was afraid and he didn't even know it.

"We had a terrible fight. I couldn't forgive him. I never have. I never will. I mean, after all, he was the one who was supposed to pick her up at school and he didn't do it. Some fucking meeting took over, so he wasn't there when he was supposed to be. And he left a phone message for me, sure, but I wasn't home. I didn't know I was supposed to be home. I was over at a friend's house with the twins—there was a pool. It had been a spur of the moment thing. We'd made the arrangements at breakfast, the three of us. Emily eating waffles, I remember, with blueberries all over them. Frozen blueberries. And Freddy with his newspaper and his coffee. He would pick her up. He made some joke about how he'd come in his chariot. So it was all set. He would come in his chariot. I think she believed him, you know. Literally. So when this girlfriend called and she had a pool, you know, her own swimming pool, I went. He left a message on the machine that I should pick her up, but I didn't get it. Why should I? I didn't phone in or anything. He called the school, too, and told them to make sure she didn't leave without one of us, but somebody screwed up. The message didn't get to her teacher. The switchboard took it, but nobody got it. He was supposed to be there. Who cares what messages he left, or who screwed it up. Who cares what trash can the information ended up in? Or what desk it fell behind. He was supposed to be there.

"And so today, it was the same thing all over again—marching in and—but do you know what? He made me feel that my marriage today is a sham. He made me feel I just settled for Roger. He made me feel that I just called this Time Out in my life after Emily was gone. How did he do that? How did he manage to make me feel that everything afterwards just took place in this long Time Out and so I just married Roger, because the game was no longer going on, you know, and so it didn't matter what I did. So I just married this guy who I didn't love. Which I always really knew. But what I didn't know was that it was *because* I didn't love him that I married him. I mean, that was *why*. Because I didn't love him. Because I would never love him. So I don't love him, and I never will."

She heard herself stop the way she hadn't heard herself speaking. The silence was a presence starkly introduced to the room, and as it lengthened, she felt herself on the verge of the formulation of something just out of reach of the language afloat in her mind. She was certain that it would emerge in seconds. But the minutes stretched on and she said nothing more; silence became her mode, silence became her speech. She hurt for Freddy, and for herself, and for Emily. But the admission of such sentiments in simple words appeared a refutation of everything she had managed to express with her effort up to this point. The force urging her to speak felt like blackmail, and her tongue refused to budge in surrender.

"Who do you love?" said Dr. Glazier.

His voice startled her, as if she had forgotten he was there. It was not his practice to interject much. He tended to let most silences flower or turn barren on their own. "What?" she said, knowing he would not repeat himself. Who did she love? Well, the boys. She loved the boys. And Roger? Was her renunciation of him real? These questions were like stones dropped into a deep hole. The ripples they elicited were distant and impossible to read. The tears tickling her cheeks had trailed from her closed eyes because of something and someone she had not spoken about. A phantasm really. Not the Freddy she had seen today, but the one she had lost. The Freddy she had loved and the Mary who had loved him. They were the people she loved. But they were dead. They were buried.

"Like the day of the funeral, the way he accused me. The contempt he had because I wanted to go. I had to. I wanted to honor her. I could barely walk, but I knew she would have wanted it. She loved parties. She was a very, very social little girl. She loved meeting people and watching them. She would have appreciated the behavior. The hats and clothes. That's what I thought about. I asked myself what she would have thought of the straw hat Susie Tilbey wore? Or Mrs. Guilson's really outlandish earrings. Or the gloves and shoes that Mrs. Samuels had on—black but with all this glitter. And her friends were there—her school friends, all dressed up and selfish, sure, preoccupied with themselves. But what's wrong with that? That's just people!

"She was a little girl. She wasn't going to graduate. She wasn't going to have a wedding. And she was a very, very social little animal. She loved the way people arranged things, all the trouble they went through for a party. She wanted to be part of the world. She wanted to be part of society. And that was the only chance there would be for her—for the world to recognize that she had been alive. What Freddy was saying didn't make any sense. She would have gone if she could have. So I went for her. But he had to—I mean, he—I mean, that's what people do! Weddings, funerals, parties— that's what they do! And she wanted to be a person. But he had to act like it was shameful, and I was shameful, and condemn us for wanting to be with her, because that's all we were doing, Freddy, you goddamn sonofabitch, Freddy!"

The emotions that she ended up struggling with left her weary. In the waiting room some minutes later she rested, letting her feelings ebb while staring at the turning pages of a magazine. Dr. Glazier came to ask her if she might want to return at the same hour for the rest of the week. She told him that she didn't know. She would come tomorrow for sure, and then decide about the rest of the week.

On the stoop in front of Dr. Glazier's door, she paused to put on her sunglasses. A car had just halted directly in front of her. The figure that stepped out, grabbing a denim jacket clear of the slamming door, was lean and blond. Walking toward her on a crooked stride that conveyed awkwardness and struggle was Bobby, his gaze both downcast and glazed; he appeared tilted by some invisible pressure. She stared as he came nearer, expecting him to meet her eyes or speak, and then when he simply passed, she turned to follow him with her glance.

"You were at the group session the other night," she said to him.

"What?" Spinning, he fumbled with his jacket.

"I was there the other night when you spoke."

"Oh, yes. Hello."

"Did it—did you find that it—I mean, how are you feeling?"

"I'm almost late for Dr. Glazier," he said, glancing skyward as if he told time by the sun.

"Oh," she said. "Sorry. I don't mean to—"

"No, no," he said. "I saw you. I think. Have you been going long?"

"To the meetings? Eight years."

"Oh, man," he said.

"What?"

He backed away, nodding and struggling to maintain a formal courtesy, his hand extending for the door behind him. His body, with its almost crippled configuration, held her captive. Everything about him appealed to her, every gesture and twitch richly expressive. "That's a long time," he said, his smile reflecting an ironic, melancholy amusement. The sheen covering their exchange was recast, something glinting out from inside it, a sense of opportunity declaring this moment not mere coincidence but a product of design. The emotion with which she had listened to him at the meeting evolved into an appetite for connection. And then she remembered the mysterious phone call the morning after the meeting and the way she had known it was this man, Bobby, on the other end.

"Now, I really should go," he said. "Or I will be late. Good talking to you."

"Would you want to talk more? Have a cup of coffee after your session?"

"What?"

"After your session."

"Well, I mean—I can't."

He looked worried and she felt rebuffed. "Oh," she said.

"I mean, today. But I could tomorrow. I'm here tomorrow, too."

"Oh," she said. "Tomorrow. Sure. Tomorrow's good."

With her forefinger against the bridge of her sunglasses, Mary blinked as he went, pushing the frame tight and looking around like a thief making certain of her mask.

20

■ ■ ■ ■ ■ ■ ■

"Excuse me. Excuse me, excuse me. I'm sorry. It just struck me. We're all white people here."

John didn't take another step. He'd been wandering through the party for hours, and he stopped near the speaker, a gnomish man, one part of a trio consisting of two men and a woman whose absorption with one another made them oblivious to John's interest in them. Edging closer, John felt the infatuation they shared was so absolute, he could lean against it and not fall through.

"Yeah, but you know what," said the second man. "The next time the riots come to town, I'm with the blacks. I'm gonna go out to Beverly Hills and do some fucking looting."

"Speak for yourself," said the woman. The two men sought each other's approval before checking for hers. Then they laughed so hard they had to close their eyes. She waited before strategically adding her giggle. When one of the men awoke to John's presence, John looked down at his plate of grease and barbecue stains, where a couple of broken potato chips lay amid the rib bones he'd gnawed bare.

A guitar called out across the room, and then it called again with a kind of country and western lightheartedness that opened the way for Peter's singing: "I was born a cowboy, and a cowboy I will die. . . ." He had a goofy rural twang, and his body language was burlesque.

"I'm sorry, Ray," said somebody behind John. It looked like Ray had been approaching when this thin guy in a T-shirt with the word "GRUNGE" stenciled all over it waylaid him.

"I'm sorry," said the guy. "But he's the one who was born a cowboy. He's the one. Is that wrong of me to say that?"

A blond girl wearing aviator glasses was hanging around and she said, "You got Ray pouting."

Ray looked like somebody who had just been told all his credit cards were stolen. "I gotta handle this, John. This mis-fucking-understanding." He raced away, with the others chasing him.

Their departure launched John into a fogbank of cigarette smoke. He passed several charged conversations. Books were all over the place, laying on tables, chairs, shelves, the floor. He stepped on one, and bent to pick it up. The title was *Manufacturing Consent.*

"John," said Peter, letting the song just stop and raising his glass of tequila in a toast. "That's a great one." Appearing to govern from a large leather chair, he lowered the guitar to his lap. His brown desert boots heeled the edge of the coffee table in front of him, crowded with party debris. Another guy with a guitar settled near Peter. Idly, the guitars started to talk to one another.

A cloud of perfume passed by John, a lingering, delicate assault. He saw a juxtaposition of long russet hair and a plaid pullover floating away. The girl was tailed by a skinny, spiky-haired guy in a smooth, black leather jacket. Coming from the opposite direction the blonde in the aviator glasses was leading the guy in the grunge shirt. "You got Ray pouting," she said.

They passed John without affecting his concentration on the other girl, as the spiky-haired guy leaned close to ask her, "Do you own a gun?"

Her skin was lustrous. He took note of her clear hazel eyes. As she said, "No," John realized how the party had pretty much been swatches of color, strips of clothing, hunks of food, but nothing whole until this second. The spiky-haired guy was characterized by a goatee and thick glasses. The girl's ears sparkled with tiny gold earrings.

"You should own a gun," he said. "Because they got a plan and the plan is internment camps."

"I hear you," she said. But her eyes flashed sideways to slip his harangue, and somewhere in the arc of her escape, she saw John and smiled. He felt a current springing toward him.

Then the spiky-haired guy stepped in the way. "Do you agree with me?"

"I agree all the way," she said.

"Thank God. No one else seems to. Like Thanksgiving is a very perilous time. Because the plan is, you eat a bunch a turkey, you got that tryptophane thing going from the turkey—next thing you're in the internment camp. I used to do a lot of cocaine, but I don't anymore, because the money goes straight to fund Black Ops. Which is not funny, because it was hard for me to give up."

" 'Hold still,' " sang Peter. He was strumming his guitar, while the second guitarist worked with him, leaning close to the neck of his instrument like he expected it to whisper instructions to him. " 'Hold still, hold still,' " Peter sang, " 'it's not the night, it's just me. . . .' "

His voice was different this time, and it caught the whole room with the quality of its hard-assed, gritty desire. He was laying claim to their attention. People responded by silencing those around them, or by moving toward him. John was caught between his interest in the girl and the general drift of the room, but then he saw the girl make a kind of spin move to leave the spiky-haired guy. She used the music as an excuse, and she did it gracefully, but it was cunning. She squirmed into a niche on the couch almost directly across from Peter. John followed, pretending to want to hear the music.

Peter had watched her approach, and now he checked John standing behind her, and then he fixed her with a dark glance, as he sang, " 'I am loaded but I'm not a gun. You're ripped, I'm ripped.' " He wheeled away, the melodiousness of his voice crushed in a growl. " 'Everything that bleeds is somehow love.' "

The audience, caught off guard, was admiring. There were still stragglers hurrying up and sitting down apologetically like latecomers at a concert. " 'If you can't find it, does it mean it was never there?' " he pined. A tall woman in an orange shirt and overalls, one shoulder strap unhooked so the bib flopped down with a hint of undress, came up behind Peter. She put her hand on his shoulder.

His response was to tilt back with a lingering glance that he severed in order to confront the eyes of the other girl, the one in front of John. Peter's layered red hair swirled as his head rocked in the overhead lights. His hawk features flushed and sharpened. He looked like the singing hurt, and yet he was addicted. " 'Look at me. Look at you. You're ripped, I'm ripped. But where there's blood, there's love.' " He clawed the strings, tearing loose a bitter racket that he accompanied with grunts, as if he were being struck from various angles. He took a breath and let out a sound like a nail driven into his foot. "Very fuckin' Catholic." He smiled.

"What?" asked the tall woman.

"The song. The blood," he said to her, and threw in a miserable chord. The way he'd gone directly from singing to talking had warded off all but a smattering of applause. It also resulted in everyone attending his conversation with the tall woman like it was a continuation of the song.

"That's not nice, Peter—it really isn't." She shook her head at him, reminding John of a suffering mother with a sad, dismaying child.

"Nice?" he said. "Nice? We're looking for nice here?" He made a conspiratorial face at John that declared the two of them in league, effortlessly and without question on this issue. "Nice, John? Nice?"

"First of all," said the woman, talking to Peter but looking at John, "I want you to explain why you think there's nothing good about a Catholic education."

"I was raised in it," said Peter. "Remember?"

"So was I."

"So you are the product of a brainwashing campaign. Do you admit that?"

"What do you want me to admit, Peter? What exactly?"

"I just told you."

Laughter skipped around the room like cheap fireworks, a lot of hissing, a couple of semi-explosions.

"Fine. Funny," said the woman. The odd part was the way her manner was remote and facetious and teasing all at the same time. "But just to attack the Church for—"

"I mean, Onward Christian soldiers, Karen, for Chrissake! Let's go to Peru and—"

"Peru?"

"And sharpen our swords on Peruvian infants!"

"What do I have to do with Peru and Peruvian—"

"How long were we married?"

"What?"

"How long were we married?"

"What's that got to do with it?"

"Just tell me, Karen, will you?" he said. "How long were we married?"

"So you admit it! You admit that it's all because of me. This vendetta against the poor Catholic Church, which has enough troubles, but still aspires to compassion, which is more than I can say for you. Because you are so damn judgmental sometimes. Cold and judgmental."

"I'm judgmental? *Me?*"

"You know you are!"

Peter appeared stricken by a return of the misery he had celebrated at the end of the song, only now he was silent, weighing her insight.

"I think you made him feel bad," said the girl who was sitting in front of John.

Karen gave her a look of almost comic disbelief, like she really doubted her own senses. Somehow she made it obvious that the girl had just presented her with an opportunity so blatantly one-sided that she feared taking advantage of it would make her look sadistic. "Well, I guess you would know, Jo Jo," she said, shrugging. "I mean, all about how to make Peter feel bad."

"The truth is, Jo Jo, she can't make me feel bad. She can't do it," said Peter. Then he gestured, declaring any and all efforts against him futile, though he seemed to need a fairly big drink of tequila. "We're all trapped anyway," he said. "The trap is sprung—"

"You're trapped? This is new," said Karen. "You're trapped? When did this happen? I thought our divorce set you free."

"No, no, no, forget about me," Peter said. "Forget about me. Just forget about me. Look at Jo Jo." He was gesturing toward the girl. "That painting I've got of hers upstairs—it's remarkable. She covers herself in paint and rolls her body on the paper. She rolls on the paper and—"

"I do not," said Jo Jo.

"Canvas. It's canvas, I mean," he said. "Trying to represent God. You look for God, you get an impression of yourself."

"That's God? That painting is God?" asked Karen.

"Because that's what all this is about. All of it," said Peter. "The Church stuff and the sex stuff and the relationship stuff—it's all ourselves. We are the trap. We trap ourselves."

"Wait a minute, wait a minute, Peter," said Karen. "I just have to get this straight. That painting up in your room is God? That painting up above your bed is supposed to be God?"

"No," said Jo Jo.

"This is an absurd conversation," said the spiky-haired guy, taking a puff from a cigarette. "Because how does anyone even know if God exists?"

"You don't have to know something exists to argue about it," Peter told him. "You can launch an armada, start a war on something that is nothing but a theory. As long as people believe in it."

"I believe in King Kong," said Jo Jo.

"Who?"

"That's good. Why, Jo Jo?" said Peter. "Why do you believe in King Kong? Maybe we all can."

She raised her wine and studied it. She smiled a *fuck you* smile at Peter that was not without sadness, though it hardened her more than it softened her. "You know, he holds her in his hand. He holds her in his hand and he just loves her. That's freedom."

"I thought we were talking about God," said the spiky-haired guy.

"We're talking about freedom now."

"But that's not freedom," said Peter "She's this little creature delivered by this big thing, Jo Jo. That's totalitarianism."

"Oh, Peter, what do you know about it? You just said you were trapped," Karen told him.

Peter was surveying his audience, when he came upon John. He lifted his glass brimful of tequila and took a swallow. "I mean, not to put too fine a point on it, but if we're going to talk about confinement, we have a resident expert here in John."

"You're not going to drag me into this," said John.

"I think you know something about confinement."

John stroked the Zippo, lighting up, and then sank back, exhaling. "I don't want to say anything."

"You have to."

John raised his fingers to the bridge of his nose. "Well, at the risk of sounding like I know what I'm talking about, I think freedom is"—if he was to judge by them, it was a goddamn joke—"overrated," he said. He was thinking about Two Tommys and the dimensions of a cell. He was thinking about waking up to find Two Tommys staring at him from the corner. About the bald guy slumped on the stairs, his blood following the cracks. The howls of the embezzler and the craziness of his attackers shouting numbers as they fucked him. Or the kid kneeling in front of that psychotic, like he was praying to madness. "I mean, freedom, it's useful, exhilarating. But if there's nothing bigger than freedom, then freedom is just . . ." a pile of shit, like the bunch of you ". . . entertainment," he finished.

"Entertainment?" asked Karen. John knew by now that her smugness was simply a trait she could not escape.

"John, this is Karen," said Peter. "We got married while you were away. And we got divorced while you were away."

"I think that what he's saying is very different," said Jo Jo. She was twisting in the seat in order to look up at John where he stood behind her.

"So the King Kong contingent has a thought," said Peter.

"I'd like to see your painting," said John.

"You mean, the God thing?" asked Peter. "It's great."

"It isn't God," Jo Jo said. "And I didn't roll in it." It troubled her to have to clarify these points so many times.

"Show him, why don't you?" said Peter. He was smiling like a man who thought burning his hand was fun.

"It's up there." She was pointing toward the stairway behind them and the loft that hovered over the room.

"I can go look," said John, walking away.

"Show the guy, Jo Jo."

John was on the stairs when the guitars started up behind him. The uniformity of the flesh-toned paint on the walls of the loft was broken by a red bookcase, a stained walnut dresser, and the rectangle of Jo Jo's painting. Much larger than he'd expected, it hung directly over Peter's black-sheeted bed. Where Peter had fucked her, it looked like. And the other one too, the ex-wife. Maybe recently. That's what he'd figured out. That Jo Jo was the ex-girlfriend Ray had told him about. The nonverbal. The instinctual but smart. The great piece of ass. And the ex-wife was the ex-wife. Peter had been busy while John was in prison. But then eight years was a lot of leeway. Time to have a life and screw it up, and fuck Jo Jo, how many times? And how many others up here talking their talk and getting laid in this bed?

He raised his glance. The background of the painting was sort of like outer space. A smooth blackness around this white icy object. He could hear footsteps behind him and he knew that Jo Jo was on her way to join him. Bringing her nonverbal, intuitive, but smart piece of ass up the stairs. The last thing he noted in the painting was two human heads inside a shape of cold light at the center, like a glass jar, or test tube.

"I'm Jo Jo," she said.

He took a long look at her. It was like she owed him something. "You know about me?"

"What? You mean, about what happened?"

"I was in prison. That I just got out."

"Yes. Peter told me. He said there was an accident."

"I was drunk."

"He said that you'd been drinking."

He could see she was confused by the messy impulses he was putting out. He liked the way it made her look. "My mom paints," he told her.

"Really?"

"Yeah. While I was in prison, she started."

"Huhhh." The information took her off on a tangent. "That's interesting."

"Is it?"

"What does she paint?"

"Acrylics."

"These are oils."

She was beside him now. They stared at the painting.

"They look like people dying inside plastic bags," he said.

"I don't know."

The inch of air between them shivered, receptors just beneath his skin prickling with a dense fibrous interest. Her nearness was rerouting his blood, like there was an emergency in his groin. "The father of the girl I ran over—he threatened to kill me last night."

"What?"

As she looked at him, he saw an image of her on a bed, her legs opening to take him in. "Last night," he said.

"What do you mean, John?"

"He threatened to kill me. Last night."

"Was he serious?"

"I think he was serious."

"But what happened was an accident."

"You're the only person I've told."

"Me?" She looked at him like he'd just said the most interesting thing she'd ever heard, even though she didn't quite understand it. "Why? You should call the police."

I don't want to fuck the police, he thought. "I think I thought it would be romantic," he said.

She glanced down the stairs, as if his remark demanded that she make certain no one was near. "Why do you want to be romantic?"

For a second he heard the voices below, and then he forgot about them. She was about to come back to him. The scenario was clear. Peter was intellectual. She was nonverbal. What did that make John? An ex-con. Jo Jo's penitentiary adventure. He could hear the tape in her head. He'd just got back from doing time with the devil and maybe he could give her a sense of it, a vicarious second-hand taste. Like a wolf regurgitating food for his mate. Like second-hand smoke. For her art. For her spirit's education. His dick was nosing around in his shorts. Eight years in the can. She probably thought he'd get hard and stay that way for a week.

"How did you get that scar on your forehead?"

It was a good story, but he thought he'd save it. Tell it later—the way he'd started yelling and couldn't stop, and the nearby con who told him to bang his head on the wall.

"Was it in jail?" she wanted to know.

"I wanted to change my mind about something," he said, "and it wouldn't change." If she looked down, she would see the bulge in his pants. She looked down. Snorting with contempt aimed mostly at herself, she stepped up onto the bed and stood on the sheets. With her eyes level to John's nose, she placed her mouth on his, parting his lips with the sweet mush of her tongue. She pulled back and bounced to the floor. She glanced at her painting, as if to remind herself of some bit of wisdom or history available in its design. John waited, putting his stock in being nonverbal.

"This is fast," she said. "This is too fast."

"You used to go out with Peter, didn't you?"

The look she gave him bore him no ill-will, but she was suddenly wary.

"He's too intellectual," said John. "He's a great guy, but I don't think that's the way you do things. I mean you—personally. I mean, you're smart, obviously." His eyes referred to her painting as if to prove his point, and she followed his example. She remained transfixed by the dark plane with its icy inhabitants, while he brought his attention back to her. "But I think you're probably more intuitive. Instinctual."

She turned the soft, receptive interest aroused by the painting onto him. "You were in prison eight years."

It was a fact he knew something more about. "I killed somebody," he said.

That had an effect on her, hearing him say it just like that. She was probably trying to imagine a portrait of him. How to capture the tangled mess he was. Her hand played in the fringes of her hair. "I want you to take my number," she said. She plucked a pen from the dresser and started writing on a section of newspaper. She wrote carefully, and then she looked up and said, "Call me, okay?"

The two guitars were mixing notes downstairs, some savage and almost out of control. " 'Hold still,' " sang Peter.

Jo Jo was gliding down the stairs, her hand light on the rail, and John watched her closely, until she sank from sight, though he could still feel her pulling at him.

But you promised. You promised you'd let Daddy kill you if he wanted, said Emily. *You promised.*

He turned to the painting, investigating it the way he thought Jo Jo had, as if it could answer his questions. Some girls are dead, he thought. And some girls are not.

He picked up the newspaper and walked to the rail. Jo Jo was standing by Peter, her hand in his hair. John looked at them for a long time, until finally he was sure that he was right to believe that she was petting him like a dog.

21

■ ■ ■ ■ ■ ■

Not giving a fuck had a gravitational attraction, and it sucked Freddy in the front door of Nicky Blair's restaurant. The view ahead was all Hollywood hotshots decked out in their high-priced accessories of designer shirts and ties, Rolex watches, and silicone-injected gash. It was a daunting mood of glitzy flesh and liquor and some egotistical chef's wet dream about himself. But Freddy was not alone; he had Verna, Tanya, and Jennifer, three strippers from the club, in tow. Two funky black girls and a white hardcase with airs, chattering like high school girls two steps behind him.

Nicky Blair himself, clad in dark, double-breasted silk cut to give his squat bulk a semblance of elegance, was mingling with bar guests. A word here, a wink, a flattering squeeze. When his glance popped up from the flora and fauna, like a predator checking for prey, he saw Freddy and squinted, then leaned to a woman in a dark gown beside him.

"He's asking the brain-trust who the fuck I am," whispered Freddy to Verna.

The woman flashed Freddy a snapshot glance, then added an overjoyed smile as she rifled through the Rolodex Nicky Blair had implanted in her brain. She tilted to Nicky, whispering, and Nicky, as if she'd injected him with speed, emerged from her briefing to stride forward, overflowing with welcome and relief that Freddy had arrived at last.

"Mr. Gale. Good to see you back. I'm sorry, but I've been scrambling since you called, and I just can't come up with the booth you requested. It's a madhouse tonight, as you can see. But if you'll follow me, I have a very nice situation for you near the bar."

Freddy scanned his little gaggle as they marched off together, Tanya and Jennifer playing impish in their shiny gowns and big glass earrings, while Verna worked at tempering her enthusiasm in order to avoid appearing naive.

"I'll have the waiter come right over," Nicky said. He made sure they were safely settled in their corner enclave of dark leather and candlelight before striding off.

"This is a nice table, huh? Good table?" said Freddy.

"It's fine," said Verna.

"I guess," said Jennifer.

"We can see the bar really good," said Tanya.

The waiter was slim and in his late twenties. Dressed in a white shirt and dark trousers, he arrived in a flurry of zest and deference. "What can I get you to drink?"

"Blow Job!" replied Jennifer.

Tanya pointed her finger at the tip of her chin, suggesting complex thought, and said, "Blow Job!"

"Vern?" said Freddy, hoping she would say the same thing.

"What are you having, Freddy?"

"A little vodka, I think."

"I'll have what he's having," she told the waiter.

"So that's two Blow Jobs," said Freddy. "And two Absoluts on the rocks."

"Right away," the waiter promised, dispensing menus before he left.

"I've been drinking Jack Daniel's, but it seems to have this effect on me," said Freddy, "where I get drunk."

"Really."

"So I thought I'd switch to vodka."

"A wise choice," said Tanya. "Although, drunk is sometimes the point, if you know what I mean."

"There are those moments," Freddy agreed.

"You should've been with us last night. We got *wasted!*" said Jennifer.

"Shouldha been there, baby." Tanya patted his thigh.

When the drinks arrived, Freddy waved his hand to immobilize the waiter, like he was a puppet attached by strings to Freddy's fingers. Raising the vodka to his mouth, as if it was a wine he had to taste before accepting, he sipped, then gazed at his companions with a thoughtful air, sipping again, nodding, and tossing the whole thing down. Tanya and Jennifer giggled while Freddy winced and shivered. "Another round, please."

"Certainly."

Once they established the pattern it was effortless to maintain, the waiter gliding up every fifteen minutes with trays of fresh drinks and sweeping away the empties in a display of cheery expertise. The girls trashed the clothes of nearby strangers. They belittled their lives at the Calypso Club, and assailed men as a worthless bunch, Freddy of course excluded. They all patted him, reassuringly. But he didn't care what they thought. He ate breadsticks and lost track of the number of vodkas he downed. Verna inhaled a cigarette, the pale flesh in her cleavage swelling above the red of her gown. He saw Tanya sucking an ice cube and Jennifer leaning over her empty glass, exploring the inside with the extended tip of her tongue. He wondered if this was how Emily would have turned out, had she lived. Like one of these bitches at his table. Would she have grown up to do shit like this? He tried to focus on them in a way he had never experienced before, as if they were Emily, or just brand new, but all he saw was their dark hair, wavy or curly, their spangled garments and jewelry. All he heard was their jabbering. He felt heat in his eyes and a fluttering in his throat, a shy sadness slipping away. He wanted to tell them what had happened to him. About Emily and the old man this afternoon. He felt ignored, but how could he blame them when he did nothing to let them in. When everything important was hidden, when his soul was a secret.

"Let me bring up a subject. Justice," he said.

The waiter arrived, interrupting with their dinners, elegantly arranged on heavy white plates, swordfish steaks, squab and a sirloin. Freddy didn't really track which order went where, just saw them sail about, as he waited for his sirloin.

"What was that, Honey?" said Verna. "Justice?"

"Justice," said Tanya. "I'm for it."

"Is that what he said?"

"He started to."

"Where's the salt? Who's got the salt?"

"Shhhhhh," said Verna, as if she had a protective interest in all of Freddy's ideas.

"Now you got a bad man," said Freddy. "He does bad things. You got a good man. And he makes a mistake. Justice. What is it? Now for the bad man, that's easy. Fuck 'em. But the good man . . ."

"Suck 'em," said Jennifer.

Tanya fit her mouth around the narrow rim of her glass and sucked.

"The good man, he what?" asked Verna.

"He's being philosophical, Verna," said Jennifer. "You don't say, 'he what?' to philosophy."

"I didn't quite understand what he said."

"He's rehearsing for death," said Tanya. "That's all philosophy is."

"Let him talk, okay?" said Verna.

"A rehearsal for death."

"Just a rehearsal for death," said Jennifer.

"You two are a couple of cynical bitches," said Freddy.

"Generic bitches!" agreed Verna, her mouth pinched with disgust.

Together Tanya and Jennifer said, "Ooooohhhh!" They seemed to be performing a routine, as if their feelings were often hurt in tandem. "Ohhhhhhh!"

"She wants to be your woman, motherfucker, better watch your ass," said Tanya, as she shook her finger at Verna. "Verna is after you, Freddy. That may be good or it may be bad, but what it may not be is false."

"Because it is the truth," added Jennifer.

Verna rolled her eyes, and flicked her fingers at them. "I wave you off like the bad smell you are."

"Easy now," said Freddy. "I think the point I was trying to make should be taken with a little more—"

"You see the orange buffalo?" said Jennifer.

"What?"

"The orange buffalo! You see him?"

Annoyed at her callous treatment of his complicated thought, Freddie looked away from Jennifer, thinking how he ought to walk the hell out. When his eyes chanced upon a red-headed guy at the bar, he put two and two together and wondered if this guy was the orange buffalo she was referring to. How the hell was that more important than his idea? he asked himself. In the seconds taken up by these thoughts, the guy's pasty skin, bulging cheeks and second-rate smile turned even more disgusting as he mistook Freddie's momentary attention for friendly interest.

"Yeah, I see him," said Tanya.

"What did you do when you saw him?" asked Jennifer.

The guy wore a black suit and shirt open at the throat, an ensemble donned for his swinger's night out on the town, as he prowled the streets in search of an alternative to his boring life, Freddy decided.

"I asked you what did you do when you saw it, Tanya?" said Jennifer.

"I shot its ass!" said Tanya.

The girls giggled and Verna snuggled closer to Freddie, trying to demonstrate her sophistication and worth by dismissing the infantile hijinks of the girls.

"Where did you get the gun?" said Jennifer.

"Same place you got the orange buffalo," said Tanya.

At this, Tanya and Jennifer could not keep their amusement safe from hysterics, and Freddie fired a glance at the red-headed orange buffalo at the bar, who managed to find in Freddie's belligerent glare an opportunity to expand their connection. His upper lip bared his teeth in a smug little flicker of phony camaraderie, and he raised his glass in celebration of some innate bond just discovered.

"I hope you still have your orange buffalo gun," Freddie said. Out of the corner of his eye, he could see the orange buffalo climbing from his bar stool and heading toward them. "Because we got the real thing, a real living orange buffalo coming up on our left."

By the time the three girls figured out what Freddie was talking about, the orange buffalo was posed above them in a cocky stance. "You ladies sure seem to be having a good time," he said. He had an unreliable voice, and his eyes danced over his audience in search of approval. "You must be a funny fella," he said to Freddy.

"I'm a riot. Now get the fuck out of here."

"What did I do? I'm just having some fun."

"Go have your fun somewhere else. Now get the fuck out of here," said Freddy.

"Freddy," said Verna, and she squeezed his hand.

"What's the matter with you, pal?" said the orange buffalo.

"He doesn't like orange buffaloes," said Verna.

"What's the matter with me? I'll kick your fuckin' head in!" snarled Freddy.

With his hand on Jennifer's wrist, the orange buffalo cooed, "Is that a Blow Job you're drinking?"

Tanya and Jennifer giggled. But then Freddy jumped up behind the table, and they stopped. His knees banged the edge, rattling plates and spilling glasses. He was standing on the seat, catapulting over the table. With his shoulders and head he slammed into the orange buffalo, who grunted and cried out, "Wait a minute!" They crashed to the rug, Freddy on top of him, the girls yelping, the uproar of nearby patrons a distant hum. With his left hand clutching a clump of red hair, Freddy was stabilizing the guy's head so he could smack it with his right fist. But the guy started growling and surging like a fucking animal, and Freddy spilled off him into the clutter where he found the handle of something, which he identified as a fork as it flashed past his eyes in an upswing in order to strike down.

Whoever stopped him was strong. It took a while to realize that a group was involved. Not an individual, and not the orange buffalo alone, but three or four strangers. He was outside by then, having been dragged through the aisle like trash by the restaurant bouncer and three other men. They were still there, guarding him. They joked with each other and brushed off their clothes. Verna wanted to sit with him, but they wouldn't let her, so she backed off, watchful and teary-eyed. Nicky Blain was standing with the orange buffalo. Freddy's captors tried to include him in the rough banter they shared, about the fight he put up and what they each had done to subdue him. But he wasn't interested. The night air was cool, yet he was burning up with a fever that he didn't dare mention to anyone, especially the cops, who were pulling up, their rooftop bubble flashing.

Nicky Blair left the orange buffalo and greeted the two cops getting out of their cruiser, like they were customers he'd been pining for, desperately. Nicky shook their hands, touched their elbows, got their names. Then, with an expression of someone whose trust had been inexplicably violated, he pointed at Freddy, who was seated on an overturned trash can.

The two cops walked up, militaristic and cold. They told him to turn around and put his hands behind his head. Nicky Blair stood nearby, looking condescending and betrayed. One handcuff clicked on, and then Freddy's hands were tugged down and the second shackle locked on his wrist, pinioning his arms behind him. They led him to the rear of the cruiser, eased him in, and slammed the door. Sealed up behind the glass and metal of the car, isolated from everyone and everything, tears filled his eyes, and he thought, I'm getting there.

The two patrolmen went from group to group on the sidewalk, interviewing customers, chatting with the girls, who sent Freddy glances full of loyalty and encouragement whenever they felt they weren't being observed. As far as he was concerned, a large unnecessary part of his brain had been removed—or injected with Novocaine—and the remainder of his consciousness was mesmerized by the phrase, "I'm getting there." He couldn't at the moment recall the use he had made of the missing parts of his brain, and that touch of amnesia didn't change when the cops returned and informed him that he was under arrest for Assault with a Deadly Weapon. Namely, the fork.

As they took him away, he had no interest in looking at the people left behind. He was hoping to leave everything behind. That's what he wanted. If he could. Everything interesting lay ahead.

At the West Hollywood sheriff's office, he was booked, and after his belt and shoelaces were removed and his personal belongings, such as his wristwatch, wallet, keys, loose change, and gold chain, were deposited in a bag, he was photographed and fingerprinted. He watched the thumb, and then the fingers of each hand, surrender something telling and mysterious. His maplike identity showed up in ink on a card, and he thought, This is practice. This is good practice. So I get used to it.

He plea-bargained down from Assault with a Deadly Weapon to Assault and Battery, and called Jeffrey to deliver the thousand dollars that he needed for bail. He had to wait in a holding cell, which was like a zoo cage for large animals. The other ten inhabitants were vacuum-packed, each in a private tube, except for a pair whispering on a bench. Trying to adapt quickly, he stood in a corner, his back to the stone, until a thin guy with a scraggly beard and an aura of puke tried to look into his eyes. Freddy entered into the man's stare, peering for a time that grew weirder the longer it lasted. It was like looking under rot at the maggoty life festering there in order to learn the tricks that would let him survive in such a place.

By the time Jeffrey showed up with the money, Freddy was facing the wall again. He seemed to have arrived at a high altitude that deprived him of his normal interest in his life. Carrying his jacket and tie, belt and shoelaces, he walked to the security door, and waited for the lock to be buzzed open. There was a small square window, and through it the lobby was visible. Jeffrey sat with his blond, laminated boyfriend. Dressed in tank tops and drawstring trousers, they were lounging on a bench in the corner. The blond was rubbing Jeffrey's feet. Jennifer and Tanya were asleep on another bench, like a glitzy pile of party debris. Not far away, Verna leaned against the brick wall, talking on a pay phone.

With a motorized snarl, the security door released and Freddy pushed through. Jennifer and Tanya stirred, yapping and trying to sit up. Verna sent him a tender pout, pointing to the phone, as if she were the one who needed to apologize. As he strode toward her, he heard her talking:

"I know, Angie, honey, and I'm so, so sorry. But you just go back to sleep, like Kerry is asking you, okay? And tell Kerry that I said not to worry, because I'll be back in plenty of time in the morning to get her home so she can get dressed for school. What? No, no. Maybe."

Freddy was beside her now and she looked up at him with a woe-is-me face, as she said, "Okay, Angie, honey, let me talk to Kerry. No. No, no, no, it does not mean I love her more than you. She's my baby-sitter. Don't you love her? Well, then, see? What? Angie, honey, that's not—No, no. That's a good girl." she smiled at Freddy. "Oh, Kerry, hi. Sorry. No, no, I already called your mom. So just go back to sleep and let Angie sleep in the bed with you if she wants. I know, I know. But, I mean, look at it this way—you're getting paid by the hour." She hung up and turned to Freddy, oozing sympathy. "Are you all right, honey?"

"Let's get out of here," said Tanya.

Verna wanted to kiss him, so he let her. She pressed her lips to his cheek, but his skin was sensitive. Her touch almost hurt, and he recoiled.

"Sorry, Honey," she said.

22

■ ■ ■ ■ ■ ■

Stuart was having a nightmare. In it John was following him from
room to room. One minute John was a normal grownup and then,
for no apparent reason, he was a gigantic, strange man. He went into
a room, and when Stuart went into another room, thinking he
would be safe, John was there, and he was a baby in a blanket on a
bed. John wanted to know the worst thing Stuart had ever done in
his life. What was it? Had he ever done anything terrible, something
as terrible as John and Hitler had done? Stuart went to the kitchen,
but it wasn't his kitchen and it wasn't his refrigerator or his table or
his spoons or his face in the mirror. It was Hitler's face in the mirror,
only he wasn't Hitler, he was somebody else. But he was as evil as
Hitler. John came up through the sink drain and told Stuart that he,
John, had done a horrible thing and he was fearful that it was in his
genes, that it was in his heredity to do such an awful, unforgivable
deed. That was why he was asking the question. That was why he
had to know the answer. Had Stuart ever killed anyone? Because
John had. He had. Then he went back down the drain and left the
water running. Stuart took a drink and the water was the truth, and
as he drank it he knew that he had to tell the truth to John, who was
gone, and in the mirror there was no one. But he'd seen the answer
to John's question. And the answer was that he'd beaten John. He'd
caught him one time for a stupid little thing, he was trying to eat the

dog's food, this was back in Seattle, and Stuart had been furious about Helen and the way he couldn't find her, he didn't know where she was. So he started beating John. He pinned him on the floor and he slapped him and held him down and hit him with his fist and he wanted to kill him. John? he said. I know what I did. John, John, where are you? He looked in the sink and down the drain and in the mirror, but he couldn't find him. John, he said. I want to answer your question. I tried to kill you, John. That's what I did. I wanted you dead. And I nearly burst into flames in that moment. When he couldn't find John anywhere—not in the cabinet, nor the basement, nor the sink, nor the toolchest, nor the mobile home, which was gone, nor his shoes—he started looking for Helen, but he couldn't find her either.

Helen was searching for a green that had haunted her most of her life, though she had never thought of it that way before. But now, as she sought to recreate the hue and quality of the spruce and pine and fir and cedar encircling her grandmother's house in Wellsbury, at the eastern edge of Seattle where she had grown up, she felt haunted. She'd taken to heart the notion, as presented by her teacher, of a palate uniquely suited to her. She had her color map and her manual. She was dabbing, adding, fussing. But it was hard, she saw, to locate memory in a mix of paints. Grandma, she thought, remembering a window of white curtains bound in bows.

It was nearly 2:00 A.M. and John was still out. Glancing at the night packing the window above the dresser, she felt her last bit of energy run out on her. His absence was hard to take.

She put the caps back on the open tubes and turned off the lights. The dark swept away her fragmentary trees. She was glad to be free of them.

In the living room Stuart was a snoring heap on the couch in front of the television, the volume low, a red car on a winding road skittering over the screen.

She paused, thinking of waking him. But then she'd have to talk to him. And all they would do was talk about John, working each other up into a frenzy. Stuart's sleeping face had a mashed quality and she decided to leave the TV on, because turning it off would probably disturb him. It all reminded her of those times when she had snuck in late at night back in Seattle during her affair all those years ago with Mac Toland, the mustached man with the plate of eggs and bagel in the painting on the wall just above where Stuart slept. Hitler, she thought, chuckling, shaking her head.

In the kitchen, she pulled a beer from the refrigerator and stood by the open back door with a cigarette. This morning after the three of them gazed up at Mac, and everybody talking about who he was at the bus stop, the miserable way she'd felt was just like the old days, when she feared she was going to get caught. She exhaled through the screen, watching smoke drift past the mobile home and toward the nearest jacaranda tree. She'd seen the inside of a lot of motel rooms that crazy year, her heart on edge, every word and breath a lie as she tiptoed through the thin ice of her life trying to decide what she wanted, who she loved, what the hell love really was, wondering whether to leave Stuart and John who was still a baby, thinking she should run away with Mac, feeling ashamed of herself for even considering leaving her little boy. But she was thinking of it every hour of the day, because Mac had filled her up, that was for sure, turned her into a stranger to herself in a wild sensual way that she'd never known with Stuart, like sex was a magical thing that could change you, and those feelings of vitality and hunger were a rapturous blur that was true.

Mac had been the real reason she'd agreed to move to Los Angeles from Seattle when Stuart came up with the scheme. To put miles of physical distance between her longing and the motel room where Mac waited, an expanse that would kill those feelings if they tried to cross. She'd never seen him after they moved. There'd been some frantic phone calls and desperate nights. She could remember the last one, and the way she'd had to whisper that she couldn't talk. He never called again. Then she and Stuart bought their house a little later, and they were still in it. John was full grown, and Stuart was retired. If she hadn't had that affair, she never would have agreed to leave those forests, that lovely, heartrending green that surrounded grandma's house. What would have happened to them all? She'd be this old. No changing that. But what about John? Would he have been to jail? And what about that little girl? That poor little Emily Gale. If Helen hadn't fallen in love with Mac Toland, and then needed to run, would that poor little girl still be alive? Or would someone else have run her down?

She opened the screen door and flipped the cigarette out into the grass. She could smell the dew, the evening primrose and the amber and tiger lilies in the beds outside. She stood there gazing through a wedge of pines to a fragment of starless sky. With her thoughts so crowded, the feeling that her solitude had been invaded was not disturbing. It was just her past, she thought. But then she realized that the thing she was registering wasn't in her mind. She whirled, expecting a mugger or Stuart. But the shadowy shape blotting the doorway was John.

"Sorry," he said. "Mom, did I scare you? I didn't know what to do. I knew I would scare you no matter what I did."

"How long were you there?"

"What were you doing just standing there in the dark like that?"

"I don't know. Lost in thought, I guess. Thinking. You know."

"Should I turn the light on?"

"What for? Don't need light to think or talk. Or do you want something? Are you hungry?"

"No." He advanced a step so moonlight revealed the upper part of him. "I saw Dad on the couch. I thought you'd be asleep in bed. I was just gonna get some water and get some sleep, myself."

"You said you were going to be back early."

He walked past her to the sink, and turned on the faucet. "What time is it?"

"Quarter past two. Do you want some ice for your water?"

"I'm sorry I didn't call. I was gonna call, but then it got so late. I really didn't think you would be up."

"Of course we'd be up. You just got home after years. We want to see you. Didn't you know we'd be worried?" She lifted the beer to her mouth and drank, though the bottle was empty.

"Any more beer?" he asked, and walked to the refrigerator. "I got the job. But then Peter and his brother threw me a coming-home party. I guess the day just kind of happened."

"When do you start?"

He twisted the top off the bottle and glanced at the wall clock glowing in the gray haze pillowing the wall. "Actually, in just a few hours."

"Oh, honey, why do you want to do this to yourself? Don't your friends want you to get your rest?"

"It was fun, Mom." Even in the poor illumination filtering through the half-lowered venetian blinds, he could see enough to know the meaning of her worried stare fixed on the beer rising to his mouth. "This my first drink of the night, Mom. I had Pepsi at the party."

"I can't follow you around, John. I'm not a policeman."

"I just don't want you to worry."

"I'm not worried. You're a grown man now and I know it. Who was there?"

"Well, there were lots of people I didn't know and a few I did. What'd you do?"

"Me? Nothing. Worried. Your father watched television."

"I thought you didn't worry." He smiled, gliding to her in order to see if she was amused by his teasing.

"I lied."

He tilted close to inspect her expression, spying a dab of something on her nose that revealed itself to be green paint. He touched it and said, "Looks like you have paint on your nose."

"Oh, my foolishness, sure. Oh, sure," she said. "I did that."

He wet his finger on his tongue and returned to the speckling that was more widespread than he had first noticed. With his eyes focused on his task, his touch seemed to smooth her breathing out. "I met a girl tonight who's a painter."

"Really?"

"Yeah."

"Where? At the party? How do you know she's a painter?"

"Peter had one of her paintings there."

"You didn't tell her about me."

"Peter bought this painting from her, that's how much he liked it. It was this black outer space kind of backdrop and these faces made out of ice, sort of."

"Oh, God," said Helen. "Abstract. I don't know how anybody does abstract kind of things. It's so brave."

"Is that what you think?"

"Can you imagine? Painting something you don't even know what it is yourself?"

As John studied her eyes, he saw how the contemplation of accomplishments she thought out of her reach notched her brow with sadness, and his arms slipped around her, and he was thinking, Mommy, Mommy, my mommy, as he squeezed until the startled recoil went out of her. They stood there in a soothing hum, a comfort in which they swayed.

"What got into you?" she asked.

He chuckled and stepped back. He wanted to speak and felt that in the next few seconds, he would begin. "It's different, Mom," he said.

"What?"

"It's just so different. You hear about this kind of thing—the kind of thing I did—and you think you know what that would be like. But when you're in it, it's very different from what you might think."

Overhead an airplane passed, a single-engine prop judging by the thin brave struggle of the sound. He was remembering how he'd felt when he stopped at a pay phone to call Jo Jo on his way home. He'd had to take a cab because he couldn't find Ray or Peter. While the cab filled up at the self-service pump, he'd called Jo Jo and asked her out to dinner. It had been like grabbing something off a shelf that belonged to somebody else. Like she was something he had no right to and he was doing something wrong. It could be that calling her was against Peter, because there was still something going on between them. That could be it.

Of course that's not it, said Emily. *Who gives a fuck about Peter! You know what it is. And you have no rights. That's why you feel it. You don't have any.*

"I was never an unhappy person, you know. As a kid. Was I, Mom?"

"I never thought so."

Oh, boo hoo. Boo-fucking-hoo!

"And I'm not now—not unhappy. That's not what it is. I don't know what it is."

Bullshit! I'll tell you what it is, Mr. Bullshit!

"I mean, I'm a person who caused unhappiness."

Be careful. Be very fucking careful here.

It was like she was screaming, it was like she was buried inside him.

"I mean, the way you stood by—and—and—" He could barely hear his thoughts for the din around them.

"You're our son," said Helen.

"That's what I mean, I think. All the things, or happy ways I felt before the accident are still there, it's just that I have this added thing, and it's hard and I wish I didn't have it, but it's—I mean, I can feel—I can feel—"

Your life! Is that what you're afraid to say! That you can feel your life when I can't feel mine! Go ahead. Spit it out. It's just your sickening, maudlin, asshole way of trying to escape what you owe. When there's only one way out. So cut the crap before I kill you myself!

"What are you two doin' in there?" said Stuart from the other room.

"Uh-oh," said Helen.

His voice arose from the dark where he lay. In the kitchen shadows Helen and John jumped apart, peering off into the glow of the TV that showed Stuart standing up. "What are you two plotting now?" he wanted to know.

"Don't you worry about it," she said.

"Plotting my murder, probably."

"Don't you worry about it," she told him. "We're just talking about how we love you."

"Oh, boy," he said, "now I'm in trouble." Stepping into the kitchen, he threw the light switch. The overhead fluorescent bulb let loose a blast that had them all blinking. "Lemme get a look at you, hiding here in the dark. Just as I thought," he said, scrutinizing them. John was by the sink, getting a glass from the cabinet so he could pour his beer. Helen had a cigarette, and she touched a match to the tip while backing toward the screen door. "Couple of guilty culprits if I ever saw them," he concluded.

"John just came home and we started talking. That's all." She had to turn away to exhale out the screen.

"Plotting," said Stuart.

"No. Just talking."

"What about?"

"Well, different things. One thing or another."

"Like what?" At the sink, Stuart put his finger under the running water, waiting for it to become cool enough to drink.

"Well, I was just going to ask him about Seattle, actually. If he ever thought about Seattle, and the lives we had there, what they would have been if we'd stayed."

"I never give it a thought," said Stuart.

"Of course you don't. I know you don't." A charge percolated beneath her casual pose, something distressed and contradictory declaring her manner a pretense. John wondered what she was hiding and doubted he would ever know. "Why don't you just go to bed, Stuart" she said. "Good Lord."

"Water over the dam," said Stuart. "That's all it is. That's all any of it is."

"Is that what you think?"

"What else is there to think?"

She sent a searching glance at John. Then the confident stride she took toward him declared her certainty that he shared her point of view. "And I was just about to ask John about the scar. I was just about to ask him how he got that scar?"

"This?" said John, touching the dead ripple above his eye, as if he needed to separate the exact scar she was interested in from a wide, confusing assortment.

"Unless you don't want to tell us," said Helen.

"No, no. I fell. Tripped and fell."

"What do you mean?"

"On the stairs. Going up the stairs after lunch."

"Is that right?" said Stuart.

"I think it was lunch. It was a long time ago. You know. Tripped and fell. I wasn't paying attention."

"I bet you thought it was going to be a whole hell of a lot more interesting than that, Helen," said Stuart. "Didn't you?"

"No."

"I bet you expected some kind of prison story."

"I didn't expect anything. I just asked. I was just curious," she told him. "You don't ask, you never find out anything."

"Curiosity killed the cat," said Stuart, strolling from the room to the hall. "And lack of sleep, you pair of night owls."

"He's right, Mom," said John. "I can still get a few hours. I better get what I can." He shot across the kitchen and out the back door.

After a few seconds she heard the door to the trailer close.

23

■ ■ ■ ■ ■ ■ ■

It annoyed Freddy that Verna was snoring peacefully while he was staring at the ceiling. After all, he'd come and she hadn't. Why should he be the insomniac? He'd sat down on the bed when they got back, probably to take off his shoes, and she'd knelt in front of him. Then she unzipped him and took him earnestly into her mouth, enterprising and straightforward. He'd thought about making the deal mutual, but couldn't gather the energy at the start and then, as the minutes went by, it seemed like a less interesting idea. Clearly, she liked running the show, if he were to judge by her groans and variations. She seemed to know what she wanted, tending him like he deserved it, and service was her hottest desire for the night. It wasn't long before she was lost, her concentration tightening, like he was a wounded hero, who had braved dangers and troubles—which, of course, he had, pummeling the orange buffalo and going to jail—and what she was doing was a hybrid of nursing, whoring, and praise. She grew frenzied and wild. Or somebody was, maybe it was him. He wished she would get it over with, and he told her. She worked harder, begging almost, a little sad and buttery. He squirmed when he came, his balls and cock feeling quarantined from the rest of him, a bludgeoning in his pelvis that made him feel left out. He slapped her, and she pulled back. But it wasn't that hard, and she knew she didn't have to be afraid. "Oh, Freddy," she said, "what's wrong?"

"You're too stupid for words," he told her, and drew her into his arms, dragging her with him as he fell back so she blanketed him in a soft stream of flesh. He thought about his dead daughter and his dead parents, one from a heart attack and the other from ovarian cancer, so he'd lived from the time he was fourteen with his father's brother, Uncle James, until he was old enough to get into the Army. He shifted, pushing at Verna, trying to shed her, wanting to escape, like she was the floodgate to a reservoir of memories he refused to receive. "I gotta pee," he told her.

When he walked back a few minutes later, she was out cold in the faint light draining through the lowered blinds. She looked dead and he wondered if he'd killed her, if he'd migrated into some altered reality where he was not who he seemed, but an imposter who could act without qualms; and so he had killed her without knowing it. He was on the threshold of such a shift; he was knocking at the door, and whoever was inside was knocking back. Maybe this other person should have a name, he thought. Maybe Richard or Tommy or Bobo or Arch. Or maybe it should be less conventional. A name like Bartholomew or Crabbe, or maybe even more crazy, such as Ezekiel, or Elijah, or maybe it should not be recognizable, like Assssunda, or Mentomabba.

She coughed. Leaning close, he heard her sighs. Sleep raised her breasts and let them fall in a motion she had nothing much to do with, her automatic nervous system maintaining things. She seemed a machine, taking in air and letting air out, her mind uncoupled and gone from the world.

Unlike Freddy, who was sitting there trying to come to terms with the feeling that he was surrounded by lessons he couldn't learn. But the really important lessons were almost always unclear. Like the sky or the sun. Or a range of mountains. What did they mean? Or a punch in the face. A tone of voice that you could not get out of your mind. The weird glance of a stranger. What did any of it mean?

Standing up, he saw that he was naked. He padded over to the desk and turned on the lamp, and without the slightest grasp of what he was doing, other than walking and turning on the lamp and sitting and pulling the envelope of photographs from the desk and dumping them and looking at them—other than that, he knew nothing. Other than that he was looking at a photo of Anthony and Andrew in matching jumpers, their arms around each other. Now what was the lesson of this moment? It could mean something that he was sitting there staring at this fragment of the past, but he found the possibility unlikely. Their glossy faces were strange. The irony that the boys were twins had always unsettled him. A dark proposi- tion in their doubleness, as if the powers that had robbed him of Emily were tempting him to trust them again. Twins were an ar- rangement of duplicates, suggesting either could replace the other.

He poured an aluminum tumbler full of vodka and gulped it down in a gesture as blank as everything else he did. But his blood altered, and with it his perspective, which sank into a dulled aware- ness, like he was a room in which the lights were going out.

He began to think that you didn't have to know much about what you were doing in order to do it. He was pulling on trousers; he was fitting himself into his jacket and slacks and socks and shoes. He was slipping out of the apartment into the hall. The brown metal double doors ahead opened into the elevator, and he knew he was pushing the button and waiting until the apparatus grumbled up and clanked open to receive him. But he had no idea what he was doing.

When he hit the street, he fumbled a cigarette from his pack, lit up, and started walking. The urban night swallowed him. Rooftops at haphazard levels cut the sky into blocks of stone and black empty air. Spurts of light plumed from windows and the street lights haloed the pavement below the neon glare of bars.

A flaming trash barrel scorched the silhouettes of the ragtag men around it, and he paused at the outer edge of their circle, as if to measure whether they had the power to pull him into their ranks. When one of them came forward, Freddy's first impression was that the man appeared about his own age, but the nearer the man got, the older he seemed, his trousers held up with a bunji cord. He stared at Freddy, like there was a rigid protocol governing such encounters, and then he asked, "What are you doing here?"

Freddy said he didn't know.

The guy's eyes beamed through their bloodshot mist with a wild suspicion. "That's what I thought," he said.

"What?"

"Gimme some money."

"No."

"Share what you got, man."

Freddy chuckled and said, "My name is Bobo. What's yours?"

"We need some money for some booze, Mr. Bobo. Want to join us? You buy, we'll share."

"No."

"Whasamatter with you, man, you're rich. Look at you. Whadya do? You work in the movies? You work for a studio?"

"I'm a jeweler."

"See! That's what I'm saying. Jewelers work with jewels, man. You could hand me twenty dollars and not even miss it."

"No, you're wrong," said Freddy and he turned and walked off.

"Don't get arbitrary on me, man," the guy called out. "You came into our natural habitat. You sought us out."

Freddy kept going, feeling annoyed at the fact that he had stopped at all. Those flickering half-shapes of men by the trash barrel were a bad set of ideas trying to confuse him, and he kept on walking.

The sign that eventually stopped him was feathery. It was a rectangle of lavender with letters printed in a darker, richer lavender, spelling out a tantalizing invitation:

D R E A M L A N D

T E R R A   S U E N O S

ONE HUNDRED BEAUTIFUL GIRLS

The sign hung over a street-level door. ONE HUNDRED BEAUTIFUL GIRLS. A hundred. Girls. Inviting him in. To a land of dreams. He was glad he hadn't stayed with the bums and their trash barrel.

The lavender mist in the hallway was dispensed by overhead lightbulbs wrapped in gels. If he'd stayed with those bums, he'd still be there. The elevator operator who opened the elevator door was a cadaverous, white-haired old man with bony hands and a fixed stare. After ascending several stories, the elevator slowed, and Freddy heard Mexican love songs playing through the walls. Soon he entered an old-style ballroom with checkered tiles flowing over the floor, a silent jukebox in the corner. Not far ahead a chunky Chicano in a cowboy hat and a pink embroidered shirt sat at a table with a cashbox under the beams of several desk lamps. Taped to the wall above him, a large handwritten sign read: DANCE WITH A PRETTY GIRL: $21.00.

Looking past the listless Chicano, Freddy saw a faintly lit bar. Girls hovered in the unsteady haze. They sat on the stools, and leaned against the bar, like pieces of fruit on display, peaches and plums that were surly. The bare wood dance floor was enclosed on three sides by a trellis woven with flowers. Above the dance floor cross beams sectioned the illumination into large patterns of blue and scarlet falling over the lone couple dancing. The band consisted of three short, fat guitar players and a tall singer.

"Can I help you?" said the Chicano, giving Freddy the onceover from under his cowboy hat. His gaze was unfocused, as if he were mortally ill.

Freddy nodded and paid and went on. Like Freddy, the musicians were exhausted, and the music they produced was depressed rather than plaintive. He knew they were sick of the sham of these late hours in which loveless couples mocked their efforts until they were so dispirited by the travesty they assisted that they could barely go on.

Ahead, the light fell through diamond-shaped holes in the trellis, touching the girls with a latticework of shadow and color. He passed a black leather couch with another gringo and a tiny blonde. The girls giggled. They were dark-haired and stuffed into dresses of savage colors cut off at mid-thigh. They clutched glasses of Coke. Shyly, they tried to tempt him, to pose for him, to anticipate his gringo taste. The bartender was an old woman whose black hair was cut as close as a coat of paint. She looked like a witch, and he didn't want to dance with her. But he wanted to dance with all the others, especially the chunky ones, who he wanted to counsel about the foolishness of eating too many burritos, too many tacos. He was smiling and they were tittering. Choosing one from their midst seemed impossible until he noticed a figure off to the side. She was the youngest, the smallest, with reddish plumes of hair, her plump little body square in her tight panty corset, garter belt, and stockings. Tilted against the trellis, with her fingers tangled there, she seemed like one of the poppies and roses winding around.

Let's dance, said Emily. Freddy extended his hand and she stepped forward, questioningly. But after a second she saw that he was sincere. Her fingers relaxed in his, so he could lead her to the dance floor. There he enfolded her, and the little band of hopeless musicians began to play with a memory of all they had once known.

They're all watching, said Emily.

Freddy, with his arms around her, leaned to her cheek.

They're all peeking through the trellis to see you dance with this lucky girl. Noses pressed against the trellis, like little kids with no money to get in. They're all so sad to see you hold her and talk to her. They know how love is so hard to find. But they have to watch, full of envy, wondering what you're telling her, desperate to know. When you're not telling her anything. Because it's me you're talking to. I'm the one you're whispering to.

"She's a beautiful woman. Did I tell you? My wife. A beautiful woman," he said. "Daytime. That was always my downfall. You're very beautiful, but you see, it's night and we're dancing, so it's safe. I could never fall in love with you. We're safe and free to dance. I met my wife in the sun. But now—well, now—you remember when you were a kid and one of your playmates made you really nervous and uncomfortable by calling their parents by their first name? I hated that when I was a kid. And now my ex-wife, well, she's a beautiful woman. But she's got my own kids calling me by my first name, what a thing, huh?"

The elevator doors surprised him when they suddenly opened to reveal the hallway of his apartment building. Freddy could see the door to his apartment. It wasn't that far. Just down the hall. But he forgot to get off. That's how tired he was. He stood there and the door closed and the elevator sank to the ground floor, where the doors parted. He remembered walking home through the gradual onset of sunrise, the sky shifting from black and serene to purple and stormy. Then it filled with a flammable chemical that burst into flames, and left behind a pale residue in which there was a faint vision of buildings and streets.

He pressed the button to go back up. As he stood in that closed-in box, his heart pinged, and he saw how his heart was running a test that was very daring for hearts. It was in fact performing feats that a heart should never do. When he tried to walk across the elevator, it took a long time between footsteps.

Stumbling into his apartment, he was perplexed to find Verna brushing her hair. She had a skirt and blouse on, and she kept brushing her hair with the black brush in her fist. Freddy walked past her and sat down in a big comfortable chair. There was a vodka bottle on a nearby end table, so he picked it up and took a swig, watching her brush her hair. Then he lit a cigarette and poured a drink into a glass.

"You are such an asshole! Where did you go?" said Verna, brushing her hair. "I mean, what do you think? I'm some kind of whore? You can just get up in the middle of the night, go your merry fuckin' way, then stumble back in here like it's not rude? Like I don't have any feelings? So I won't notice rude, for some goddamn reason, such as what? Because I dance naked, I mean, half naked, on a stage, and I shove my tits and ass in some faceless asshole's face, so that means I have no emotions and I'm a whore?"

He inhaled the cigarette and wondered if she was done brushing her hair, because she had stopped to say these words. He hoped she wasn't done.

"And I liked you. I don't fuck very many guys, you know."

He inhaled the cigarette and took a sip of the vodka, and decided to tell her that, strictly speaking, she hadn't fucked him either. "You blew me." That seemed to disgust her so much that she started brushing her hair again.

"You are such an asshole! Where did you go? I mean, what do you think? I'm some kind of whore? You can just get up in the middle of the night, go your merry fuckin' way, then stumble back in here like it's not rude? Because I dance naked on a stage, and shove my tits in some asshole's face, so I'm a whore?"

He dreamed it went on like that for a long time, Verna scolding him, trying to make him care, trying to make him unhappy, and always brushing her hair. It didn't matter what she said, how angry she was, how bitter, how hurt, how accusatory, as long as she kept brushing her hair. It made him happy to see the motion of her arm, the way it went up and down, stroke after stroke, the hair snapping and fluttering, her body tilted with energy and purpose, making her so concentrated, so determined, so lively.

"I made the bed," she told him, walking away, shutting the door, leaving him.

But he wasn't alone long. Because Emily came and smiled down at him and reached for the cigarette that he'd gone to sleep with burning in his fingers. Protectively she picked it up, being gentle and considerate so she wouldn't disturb him as she crushed it out in the ashtray, and took his head in her hands.

Sleep, Daddy, she said. *Sleep.*

24

■ ■ ■ ■ ■ ■

John was leaning near the bow of the seiner *Southern Gal*, his arms
folded over the black fisherman's apron he wore, as he studied the
expanse of water shrinking before the advancing bulk and detail of
the shoreline. Harbor traffic was plentiful, some vessels setting out,
others returning past the oil rigs and buoys to the warehouses edging out into the waves. Parked cars waited where the ribbons of
weathered docks ended, and then a backdrop of gleaming metropoli-
tan shapes arose, and higher and further still drifted a mist of mountains. The grinding engine below shook the soles of his feet. Gulls
prowled the wake, snooping into the foamy furrows to nose the
crud, their squawking homey, like pets.

He glanced over his shoulder, as if to reconsider the hours he was
leaving. At some point a peculiar feeling had come over him, a kind
of disorientation at meeting confinement and vast spaces side by
side. The horizon seemed infinite, yet the boat locked you in.

When Ol' Hank rumbled up and directed him to get ready to
dock, John backed along the gunwale and seized one of the huge
hawsers lying in a pile. He kept his eyes fixed on Ol' Hank, who had
set up near the bow with another thick hunk of rope. Ahead, John
saw Ray waving, and he was glad Ray had made it for the pickup.
Ray'd missed the delivery in the morning, phoning and screaming
about his hangover. Waking John's parents and offering to pay the

cab fare, if only John would let him off the hook this morning. Now he was propped up against the rail at the edge of the pier, sunlight sparking from his fist around a can of beer.

As John flexed, getting ready, his fingers ached and his back muscles felt strained. His hamstrings were a tight burning line. The day's work hadn't been a problem of strength. He was strong enough. But he'd been clumsy. The waves had seemed misaligned, so he never felt in balance. He'd undermined his own power, as the crew set out in a rush to ensnare a school of tuna. They had six hundred feet of rectangular net to deploy, one end locked to a lowered skiff, the other towed by the *Southern Gal* in a swift circle around the panicky fish. The water swirled, then came to a gradual boil of foam slicked with blood as the net was drawn to the decks, and the fish, in a waterfall of squirming stink, gushed into the hold.

He waved at Ray, hoping that he wasn't too hung over now. Otherwise it would be taxi cabs and long walks, and he would never have time to get together with Jo Jo. He'd talked to Ray this morning about dinner and Jo Jo, but who knew what Ray would remember, and now John had another favor to ask. Somewhere in the middle of the day, all land out of sight, he'd realized he wanted to go to the cemetery. Maybe just to see what it felt like to be at Emily Gale's grave now. He'd gone there once during the trial when he was out on bail. He could recall the cypress on the horizon. The field of markers. Her stone in the grass. He hadn't stayed long. But it might be different after all these years. Maybe he could try to speak. To what? To himself. To whatever was there.

"How'd he do?" Ray yelled as the boat bounced on the pilings and the lines were hurled ashore.

"Keeps his mouth shut," said Ol' Hank.

"Yeah. Hey, John, how long are you gonna be?"

"Ask him," John said, gesturing at Ol' Hank, who was grizzled and paunchy, yet oddly dainty in his movements, as if years at sea had taken the weight out of his step. He wore a gray sweatshirt and a stocking cap, and he took his time with the rope.

"Hank, how long?" yelled Ray.

The old man wheezed, trying to catch his breath. Then he started coughing. He struggled onto the pier to stand beside Ray, his eyes wet, his throat wrestling with a mass of phlegm as he pulled a cigarette from his pocket and huddled with his lighter.

"I need to restock the beer and soda cabinet. Anything else?" John asked.

Ol' Hank pointed toward the stern where seagulls formed a ranting swirl over several crew members dumping barrels. "I'll have Frank and Rabbit hose down the deck. You're probably tired and sore as an old whore. Sammy can check the bait buoy."

"It was pretty full this morning."

"Make sure when you do that, when you check the bait buoy in the mornings, if there's any dead ones floatin' on the top, go ahead and grab 'em out of it."

John nodded, heading around the wheelhouse where he disappeared below deck, and Ol' Hank, after squinting at his cigarette as if it were a strange item someone had stuck into his fingers when he wasn't looking, nudged Ray with his elbow. "Fish die for no good reason, you know, like me. No good goddamn reason. When I die, some other fuck'll come along, do what I do just like me. You, too, Ray. Same shit is true of you."

"You think so?" said Ray. "Me?"

"Well," said Ol' Hank, "maybe not you."

"Cheery sonofabitch," said Ray, a few minutes later as he and John were hastening along the pier toward the parking lot. John carried a small satchel and a garment bag. Peeling off his gloves with his teeth, he managed to stuff them, along with his dark watch cap, into the satchel. The sea still filled his legs, giving the planks of the walkway an odd fluidity.

"Listen, I spoke to Jo Jo about directions, and she said she'd meet us at the restaurant," Ray said.

"So you remember talking to me this morning. I wasn't sure you would."

"Doesn't she have a great telephone voice? She invited me and my girlfriend Cammy to have dinner with you guys, if it was okay with you. Did you meet Cammy last night?"

"I don't think so."

"We can stop by my place, have a couple beers, and clean off the postal crud and the fish."

They went on a few steps before John said, "Listen, I got something to ask you. Okay?"

"Sure. But first you gotta tell me somethin'. You gotta, okay? Jo Jo, see, she's like my dream."

"Really?"

"So you gotta tell me, fucker, what is she like in bed? You gotta fill me in. Gimme details."

John glanced off at the shoreline, the waves hissing to an end on stones. "You're asking the wrong guy, Ray."

"Whadya mean? You went home with her."

"What are you talkin' about?"

"Everybody said you went home with her."

"You got drunk, Ray. You disappeared."

"I know what everybody said."

"Who?"

"I can't remember."

"What do you do with information like this?" said John. He spit in the shallows where seaweed danced over dim stones and fanned a discarded quart bottle of Schlitz.

"Look at me. Look at me closely," said Ray. "My range is limited."

John knew that Ray was trying to get some ironic mileage out of the fact that he was short, with a receding hairline and a blunt nose.

"You think I got laid a lot?"

"Yes," said John.

"Well, you're right. But Jo Jo's my dream."

"I thought she was Peter's girlfriend."

"Wait a minute, wait a minute, John. It's called heterosexuality. Hello!" said Ray. "She's made for it. And you've been—not that I need to remind you—in prison. Of course I want you to fuck her raw. I'm your pal. I support you."

"Can I tell you something?" said John. He felt like he was reading an instruction manual for an appliance that bored him, and yet he couldn't stop turning the pages. "Have you ever seen a dog or a cat chase its own tail?"

"Yeah."

"It's funny, right?"

"It's hysterical. It's very, very funny."

"Because it's confused. That's why it's funny—that's what makes it funny." He thumbed and raised the Zippo to the cigarette in his mouth. "And when it comes to women, you're a cat chasing its own tail."

Ray plucked the cigarette from John's mouth. He stole a long drag, and stopped to stare at the water. He furrowed his brow and pinched his lips so his cheeks took on little indentations, and he gave the impression of someone for whom thinking was like hitting his thumb with a hammer. "I'm not stupid," said Ray. "I know what you're saying. It's the respect thing. But I gotta tell you—taking into consideration the fact that you know me as well as you do—there is no way you could have believed that you could get that idea through to me. But you said it anyway. So maybe you needed to hear it."

"You're a dog chasing his own goddamn tail, Ray," said John. "You're a dog, and you think your own tail is worth catching." He pushed off the piling, and set off. Ray started barking. Dirt coated John's palms, so he was slapping them clean as he strode along toward the parking lot, with Ray trailing him, panting and snarling.

The maroon Riviera was only a short distance off now, and John grabbed the front of his jacket and worked it open button by button. What he was trying to figure out was whether it would be best to ask Ray now about taking him all the way to the cemetery, or if he should wait until they were on the road.

"Cammy's in the car and she's in a bad mood," said Ray as he slipped ahead of John and grinned at him.

The look John gave back was a mix of half a dozen questions. "She's here?" he asked, forgetting the rest.

Ray swung open the front door and said, "She's a schoolteacher. You'll hate her."

"I heard that!" said a female voice inside the car.

Peeking in, John saw a sultry girl in the passenger seat. She was dark-haired and heavily made up; blue tint around the eyes, and her lips coated in a purple gloss. She looked vaguely familiar. When she saw John, her mouth moved in the motions of a smile, but the effect was unnerving. "You just have to say shit like that, don't you, Ray," she said, staring at Ray. Her rough-edged voice had more alley in it than classroom.

"Can't you see I have a friend with me? Be polite just one time."

Cammy gave John another opportunity to experience her edgy

smile, took a breath and, sounding like she'd just taken a hit of helium, said, "Hello, I'm Cammy."

"Pleasure to meet you, Cammy," said John. From the back seat, he took the opportunity to extend his hand, which she grabbed and let go.

Ray got them to the freeway fast. He fired the Riviera up to sixty, then seventy. John could feel the frame trembling, as if the car was experiencing some form of apprehension. Cammy said something that John couldn't follow, and Ray answered with a mocking look. She made a gagging noise, her middle finger in her mouth. Ray snapped on the radio, jabbing buttons until he found a ton of heavy metal screeching, like cars getting squashed in a compressor. By this time Cammy was railing at him, and John, edging closer, managed to hear.

". . . she is a whore and you were definitely one hundred percent without a doubt flirting with her!"

"She's not a whore. What do you mean, she's a whore?" said Ray.

"She's a whore! She's a whore!"

"But why do you say it? What do you base it on?"

"In her fucking postal uniform and her 'I'm a little postal worker' walk."

"That's her goddamn job," said Ray, and he jumped on the gas. The speedometer needle touched ninety where it fluttered, then backed off, like it had seen something scary.

"They're all whores. That's all that turns you on," said Cammy.

"You turn me on, Cammy. You really, truly, honestly—"

"Shut up. You're disgusting—I hate you—your breath stinks, all the time," said Cammy. "So shut up and don't talk to me."

Ray lunged, as if to force the Riviera past ninety by means of bodyweight and Stone Age will.

Somehow nothing in the situation struck John as legitimately his concern, even though he thought Ray was maybe a little drunk. In prison you stayed out of things, minded your own business. You walked on by.

"He's such bullshit, isn't he?" said Cammy, turning all the way around so she could smile right at John. "Don't let him scare you, John. He's just driving like this to scare us. But don't give in."

I'd like some flowers, said Emily.

John looked out the window, thinking he would probably die before he got to the goddamn cemetery. A bank of wildflowers foamed yellow and scarlet up a clay bluff that led to a field full of oil pumps.

I'd really like some flowers, John. I really, really would.

"I don't hear you denying that you were flirting," said Cammy.

"You said not to talk to you, Cammy."

"Oh, great. That you hear," she told him.

Would you, John? Please.

With the heavy metal band mutating their misery into a shrieking that no amount of human viciousness and insanity could explain, Ray suddenly recoiled, his foot lifting off the gas. "I think I just scared myself," he said, as he pumped the brake.

Beautiful, beautiful flowers. From you, John. Surprise me.

"Ray," said John.

"What?"

"Would you stop at a florist for me?"

"What?"

"Is there a florist near your place we could stop at? Would you do that?"

"A florist? Sure. What for?"

Flowers for my grave, said Emily.

The woman behind the counter was in her seventies. Together, she and John looked into cases of myriad colors and shapes and she asked him questions. Eventually, he emerged from the store with petunia and larkspur and dahlia glowing in his arms. Cammy and Ray were on the hood of the car. Cammy stuck her nose into the batch. "Jo Jo is a lucky girl," she said. "But then love always starts out great."

"They're not for Jo Jo," John said. "I don't know how to say this, but—" Not only did he lack the words but it was difficult to look at Ray. Had he been able to drive, this was not something he would have asked for. "I mean, Ray, you know, if I had a license, I wouldn't ask you for this, but I want you to drive me to the cemetery."

"Cemetery?"

"What?" said Cammy. "I thought we were going to dinner."

"I just want to go to her grave. To Emily's grave."

"Who?"

"Who's Emily?"

"That's okay," said John, and he started across the street. "I can hitchhike."

"What?" yelled Ray behind him. "What are you talking about?"

John had reached the opposite curb by the time Ray caught up. "John, Johnny, help me here. I thought we were—I mean, I thought the plan was—"

"I want to go to her grave. The little girl I ran over."

"Oh," said Ray.

"I can't drive. I don't have a license."

"Oh," said Ray. "Sure."

The cemetery was bordered in cypress, the uppermost limbs blooming with a dull, gray-green crown, an autumnal mood. The Riviera cruised through the entrance and on past several large gray monuments, a series of mausoleums. John was trying to remember the way. His visit was a long time ago. He felt disoriented by the repetitive landscape. The radio was off, Ray's handling of the Riviera sedate. Cammy puffed a cigarette.

On their second pass, he began to worry that he was lost. But then a marker he had somehow missed the first time around appeared on the right. It was a wrought-iron sculpture that depicted an angel in an abstract way. "There," he said. "It's just down there. Sorry."

It was about a quarter of a mile further on that they parked, and John climbed out with flowers in his hand. "I won't be long," he said.

"What difference does it make? She can drive me crazy here as well as anywhere," Ray told him.

"Oh, man," said Cammy.

"Don't start."

"Why? It's what you want."

Glancing back over his shoulder, John saw Cammy slide across the seat, and then her torso merged with Ray's as she wriggled onto his lap. Her head crowded his, and the definition between them disappeared in a kiss. Her hand, visible against his cheek, slid out of view.

John crossed the yellowing grass under intermittent maple and teetering cypress in their green, torchlike swirls. Not far ahead, he saw the monument he was looking for, a large rectangle of speckled, amber marble on a stone platform in a semicircle of shrubs. Two bronze statues, one of a child, the other of a lamb, were mounted on the smooth top. The child was a little girl with a big forehead and cherubic cheeks. A scarf with stars dotting the hem was molded over her hair. She crouched low on her haunches in order to peer with an intense, confrontational curiosity into the lamb's eyes. The engraved inscription read:

OUR LITTLE LAMBS

Emily's grave was on the downslope of this burial field for children spreading out beyond the monument. In seconds, he would be there. The sun was lowering. Beyond the cypress that banked the end of the cemetery, a reddening tinge streaked over a distant slope. His knees felt brittle and he was giving himself a minute to get ready, when he heard children laughing. Their joy startled him, sounding surreal in this place. Laughter sprinkled the afternoon. He cleared the monument and saw a pair of small figures racing across the grass. Maybe fifty yards away, two boys sprinted toward each other, and he had the uncanny sensation that they were the same boy split in some weird way. Whinnying like horses, they sped on a collision course, and then, like daredevils, they missed each other by inches and went circling off. At the center of their orbit was the dark figure of a woman seated on a wide black blanket or cape spread out beneath her on the ground. Her hair was black, and her arms were propped up behind her. Her legs were stretched straight and crossed at the ankles. She gazed at the boys and seemed to luxuriate in them the way sunbathers drink in the sun. As John returned to the boys, he realized that they were in identical clothes. They were twins, he saw, and then he understood that the dark-haired woman was Emily's mother.

He dropped to his knees. He retreated until he could pull himself behind the marble slab. Crouched there, wanting to flee, he peeked through the legs of the lamb and spied on Mary. She sat with the black folds beneath her like paint on the grass. The boys frolicked past her again and she sat without moving. He wondered what she was doing sitting there so relaxed and serene, her manner more suited to a beach, or a playground. Unless that was where she was in her mind, and that was why she came here. So that these running boys could play with their sister. So that her living children could play with her dead one.

See the flowers in your hand, said Emily. *The blaze is blinding, isn't it? Smell the scent, each breath, so singular. Subtle, endless variations. That's the living.*

He opened his eyes and glimpsed the exuberance of the boys again. He saw the spangle of their red and blue sweaters. He heard the uninhibited glee of their cries as they galloped and turned to come back.

And my mother with them. Look at her calm beauty, her face uplifted to the air. She's here. And my brothers. They're here. You're here, John. That's who's here. But I'm not. I'm like the scent and color of those flowers fallen all over the ground. See the count-less bouquets forsaken all over this place. Look at them. See how they're withering. Look at their lackluster tone. They would be brittle to touch, a stink in them. Once they were like the flowers in your hand, scented and vibrant. But where is their luster and per-fume now, John? I'm like that, John. Like their perfume and luster. I'm gone.

"What the hell? I thought you said you were just gonna be a cou-ple minutes!" grumbled Ray behind him. John wheeled, an alarmed look in his eyes. But Ray wasn't interested, or else he was oblivious, because he said only, "I mean, what the hell are you doing here, John? We gotta go."

The twin boys stopped yelling. John imagined that they came to a standstill. He felt he was at the bottom of the hill with Mary, having been jarred from her reverie by Ray's arrival. She looked up the hillside toward the monument where Ray was jumping around. From her vantage it must seem that this skinny, dark-haired figure was talking to no one. Speaking to the air, or to the marble statues of the little girl and the lamb.

Ray was distracted, his attention drawn down toward where Mary stood.

"Is she looking up?" asked John.

"What the hell's her problem?" said Ray.

"She's not coming up here, is she?"

Suddenly Ray started yelling and gesticulating wildly. "How could you die on me?" His voice was maudlin and mocking. He bent down to the lamb. "How could you die on me? How? How?"

John lunged at him, wrestling him into his hiding place, slamming him against the ground.

"Owwwww, owwww," said Ray. "Jesus."

John scurried off in the direction he had come from, searching for Ray's car, jogging at a crouch.

"Hey!" said Ray.

John started to run. It couldn't be done, whatever it was he'd wanted. It couldn't fucking be done.

No, said Emily, *it can't.*

He hurled the flowers down. He looked back and saw Ray jogging after him. Now he was high enough to see Mary herding the boys toward a white car parked at the curb. She clutched their hands, one on each side, while her wary attention was aimed up toward him. He had no idea whether she had recognized him or not, but clearly she was looking at him. He whirled and went on.

25

■ ■ ■ ■ ■ ■ ■

Mary arrived for her session with Dr. Glazier in a mood shadowed by the events at the cemetery, where she'd gone impulsively after picking the boys up at school. Initially, when faced with their outburst of coltish play, the protocol expected in such a setting pressed her to stop them. But then, guided by a feeling in which she placed a tentative trust, she delayed. They streaked about the grass. They darted toward one another, then toward her and off again. The satisfaction that they introduced her to began as amazement and turned into pleasure.

In the end, though, just as she had first feared, they offended someone. Startled by shouts at the top of the hill, she spied a young man screaming near the monument. Though suspicious of something in his behavior, the possibility that he was really distressed and that the boys were the cause led her to end their visit.

She tried to explain some of this to Dr. Glazier, because it touched many of the things that concerned her, the lack of trust she felt in her emotions, the lack of life in her relations with Roger, the repressive power Freddy still could inflict on her. Everything was scrambled and displaced and rearranged, but somehow all present, and she talked in an effort to sort it out, scrutinizing Roger and fighting against Freddy, while the strange invitation whose existence she sensed in Bobby hovered just outside the shape of every sentence, but went unmentioned. Roger, with his lack of personal involvement in Emily, seemed brittle and superficial, a repository of unearned happiness, at the same time that Freddy, with his mad plans, struck her as overwhelming and untenable. But Bobby suggested a third secret alternative.

After her session, she drove through the neighborhood scouting for a coffee shop. She found a McDonald's in a mini-mall a few blocks away. She had coffee while reading the newspaper, and headed back as the time approached to meet Bobby. He was at the curb when she reached the street where Dr. Glazier had his office. She cruised to a halt in front of him and lowered the window to tell him about the mini-mall. He shifted from one foot to the other and said he'd ride over in her car, as long as it was that close, and then she could drop him off back here when they were done.

For the first minutes, they drove silently. His proximity made her nervous in a way that left her unable to look directly at him. The road offered a good diversion. With the McDonald's in sight, she slid into the right-hand turning lane.

"What'd you want to talk about?" he said.

The directness of his question flummoxed her further and she said, "Well, you know. . . ."

"I don't, I guess," he said. "I mean, honestly."

The Tiempo bumped up the driveway into the McDonald's parking lot. He looked away from her, communicating a wan bewilderment as the car stopped and he moved quickly out the door. She followed and they lingered awkwardly. She couldn't tell what he was thinking, and while he turned his attention to the pavement beneath his shoes, she scouted her surroundings, the walkways and storefronts, like someone wary of being spied. Standing there in the sun with him felt illicit. He let out a noisy breath, sounding like a weary, frustrated horse, and strode away.

Once they were seated, a large, despairing waitress brought coffee to the booth where they waited, their hands resting on the dull tabletop. She was overweight, distracted, and surly behind her weird smile, and as she trudged away, he said, "Miss," calling her back. "I think I might have a double cheeseburger and fries. You got time?" he asked Mary. "You want something?"

"No, no. You go ahead, though." The blue of his eyes was less vibrant than she remembered. But then she had never been this close to him before, she realized. So the blue she remembered was a blue she had imagined. The lump on his nose suggested damaged cartilage, and both cheeks, beneath the fuzz of his day's growth of beard, were grimy and infected with pockets of blackheads.

"My brother's still dead," he said.

"What?"

"He's still dead. My brother, I mean."

"Well," she said, studying the space just to the right of his head, as if a sign might appear to explain his tone.

"I mean, he is still dead. I've gone to a meeting and I've gone to Dr. Glazier and he's still dead. You know what I mean?"

"Not exactly."

"I mean, well—Who'd you lose? You lost somebody, right?"

"My daughter."

"Young, probably, I bet," he said. "I mean, you're young."

"She was eight."

"And you said you'd been coming to the meetings for eight years, right. That's what you said the other day."

"Yes."

"So it happened eight years ago, and you're still coming to the meetings, right?"

"Yes."

"My father thinks I'm making it up, the way I feel. You know—that I'm just making it worse. That I'm wallowing in it. That's what he says—'You're wallowing in it.' That's because, if he were to tell the truth, the whole truth and nothing but the truth, he never liked any of us kids much." With his left hand serving as a kind of tray, he presented his right fist to Mary, palm down, fingers clenched, a bracelet of ripped knuckles, the raw inner tissues peeping out. "He popped me last night. Slapped me across the face, you know. So I took a shot at him and missed. Hit the wall. Look at that. 'Wallowing in it.' Yeah, right. We were going to start an autobody shop. Danny was very talented in the area of business. You know, he was a talker. He could charm people. They liked him, my brother Danny, while I loved the grease and the smell of the new parts and banging away with a padded mallet. But that's gone now. So I'm wallowing. Yeah, right. Wallow, wallow."

After the double cheeseburger arrived, Bobby covered it in catsup and took a snarl of a bite. Mary felt a kind of nimbus around him unzip and disappear, eliminating the magical appeal he had seemed to exude and leaving behind a very ordinary middle-aged man chomping on a hamburger. She looked out the window, wanting to go home, and saw the McDonald's playground with its brightly painted geometry of rides and structures hemmed in by a fence of tall green, yellow, and red metal spikes. Bobby was amplifying his story with details about his brother and the plans they'd hatched for the autobody shop as a means to escape the "old man's domineering bullshit." He gave a quick rendition of his odd unhappy laugh, while Mary watched a rotund blond woman break out of a conversation on an orange playground bench with a rotund redhead. The redhead was crammed into shorts and a sweatshirt, while the blonde wore stretch pants and a white T-shirt that, under the pressures of her sagging breasts and tiered gut, looked like puddled ice cream. The blonde was yelling and waddling toward a kind of enclosed sliding board, a large green tube. She plunged her hand into the opening, shook with effort, digging her heels in as she hauled a small boy out by one leg. She lifted him high enough so that, as he hung there upside down, his eyes peered into hers. She slapped him in the face and when he wailed, she slapped him again. The redhead was laughing as the blonde set the little boy down on his head. The redhead opened her arms in welcome, and the little boy ran to her.

Bobby was still talking. Finishing up about a rebuilt engine, he went on to repeat many of the things he'd said earlier. Mary noticed that certain phrases that had been striking when she first heard them at the meeting were being reissued now, and their repetition diluted their original power. He was broken. That was all he had to offer. He was like a man in a pitch black alley being mugged by bullies he couldn't see. She had no idea what she was doing there with him. He wiped catsup from his mouth, using a brusque gesture, almost a blow to his own face, as he grinned darkly at her, reminding her of Freddy.

Still, it was another hour before she could get him out of the McDonald's. As she dropped him near his parked car, and watched him stride off, his losses an invisible burden pitching him off balance, a tumorous growth that he had no choice but to carry, she saw the specter of Freddy walking in his place. She remembered Freddy's haunted expression as he crashed around her house, bellowing and trying to hurt her. He'd claimed he was lugging around misery that rightfully belonged to her, and the mysterious thing was that she knew what he meant, because somehow his claim was true. She called up a memory of Bobby at the meeting that first night, and made him tell Freddy's story. They were a double image, a picture suffused with a background of haunting music. Mistakenly, she had projected her softheartedness onto Bobby. Because she'd refused to permit herself the slightest sympathy for Freddy, she'd misunderstood what she felt. Even that phone call. It was clear now that Bobby had never thought about her before she saw him on the sidewalk at Dr. Glazier's the other day. In all probability, if that call was anything but a wrong number, it was Freddy wanting to tell her what he ended up coming to her door to announce.

Like Bobby, whose wave she returned as her Tiempo glided past his red Mustang, Freddy was an ordinary person, who had failed to recover from a terrible blow. She saw his plight now and how she was part of it. She felt bad for him. She pitied him. She felt pity and wished she could tell him how she felt, but knew she would never have the chance.

26

■ ■ ■ ■ ■ ■ ■

John had his first real drink, a scotch and water, as they waited for dinner. Jo Jo sat to his left. On the other side of the table, Ray and Cammy drank wine and tortured each other with a spirited sadism that had them both totally mesmerized. John's second drink was scotch again, but this time, he skipped the water. He wasn't driving, so he thought, what the hell. He'd left the cemetery feeling wild and depressed in a way that made him want to bag it and go home. When he expressed just a portion of what was on his mind, Ray and Cammy insisted that he stick with the plan. He had to go out. He had to have fun. That was his job right now. His job was fun. Cammy talked for a long time about a television special she'd seen on halfway houses and healing. It was called "The Difficulty of Transition." His confusion and despondency gave Cammy an advantage in the argument, because after a while, he just tuned out. Besides, he didn't have a car. At Ray's they cleaned up and changed clothes before driving to the restaurant. Jo Jo, having come from the opposite direction in her own car, was waiting.

Shown to their table in the corner, where a large Hawaiian totem carved out of a tree leaned over them, they ordered drinks and started ripping apart the bread and devouring it along with the breadsticks. John drank the first scotch, and then the second. As far as he was concerned, the events of the afternoon had crushed his hopes for amends in a set of shadowy circumstances determined to take him back to his cell, to return him to prison, and a part of him had gone. It was ridiculous—the idea that he could somehow work things out with an armful of flowers. That's what he'd thought. But not anymore. He couldn't work things out, and he was sick of trying. But what he could do was screw Jo Jo. With lengths of honey hair, she sat to his left in an orange slip dress patterned in hieroglyphics, and he wanted to screw her. He might not know what else he wanted, but looking at the nearly invisible straps creasing the skin of her shoulders, he felt clear about that. The part of him that had been shoved back into prison wanted her. Along with the part of him drinking the scotch. And the part of him that had given up on everything wanted her most of all. He might not be able to make up for what he'd done. He might be locked back up in prison, but he could screw her. Maybe he would drag her into the cell with him.

So he made banal chitchat, and he sat and stared at her, like she might explode and light up the dark room he was in. Every once in a while she caught him and she had to question him with an embarrassed little squint of her eyes. But there was no way he could explain what he was doing, even if Ray and Cammy weren't there. But they were, slashing away at each other, leaving little psychic splatters of blood all over the table.

Then Peter strolled up. The mood they were balancing, already full of undercurrent, started to slide completely out of kilter. Peter smiled and stood over the table, the strangeness and awkwardness falling far into the surreal.

"C'mon, c'mon, sit down. Join us," said Ray.

"No, I've eaten. And I'm due over at Ruskin's." He checked his watch and found that, as he feared, it was time to go. "There's a hot new young jazz pianist there tonight—making his debut on this coast. But he's got a great reputation in the East."

"Maybe we'll drop by. Okay?"

"That's up to you," Peter said, smiling at everyone before he left. Then he nodded at John.

Once he was gone, Ray told a joke about a welder, a hooker, a broomstick, and a blowtorch, but the set-up was so elaborate that John couldn't stay with it. He went in and out of distraction so often that, by the time the punchline arrived, he had no idea what any of it meant. Still, he laughed. But all he really felt was amazement at what an asshole Ray was and how full of shit he could be himself. They ate big salads with a sugary dressing and then went on to steaks and surf and turf and lasagna and fried onion rings. Coffee came, then desserts of ice cream and pie.

When it was over, Jo Jo offered John a ride home since she lived in his direction. It would be silly for Ray to drive all the way over and all the way back.

"Like I don't do silly things," said Ray.

"Shut up, Ray," said Cammy.

"Right," said Ray. "I'm reforming."

Ray's Riviera cruised off. John and Jo Jo stood in an enclave of trees on a wooden platform at the edge of the restaurant parking lot overhung by vines. Garish flowers dangled in the lightspill from several nearby windows. A young blond valet in a red jacket trotted up to them, and Jo Jo gave him her parking ticket. She had a jacket that needed buttoning, so she played with the buttons. John counted his money, getting the tip ready. Her body was breathing beside his. He'd changed into a blue pullover and jeans. He was carrying the black leather vest he'd brought to work in the garment bag, and now he pulled it on.

"I keep thinking about you in prison," she said. "I don't see how you survived."

If she wanted prison stories, he'd tell them. That was okay. He'd tell her what she wanted. He'd be research, if that was what she was after. Scare the hell out of her if she wanted.

Then the guy delivered the car, a blue, very clean little Honda Accord, and they got in, Jo Jo behind the wheel and John beside her. They drove off and she stopped at lights and turned corners and slowed for pedestrians.

"Did you make any friends?"

Two Tommys, he thought, ought to be worth something special. He'd save that. "It's not about that, I don't think. You kind of make deals, you know." He'd pose, give her the pose. He'd play it however she wanted. Expand her range. Darken her palette. As long as she let him break out of the cell holding him. As long as she let him screw her.

They were halted at a traffic light. He leaned up to the dashboard, pointing out a freeway sign. Then he started instructing her about the best way to get to his parents' house from the intersection where they waited. She listened closely, and when the light changed, she tilted toward him, her hand floating out to his knee. "Wasn't that weird with Peter showing up like that?" she said. She wheeled them off in a direction that had nothing to do with his instructions.

If she wanted to go back to Peter, it was fine. If he was just a decoy, some kind of an experiment to make Peter jealous, a developmental stage in the necessarily unconventional progress of their modern, difficult, long-term relationship, that was okay. He'd be a juncture for her and Peter, a demarcation they could look back on to measure the weight of their connection.

"Was it hard seeing him?" he asked.

"In what way?"

"I mean, seeing him like that and just—we're all—I mean, I've known Peter a long time and—"

"How long?"

"Counting the time I was in prison, maybe twelve—Let me see . . . Nineteen eighty-eight was—"

"Look, that's over. I mean, between him and me. It's over. Did you see how he handled it?"

"What?"

"What was wrong with how he handled it?"

"I don't know. You mean bumping into us?"

The possibility that he might say something that she wouldn't like, or might misconstrue, kept him silent for a minute, searching carefully.

"No, no, you do, John. I know you do."

It still didn't feel safe to speak, so he stayed with a slow, serious process of thinking.

"What was wrong, John, was not *how*. But that he did it. What was wrong was that he *handled* it. That's just what he did. He handled it. It was in some category to be handled. He made some mental adjustment, and there we all were in his head. The rest of us were wherever we were and that was fine with him. He was just thinking away. But you—you were squirming. Weren't you? I mean, I don't have to ask. I saw you."

"I guess."

"And I was too. I was squirming. As any human being would be."

At the end of a suburban street, she brought the car to a stop and directed John to get out and open an aluminum gate—a lunarlike fragment embedded in a brick wall. He shoved it aside, and the Honda cruised past. She led him up a narrow concrete path. She opened the door and he followed her into her apartment. She shut the door and there were other doors and she showed him the way through them without turning on any lights.

"That story you told about the scar," she said, and stopped. He waited in the dark. A small lamp on a shelf came on, and he saw that her eyes were inquisitive and sad. She took off her jacket, and then, as if some crucial fact had finally been established, she flicked the lamp off before walking away. If she wanted to treat him like he was a specimen of something that belonged in the dark, he didn't mind. It was okay. He followed and found her in her bedroom lighting candles. On the wall above the bed was a different version of the painting he'd seen at Peter's, the straining faces shrouded in mucus. The perspective was altered, the image bigger. Shepherding a burning match to the wick of a tall fat candle, she huddled in a corner with her back to him.

He'd go along with it. Sure. He'd give her a pose. He'd play it, and if she wanted to paint him, he'd let her. He'd actually pose, if that's what she wanted. Be one of those people screaming in the ice cubes. He knew about it. He'd been there. Locked up. Yelling. She wasn't all wrong. He could verify it for her. Give a first-hand account.

When she stood after lighting the candle, she stayed facing the flame and he walked up behind her and fit his arms around her waist. She leaned into him and they swayed, and he raised his hands to her breasts, where he flexed slowly, seeking the nipples, and when he had them, she sighed, as if someone had just relieved her of a terrible burden. He didn't care what her reasons were, or even if there weren't any. Her reasons were her business, just like his were his own.

Wordlessly she revolved in his arms, and pressed him back to sit on the edge of the bed. For minutes they stared at each other. Then she reached toward his vest, so he took it off. She slipped out of her dress. He took off his shirt. In her bra and panties, she straddled him as he lay on the bed. Gently, she touched his chest; his hands slid up her arms to her face. They kissed, and when they parted, she whispered, "God, this is wild." She tugged down his jeans, and pushed aside the crotch of her panties. He entered her, and it didn't seem possible that this could be human. It didn't seem possible that anything could be so soft. It didn't seem possible that such softness could be inside someone and they would let you go there. He didn't mind if she wanted him to live in the dark. Or if he was just an experiment. A diversion. Then she squeezed and it was just like the cemetery. He didn't have a chance.

"I was reading," she said, "in this book, and it says when you come, when a man comes, the sperm comes out at almost thirty miles an hour. That's a lot of pressure," she said, fitting her thumb inside his lips.

It was the nicest thing anybody had ever said to him, and he nodded. He'd pose for her, if she wanted. Show her the truth. Sure, whatever. Somehow she squeezed him again, as if somebody very tender and caring was in there taking care of him, and he reached up to her breasts. Her reasons didn't matter. She could go back to Peter if she wanted. She was above him, wheeling left as far as she could go, and then right all the way back, but slowly, like she didn't want to miss even the smallest notch of each turn. Then he went blind and he stayed blind. And when he saw her again, he was hard again. He'd tell her whatever she wanted. All she had to do was ask. But now he was going to break through the walls and be alive again. He pushed her over, his hands clamping her ass to him, and he didn't want to be locked up anymore, as he looked down at her distorted face. Lit up from within, her skin projected a coursing thirst that settled in her eyes, a desire fixed on him, and he felt sad that she needed so much, and desperately apologetic, but his sympathy was of no use, his remorse and sorrow pointless against an appetite driving him to pinion her wrists to the bed, and then lift her and shake her and lift her and shake her like his hands were chains shackling them together, so he could not get away.

The last thing he heard was her whisper. "King Kong," she said. Then he was gone. He didn't know where he was going, though it was a kind of sleep, and he was willing. Not that there was much choice. Still, he reached for her as he sank, hoping not to be all by himself in the vast and lonely bed, so he curled his mass around her small, galvanizing shape.

John, said Emily. *Do you have a minute for a question? I was wondering if you noticed something? When you were over her, kneeling over her—did she remind you of anything? Anything at all? That's what I'm wondering. When she was making that noise you enjoyed so much, her face in this sad ecstatic contortion, didn't the whole thing just remind you of when I was lying on that pavement, blood in my teeth, looking up at you, trying to speak? Didn't it remind you of me? Of us? There you were, over me, just as you were over her. Kneeling. Looking down. It reminded me, and I was wondering if you noticed the resemblance? John, can I tell you something? I really, really, really want to. And, I don't want you feeling imposed upon or pressured. But I know what I felt in that moment, and I think you felt it, too. So I just have to say it. I love you, John. I want to see you. Come to me, John. Don't you love me?*

He woke up thinking he wanted a drink of water. The face inches from his own was Jo Jo's, and he contemplated her a moment, like sleep had turned her into a stranger. Painstakingly, he disentangled himself, and though he wanted to be considerate and avoid disturbing her, his more pressing desire was to remain alone. He wanted to get away, as if her proximity endangered him. He slipped from the bed and snuck into his underwear. Carrying his socks and shoes and trousers and shirt, he wondered if he was leaving. In the kitchen he found the refrigerator and on the bottom shelf a bottle of Coke, which he grabbed. He went to the door and found that it was unlocked and that scared him. It infuriated him. He opened it, wondering if Freddy Gale might step in.

Was that what was troubling him, that Freddy was out there somewhere, stalking him with a gun, and if he found him here, would he kill Jo Jo, too? The stoop and the walkway below it were empty. The night and neighborhood were still. Where was Freddy, anyway? The poor fuck. What was he doing, wandering the night, like some lost soul, thought John, with an affectionate regret more apt for an estranged relative or a withdrawn, contentious friend.

"John," said Jo Jo, calling from within the apartment. He pulled a cigarette from his pocket and prepared to light up, bending low in hope of hiding the flame.

"John," she called again. Though trying to sound simply curious, she was worried. "John?" She thought he was gone.

"Out here," he said and struck the match, and with the cigarette in his mouth, he pulled his trousers on.

The patter of her footfalls brought her into view. Naked, she advanced through a distant doorway and then a nearer one. "What are you doing? Are you okay?" she asked.

"You should lock your doors," he told her.

"Oh, well, they wouldn't keep anybody out."

"You should still lock them."

She plucked up something and dropped it over her head. It turned out to be his T-shirt. "Couldn't you sleep?"

"I thought I heard something."

"What? A prowler, you mean?"

"I don't know."

"Or is it that man?" She edged closer to him, wanting to measure the accuracy of her idea in the response of his eyes. "Is that what you're talking about, John? That man, the father of—"

"What about him?"

"I mean, that it was him, the noise you heard, or thought you heard. Are you worried that he's still after you?"

"He is still after me."

"Well, then, let's get back inside," she said, taking him by the arm, and pressuring him to move with her to safety behind the door and the locks she set, a drop bolt on the frame and another delicate little switch built into the knob. "Did you call the police? What did they say?"

"What?"

"The police."

"I didn't call them."

"You didn't call them?"

"No."

"Really? That's weird," she said.

"Weird?"

"I don't understand what you're saying."

"I didn't call them."

"So it's weird. You think he's after you to kill you but you don't call the police."

"Maybe I should go."

"Go? John, what are you talking about? Is that what you're talking about?"

"I don't like the way you're going about this—you're all over me."

"What? No, no. Is that what you—? I'm just trying to figure out how you could have somebody after you threatening to kill you and still not call the police. I mean, that's nuts. It's suicidal. I mean, do you want to die?"

"I don't know."

"You don't know? Is that what you said?" She wheeled away, tossing her hair. "You don't know if you want to die. Great."

"I mean, I've seen more shit than this guy. Worse fucking guys day in and day out in prison. I mean, being threatened is a routine event. This guy's strictly an amateur compared to your average, garden variety psychotic in prison. I mean, in prison—you wanna hear about prison?"

"No. No, I don't. God," she said. "I really know how to pick 'em."

"What? What's that? What'd you say?"

"Nothing."

"Can I have my shirt?"

"Of course." Jo Jo whipped the T-shirt up over her head and handed it to him. "Did you see her die?"

He was turning away, but that brought him back. Now she was getting down to it. Prison wasn't crazy enough for her. She wanted the real gore. "What are you asking me? What the hell are you asking me?"

"Maybe you should go," she said, like she suddenly saw the value in the idea.

"Where the hell do you get off asking me something like that? I'm not some fucking piece of research for you! Is that what you think?"

"What?" She walked away, searching as she moved from room to room, angling one way and then another, as he followed her, and she looked for something to put on. "Forget I said it," she told him. "Okay?"

"No," he said. "No. I was drunk, you know. Out having a good time. On my way home from a softball game. We got off work early to do it—it was a company game. I'd had some beers. Too many beers. Just beer, you know, but who counts? I didn't even know what happened. I just heard a bump. And when I stopped and got out, then I knew. She was lying on the street all torn up. There were other people there. Already. This crossing guard. Some old guy. He was staring at me. She was like this little pile on the pavement, this little bundle of clothes, and I went over. I could see her moving a little, her mouth was kind of moving. I thought she was talking to someone, you know. I mean, not me. I mean, someone who wasn't there: her mother or her father. When I got up to her, I knelt down. She wasn't talking to someone else. She was talking to me. She was apologizing to me. She was apologizing for not having looked both ways."

Jo Jo had found an indigo silk Japanese robe and she was putting it on and tying the belt. She finished, and then for a second, she fussed with the lengths of the bows, tugging them until they were even. "You have such a beautiful face. The ways your eyes slope. Like a puppy."

"What are you talking about?" She was going to put a plastic sack over his head, and then, when he was suffocating, she would paint him.

The robe was trembling, the pattern of stitched trees and white birds shivering with a windy violence, as she turned away. "I think your guilt is just a little too much competition for me. I think you should let me know when you think maybe you want life. That's what I'm saying. You know, if you decide."

"I gotta get to work," he told her. He went back and gathered the rest of his clothes and started dressing.

"I'll drive you."

"No."

"Yes, I will," she said. "I'll drive you."

Daybreak was a beatific crescent of bloodred sun over the sea, a surface of foamy hatchets coming in from the wide horizon to the foreground of surf. Jo Jo drove with John in the passenger seat, a container of coffee on his lap. He sipped a little, lit up a smoke. She watched the road and they spoke only enough to make sure his directions were clear.

At the fishing pier, he pointed to the parking lot nearest to the

Southern Gal's berth. There were other cars gathering, doors slamming, men leaning in windows, collecting gear. She glanced at him, but he didn't even try to fight through the cold color in her eyes. As if she expected nothing more from him, she turned her attention to the dashboard.

The morning was clear, the water already plowed by several seiners, and a trawler dancing out past the orange scheme of a barge crane grinding into motion. Engines were awakening, then idling, the stench and fumes of diesel rising into the lenslike glass of the air, as he started toward the boat.

When he heard the door slam behind him, he just kept going, neither slower nor faster. It was like the world around him, at least in this morning of gulls and waves slapping against the pilings nearby, was not the world he occupied. Then she touched him from behind and the pressure of her fingers was a request for him to wait. He stopped, but he didn't turn. Her head knocked against his back twice and her hand came around, feeling its way across his chest until it reached the muscles over his heart. "It's in there somewhere," she said, and then she walked away.

Yes, but I have it, said Emily. *It belongs to me.*

He watched her drive off. He missed them, he realized, Emily and her father. His heart wasn't in where Jo Jo had pressed. It was gone, and the girl who had taken it was possessive. She was achingly, fearfully insecure. But she didn't have to worry. He missed those sad eyes, shy and childish, looking up at him with their bloody, spellbinding claims.

As he swung over the gunwale and dropped aboard, Ol' Hank came up from the hold, yelling, "You need to double-check that the beer and soda cabinet been stocked."

"I know."

"Check the bait buoy."

"All right."

"Make sure, if there's any dead ones in there floatin', that you just go ahead and grab 'em out of it. Get 'em out."

"You told me," said John, trying to escape by heading for the bait buoy.

Ol' Hank trailed him, the cigarette stuck in his mouth bobbing and wiggling. "Gotta do it every morning, every night."

"You told me, Hank."

"They're fine one minute, gone the next. Fish just up and die like the rest of us. When I die, who you think is going to come along and do just what I do—same damn thing? Stand here talking to you just like me. You'll have to blink and do a goddamn double take if you notice at all. 'Where's Ol' Hank?' 'I don't know.' 'Dead.' 'No shit.' 'Who are you?' Some poor fuck. Who you think it'll be?"

"I don't know."

"John, John, John," the old man said, and he squeezed John's arm in his big clammy hands.

"What?"

He just smiled, and turned, relishing the taste of absurdity, as he spit a black gob of phlegm into a blaze of water, where the reflected sun was huge.

It's the third day, John, she said.

Tonight after work, he was going to find Freddy Gale. The paradoxical ache had to be obeyed, like nostalgia for a time or place, a decade or city, where your life had been lived and even your enemies were a part of it. It was just what you did when you missed somebody.

But now the *Southern Gal,* shaking loose from the dock, was bearing him on an opposite course, chugging out into a gleam of water, the stride of the waves lengthening.

27

■ ■ ■ ■ ■ ■ ■

Freddy was concentrating on his heart, as if each new beat was an unprotected valuable lying on a table. Seconds ago, he had felt a very large door starting to close on his chest. The edges of a dark sack slipped over his brain, and he lay down on the floor. The blank paleness above him was the ceiling. His father had gone this way. Oxygen deprivation. Ventricular fibrillation. An electrical confusion that stupefied the heart, robbing the brain of breath, turning the old man into an appliance with a power-supply problem. There he was one minute, a little green maybe, but yammering away with some story. In seconds, he was like a disconnected TV. A gray empty screen that Freddy could not see into, and nobody was looking out. The moment between was shocking. Ronald Gale made a stricken complaint like a dreaming dog announcing trouble in the animal world. Twice he slammed fists into his chest, in a comical imitation of savagery, or a futile display of physical strength. With Freddy watching in frozen amazement, his father's eyes bugged out into hardboiled eggs which some expanding science fiction monster inside him was trying to spit across the room. Then he just stopped the whole thing, like it was a humiliating undertaking that he refused to dignify with further opposition.

Freddy, however, saw only the shadow of the door, the promise of an ominous, excruciating closing. His fear had been as much a memory of his father as anything actually happening to him. He was lying on the rug, thinking. The fact that he was thinking argued that he wasn't dead. The handgun that he'd placed on the couch on his way to the floor hadn't been fired into anybody's head. His heart was bouncing along, happy with his attention, like a spoiled child who had thrown a tantrum.

The gun lay next to the marked-up calendar like they were two parts of one set of something. He needed to cross out the day. But then he realized that he had lost track. He had no idea what day it was. He grunted at the absurdity of what he was doing. He spat on the calendar and stood up. He dressed quickly, and on the way to the door stopped to take a long piss in the corner. Facing the wedge of the wall, he peed all over the rug.

Great, Dad, said Emily, giggling. *This is nuts. This is really fucking nuts.*

It was noon when he arrived at the store. Jeffrey, who was engaged with a female customer stuffed into a purple catsuit two sizes too tight, looked at him like he didn't belong there. Freddy squinted at Jeffrey, whose returning glance suggested that it might be best if they both explained themselves later.

"This is outrageous, such ineptitude. How can you screw up a ring size?" said the woman as Freddy tried to cross behind her.

"We haven't," said Jeffrey.

"And then lie about it," said the woman. She had Freddy in her sights. She was trying to watch him without losing track of Jeffrey.

"You have a swollen finger one day and not the next," Jeffrey told her.

"I don't have a swollen finger," she snarled, looking at Freddy, but unable to decide whether or not he belonged to this argument.

"I'm here to help you," said Jeffrey. "Let me help you."

In his office, Freddy snatched up his phone messages and sorted through them. The surveillance monitor on his desk showed Jeffrey and the woman still arguing. The camera, suspended in a rear corner of the store, had them framed from a high angle. They were saying the same things over and over. Shoehorned into her goddamned catsuit, she was deluded about the size of everything.

Rifling through the pink pile of messages once more, he realized how fucking disappointed he was that Mary hadn't called. He'd expected to hear from her. Or maybe it was John Booth he wanted to hear from. Somebody that mattered. When he sagged in his chair, the gun in the back of his waistband stabbed into his spine.

The woman was saying, "Look! Listen! Wake up! I have had these fingers all my adult life and they don't change. They are my fingers."

"Water," Jeffrey said. "People hold water."

"I don't"

"People retain water!" said Jeffrey. "Especially women."

They were driving Freddy nuts. He lit a cigarette and tried to remember the last thing Mary had said at the house yesterday, her final lie.

"You have a swollen finger one day and not the next. This is your problem. I'm sorry," said Jeffrey.

Freddy popped the magazine from the butt of the handgun and removed a cartridge, then jammed it back in, testing the spring. The fact that Mary hadn't called made everything he was doing feel shallow and wasted. He was glaring at the denatured images of Jeffrey and the woman, listening to their tinny voices. They were the stupidest, most boring TV show he'd ever seen.

"I was seven on Tuesday and I'm seven today," said the woman.

"I've measured it several times, madam."

"It won't even go on my finger! It is not—I say *not* a seven."

"Why did it fit you perfectly three days ago?"

"It didn't."

"Then why did you walk out with it?"

"I'll report you to the Better Business Bureau! You can't get away with treating a customer like this."

He ought to put the gun in her ear and take her fucking temperature. Let her report that to the Better Business Bureau. When the magazine clicked into place, Freddy eased a round into the chamber. He enjoyed watching it rise and seat itself. Excuse me, ma'am, but I would strongly suggest that you start paying closer attention to the lessons you were taught in manners class, or I will revoke your license for noise. He turned down the volume but within seconds flipped it back up because their pointless, idiotic squabble was somehow liberating in its shameless stupidity.

"May I help you, ma'am?" said Freddy.

He stood at the rear of the store, having flung open the curtains that covered the stairway to his office.

"Are you the owner?"

"Yes, I would be the proprietor in question."

"Thank God. I told this Jap faggot I ordered this ring, size seven. My finger has always been seven." The fingers she thrust at him ended in glued-on nails like painted bear claws.

The ring was dangling on a front joint, and Freddy grinned at her like he wanted her to understand that he intended to hurt her severely, as soon as he figured the best way to do it. He plucked the ring between his thumb and forefinger, handling it like her touch had contaminated it, as he raised it to the light before his experienced eye.

"It's a seven," he said.

"This is a six and a half, or a goddamn six and three quarters, maybe. At best—at the very outside!" said the woman.

"No," said Freddy.

"Don't try and run the same shit on me as your pet asshole here," she sneered.

He slammed the handgun down on the display counter, exploding shock waves of glass out from the point of impact. Both Jeffrey and the woman turned to look at the snowy shape in the shattered glass, which exhaled a crumbling sigh, like it might be asking for help. Freddy brought the woman's face to him, moving her by the tip of her chin. Then he jammed the ring against her forehead with his finger, pinning it where she could never see it. "Does this look like a fucking six and a half, six and three fucking quarters to you?"

Her darting eyes suggested she was trying to see the ring and answer his question, but he canceled her effort by shoving her fingers deeply into his mouth, sucking them, and pulling them out thick with spit, a strand of saliva connecting her ring finger to his lips until he severed it, driving the band past the knuckle to the meat of her hand. "You were right," he said. "You are a seven. A perfect-fucking-seven."

She was mesmerized by the ring, as Freddy retrieved the gun and whirled for the door, thinking how they were all on videotape. He shot a glance up at the impervious lens of the surveillance camera and gave it a macabre smile.

"Mr. Gale," said Jeffrey.

"What?"

The woman was like an old piece of furniture he had never really cared for, and he looked right past her. Jeffrey was poised, the unfinished words on his tongue urging him toward the question he somehow couldn't bring himself to ask.

"Jeffrey," said Freddy, and he reached into his pocket, pulled out the vault keys, and flipped them. "You close up tonight, okay," he said. "And open up in the morning. Okay?"

He drove for forty-five minutes, plunging into and through neighborhoods and business districts, racing onto this or that freeway and then veering off. He darted into a parking lot, and he cruised around a shopping mall, trying to burn off the excess adrenaline.

Finally, he was on Sunset Boulevard, commencing a long curving descent like a banking airplane toward the Pacific Coast Highway, and when he got there, he turned right to Malibu. He pulled into a liquor store. He bought a pack of cigarettes, a pint of Absolut, and a half dozen airline bottles. As he was collecting his change, he squinted at the grizzled clerk with his fifty-year-old potbelly, jeans and Bon Jovi T-shirt, and he said, "Do I know you? Did we meet at a party up at ah—I mean, was that—Wait a minute, wait a minute."

"I don't think so."

"Bartholemew is my name. I mean, Bart Samuels."

The guy was puzzled but polite as he took Freddy's offered hand. "Sorry. But I don't think so."

"Wait a minute, wait a minute. Now I see it. No. You're not the guy."

Outside, Freddy spotted a bank of pay phones, and when he got to the last one, he dumped in some quarters and dialed Mary's number. But he had nothing to say to her goddamn machine, so he hung up. There were more quarters, so he dropped one in the slot, and just for the hell of it dialed E-M-I-L-Y. But it didn't provide him with enough numbers. He thought of adding G-A-L-E. He counted and saw that when he got as far as G-A, he would have enough digits. He dumped three quarters in and started dialing, but after a couple numbers he stopped. He lit up a cigarette before beginning all over again, only this time, he dialed John Booth's home.

"Hello?" said a woman.

"Could I speak to John?" If she said "yes" Freddy was poised to hang up and drive over right now.

"Well, he's not here just at the moment," said the woman.

"Yes, I'm looking for John Booth."

"You have the right number, but he's at work. Can I take a message?"

"Uh, do you know where I might . . . , uhhh . . . is this Mrs. Booth?"

"Yes."

"Hi. This is Richard." He thought a second. "Crabbe," he added. "John knows me as Bobo Crabbe. I'm a friend of John's and I've got a coming-out present I wanted to give him."

"Oh, that's very nice."

"What time do you expect him home?"

"Well, he gets home five or six o'clock. Sometimes."

"Oh geez. Oh, God," He was scrambling. His grasp of what he wanted was flying around and he couldn't make it settle enough for him to get a good look at it. "I'd love to surprise him with this thing, and as it turns out, I've been summoned out of town on business and I have to get to the airport by five. You said he was working?"

"You could drop it by our house."

"Well, sure," he said. "I could." And wait for him. But then I'd have to kill the whole bunch of you.

"But you probably want to give it to him personally."

"That is what I was thinking. I didn't know he had a job."

"Oh, yes. Friends got it for him." She sounded so fucking proud. Like her son was something to be proud of. "He's out at the Long Beach fishing pier," she said, just sounding so fucking self-satisfied and sickening about her goddamn son, as if getting a job was this big earth-shaking deal. "Working really long hours. So I don't think you'll be able to reach him because he's out on the boat most of the time."

"He's out on a boat?"

"It's hard work."

"Do you know the name of it? The boat? I mean, if I should get down there and try to find him."

"Oh, sure. *Southern Gal.* Isn't that a good one?"

"Uh-huh, it sure is. Well, maybe I'll scoot down there. Although I really don't think there's time. But I'll tell you what, if you could just leave the message that I called, and uh, if I don't get down—No, no, don't tell him. Don't tell him about the surprise."

"Oh, this is a shame. It's really a shame."

"Yes it is."

"But there's worse things."

"I guess so."

"Oh, that's for sure. Did you hear about the earthquake in Mexico on the news this afternoon? It was centered in the suburbs of a city, and the epicenter was right under an old folks home. Right under it. Isn't that terrible? I just heard it on the radio. What is God thinking, do you suppose?"

"I have no idea."

"All those poor old people."

"Maybe He doesn't think. I mean, maybe He doesn't think. Maybe He just does things."

"Wouldn't that be a kicker?"

"Well, thank you very much, Mrs. Booth. 'Bye."

"Okay. Thank you, Mr. Crabbe. 'Bye."

Getting to Long Beach was simple, and finding the harbor wasn't very difficult. But locating the exact pier for the *Southern Gal* took some time. He had to accost this security guard put-putting around on his motor scooter. He had to wave the guy down and give him a bullshit story. It was boring, trying to come up with the details and then having to spell them out for this asshole who was obviously thinking of something else, probably how to handicap a horse race, or how to come up with some scheme to pick a winner in Lotto.

Then he drove to Pier 8, where he parked and started down a walkway identified with a crumbling old placard. He despised the way the platform kept shifting. First to the left, and then back again. And what did it do next? It shifted to the left and then back again with the same sloshing noise. The seagulls kept plunging and tending the same scummy patch of water, wheeling like rubbish in the wind. The sound of the diesels was boring, and up ahead were these idiots in sailor suits. The nearest guy was lugging a cumbersome box that blocked his view, so that he didn't have a clue what was in front of him.

What a bunch of doofuses, said Emily.

"Assholes," he told her.

At the sound of Freddy's voice, the guy peeked around the box, this look of righteous irritation in his eyes.

"Whoa," said the guy.

A pompous voice boomed over a public address: "Sir, get off the dock! Yes, you, sir, get off the dock, GET OFF THE DOCK!"

As Freddy searched the sky for the source of this unbelievably boring voice, Emily sang to him, *Sailing, sailing, over the bounding main.* And then he patted the handgun, the nine-millimeter Glock, the lethal fucking thing in his waistband, and he thought, *Bound this!*

"They don't like anyone down here, that's all," said the guy. He was straining to stand there with his box.

"Oh, yeah?" said Freddy.

"Yeah."

The P.A. was still blaring, but Freddy just shut it out. "You work down here—on the *Southern Gal?*" Freddy nodded at the boat, which was no more than sixty feet ahead, the name stenciled on the bow.

"Yeah."

"I'm just looking for somebody, he works on that boat."

"Who's that?" The guy was searching the sky like he was the one who had annoyed the P.A. voice, and he was looking for the source. He shifted the box for a better grip, when, if he had a brain in his head, he would have set the goddamn thing down. Clearly, he had no idea how much he was boring Freddy.

"You're boring me," said Freddy. "John Booth is his name."

"I'm boring you? I'm boring you? Fuck you!"

"John Booth."

"He's gone. You missed him by about twenty minutes. Now get off, okay!"

"Oh yeah," said Freddy, because he didn't believe this guy. And suddenly he knew why. Past the stupid fucking box, he saw John Booth's large, unmistakable shape scurrying along the side of the boat's cabin and disappearing in the hold of the *Southern Gal.* "Then who's that?" Freddy shouted, and ran past the guy.

"Hey!" he heard behind him, and he could imagine the guy finally setting down the box.

With his hands on the railing, Freddy was just about to leap aboard when an old white-haired guy appeared, smoke and ashes bubbling around his head and out of his mouth. He had a big pole in his hands and the instant his eyes chanced on Freddy, he started coughing, but he knew to raise the pole with a slight suggestion of warning. "Can I help you?"

"I just want to talk to John Booth."

"He's not here." The old guy had a greenish tint like his bones were corroded, and he slobbered the cigarette out of his mouth without using his hands. He kept spitting and spitting.

"I just want to talk to him," said Freddy.

The young guy sprang past Freddy, and after a quick dance around the deck, lunged to grab up another pole. This one ended in a huge metal hook jabbing the air in a nasty question mark.

"I don't know what's goin' on here," he said. "Ol' Hank, what's going' on here?"

"Hey, hey, all right." Freddy opened his jacket, like he was proud of his shirt. With the front panel parting, there was the gun. By now the old guy was coughing so hard, he had to sit down on a storage chest attached to the wall of the cabin. The young guy lowered the pole, but he was hesitant to drop it. He was acting like he was making a really important decision. Just then, the big guy Freddy had seen run to hide in the hold came strolling up like he was on his way to a picnic. "I can't find it, Ol' Hank," he said. "You sure you put it down there."

Freddy had no idea what the guy was talking about, but it was clear that he was not John Booth. He was just another asshole in a sailor outfit.

"I'm just looking for a guy. That's all," Freddy said. "I just want to say hello to him, you know. Maybe I have a present for him, maybe I don't. Then you guys start jumping around with clubs and hooks and shit. Waving 'em around. I don't wanna end up fish bait, you know. I think we all misunderstood each other. That's what happened. For my part, I apologize. You just tell John that Bobo was looking for him. Bobo Mannassadada. Tell him," Freddy said, and then he turned, heading back toward his car.

That's a good one, said Emily. *Wow, Dad. Wow. Mannassadada.*

"It ain't boring," he told her.

Behind him he could hear the men on the boat.

"Who is that asshole?" the old guy managed to squeak between coughs.

"I think he thought you were John."

"John's gone."

"Ex-cons," said the old guy. "This is what happens when you start hiring riffraff."

28

■ ■ ■ ■ ■ ■

As the bus jerked to a halt along jeweler's row, John came out the door like a skydiver stepping into the air. Then he stood there. In seconds, he would walk in on Freddy Gale and tell him something. Kill me. Don't kill me. Hello. Let's talk. Fuck you. The next time I see you you're dead. I'm warning you. I'm begging you. How you been? Long time, no see. He lit a cigarette, his lungs reaching for the hit, as he counseled himself to enjoy the confusion. It was all he had.

The street teemed with cars struggling in both directions. In the company of a band of teenage Chicanos, he dodged through a brief crease in the flow. Once he stepped up onto the opposite curb, he headed for the sign saying GALE'S FINE JEWELRY. Without breaking stride, he went past the dazzle of the display window and in through the door.

Whirling around in the main aisle, a young Asian man was tending a vacuum cleaner, his arm pumping the hose and nozzle back and forth. Glass was splattered all over the rug. With his concentration downward, and the whir of the motor drowning out the bell above the door, he failed to notice John's arrival. Just to the left of where he was working, the surface of a display case was shattered. John hesitated, wondering if Freddy were around somewhere. Maybe in the office. There had to be an office. The young man was turning as he swept and, when he saw John, he did a kind of double take. John nodded. Still trying to locate the office entrance, he studied the dark curtain partitioning off the rear. The appliance shut down in response to a nudge from the young man's toe. He was a fashionplate, brown baggy trousers with an infinity of pleats, a double-breasted sport coat with a sweatshirt hood.

"May I help you?" he asked, grimacing like the splinters on the floor were cutting into his feet.

"Well, I was looking for Mr. Gale, the owner."

"He's insane, you know."

"What?"

"The man is certifiable. Leave your neurosis at home, that's my motto. I mean, we're all capable of acting out, right? I am, and I'm sure you are. But keep it in check, I say. And why here, why in a place of business?"

"What happened?"

"I have no idea. None. And I was right here when it happened. When I get home, I will say, 'He went mad.' That's all. 'He went mad.' "

"I want to see him. Is he here?"

"Of course not. Why would he be here? It's only his business."

"Do you know where he is?"

"I mean, I would appreciate it, sir, if you would just leave. Since you're in pursuit of Mr. Gale and not shopping. I want to finish up and go home. I have a terrible headache."

The young man banged his heel on the "start" button and the vacuum cleaner grabbed some air. "There was this lovely woman here," he yelled over the machine, "and she was disturbed about something; she was insecure about having perhaps made a bad purchase. She was being a little troublesome, a trifle obnoxious, of course, but so what? I don't understand what he did."

"He broke this? *He* did this?" John walked to the damaged counter, the atomized glass over tiers of silver bracelets.

"With a gun! With a gun!"

"He shot it?" Then he turned to inquire more definitely. "He shot this?"

"No, no. Like a hammer." The young man waved his hand in a demonstration.

"But you don't know where he is?" John was drawn back to reconsider the wreckage.

"Probably with his sluts."

"What?"

"If he's anywhere, that's where he is. With his slutty dancers and friends over on Seventh Street. It's this upscale strip joint near where he lives."

"He lives around here?"

"I'll write it all down for you. It's just a few blocks. Maybe you can talk some sense into him." Once more he prodded the vacuum cleaner into silence, before plucking a pen from his breast pocket.

It took less than ten minutes for John to reach Freddy's apartment building. A bus, arriving at its stop precisely as he walked by, startled him. He stared at the opening door, but the idea of jumping aboard wasn't a real temptation. It was the coincidence that intrigued him more than the possibility of leaving. The discoveries he had made in Freddy's store had altered things. It was like Freddy was running from him now. Breaking things and running away and hiding. He rang the buzzer for five solid minutes before he returned to the street, put on his sunglasses, and stood looking up, like he expected to sense the right window, or even see Freddy up there. He paced and waited through a whole cigarette.

The door to the Calypso Club slid open on a dull, sober mood. Clearly, the place was not ready for business. Still he proceeded, peering through a beaded curtain and feeling wary, like a child in an adult's hideaway. He took off his sunglasses, and the first thing he saw was the bar, a slab of black vinyl segmented by lines of silver studs. The bartender was a redhead in jeans and a halter top that left her belly exposed. Seated at the bar was a brown-haired girl in a robe; she was bent over a paperback book. A field of tables stacked with chairs led to a small stage with a barren quality in the daylight. At a corner table, a stubby, dark-haired guy was scowling at a ledger and a small computer. Chomping on a cigar, he glanced at John Booth through a veil of smoke and then went back to scrutinizing receipts and punching in numbers. A nearby booth overflowed with a sprawling male shape, the bulk of a gorilla, his head back, his breath snores.

The bartender was watching John as he approached, her stomach emitting this glow like her abdominal muscles were gold bars.

"We're not opened yet," she said pleasantly.

John set down his sunglasses before asking, "Could I get a glass of water, please?"

"You want some water?"

She shuffled away, sliding her feet rather than picking them up. The girl with the paperback smiled and John returned the smile and she squinted like she was rearranging a set of very interesting objects in her mind. The cover of the book flashed as she moved to flatten it out on the bar surface, before sinking back into its pages: *Men Who Hate Women and the Women Who Love Them.* He noticed that she had several others piled up by her elbow. *Men Are from Mars and Women Are from Venus* was the only spine angled so he could read it.

When the bartender returned with the water, he took a sip and scanned the room. "Do you know a fella named Freddy Gale?"

" 'Course I do. He's here every night," said the bartender.

The girl left her book again, only this time her expression was intently curious. It looked to John like she had something to say.

"*She* really knows him," said the bartender in a tone that told the whole story.

"Hello, Maggie!" said the girl to the bartender.

"Hello."

"We both know him."

"I don't know him like you know him, Mia."

"Never?"

"Never say never."

"But he's not here now?" said John.

"No," said the girl. She was elbowing her pile of books to a site she could obscure with her body.

The bartender stretched her arms out on the bar, and rested her chin on them. "He usually comes in about nine-thirty or ten."

"You a friend of Freddy's?" asked the other girl Mia.

"I know him."

"You want us to give him a message?" the bartender said into her forearms. "God, I'm beat. I'm fucking exhausted. I think I have Epstein-Barr or some shit."

A burst of static announced that the sound system was being activated, and then several startling chords sprang from speakers around the room. Mia, grabbing her books, jumped to her feet and said, "Okay!" She sounded like her name had been called as she hastened away, a schoolgirl late for class.

"She's gotta practice," said the bartender.

A male singing voice emerged from the cloud of music, this echoey rip-off of an American Indian chanting. Synthesizer chords interjected a spooky hint of otherworldly interests. On stage, Mia abandoned her robe. Dressed in a white garter belt sustaining a vapor of hose, she wore a white bra and bikini panties. She stood on the sidelines for a moment searching for a place to enter the music, now dominated by a ghostly female voice, this witchy hybrid of pop ambitions and dead chanting monks. She pranced onto the barren stage in the flat daylight. She stalked and humped, and John stared, imagining he was Freddy, fucking this girl. She was sinewy and graceful, her legs long and delicate, her smooth brow suggesting, with the power of her concentration, a kind of academic strain.

"Freddy comes here a lot?" he asked Maggie, the bartender who was still slumped on the bar beside him.

"All the time."

He pointed his chin at Mia, singling her out for both of them to study. Maggie nodded, as if they'd just shared a lengthy, detailed communication. "She's mad for Freddy, if that's what you mean?"

"I don't know what I mean."

"Well, say for example, if you asked her out, she might go. If that's what you're thinking. But her world view is more or less Freddy-based, so you would find yourself related to her grand Freddy strategy somewhere. You'd probably never know it. In your case, she would see you as some kind of useful tactical move, since you know Freddy. One can assume that you talk. If you talk, well, you talk broads. You talk gash. That's what she would figure. Which of course is a situation you could take advantage of, if your goals were limited. You could bag her, I'm sure—and if that's all you wanted, what do you care if she's using you to get into Freddy's head? She's got a master plan which I don't think even she understands. She hates to try to explain it. Not that she's alone. Any number of girls—Verna, for example—find Freddy a wet dream who cannot serve up enough confusion to keep her off. But then she's older, and she loves to complain. Where do you know him from?"

"Freddy?"

"Yeah. Listen, I gotta have some coffee, I'm dyin'. I feel like I'm drugged, and I got ten hours sleep last night." She raised her head and then her arm from the bar where she had been lolling.

On stage Mia was wrapping herself in a plume of white chiffon from which only her head and feet extended. Otherwise she was this cloud. The music was a sort of spaceship sound. Then the guy who knew that Indians had spiritual affiliations started trying to sing like one again. As the lights transmuted from ordinary daylight to a nocturnal mood, Mia gained a spectral quality. A diaphanous shroud hovered over the faint outline of her body. Because the floor was painted black, it vanished, and she appeared suspended. The witchy female voice was back, sneaking lyrics about believing in destiny into the corners of the arrangement like it was the back of John's head.

"I find that personally Freddy is mainly smug," said Maggie, bringing two cups of coffee. "You know, pretty much vain, and cut off and remote. I think I could connect with him on a physical level, sure, but does he have a heart? And if he does, will he share? Now those kinds of questions can be a real turn-on, but in my case, it's a long road, I've seen it before, it's a lot of mud. So I am more inclined to back off and tell myself 'Whoa, Maggie. Look where you are! Check your surroundings, you know. Is this alley safe?' I say study the floor plan so, if the cabin starts to fill with smoke and flames, you know where the exit doors are. But not everybody sees it the same. Do you know anything about Epstein-Barr?"

"No."

"It makes you tired, right?" She stretched her arms across the bar and, turning to face John, settled back down on them.

"Does he talk much about his daughter?"

"Who?"

"Freddy."

"Freddy? Freddy has a daughter?"

"She's dead."

"I didn't know he had a daughter. When?"

"She's dead."

"Really. I don't think anybody knows that. She's dead?"

"She was killed by a drunk driver."

"I didn't even know he was married. He's just got this little apartment. It's nice, but little. Does he have a house, too?"

"He's divorced."

"God, Mia is going to be forced into some serious revamping over this one. He's divorced? He's fucking divorced? I mean, I don't think the guys at his table even know about this shit, I really don't, because we know what they know, pretty much. Mia is going to go into orbit. What else do you know?"

He thought about her question but could find no quick answer.

"And his daughter was killed?" Maggie asked.

"Eight years ago."

"Eight years ago? God, I was in high school. Or was I? No, I hadn't even started. I was in middle school."

The music turned weirdly devotional. Mia, after discarding the chiffon, was strips of lace and silk interrupted by skin, her body shifting, a white liquid dripping down her shoulders in these spiraling streaks emitted from her hands in which she clutched paint tubes. The chords of the music were like animal prayers in a cave. Then it was spaceships. White paint was tracking her back, like whipmarks, dripping white blood. The witch was talking. It sounded like she said, "Innocent." It sounded like she said, "Devotion." John felt incredibly sad.

Mia fell to the floor, she posed and writhed, her head thrown back, all underwear and paint. She rolled onto her stomach and lay there, her feet pointing off behind her. The rest of her progressed through a series of curves, her calves and thighs and butt cheeks and spine flowing into her arms pointed out in front of her like she was diving somewhere.

I'm like that, said Emily. *Flying. Alone.*

"What the fuck is going on here?" yelled a swirling bulk in the corner. The lights went on and the music shut down, and they were all staring at the guy who had been sleeping in the booth before. It was daylight again, and the guy was upright. With nothing to accompany her except traffic sounds, Mia was grabbing her white chiffon and her robe.

"That's paint! She's getting paint all over the goddamn floor! *Sunny!*" the big guy roared at the pock-faced guy doing the book-keeping at the table.

"Sunny, it's water-soluble paint," yelled Mia.

At his table, Sunny looked interested but noncommittal. He chomped, and the cigar jumped around in his mouth.

"Who the hell is going to clean this up?" said the big guy, rushing onto the stage like he was going to knock her down.

"Come on, Joe," said Mia, "I've been rehearsing this for a week."

"Look at this mess!" He was stomping around on the stains, kicking at them.

"It's water-soluble paint, Joe. It washes right off."

"She's an artist, Joe," said Sunny. He was standing up from the table with the ledger tucked under his arm.

"She's an artist? Give me a fucking break," said Joe. "I have been to the museum. Right, right," he snarled at Mia, crowding her face with his huge head. "You're a regular Vincent van Gogh and fuck-yourself artist. Get off the dance floor."

Mia slipped past him to the stage apron, her hand slanted to shade her eyes like she was still blinded by stage lights. "Sir," she said, covering herself with her scarf. "Sir. Excuse me, sir, but you've been here a few minutes. You think it's erotic, don't you?"

Joe lumbered up to her side and bent at the waist, his hands on his knees like his stomach hurt.

"Sir!" said Mia.

"They're talkin' to you," said Maggie to John.

"Who are you?" said Joe. "What are you doing here anyway? We ain't open! Who is this guy? Does anybody know this guy?"

"Let him speak, Joe," said Mia. "He can be an objective witness. Why can't he? Is it erotic, sir?"

"All right," said Joe. "I'd like to know his opinion. I certainly know mine! Would you give us your opinion? Is this bullshit erotic?"

"Yes," said John. "It's erotic."

"Who are you?" said Joe.

John was approaching and when he was close, he looked up at the two of them. "I'm nobody," he said.

"Listen to this fucking guy!" said Joe. He jumped down, lost his balance, stepped to correct himself, said, "Fuck!" and started pushing at John. "Get out! We're closed. Hey, why don't you do yourself a favor, go home, get a gun, put it in your mouth and pull the trigger. Relieve some of the pressure."

"It's erotic," said John.

"Just keep walking," said Joe. And then he came to an abrupt halt and scanned the room, his gaze growing disappointed as it bounced around from Maggie to Sunny to Mia to some thin guy in a red T-shirt who had emerged from backstage. "What? Am I alone in this?"

Momentum kept John on a course to the bar, where his sunglasses lay and the bartender waited, her chin in her palm.

"What was that group? The music?" he said. "Do you know?"

"Enigma," she told him.

Joe all but jumped onto the bar to jam his head between them. "Hey, you working for me here, Maggie, or the *Daily Gazette*?"

"I'm going," said John, marching for the door. He was sick of Freddy's hangout.

"I know that," said Joe.

None of them even know I exist, said Emily. *Isn't that weird? He never came here when I was alive. He never came here until you killed me. Then he started. Looking for me here, somehow. Trying to find me here. In this place.*

"He seemed like a nice guy," said Maggie.

"Go fill some ketchup bottles."

When John came out onto the street, it was still day. The streets and buildings were distinct in the light, but the rooftops probed a sky that was growing metallic, its colors dulling with the coming night. He wanted nothing more to do with Freddy's life. He felt almost as if he had been hypnotized, and now he was waking up. Told to do things and so he'd done them. Now he wanted to do something else, be somewhere different. Before he had felt a kind of nostalgia for Freddy, a form of empathy or identification, but now he wanted only to break free. He'd just sat in Freddy's bar, Freddy's hangout, talking to Freddy's friends, and watching Freddy's girlfriend take off her clothes. He'd tried to be Freddy, sort of, imagining Freddy sitting where he sat, conjuring up images of Freddy fucking the girl, and now he wanted to be himself.

At the corner pay phone, he dialed Jo Jo's number. That was what he needed, another night with her. Maybe a movie. Something simple. And if he was at her place, Freddy would never find him. He scanned the crowd around him in a hurried hunt for Freddy's face.

The ringing phone roused nothing with its first three tries, and then it summoned up her voice: "Hi, this is Jo Jo. I'm not in right now, but you can leave me a message at the beep. If you need to reach me, I've gone to Big Sur for a couple days. Something spur of the moment. An old friend. If the feeling's strong, I can be reached at 409-555-9085."

John crossed to the bus stop on the opposite corner, and then he had a hunch, and he went back to the phone and dialed Peter's number. "Hi," said Peter's machine. "This is Peter, or what was once Peter, and is now his recorded voice. I'm out of town for the weekend. I mean, till the weekend. Through the weekend. But I can be reached in regard to earthshaking matters at 409-555-9085. And remember. I was born a cowboy."

When the bus came, John got on. He watched the urban life stream by like crushed bugs on the glass, and thought how he had conspired against himself to bring this about, treating her the way he had last night. Then he'd run around after Freddy instead of getting ahold of her and apologizing, or at least letting her know that he wanted to see her. No, no, of course not. He hadn't felt like doing that until it was too late, until the hypnotist's spell had been lifted, and his option of Jo Jo, a possible refuge, had been removed. It struck him as apt, actually, as the way things ought to be.

It's very apt, said Emily. *It's what I want.*

He'd be home tonight where he belonged, where Freddy could find him if he wanted. Unless Freddy was off banging that Mia and talking about art and blow jobs and having a good time. John laughed. What an asshole he was. Ridiculous. Was this what he wanted, being alone like this? He'd sentenced himself to isolation. Just like he had for the last eight years. Offending her, hurting her, driving her off. Screwing things up just like he did in his car eight years ago. Maybe you knew what you wanted by what you had.

Dusk was speeding toward night, and his parents' car was gone from the front driveway when he got home. He let himself into the empty house and drank a beer while reading the note they'd left. They'd gone out to dinner with another retired couple and they were going to go to a movie. John watched the evening news, while night came on in a rush. The glow of the TV blinded him to the scope of the dark raining down.

By the time his parents came home, he was in bed in the trailer, the bedside light burning. He heard them inside for a while, banging around. Then the kitchen lights went out, followed minutes later by the glow from their bedroom window. He stubbed out his cigarette and picked up the phone, intending to get the number from Jo Jo's machine so he could call her even if Peter was there. So he could tell her what he thought. What he wished he'd done. Or maybe tell her nothing. Just sit there on the phone. An anonymous caller. But at least fucking interrupt them. He'd barely started to dial when he froze and hung up, realizing it wasn't her he wanted.

No, said Emily. *It's me.*

He turned out the lamp and lay in the dark, listening to Emily. Listening closely, simply, openly, to all she had to say, his eyes shutting and staying shut until he heard a muffled snapping noise from outside and he knew something was there looking in the window. Freddy Gale? No, no, he thought. He wasn't coming. He wasn't that nuts. It was a dog, or a bird. Or a cat. John closed his eyes, drawing air in and letting it out, trying to tranquilize himself with a calming rhythm in order to sleep.

Good night, she said, and he thought he saw her.

He bolted up, grabbing the walls. He was in flight, even though he sat there, his breath coming in huge ungovernable gulps. His ears hummed and his skin tingled. He put his hands over his mouth and jumped from the bed and started moving around the trailer. He had to stop. He squatted against the far corner, perspiration dripping into his eyes. Whatever was outside his window was going to get him. He leaped and jerked back the curtain and saw the huge shaggy shoulder of a wavering tree.

He fell onto his bed, the hot jets of adrenaline ebbing, and with their departure he was feeling heavy and stuporous. He was overwhelmingly tired. Drained. Exhausted. Now nothing could keep him awake.

There, said Emily. *See? Everything's all right.*

29

∎ ∎ ∎ ∎ ∎ ∎ ∎

"You want to know why? Why do I keep my hand in my pocket? Because I'm warming your lunch, Dick Breath," said Sunny.

The audience made a loud barking noise. Sunny was doing his MC schtick under lights so red his face was burned away. Freddy scanned the distorted mouths around him. They thought they were laughing, tongues and teeth gnawing the air, gums and spit everywhere.

"We have another one of our regulars comin' up," Sunny announced, looking like he had bitten into something with a terrible taste. "Ina! Ina was Miss America in 1912. Oh, you lonely fucks!" he shouted. "You stupid, stupid fucks."

Freddy laughed. He liked that. He was a visitor, a mocking observer gathering evidence about the odd lives lived here, one of which used to be his own.

"The truth is," Sunny groaned, "I like ugly strippers, saggy tits, the whole thing. It's a show of courage. Let's hope you're a group with a stomach for courage!"

The bubbly sound to Freddy's right was the word "Exactly" being passed from one mouth to another on the nodding heads of Coop and Silas and the rest of them at the table, as if Sunny had just let them in on a rare kernel of wisdom.

"Oh, fuck this bullshit," said Sunny. "I'm just jerking you jerkoffs around. The truth is I like 'em young and firm and totally strange. So it's time to get on to my very own fucking favorite moment of every evening here! How and why we deserve our name! The Calypso Club!" Sunny shouted. He made a gesture with his right arm like he was throwing away something disgusting that he didn't want the wind blowing back in his face.

The loudspeakers boomed with a calypso beat, and dancers, feathered and fruity as a bunch of birds and bananas, stormed the stage. Sunny looked grief-stricken as he fled. It was a brief expression, and you had to be watching closely to see it. Freddy was riveted, wondering if Sunny, like himself, had some hidden misery about to be laid open. Arriving at the table, Sunny did nothing with the drink he had left earlier except sip it and then shove it aside. Freddy leaned in so that he would not miss any clues, especially those accidentally exposed. "This is what I hate, this fuckin' thing," said Sunny. "I've timed it. It takes them five full minutes to show tit by the time they get all that flash off 'em, and in the meantime we got to listen to this. What is this music? What's it for? I hate this fuckin' number."

"Can I tell you something about this garbage?" said Coop to Sunny.

"What?"

"Why do you have it?"

"I know. It sucks."

"I like it," said Freddy. "I like it. It's called tradition—without tradition, new things die." He smiled, waiting for their confusion to solidify into a single state from which they would all stare, like dogs, needing his explanation.

"That's good, that's good," said Coop.

"What'd he say?"

" 'New things die.' That's what he said. I'm tellin' you, this sonofabitch is a poet. A jeweler-poet. The only goddamn jeweler-poet I ever saw," said Sunny.

"A Jew-jeweler-poet," said Coop.

Freddy was stroking his own cock. He could feel it through the smooth weave of his trousers. Using the ends of the tablecloth to conceal what he was doing, he wedged his hand inside his trousers. He fought through the elastic of his underwear and found the skin, the fleshy stirring lump of nerves, waking up like some brainless thing looking for food. He imagined a woman. He didn't know who she was. But he wanted her.

"No, no, no. Let me tell you the problem with this crapola," said Silas. "This is the fucking finale. Don't you understand? This is the last thing we see. From this we go home. It oughta make us feel happy instead of that we have been invaded by Mars."

For a second, they all contemplated the hubbub of feathers, the bird calls and spasmodic wavering on the stage. It looked like a rainbow being ripped apart.

"I don't like it," said Coop. "You wanna do this multicultural shit—do it early—do it in the daylight."

That sent them all into fits of snorts and giggles. Freddy downed his drink while the rest of them kept on reeling, and then he put his hand on Coop's shoulder and he said, "I'm gonna kill a guy."

"You're what now?" said Silas.

Coop was squinting at him, trying to anticipate the punchline he didn't want to get duped by. "What?" he said. "What, Freddy?"

Freddy x-rayed them with his eyes, his mouth smiling like his teeth were burning. "Nothing," he said.

"He said he's gonna kill a guy. Who you gonna kill?" said Silas.

"I missed something. What are we talking about?" Manny asked.

"Maybe if you guys shut up for two seconds, Freddy could talk," said Sunny.

A "shhhh" was passed around the table, and when it completed the trip, ending with Buddy, he said, "What are we doing?"

"I think maybe the way he told us about his vacuum cleaner, he is now going to maybe tell us about a washing machine," said Coop. "Right, Freddy?"

"Right, Coop," said Freddy, and then he told them, "You fellas are something, but I have to hit the road. I changed my mind. I agree with Coop. I hate this fuckin' number. I don't want to go into the night with this shit polluting my brain."

He was on his feet by the time he finished, and he just kept on going. They were talking behind him, relying on their bush league scorn to tame what they sensed in the moment, to worm their way out of the dark conspiracy of murder he had invited them into.

Their words were the loud grunts, the banter of some subgroup he was leaving. He had his hand on his dick, and he was glad for the tingle. It was good to have a friend, at least one in this world, because his last memory of them was of piles of shit rotting around a table.

When he pushed open the door to the girls' dressing room, he started looking for a woman to take home with him. Peeking over the wood partition into their lair, he saw Verna with a phone to her ear stationed at her makeup table. Mia and two other beautiful girls, all of them seminude, sat in a row at matching makeup chairs sorting their outfits and lipstick and chatting.

"Did Kerry brush your teeth?" Verna was saying. "That's my good little Angie that you let her. Good for you."

"Chiffon, I think, is emotional," said Mia. "Red is spiritual." She was packing some paperback books. "Hi, Freddy."

They all looked over, but Mia, perhaps because she was the first to spy him, was excited. She clapped her hands soundlessly, like a child watching the arrival of her birthday cake.

"Aladdin is handsome, isn't he?" said Verna to her daughter on the phone. She waved at Freddy and her eyes skipped from him to Mia, as she scrambled to decode what was happening. "I gotta go, honey," she said, racing to understand whether events were headed in a direction good for her or not. "Yes! Okay, sweetie, you be good and let Kerry put you to bed. Okay? I love you—I gotta talk to Kerry now."

"Ladies," said Freddy. "Who wants to get off early this fine night?"

"Who are you talking to, Freddy?" said Mia, rising and pulling on a pair of jeans.

"Guess."

Mia giggled and Verna snatched an alarm clock from the makeup table. Time seemed a crucial factor for her, as she said into the phone, "Can I talk to Kerry, honey, please! Night-night, honey. Please!" She was glaring like the silk blouse Mia was throwing on belonged to Verna and it was being stolen right before her eyes. "I've only got one more show, Freddy," she told him.

"I'm off," said Mia.

"Kerry, honey?" Verna almost shouted into the phone. "Something just came up. Is it possible for you to stay overnight?"

She was such a slut, thought Freddy. He wanted to reprimand her. He wanted to take her aside and assail her with an inspirational harangue, then send her home to her daughter. Instead, he simply reached his hand toward Mia.

"Let's party," said Mia.

Verna's disappointment was as naked as much of the rest of her. She hung up the phone, and watched Mia gather her bags, a black leather one slung over her shoulder, and then a red suede satchel. Freddy raced her to the laptop electrical keyboard in its carrying case, snatching it up.

"Anything else?" He grinned, putting his nose right against hers.

"Whore," said Verna, as if she was saying good night.

Freddy threw a disapproving scowl over his shoulder. Mia waved until they were gone.

They left through the stage door, and the outlaw mood of the alley made the cracked concrete and walls of brick into a perverse primordial place. He put his hand between Mia's legs, cradling her crotch the way he'd seen her hold herself somewhere, sometime, and then he leaned into her so she had to scramble backwards. She staggered, prancing, and preoccupied with her desire to hang on to her bags. When she collided with the bricks, she emitted a soft "Oooofff . . . !" and he put his mouth to hers, entering her effort to breathe with his tongue. "Mmmmmm," she said.

Reluctant to hear her, he trapped her tongue so she couldn't speak, pressing it as it squirmed.

"Don' 'rop ma 'ey'or'!" she said.

No, he thought. I won't drop your keyboard. And as he raised his free hand to her breast, he was thinking about Verna, poor left-behind Verna, and he wanted to make sure she was hurt. He wanted to inflict irreparable damage on Verna by kissing Mia. The wall against which he had her pinioned was fuzzed with music, the bricks emitting what they were built to contain. He could hear the Cranberries singing "Linger." He kissed Mia harder, needing to do Verna serious harm so she would go home to her kid. He could see the eyes of the crowd inside, and the object of their attention was Verna in a mirror behind a tinseled curtain, poised to perform, her eyes dripping tears she wiped like a child struggling to accept a hard lesson. Then, with the music turning dictatorial, she started to dance, but no one cared. Everybody was jabbering and distracted. Sunny was feeding the fish in the fish tank, and you could see Verna through the bowl, dancing past the fish; but Sunny didn't even look, and Freddy pulled back and released Mia. He set off down the street, tugging her along by the hand.

"How old are you?" she said.

Now Verna was packing up, putting her clothes in a bag, and she was glad to be done for the night, because she was going home to her little apartment where her daughter slept.

Mia started skipping along the street. Freddy didn't want to let her get too far ahead, but he wasn't going to run. In the elevator, she faced into the corner and would not look at him except to peek provocatively over her shoulder. In the hallway, she took off her blouse. In his apartment, while he paused to put the gun on a chair by the door, she dove into his bed. She unhooked her bra. She unbuttoned his shirt, and jumped up on the bed and stood over him unzipping her jeans. He pulled off his shirt, looking up to see her bra fall past him. He grabbed her legs, which seemed heartbreakingly perishable, and he kissed her thighs, the sides and back of her knees. When she took his head between her hands and held it, he looked up.

"I mean, I really want to fuck you, Freddy, but I want to read you something first. Can I read you something? And I want to play you a song!"

His desire for her made him prone to grant her anything she wished, even when he didn't know what it was, and she was already off the bed, anyway. She was over by her bags, bending and unzipping and reaching into one. She stood up with a paperback book. Very carefully, she opened the pages to a playing card used for a marker and she read, " 'Mark was so loving in bed, so how could it have been so bad? I just didn't get it. He was never brutal, he was rarely insensitive, and it was never a quickie. I simply couldn't believe that someone who could be so wonderful and so giving in bed could be so appalling outside. I think if we could have just stayed in bed all the time everything would have been fine.' " She shut the covers between her palms and he knew she was studying him, though her eyes were obscured. Her expectation was palpable. "Does that sound familiar, Freddy?"

"What?" he said, laying there. He wished he knew what to answer, as she approached and knelt down, lowering her head until her eyes aligned with his.

"I know everything, Freddy."

"What?"

"Someone came and told us. I know everything. I know your sorrows. Someone told Maggie and Maggie told me."

She was so earnest that it didn't matter that he had no idea what she was talking about. He started trying to bring her to the bed, because he wanted her closer.

"I wrote a song for you, Freddy. I want to play it."

"No," he said, trying to draw her toward him.

"Please."

Maybe it's pretty, said Emily. *I'd like to hear it.*

He couldn't deny her; it wasn't possible.

"Okay. But hurry."

"It's for us, a song for Mia and Freddy." She was pulling out struts and popping up little lids. The keyboard materialized next to the bed. It stood with white and black keys on spidery legs, emitting a few eager chirps as she fiddled with dials. Then she flicked a switch, and multicolored lights sent their reflections bubbling through the air. The introduction was romantic and simple, and he waited, listening. Then she started to sing. He heard his name and her name. He heard the word "sorrows," and he reached out and stroked her thigh, and eased his fingers into her.

Mmmmmmmmmm, said Emily. *It's a pretty song, I think. I'm glad we let her play it.*

"It's pretty," he said. "We like it." He wasn't sure she actually heard him, because she didn't answer. Not that he was surprised, given the world she was in, the chords she had to manipulate, the lyrics she had to remember, while his fingers intrigued and coaxed her.

"One thing at a time, okay, Freddy?" she said and moved his hand away.

"Just promise me you won't put me to sleep. I've got business tonight." The kaleidoscopic lights took over the room and left him trying to figure out where he was from the bottom of a deep space like a swimming pool, while the departing world flickered above.

Emily said, *Don't worry. I'll wake you. Don't worry. It's a pretty song. And she's sweet. And she really likes you. She's silly, I think. Maybe stupid. I don't know. But sweet. She's goofy. But a lot like me. You're right about that. A lot like I would have been if I had reached her age without ever growing up.*

With the lights still pulsing through the room, Mia was on him, kissing his belly, licking his dick so he groaned. As she wheeled and parked her crotch over his face, he kissed her, lovingly. Ahhhhhhh, he thought. Ahhhhhhh. It was more than he bargained for. But what had he bargained for?

Don't worry, Dad. We'll get there. You couldn't stop if you wanted to, anyway, could you, you crazy man, my wild wild dear dear Daddy. You just go ahead. I'll see that we do what we have to. He'll be in his bed. Just like last time. But that will be the only resemblance. We're different now. The both of us! You can't live without me. We'll find him on his back asleep in that trailer. Why wouldn't he? I mean, he thinks we're fools and he's free. Like a breeze through the window, we'll enter. A ghost with a gun. Our heart removed. Cut from my chest. Dead in the road. But our soul will face him. Poor John. What do you think he will think? With a bullet in his brain. How will he feel? Not so good, I bet. Not as good as you. Wouldn't you like to know? As the skin rips apart and we rush in, roaring like wild bears, like lions, like demons, what do you think he will feel? Or know?

30

■ ■ ■ ■ ■ ■ ■

So you're there, John, and you're sound asleep. Dreaming? I doubt it. Unless, of course, you're dreaming of me. But asleep in your bed. Dead to the world. Out like a light. How stupid, John! Were you tired? With your life about to end! A nap! Or is it maybe what you want! You can just forget about everything—all of it—but especially her. Just like I had to forget about my dresses and brothers and classes and dolls, all my silly dreams. No more touching for you, John. No more honey hair. No more tasting that softness. Because you'll be gone. Without a word. Remember how cold you were, and mean? Where is she now? And when you called, what did you think you were going to say? You didn't even leave a message, did you? Were you going to apologize? Well you didn't, did you? Said nothing! Hung up! So you'll take your apology to your grave. Daddy's gun in your ear, his shadow in your room. The hammer driving the firing pin, as small as a needle. It sinks into the rim of the cartridge which explodes—you'll hear it. Thunder? you'll guess. The bullet launched like a locomotive down a tunnel straight to your brain. Will you feel your skin rip? What will your mashed skull sound like? Bones give way like crumbling stone, the walls of your life shown up for the bullshit they have always been, all your doors kicked open, so anything can get in. Feel that cold metal in your ear? Better wake up, John. Run, if you can. Who's in the hall-

way? Who's in the yard? Who's stealing up to your door? Is it Daddy? Or just the blackest thought you ever had? Who is it? Mr Death, John? No, no. Don't worry. It's just me. Little Emily. That's all. Hello, I'm here.

John sprang from bed. Without dressing, he stepped into the yard, ducking as he crossed to the house. If fucking Freddy Gale was coming, he'd just missed his best chance. In the kitchen, John went straight to the basement door and fled down the stairs. He knew where the cabinet with the guns stood against the wall. He knew that the old rubber boots in the corner contained the key to the padlock. In seconds the cabinet door swung open. The weapons stood in a row, the two rifles beside the pair of shotguns. The smell of oil and metal hit him like a stimulant, sharpening his senses. The four metal barrels were inset into stained wood. He thought things over, reviewing the likelihood of close quarters, the need for quick reactions. He reached for the pump twelve gauge. Three boxes of shotgun shells were stacked in the left-hand corner of the shelf, two opened, one brand new. He grabbed the fresh one and undid the flaps on the lid. He opened the breech and looked down the barrel, aiming at the light bulb in the ceiling where he saw a circle of light. Then he started loading in the shells.

Really, John, do you think that will help you? Do you?

One, two, three, he counted. I'm not letting it happen. I'm not going to just lay there and let it fucking happen. He pumped a round into the chamber and went up to the kitchen, where he turned on the faucet. He cupped water in his hands and soaked his face.

31

■ ■ ■ ■ ■ ■ ■

He's ready, Dad, said Emily. *He's ready now.*

Freddy's heart was starving. Nothing could get in and the tissues were dying, blood lapping at the valves as panic turned it wild. In a fit of abnormal rhythms, the ventricular muscle thickened, because growing bigger would help it beat faster. But to do so it needed more air, and so it beat harder, blustering and bloating, overgrown and more and more impoverished, until his pulses short-circuited, rocketing him toward a distant dark point where he died.

Mia was unconscious and snoring. Freddy untangled himself, and she managed only a grunt of protest against the way he moved her limbs around, and then she swooned happily back to sleep. How could she just lay there? he thought, looking at her and picking up the gun. She wouldn't be so calm if she woke up to this, he told himself, setting the barrel directly over her head. And when he thought of his finger on the trigger, and then of his finger pulling the trigger, he remembered a dream. Ohhh! He gasped. Why would he dream that? It was true that he'd been late. That he was supposed to pick her up and he was late. But why would he dream that? It was wrong. It was insane, though its appalling claims seemed to convey a slowly emerging truth. But it couldn't have happened that way. Or did it? Suddenly, he felt that what he was facing was a set of facts that he had denied, and now they were arising before him with a shocking authority. Except they couldn't be true. Somebody had to tell him. Somebody had to help him. Somebody who knew. It was Mary he needed. Mary, his wife.

He was in the bathroom, hugging the phone to his chest, as he leaned into a slant of moonlight to jab the number that he knew by heart. He closed the bathroom door so Mia wouldn't overhear and he waited and prayed for Mary to answer.

"Hello . . . ?" she said, sounding afraid.

"Mary? It's Freddy."

"Freddy? Freddy, what are you—?"

"Mary, please don't hang up. Please. I need . . . to . . . ask you." He laughed. It was strange to laugh, but he did it because she always liked a joke. But then something else started to happen to him, something awful. "I'm fallin' apart here, Mary," he said. "Oh, Lord, oh, God." The awful thing kept happening and he couldn't stop it. "I had this fucking dream. It's sunny outside, I'm driving my car, and my car feels big. It feels like it's driving me. And I'm passing Em's old school, the elementary school. And there's a crosswalk. All these little kids are being taken across the street by this crossing guard, and the crossing guard is John Booth. He's showing them the way. And Em is one of the little girls he's taking across the street. I'm getting closer and closer and I'm hitting my brakes and they're not slowing the car at all, and the wheel won't turn . . . And I . . . I just plow straight through them. I see Em's face just before I hit her, that sweet, innocent face. Mary, I don't know what to do."

"Oh, Freddy," she was saying. "Freddy, don't cry. Please. Oh, Freddy."

Was he crying? It didn't felt like crying. It felt like being eaten alive. This was how he was going to die, with his heart shutting down and his father's face replacing his own. His eyes spewing out of his head like puke. Beating his chest like an ape.

"Freddy, please, okay," she said, sounding so sad, so concerned. "It's all right."

"No."

"Shhhhhh."

She was right there with him. Beside him in the dark. Like she used to be. "I just want to see you. Can I see you? I just want to see you, Mary." Maybe she'd like him better if he made a joke. That was a thought. She always liked jokes, especially in tough situations. "You're real, right?" he said. "Mary. I'm real. We used to be real. I just want to see you. Okay."

"Now?"

"Please." He was making so much noise trying to breathe that he wasn't sure he heard her, but it sounded like she'd agreed. "What?"

"All right, Freddy."

"You will? You will—yes? You're saying yes?"

"Izzy's Diner. Could you come there?"

"Anywhere. Anywhere."

"It's open all night. And it's sort of halfway."

"I can be there in fifteen minutes, okay?"

"I'll need a half hour. I have to get dressed."

"That's okay. Sure. Half an hour is okay. I'll see you there in half an hour."

"All right."

"Thank you, Mary. Thank you."

He was so excited. It was like the first time she had said yes to a date with him. He felt such an incredible buoyancy, such a surge of optimism. Just like all the other times that Mary had made him feel good. It had been way back in high school, but he could see it so clearly, the pay phone he'd paced around, a senior finally getting up the nerve to call this amazing sophomore, who almost instantly agreed to go to a movie with him, and after a while she'd fallen in love with him. The miracle at the moment was that it was happening again.

Mary parked her Tiempo in a single graceful swerve up from the traffic into the first space in the diner's mostly empty lot. Freddy, in the process of lighting a new cigarette with the stub of a butt, ground them both out on the pavement and ran to open the car door for her. She was out before he could get there. Her narrow glance appraised him with a wariness that made him nervous about the gun in his belt.

"I almost forgot where this place was," said Mary.

"You're right on time."

"Good."

"Listen, go on inside. I just gotta get something from my car."

"Okay."

It was a small, unimportant lie, because it was the right thing to do, he reassured himself, hurrying to put the Glock in the glove compartment.

No one occupied the booths, and only a few scattered customers sat on the stools along the counter. Mary, dressed in beige slacks and a sweater under a light raincoat she had unbuttoned but not taken off, was waiting for him in a booth against the windows opening onto Wilshire Boulevard. As Freddy settled across from her, he took a deep breath and blinked, sighing with bewilderment.

"Oh, Freddy," said Mary. "Poor Freddy." She added a little sigh of her own. "What a mess it's all become."

He smiled and shook his head, mostly out of amazement that they were together like this. A sense of irony threw itself over his mind, as he considered the enormous task awaiting him if he were to say all that needed to be said. Yet he understood that no matter how imposing it all might be, the only way through it was to begin. He managed another smile, this time acknowledging his inadequacy, at the same time that he vowed a sincere effort to try. "Mary, I—"

"No, Freddy. Let me talk." She raised her hand, like an official whose authority was larger than his. "I've been so angry at you for so goddamn long. Too angry to hear you, or see you, or care about you. But when you left the house the other day, I did see you. For the first time since Emily was killed. I can see that you are a good man, and you loved her so much. But I loved her, too, Freddy. And I needed you so badly when . . ."

She stopped. Her thoughtful silence suggested a task more complicated than a search for the right word. He wondered what she was thinking. Not knowing made him nervous. He wanted to speak, and yet he hesitated, fearing he might appear rude.

"You remember?" said Mary. "We were coming back home from Las Vegas, and the wind, God, the plane was bouncing all over the place. I got so scared. I was shaking! Do you remember what you said? I couldn't believe how calm you were, and you took my hand, and you said—do you remember?"

Though he recalled the chaos of the plane and the feel of her fingers squeezing, just as they were now, he couldn't salvage his own words. "Tell me," he said.

"Do you remember?" said Mary.

He sensed compliments waiting for him in the memory, the details of something exemplary that he had done to please her. "Tell me."

" 'Pray we crash,' you said. 'Because then we can call ourselves survivors.' You were so . . . what?"

"I don't know," he said.

"Unshakable."

The idea of once possessing such an off-the-cuff, toughminded savvy that he could mock their peril with a joke that remained in her memory after all these years gratified him, and made him beam at her, as if he had regained that heroic stature.

"Where did that guy go?" she asked him. "Emmy died, and this terrible anger. It made you so small. Weak. I needed you to be big and strong and I hated you for your weakness. I hated you. Now tonight, I'm pitying you, Freddy. I'm pitying you. I don't know how to help you, Freddy."

She tightened her hold on him. Their intertwined fingers confused him, because she was touching him tenderly, though he felt that something had pierced him like a needle, jetting a chilling chemical. He didn't understand, but he wanted to hang on to her, and he laughed, trying to tough it out, trying to be savvy. "Look around. Look at the marriages people have. We had a good one, didn't we?"

"Yes, we did."

"Good times."

"Very good."

"No hidden agendas, none of the nasty bullshit. We were hot for each other."

"It was a wonderful time."

"You tell me if my memory is distorted here."

"No."

And then the icy sensation inside him revealed what it was. From the cold vaporous breath she had fed into him to covertly spread its poisons, a word emerged. Pity. She pitied him. That was the sly needle, like a witch's insertion. "You pity me?" he said. "You pity me? Is that what you said?"

"What?" she squeezed his hand.

"Whadya mean, 'what'? 'Freddy, I'm pitying you.' Oh boy!" His contempt was like vomit slopping from his mouth all over the table, and she didn't like it.

"Freddy, whatever you're doing, stop it," she said.

He couldn't stop it, and he didn't want to. " 'Freddy, whatever you're doing, stop it,' " he mimicked her, belittling her voice with a witchy imitation, laughing at her inability to damage him, no matter how she might try. The way she averted her eyes, grabbing her purse to rise, it was as if his face had sprouted sores. But he wasn't going to let her go now that everything was just starting to go his way. He wanted his turn on top, and he caught her by the wrist, snaring her so she fell back. Pinning her to the seat with the rage in his eyes, he released his grip and said, "I hope you die. I hope you fucking die!"

While her curse had failed in its underhanded cunning and sabotage, his was a total success. He blinked and she was gone.

32

∎∎∎∎∎∎∎

By the time Freddy shot up the freeway entrance ramp, he had the radio blaring. It was some deranged group and he was yelling along, as he reached to the glove compartment and brought out the Glock just in case it wanted to sing, too. He gave it a conspiratorial squint, and a pat, like the chill steel contained the brains of a wild beast whose soul was pledged to him. By now the music struck him as annoying, so he snapped it off. The clatter of the glove compartment door, which he'd left open, was even more annoying. He scowled at it. Then the high beam prodding of some asshole who had just drifted in behind him started to really piss him off. He slammed the glove compartment shut, but the stupid fucking thing flopped open. He flung it up again. The assault in the rearview mirror was so bright it looked like the back seat of his car was on fire. What did this jerkoff have in mind back there? If he had a fucking mind. The glove compartment rattled. He swatted it and it caught. He honked the horn. Hadn't this dickhead ever heard of low beams? It was like a pair of searchlights behind him, these huge violent orbs obliterating the shape of the car pursuing him. He hit a bump, and the glove compartment sprang loose. "Shit!" He leaned all the way over and punched it, then jammed on the brakes, thinking, Take that, fuckhead. He hit the gas, speeding away.

The red gumball light of a police car swelled through the flaring headlights. Like burning gas, the scarlet emissions wiped everything from view. The short siren burst jolted him, and his heart disappeared.

"Pull over to the right! Pull over to the right!" said a voice, superhuman with its P.A. amplification. The command drilled into the back of his head. He looked at the gun on the seat beside him.

Be careful, said Emily.

"I know." He braked to a cautious halt on the freeway shoulder.

Now he could see the patrol car in the rearview mirror, the headlights dimming as the car inhaled them. The gumball cast a bloody web over him. What the hell was he supposed to do? he thought, looking down at the gun. It seemed to await his instruction. It had no plans of its own. But anything he wanted was fine. Though a goddamn shoot-out on the highway was not what he wanted. At least not until after John Booth was dead.

Don't you have a permit? asked Emily.

What the hell, he thought. "Sure." He could scam this thing, he knew the tricks, the good citizen pose, the polite tone and groveling babble. He grabbed the door handle and shoved.

"Remain in your car, sir!" shouted the cop.

Lifting his hands high above his head, Freddy hunched his shoulders, like a timid hobo. "There's a gun on the seat. That's why I'm getting out. There's a gun on the seat."

"There's a gun in the car?" said the cop.

"Yeah." He peeked at the approaching cops, a burly bulging uniform, tailored and starched, in the lead, and a slighter figure trailing and flanking him. The guy in the front had a black mustache and thick hair. Keeping his hands over his head, Freddy watched the pair exchange a quick look, and he saw that the second cop was a woman.

"Step back here, sir. Step back toward me, sir," said the male, with a nod that sent his partner sliding past Freddy.

Pushing his hands a little higher, Freddy moved toward the spot indicated. He figured the woman was going to get the gun. But he would get it back. He had a permit. The permit was in order. He took tiny, deferential steps, so there could be no doubt that his intentions were cooperative and he was a good citizen.

"Okay, stop right there."

Obeying was clearly the thing to do. He searched the cop's blank expression for a clue to his attitude, but it was like trying to make sense of a rock.

"Turn around, raise your hands, and interlace your fingers behind your head. You got any more weapons on you?"

"No." He'd done all this last night on the sidewalk in front of Nicky Blair's.

Practice makes perfect, said Emily.

"I guess."

"What?" said the cop.

"Nothing. No, no."

"Spread your feet for me."

How long is this going to go on?

With his arms up in the air, elbows out, hands hugging the nape of his neck, Freddy had no idea how long this or anything else would go on. This minute. The night. His life. Cars whooshed past in both directions, the nearest lanes throwing a surge of wind over him, passengers in a gray sedan peering out at him, their heads turning to watch every second of the spectacle he was providing, as the cop patted him down from his armpits to his ankles. I'm getting good at this, thought Freddy. It was an unsavory intimacy, this stranger's touch sinking along his thigh until the cop's fingers took over Freddy's ankles like Freddy wasn't even there, and something in him started to leak rage. Fuck this, he thought.

When the cop stepped around in front of him, Freddy said, "I've got a permit for the gun."

"You got a permit for the gun?"

"Yes."

"Why do you carry the gun?"

"Because I'm a jeweler. I have a jewelry store. It's all I got. The gun is to protect what I have."

"You can put your hands down. Do you have the permit for the gun on you?"

"Yeah, it's in my wallet?"

"Is your license in there also? Give me your wallet."

"Yeah," said Freddy, reaching into his jacket pocket, as the female cop came around the car.

She gave Freddy a look, like she was asking herself a very unsettling question about him and she was anticipating a provocative answer.

Freddy hated seeing the gun in her hands. It was obvious the gun was uncomfortable. It was his gun. It could barely tolerate the touch of her fingers.

"Dennis," she said. "It's a nine millimeter auto loaded, with one in the chamber."

"Oh?" said Dennis. Whatever his opinion of Freddy had been up to this moment, the arrival of this information gave it a twist. He seemed to dislike Freddy, instantly, at the same time that he found him more interesting. Moving slowly, Freddy handed his wallet over. Freddy Gale, he thought. Who the fuck was that? Names, dates, numbers. Who cared?

"He says there's a permit for the gun in his wallet," said Dennis. He passed the wallet to the woman, but kept his eyes trained on Freddy. While the woman cop set the gun and the billfold on the trunk of the car, the male cop studied Freddy. His eyes were rifle sights, and he seemed to consider Freddy something he should have shot long ago. She removed the driver's license, credit cards, and the rest of the bullshit, dealing them out in a hand of solitaire on the sheen of the metal.

"The reason we stopped you is that you were driving erratically," said the male cop. "You been drinking tonight, sir?"

Fighting the urge to just stalk away, Freddy said, "I had a few drinks hours ago." His mini-shrug was meant to slip the hook they were trying to catch him on. The casual flip of his hand tossed the whole thing aside, every part of it, but especially them with their fucking uniforms and their attitudes.

"Blow in my hand for me," said the cop.

"What?" The request seemed a demand for an outrageous familiarity. In a very businesslike manner, the cop put his palm directly in front of Freddy's mouth. Feeling inexperienced and embarrassed, Freddy breathed, trying to pick up the cop's real intent, his private appetite.

"Harder, please," said the cop. Freddy inhaled and exhaled, his gaze questioning the cop to see if he was doing it right, and the cop drank in some night air, but gave no clue to what he thought of it. "We're going to conduct a few tests on you. I'm gonna explain them to you. I want you to perform them like I explain them."

The freeway shoulder spilled down at a steep grade to a thick patch of foliage. Lights poked through the branches and leaves, a few wedges of rooftops inset like stepping stones across a creek. "All right."

"In this first test, I want you to put your heels together, extend your arms with your index fingers out. I want you to tilt your head back and close your eyes."

He was trying to think how many drinks he'd had. He saw the sweep of the night sky. He hoped his breath smelled more of cigarettes than booze. Overhead, the transit of a jet sealed from view by smog dropped a sound like rain on another part of the planet. He imagined John Booth sequestered inside the cabin, sipping a Bloody Mary, and imagining that he could fly away with the assistance of these two cops, who were harassing Freddy, when they should be hunting John Booth down, locking him away forever, shredding him in some fucking alley, if they were interested in fucking justice.

"I want you to take your right finger and touch the tip of your nose."

Freddy felt like a clown on a tightrope, wondering about the penalty for opening his eyes. He wasn't sure he could do this. Stay upright like this. The fuzz in his head was getting heavy and threatening to pull him over backwards.

"Now, touch the tip of your nose with your left finger."

This is really bullshit, said Emily. *What the hell are they doing!*

"Okay, sir, put your hand back after you touch the tip of your nose. Okay, let's do your left finger again, touch the tip of your nose. Okay that's fine. Just put your hands down at your side now."

"Dennis," the female cop said, "the permit's good."

While Freddy was waving his arms around, giving John Booth time to jet off to places unknown, she must have been radioing in. He'd be out of here soon, and the thought was a darkness that tempted him to smile.

"The permit's good? Okay, sir, on this next test, I want you to put your right foot on this line, okay?"

The impulse to tell Dennis to go to hell was startling, and it took Freddy several seconds to escape its appeal.

"Sir?" said Dennis.

Freddy nodded. By then his foot was complying with the instructions. The foot seemed separate and far more cooperative than the rest of him. He hoped his leg knew what it was doing, as he watched it lift and then lower the shoe shape on the end of it down onto the white paint.

"On this test, sir, I want you to take ten steps down the line, walking heel to toe. In other words, sir, you take your left foot and place it so the heel is touching the toe of your right foot, and then vice versa. And I want you to count them as you go. I want you to take ten steps and turn around and take ten more back this way. Will you do that, sir?"

No, dammit! You're just letting them push us around!

"One, two, three . . ," he counted, feeling humiliated and childish, like he was playing a schoolyard game, his feet like little children marching in a line. "Five, six, seven. . . ." Like little schoolchildren walking home from school. The line wavered, appearing freshly and sloppily painted. The first steps had been so simple, he couldn't fathom the force enticing his foot into a pointless veer, and he tried to fight it. How could the road be tilting? It was obvious, his next step was destined for a spot far beyond the edge. Struggling to compensate, he lunged, momentum forcing him to scamper toward the roadway in order to keep from falling. He giggled, knowing he didn't have to see the cop to learn he'd screwed up.

"You don't have to walk back this way, sir. In our opinion, you've had too much to drink tonight."

He didn't give a shit about their opinion. *Who the hell cares!*

"Your ability to operate a motor vehicle is impaired. I want you to turn around and face the trunk of your car and put your hands behind your back."

I'm sick of this shit! I'm sick of this shit!

Freddy was struggling. He was ashamed of what was happening and the way he was giving up to them. What he needed was a minute, just a minute to think, because he had to come up with something better than just scolding himself for failing again, for fucking it all up. For somehow screwing it all up and then surrendering to these jerks. But that's what he was doing, following their orders and turning to face the trunk of the car, like a good little boy, a good little jerk, who looked down at the silver Glock lying directly below him where the cop had left it after dicking around with his wallet.

"You're under arrest for drunk driving."

He couldn't go to jail, because then John Booth would live out the night and Freddy would have to start all over again. Nobody could expect that. He heard the clink of handcuffs opening behind him. On the waxed surface of his Cadillac, the gun had an idea. *Take me!* it said. But it wasn't the gun, he understood, as he stared at it laying there. Guns couldn't talk. It was Emily. It was Emily screaming, *Take me!*

"Freeze! Stop!" shouted the female cop.

He was skidding down a dirt slide toward the trees.

"Jesus Christ! Show us in foot pursuit!" the man was calling behind him.

Limbs and shrubs reached toward him. The receding sounds of the cops had the sense of a radio signal breaking up. ". . . four nine. We are in foot pursuit! Southbound . . . viaduct . . . !"

The foliage slapped him. He had to fight through with his forearms and hands sweeping back and forth in front of him like windshield wipers. He picked his feet up high so he wouldn't trip on roots or loose stones. The scraping and slapping of leather on concrete was the pursuing cops running off the pavement into the trees.

He felt clumsy in his coat and jacket. He wasn't dressed for running. By the time he pushed aside a mass of steely shrubs and came into a clearing, he was gasping for air, the worn fall of a pathway visible under his feet. Probably a place where kids played. Snatches of stucco walls and lighted windows flashed at him through the spangle of leaves and white birch bark to his right.

The sudden appearance of a chain-link fence atop a stone wall high above halted him, his darting eyes seeking an exit. He took a chance that the concrete stairway twenty yards off in the shadows would lead to a gate, and it did. Veering into a narrow street with one-story houses on both sides, he crossed somebody's yard, then stepped into a pocket of murk and sank into it, hoping it would swallow him as he pressed against its source, the splintering wood wall of a shed. The heave of his lungs made it hard to hear anything else above their din. But he had to locate the cops. He gulped air and held it, his eyes bugging out, and then he heard them calling instructions to one another as they grew near. They were blocked from view, but their panting, along with the slap of their shoes, enabled him to trace their approach.

"I'm checking behind that shed," called Dennis.

Freddy turned to seek a way out, his elbow bumping a shape. He reached to stop it from falling. It was a rake, but he missed. Before it hit a bucket or something with a clatter, he bolted. Dennis shouted behind him, a wild bark like the cry of a surprised dog.

Freddy was huffing and groaning with every breath. His legs fired misery from his ankles to his chest. He was afraid he was going to puke. Though he admonished himself to sprint, he was lumbering. He was going to fucking die if he didn't try something other than running. His heart felt like it was trying to eat him. He knew what was coming, he could sense the way it would start, the rattle and ache in his chest turning into a thunderous burst of electrical pain filling his arm with a widening agony he could only escape by dropping dead on this stupid little street. He had to stop running. He had to get away from the cops, and he had to kill John Booth. But more than anything else, he had to stop running.

Ahead the walkway split, with one fork leading up to a small red house. He lunged toward it, wanting to get in so he could hide and rest. He just slammed into the door, grabbing the knob, and when it wouldn't open, he kicked it, and then he rammed his shoulder into it, kneeing it and pounding, like it was unreasonable in its refusal to admit him. When the wood splintered under his charge, the lock giving way, he staggered into a strange living room.

To his right, scuffling sounds led to a spill of light seeping out over the rug. He went down a corridor until he saw the back way out. He'd taken too long to get in, and made too much noise. He had to keep going and he knew it. He unbolted the door and pushed it open, and almost stepped into the tidal surf and roar of a police chopper sweeping toward him. The searchlight stripped the night from red and blue tile rooftops, silver garbage cans and grass, and a car on cinder blocks, as it plunged toward him. He shrank back.

He was retreating down the hall, wondering how far he could go, when an escalation of sounds in the living room informed him the police had arrived there.

He heard Dennis say, "Police officer, sir."

"What's going on?" asked a new male voice, the owner of the house.

Let's hide, said Emily.

There was a door just to his right. It seemed his only chance, so he took it, pressing it closed behind him. In the lightless room, he grabbed the edge of the nearest bulk and it turned out to be a dresser. He was fighting for air, yet his gasping put him in peril if they heard it. The passing chopper spilled its beacon through the window, disclosing inches from his face a painting of a dog dressed up as a clown with big blue eyes.

He could hear the cops and the homeowner, and they were moving in his direction. He started backing across the room, scrambling to figure out what to do. If they decided to search room to room, it was over. They had him. Though he still had the gun. At any second, they were going to walk in. He turned, hunting for a way out. And then he saw a child in a bed in the corner, a girl lying on the opposite side of the room. She was staring at him out of dark eyes shaded in black bangs, her chin tucked down onto a sheet pattered with clown decals.

Outside, Dennis wanted to know, "We just chased a guy with a gun in here, have you seen him?"

"A gun? In here?"

The little girl didn't move, she barely breathed. Freddy looked at the door, then back to the girl, her expression unchanging. He lifted his finger to his lips in a petition for silence with nothing to enforce it except the begging in his eyes.

In the hall just outside the door the woman cop asked, "Have you seen anybody here, sir?"

"I just heard my door bashed in—this crash, and I came out and I see you guys."

"Look," said Dennis, his voice receding as he moved away from the others. "The back door's open!"

"Aerobic time!" said the woman cop.

It sounded like they thought he'd gone that way and they were going to chase him. He couldn't believe his good fortune. But then the homeowner said, "I got kids in this house! What if he's in here?"

Freddy winced, trying to find an escape, but there wasn't any. No doors, just windows. If they were on their way, he'd never have time to climb out. With his gaze riveted on the little girl, he listened to the nearing footsteps in the hall. As he retreated into her closet, the fluff of her dresses brushed his ears. He heard the door open. He held his breath, the angle allowing him to stare at the girl.

"Honey, are you all right?" the father asked. "These policemen are looking for someone."

It took her a long time to speak. When she did, she seemed to be reading a faint lettering in the air above her. "What was the noise?"

"Did you see anyone?"

She fell silent again, her olive skin, her shimmering hair and bright eyes as immobile as the clown faces on her sheets.

"Look, sir, we gotta keep searching for this guy," said Dennis. "We'll send another officer to take a report."

"I'll tell you what happened in the morning, sweetheart," said the father. "Go back to sleep."

"You lock up now once we're gone," Dennis said.

"Lock up what? My front door's a mess. Look at it."

The bedroom door shut and a shadow fell over the girl. The muffled quality of the voices let Freddy take a breath. With his jacket sleeve, he matted sweat from his face. He peered over the hem, wondering what could have inspired her to protect him. He eased forward, approaching to thank her, and that's when he saw how her pupils were dilated and almost sightless with fear. The lids started batting as he got near. It was terror that had muted her and saved him, a nightmarish fear of the crazy man. As if he was there to harm her. As if he was one of the monsters running loose. Like John Booth. Or the guy who kidnapped little Sally Renne, the monster who slipped into the room where she and several other girls slept with adults just inches away and the monster took her off and killed her. This little girl probably even knew about Sally Renne. It was in the papers. On the cover of *People* magazine. Bob Russel Smith out on parole. That's who she thought he was.

She looks awful. She's so scared. Help her.

It felt like she was going to explode with fright, as he looked down at her. But he couldn't stop himself. He bent and kissed her brow. "Good night, sweetheart," he whispered.

Peeking into the hall, he saw the back of a man shoving furniture across the living room in order to create a barricade where Freddy had broken in. To his right, the back door was still open. Freddy sped over the carpeted corridor without a sound and dodged out the door.

At least four blocks away the chopper, with its thrashing engine and wheeling beacon, roamed about snatching shapes from the dark. He crouched, keeping close to the house as he stole off in the opposite direction.

He slunk through several backyards, then ventured to the street and the sidewalk where he tried to stride along normally. Some people were on their porches, having been drawn out by the commotion. No one paid him any particular attention. He didn't know where the hell he was, but after a few blocks, he saw a twenty-four-hour gas station, with a Stop and Shop. He went straight up to it and walked in. He bought a quart bottle of Coke, a cup of black coffee, and a pack of cigarettes. When he came out the door, pocketing his change, he paused and lit up a cigarette.

Let's take a cab, said Emily.

With the cigarette dangling from his lips, he strode to the nearby pay phone jutting out of the wall where it appeared to float in the fluorescent glow.

33

■■■■■■■

In the thicket of shrubs, John Booth lurked, the shotgun cradled in his arms. He'd been ready for hours, smoking cigarettes, grinding them out. Embarrassment swept him suddenly, and he felt ridiculous at the way he was acting like a fucking madman hiding in these suburban bushes. A shift in the breeze could alarm him, the stride of a cat or a squirrel passing unseen. He rose from the shadows. The hell with it. He was tired. He stepped toward the trailer, but then he stopped, ordering himself back into hiding. Do it, damnit! he told himself, sinking into the bushes. So you lose a night's sleep. So what. He looked to the ground and reached for a cigarette.

Without warning, a figure careened around the corner of the Booth home. At the sight of Freddy Gale trudging along the driveway, a flame of adrenaline ignited John's nerves and skin. Disheveled, his shirt tail out, Freddy staggered around, wandering from one side of the driveway to the other. Silhouetted against the house, he was a shambles, his eyes downcast. Not even looking where he was going. When he reached the back of the house where the trailer faced him, he faltered. He stood, staring at the silver gleam of the walls. He appeared to be gathering his concentration, steeling himself for the nearing task.

Watch it! Watch it! said Emily.

Freddy knew he had to be careful. He felt vague, as if exhaustion had distanced him from his body, so he could not abuse it any more. His shirt and undershirt were soaked. The label with the cleaning instructions jabbed into his neck. It was like he was fevered and abandoned in some tropical night. The trailer felt bigger than he remembered it. It seemed doorless and hard to get into, the fallen discarded body of an old-fashioned aircraft. He studied it, then stepped toward the window preparing to look in.

Get ready. Get ready.

John tensed, because he knew that once Freddy peered inside, he would spy the empty bed. Then John would have to make his move. Maybe he should make it now, before the guy took another step. But Freddy was behaving in such an odd way, it was hard to be certain what to do. He looked befuddled, just standing there like the pavement was mud and he was sinking several feet away from the window. Then, without taking another step, certainly without looking in, Freddy staggered backward. He sagged into a crouch, leaning against the wall of the house. He pressed his hands to the sides of his head. Collapsing further, he ended up on his butt, looking like he intended to rest for a long time.

C'mon. C'mon. A little depraved mind murder. Let's have a little depraved indifference to human life.

Freddy had a sour taste in his mouth. His stomach was queasy. He took a deep breath and belched. He tried for another. Bile kept bubbling up into his throat, staining the back of his mouth, just as the image of that dark-eyed child in her bed kept blackening his mind, her terror haunting him with a reprise of Emily's fear before the onrushing car. He had been late, of course, hadn't he? On that day. Busy with some fucking deal. He ought to put the gun to his own head. *A little depraved indifference to human life.* The phrase had been absent from his thoughts until he jumped into that room and saw that child's face. *A little depraved mind murder. That's our motto.*

He nodded. He agreed. She was right. He lifted the handgun from his jacket pocket. He stuck it in the front of his belt. He had to get going. He placed his hands against the concrete, and shifted his sore body onto his knees, preparing to stand up. But then he just knelt there on all fours. He didn't feel good. He felt sick. Just one more minute. He was trying to remember something. He didn't know what it was but it hurt not to know it. He was sick of not knowing it. Straining, he pushed, scrambling to get the leverage that would start him to his feet.

Let's get him! Let's go.

John sprang from the shrubs. On a wave of raw, unexamined impulse, he erupted from hiding with a rattle of bushes, a patter of feet, the tip of the shotgun barrel a jittery leaden flash he couldn't keep aligned with Freddy's jacket.

Now, now!

Freddy jumped from his reverie to find John Booth flying toward him and almost landing on top of him, a big pump action shotgun in the huge slabs of his hands.

We got him!

Freddy stared in disbelief, trying to grasp what was happening. John had a gun. Clad in faded jeans and a white tank top, he was settling into a low squat, the barrel mouth gaping at Freddy's chest. Freddy glanced away, finding nothing of interest in the grainy pavement beneath him, a sickening sense of surrender rising to steal over him.

All right. Now what!

John didn't know what to do. The guy was acting so weird. But the heft of the twelve gauge with the long barrel sticking out to keep Freddy away felt like a solid, dependable fortification that would protect him, even if he never fired. Because he was in charge now, and as long as they remained like this, he would stay in charge. The butt of the handgun jutted up from the waist of Freddy's trousers. Any move to grab it would have to occur in full view. Would he be crazy enough to try that?

Of course. If he was here, he was crazy!

Freddy was glaring at him, his bizarre expression of surprise evolving into a cynical gleam.

He thinks he's got you. That's what he thinks.

"I'm gonna tell you a good one, kid," said Freddy.

"What?"

"A good one, don't you want to hear a good one?"

"What? What?"

"I got pulled over tonight. Police, right? The whole bit. You wanna guess what they got me for? Drunk driving. That's what.

And then I run from them. So that makes me technically on the run from the law. And I got my gun. Now I'm not particularly acquainted with the law, but I'm on the run, and I'm on your property. My guess is you could shoot me and come out clean."

"What?" said John.

Killer with a car. Killer with a gun.

"So I'm gonna get my gun outa my pants here," Freddy told him with a weird, mischievous squint, as his fingers closed on the Glock's handle.

I came out of school and looked all over for you, you know. Up and down the sidewalk. I peeked around the building. Trying to see the parking lot. Maybe you were there. I looked and looked. Then I stood at the entrance waiting for a long, long time.

Freddy tugged. The gun slipped free from his belt, the weight filling his hand, and as it did, he looked directly into the shotgun barrel, anticipating the exploding candle he would get to glimpse at the pull of the trigger.

Where were you? I waited and waited.

I was in a hotel room making a deal, doing business, getting ahead, conniving with this asshole. For African earrings in leather cases, fine animal carvings in ivory and stone that you would have loved. I had a pair all picked out for you.

You were coming in your chariot, you said.

The muzzle was a ring of dark steel defining an inky hole receding to where the bullet lay concealed in its lethal nest. The socket of the barrel was lightless and black, and it made Freddy exquisitely aware of his own thoughts. The black was like the bedroom window through which he'd stared eight years ago, the night eroding under the onslaught of dawn bringing the day of her funeral, his bleak anguish unrelenting until he saw that he must not go to the cemetery that morning. At first, the idea was startling and scary, but quickly, it gained a magnetic, compelling appeal. Defiance filled him. With it came a sense of strength. It flowed from the wound where his life had been cut out of him, but the gash remained, and he wanted to keep it. Every offer of consolation, every sanctimonious touch or word or show of sympathy felt treacherous and obscene, like people were trying to remove something real from him, the last living sanguinary thing he had of her, his grief. So they could replace it with their rote formula, their trite gestures. And to put her in the ground, he wouldn't do it. He might not be able to take her in his arms, but he could refuse this ceremony with its empty offer of a grace equivalent to the blasphemy of her death.

That's right. My death. My death.

Free for several seconds, the Glock lay in his lap. But now it was coming up. Freddy's hand was moving with it, rising slowly.

Just a little at a time. And don't fire. Aim, but don't fire.

"And I figure I'm gonna try and shoot you," he said. It felt like the mass of the gun had grown enormous. His arm was quivering as he tried to align the bead and crease of the sight with John's head. John was like a pile of rocks, his legs sticking out at angles as he crouched. He hadn't budged. Only his chest moved with his breath, the protruding barrel advancing toward Freddy, its aura mesmerizing as it searched for him, targeting him like the tongue of a deadly serpent.

Wait until he fires, and then, after you're hit and sailing backward, then let him have it.

But it's a shotgun, Emily. It's a shotgun. I'll be dead.

He's going to do it. He's going to do it.

The way the automatic was trembling, John was positive the hammer would fall by accident long before Freddy ever managed to fire deliberately. Cocked the way it was, a nervous breath, a twitch, or a cough might make the gun go off. He knew he could easily be dead in the next seconds, and yet his own finger failed to draw back on the shotgun's trigger. He just kept squinting down the gleam of the barrel into this awful expression on Freddy Gale's face. He kept staring and waiting with a sense of anticipation, like something was coming and when it got there, he would know what to do.

The tiny shiver you felt like a feather through the huge machine of your car was all the impact my little death could make. Why were you going so fast? Why weren't you looking?

The flash of the metal barrel was a mesmerizing question. Behind it hovered Freddy Gale's dazed, chalky face. His skin was greenish, his eyes drugged with secrets. He looked sick and faint, but he was powerful and dangerous. John was no longer in charge. Not the way he had been. The balance had shifted. They both had guns now, the tips of the barrels separated by a few yards of thin air.

Freddy took a breath and blinked and shifted his base, as if to steady himself.

In the graveyard. In the dirt. My tiny box. There's room for you.

She wanted him, and John stood up, slowly.

Now, now.

Watching John straighten, Freddy flinched, but didn't fire. John flashed with an intense emotion and tossed the shotgun into the air. Freddy watched the weapon sail toward a soft bed of grass. It thudded bewilderingly into the dirt and into his thoughts. When he looked back, he found John moving off down the driveway.

"Hey!" said Freddy. John was picking up speed, racing toward the street. As Freddy struggled to stand up, he felt weird and deceived. He felt oddly left out and abandoned, as he trotted in the direction John had gone.

The distance spangled with the 7-Eleven where John had bought all the food the other night. The glow of the windows was a solitary outpost of festive illumination with a car pulling to a halt through the shimmer of neon and pavement.

Run!

When Freddy cleared the barrier of the siding and the front stoop, John was a faint figure more than half a block away. Oh God, he thought. No, please. John's lumbering shape dissolved in shadows, and reappeared in a spectrum of street lights. No, no, Freddy thought, watching. Please don't make me run again. I can't. But already he was doing it, his jacket flapping, his legs pumping.

He's getting away, Emily cried.

"I know, I know."

John was ephemeral, his form flickering and fantastic with the intervening space. Freddy had no idea where they were going. The sky was blank slate above the far off buildings, and the concrete was hard under the slam of his feet, sweat pouring from him almost instantly. Studying his drumming feet, and then the sidewalk ahead, Freddy tried not to think. Trees jumped past on his left, houses on his right, and every now and then a streetlight flew overhead. He jolted down from the curb to the road, then up on the other side. John departed the residential area. Freddy watched his quarry sprint across a wide boulevard, float for a second in the light of a 7-Eleven and then dodge from view between an auto supply and an electronics store.

Struggling to keep up, Freddy found himself plodding across that same boulevard John had seemed to bound. He labored alongside the 7-Eleven, glancing in at the attendant bent over a book at the counter. He entered the gap between the auto supply and the electronics stores. When he emerged from the small gully they formed, he was gagging. He could feel his heart heaving, but John was visible again. They were on a narrow street full of cracks and filmed with a dust like unmixed cement. Little clouds came up around John's feet. Freddy glanced down and saw the same residue in a faint surf around his ankles.

If you'd done what you were supposed to—if you'd just paid attention—if you'd kept your promise, been responsible—we wouldn't be here now. Where would we be? Where?

John had lengthened his lead. It seemed more than a block. When a gray mass of building swept past him, John groaned and fretted for the time it took to get to the next corner. With sweat in his eyes, he was blind to the quart beer bottle in the middle of the walk. His foot skated on the glass cylinder, and the only thing that saved him from crashing down on his ass was the way the bottle shattered beneath his weight, so he came through to the pavement and managed to recover.

He's gone. He's gone. You lost him.

John stopped. He looked back to where Freddy should be, and then he bent over, his hands on his knees, the way distance runners do on the verge of collapsing. Freddy catapulted into view so hard he was staggering and out of control. He nearly fell, trying to stop, and then he raised the handgun straight at John.

Easy, easy.

Freddy was praying he would get off a shot. But his effort to steady his aim was sabotaged by his tumultuous breathing. The gun sight streaked back and forth over John's shape at jagged angles, like maybe the idea was to X him out. He couldn't even get a half-assed alignment. His only hope was a wild shot, or maybe two or three.

Now! Now! Go ahead!

Scampering backwards like a linebacker sinking into pass coverage, John dug in his left foot and leaped off to his right.

Now! Damnit! Now!

Oh, goddamnit, thought Freddy. Goddamnit. It was too late. His pulses were razors when he tried to run. His heart was having a fit. It was malignant and hate-filled. It was corpulent with hate. Poisoned with bile. His heart was repellent and breaking. And Emily was screaming at him, but he was too exhausted to hear her anymore. Nothing except her tone. The embittered, carping, censorious nagging that even his fatigue couldn't save him from.

Damn you!

John fled down a crevice under a promontory of shadowy concrete, a freeway overpass. It was like running toward a hive of raging bees, the repetitive roaring. Cars shot back and forth in bursts of light. Freddy found a set of stairs that took him into a lightless tunnel leading to the other side. He was coughing and reeling, as he flailed down that narrow corridor echoing with his passage, a steady thunder overhead, debris underfoot, a stink of urine, broken bottles and old clothes and graffiti. Names like banners in spray paint exploded on the walls. The garish secrets and mad slogans of strangers, their grandiose visions and vows scrawled in block letters as big as bicycles. People who weren't there. People who he didn't know and who didn't know him. But they had left gaudy shouts all over the walls. Like prayers in the dirt of the catacombs, messages he would never read.

He slogged up the last two stairs on the other side, and he saw John less than thirty feet away standing at a bus stop on a well-lit city street. John was alone at the painted curb, watching an approaching bus whining and preparing to stop. It was obvious that John was waiting to get on. A bus? A fucking bus? He was getting on a bus? Freddy had to start sprinting, or he would be left behind. The doors sprang open and John jumped aboard. Freddy was almost there. He yelled. The back door spasmed, as if to shut, but then it popped back open, and he floundered on just as the bus rocked into motion. A white, blinding faintness assaulted his thoughts, so he had to flop into a seat, his head in his hands. He feared he was going to pass out for sure. Still he tried to peek, and what he saw was John standing with the driver. John was indicating Freddy and bringing out enough money to pay both fares.

What the hell is going on? said Emily.

He had no idea what was going on except that, sooner or later, he was going to shoot John. Or maybe he wasn't. Maybe he was never going to shoot him. Maybe he was just going to chase him. Do this forever. Maybe he was in some kind of hell, and in this hell he would just chase John Booth. Maybe he would never shoot him. Just chase him and chase him in hell forever. His heart was a knot of acidic fire; his stomach full of the same poison. He was sure that if he didn't just sit there quietly, he would puke.

John settled down near the driver. He leaned back against the window. The only other passengers were situated about midway between Freddy and John: a skinny, college-aged kid and a woman in a cheap coat, the two of them squabbling loudly without looking at each other.

"You don't have a cent to your name," she was saying. "I want to know what you're doing out here. I don't get how you're making any money. You're not making any money."

"Well, I have a job. Yes, I am making money! How can you say I'm not making money? If I'm paying my rent and I'm eating, I'm making money, right?" He was bespectacled and balding, the little hair he had cut very short.

"Right. Except you can't even take me out for breakfast when I come out here."

"Oh, I'm so sorry, okay? I'm so sorry I can't afford that right now. It just so happens to be that right now when you're here, I don't have money, so it becomes like this issue with you."

Freddy wanted to stop listening. He wanted to shut his eyes and steal a little rest. But he knew he didn't dare. Because John was trying to trick him and he knew it. He didn't know how, but it was close. It was going to happen. He could feel it.

It's very close, she told him.

The bus made several stops, and at each one, he scrutinized John and prepared to jump to his feet if John tried to exit. But John just sat there, like he was going to ride for a long time. Freddy wondered if he should walk up and shoot him right then and there. He tried to exude his murderous thoughts from his eyes, and the result, whether he succeeded or not, made him sad. It was strange the way the moment and its aftermath brought him back to the kid and the woman, who was obviously his mother, the two of them attaining a vivid focus.

"You're not feeding yourself," she said.

"I am too."

"No, you're not. I don't understand what you do for a living out here."

"You don't have to."

"I do have to. I do have to."

The flash and blur of the street outside, where cars whizzed by, agitated him. The illuminated windows of stores were jarring, like they shouldn't be situated so close to one another, and so close to the street, and they shouldn't be blazing so violently.

"It's telemarketing. I do telemarketing," said the guy.

"Telemarketing? You answer the telephone? You make phone calls. I hang up on people like you."

"I don't care. I really don't."

As the bus slowed to a halt and the doors, with a hydraulic squeal, parted, Emily said, *Watch him! Watch him!!*

And she was right. Freddy caught John trying to conceal the fact that he was studying Freddy. Guiltily, John glanced out the front door, hoping to appear casual, but it was obvious he was measuring something, making calculations. It seemed to Freddy that John was trying to determine the exact number of passengers about to enter from the street. Freddy checked and saw that there were at least two, though there might be more. His angle of vision was bad. John leaned forward, as if relaxing. He pretended to look at the floor, but Freddy suspected that this change in position was really a weight shift to prepare him to run. The last passenger stepped aboard. The driver reached to activate the control that shut the door. And John sprang for the street.

Now!

Freddy vaulted to follow. But for all his readiness, he was late. The rear door clamped its rubber grip on his leg, and he had to shout and struggle. By the time he broke loose, John was climbing into the dark. He was running away from the business district and heading for the outskirts of town. There were still street lights and homes, but they were becoming fewer. The uncivilized gaps grew larger, until they reached a point on one side of the street not far ahead, where they stopped completely.

Pulling out the Glock, Freddy worked a round into the chamber. The bus ride had been good for him. He felt rejuvenated, and he was determined to gamble with a spurt. Concentrating on breathing and holding a pace, he saw John veer, wafting like a large piece of paper into the road. On an upward diagonal, John cut for the darker, uninhabited landscape.

Freddy was still gaining. But his mood was emptying out, a sudden weakness overtaking him. He had to cross the street, and when he pushed off, he felt a twinge in his knee like a nail being driven in from the back. The sensation hobbled him for a stride, and he slowed, grabbing his leg. His heart was hammering again. The odd breath that came out of him was a kind of bleating sob. If he kept this up, he was going to blow a fucking valve. On his own stunned face, he saw his father's dying stupefaction and disbelief.

John appeared to be entering a cavern. It was the mammoth shadow of a hillside crowned with the saw-toothed jaggedness of fir trees. But it looked like a fortress creased with bulwarks and watchtowers. Before it stood a silver, gleaming net, girding the base of the opaque mouth. Freddy identified a chain link fence. John was against it, beginning to climb. Freddy toiled into the road, his eyes fixed on John who was scrambling for leverage and starting to rise. Freddy could hear the clatter and was about to shout when something snatched at his foot, ripping it out from under him. He'd tripped on the median in the center of the road. He slammed onto his outstretched hands nearly losing the gun. He was on his belly as a honking car boomed toward him, and he lunged back. The car made a metallic, explosive whine, and its velocity sucked at him. Scampering the rest of the way across the road, he caught the tip of his toe on the curb, but fought to stay upright. John was straddling the top of the fence. Once he was over, he could make it into the woods. Freddy thumbed back the hammer.

It's dark, and I'll never see you again.

It was like John was flying six feet off the ground at the top of the fence. Below him, a foam of water rushed down the hillside through a cement bed that flowed under the fence onto the street.

Drop him! Drop him!

John looked back.

Finish it! Be a fucking man!

The Glock flung Freddy's arms up, leaving a trail of sparks. The report was a door slam in a huge cavern. Freddy grunted or John cried out. There was a noise, a human noise. Then John plummeted straight down on the opposite side of the fence. The water jumped up around him, struggling to get away.

Freddy was staring. It was amazing how that huge vigorous figure had pivoted, and then dropped like the earth was no longer its element. Gravity had overwhelmed him. He was climbing the fence and then he stopped. Now he was sprawled motionless in the shallow creek pouring a small rapids over him.

Oh, God. Oh, God.

John Booth was dead. He'd done it. Freddy was walking up to the fence. Emily was dead. Freddy leaned and looked into the shadowy, whispering water, a strange dread starting. He was the only one who wasn't dead. Only Freddy wasn't dead. Though he tried to block it from his mind, he saw it all again. Like John yielding to the bullet atop the fence, there was no way to escape the image of that enormous shape overwhelmed by falling.

I'm waiting.

He looked at the gun in his hand.

What are you waiting for? Don't you want to join me?

John heard her and wanted to respond. He looked, expecting to see her over him, but it was the sky and a street light blurred by the violence of the bullet and the shock of his fall. Water poured across his eyes. Everything was coming back, the night, the sky, the trees leaning over him. He placed his hands to the ache just below his ear. There was blood, and a deep gouge of torn flesh that stung under the touch of his fingers.

Look at that. Look, damnit.

Stunned by the sight of the moving hand, Freddy was staring. He was tilted against the fence, peering in. He saw that John's eyes were open, and he saw that they were aware. In the strings of white water veiling John's face, and blanketing his chest, he was stirring.

Did you think it would be so easy? Is that what you thought?

John snorted three times. They were distinct and sequential, like a series of hard physical objects. He pressed his hands into the water until he found the concrete surface on which he lay, and he wrestled himself around onto his stomach and then up to his knees.

Freddy was scrambling to find another explanation for what he was seeing. His mind, in a fog of disbelief, was throwing around a hodgepodge of ideas. Anything was better than the thing he knew he was staring at. He'd shot the guy, and the guy hadn't died. And now the sonofabitch was panting like a bull and rising up, forcing his way free of the gushing rivulets that could not detain him. Like a sprinter ready for his race, he was on his hands and knees and he was pushing to rise to his feet and start away.

No, thought Freddy. What am I supposed to do? Shoot him again? Do I have to shoot him again?

John lost his footing, but the instant his knees hit the matted grass and dirt, he struggled upright, clawing at trees to work his way up the slope.

I shot him! *I did it!* He grabbed the top of the fence, kicking and straining. He fought until he straddled the strut that he held in both hands. Swinging his leg over, he let himself drop, landing in the water where John had fallen minutes ago.

Up the slope John was swallowed in a whispering curtain of shrubs. Freddy looked at the gun. He started to climb. It was a pathless labyrinth, a muddle. Tree limbs and shrubs and their shadows fell in a coalescing density that appeared impassable until he strode through. Low branches and drooping wet leaves crawled over his face like the bellies of worms. He couldn't see John, and the uproar of his own advance drowned out every other sound. Then he shoved open a thicket and stepped through the gap into the wide, uninhabited spaces of a field. He had to find him.

Rolling terrain marked with stones lay before him, a dispersion of rocky fragments widespread in well-tended grass. The moon shed a chill gleam. Fifty or so yards ahead, John was walking along a pathway. He veered abruptly, staggering among the stones.

Well, I've been waiting.

It was a cemetery, Freddy stood facing a marble slab on an upraised platform with two bronze statues, a bold little girl squatting to peer into the eyes of a sturdy little lamb, as if she were about to demand the answer to a challenging question.

Look at all the dead. All except you and John.

The icy sensation spreading in the back of his throat threatened to set his teeth chattering. *Did you ever stop to think that life could go on without you?* He took little sips of air, fearful that he might suddenly become unable to breathe at all. *And your foolish pride burn a hole right through you.*

Beyond the sturdy metal figures of the lamb and child outlined in moonlight, John was a distant white blur crumpling to the ground. He lay on his belly with his arms outspread, a haze of moonlight covering him with an underwater texture, the floating gravestones hunks of coral. Though Freddy still carried the gun, he knew he was not chasing John anymore. He had chased him and chased him, but now something else was happening. He felt he was following.

Yes, said Emily. *Yes.*

Maybe that was what he was doing all along. Right from the start.

Let me go, she said.

Following him to this place.

Dread arose from the ground, enshrouding him with its damp and foggy powers. He could feel it wrapping around him, numbing him, encrusting him.

When he arrived over John on his belly in the grass, Freddy knew exactly where he was, before John rolled over and uncovered the grave. Still Freddy was startled to see it and to read it.

EMILY GALE

1981–1988

Tender Child Rest In Heaven

And to see the color. "It's pink. Emily's stone is pink," said Freddy.

It was a rosy square of flat, speckled granite set into the dirt. It was level with the grass, and he was kneeling in order to reach toward the stone.

Once more she said, *Let me go.*

No, he thought. No, no. But something was erupting when his fingers touched her name, and he couldn't stop it. Only the gravestone seemed to hold it back, and then that was not enough. The thing started to reach out to him, rising against the plug of her little pink tomb, until it burst out to wrap around him, an excruciating pain and a feeling of light, like diamonds disgorged from the belly of the earth in a spiral whose adornment was awful, a violent, savage radiance swaddling him, and he writhed and wailed in its embrace.

He reached for the gun, wanting to end it. Wanting to escape. But he couldn't find it. He'd dropped it, and it was gone. And the light was everywhere, and it was inexplicable, and it hurt.

"FRED GALE!" said a bellowing voice. "DOWN THERE! FRED GALE, WE WOULD LIKE YOU TO STAND AND PLACE YOUR HANDS OVER YOUR HEAD!"

Through the crookedness of his grief, Freddy saw great wheels of illumination sweeping over the field toward him. They covered him. And their source was a fiery figure on the crest of the hill, a bonfire around a smoldering shape. It was a car stationed behind the blaze of its headlights, and a searchlight, too, all trained down the sloping landscape toward him, flowing over the graves to where Freddy and John lay in the grass.

A fragmentary pair of lights broke loose, two figures bearing them away from the car. They were coming toward him. It was people with flashlights, he realized. In the hands of people, flashlights were dropping down the hill. Then he recognized the voice; he remembered the face. It was Dennis bellowing on his loudspeaker. Dennis was walking down the slope with his partner. The police, he thought, wondering if he should stand, as they had ordered, wondering if he should raise his hands. The police were walking down to arrest him. Well, okay, he needed a rest.

34

■ ■ ■ ■ ■ ■ ■

Letters were dropping through Mary's sleep, like starlight crossing
light-years. Other galaxies were poised beyond her patient, waiting
gaze. Though visible, they could not be seen, their site so remote no
evidence of them had arrived yet. Only the Andromeda nebulae, a
ghostly haze, had traveled the hundreds of millions of light-years to
proffer its existence. Like the sender of the letters Mary was eager to
read, the Andromeda nebulae could have already ceased to exist
before this moment in which she saw its aura approaching on a gesture flung out long ago.

Dear Mommy,
  The wind, the wind, the wind.

Dear Mommy,
  The ship, the ship, the ship.

Dear Mommy,
  The sea, the sea, the sea.
                    All my love, my little Mommy.
                            Emily, Emily, Emily

Mary woke reaching for Emily's pen on the bedside table, intending to jot down a thought. Directly before her the window framed stars and inky streaks of darkness. She had no idea what it was she had awoken to write. The stars were unreadable. With their spangle and dispersion, they struck her as melancholy musical notes. They seemed the elements of a mournful language, like Chinese characters raining down the page. She'd heard sadness in her sleep. That's what had awoken her, not a thought, but sadness. And now, as the edges of her waking consciousness were stabilizing, she realized it was in the room. The feeling filled the room. The gasps of a child, losing all hope of assistance. It seemed to come from the walls. As she raised herself on her elbow, her eyes were trained on the corner where her senses, sorting the matter, zeroed her in. A pile of shadows trembled, sections shifting under an insistent moonlight to reveal a patch of cloth, a family of jolly bears in red shirts eating bowls of soup around a campfire.

"Anthony?" she said.

The sobbing was swallowed in a gasp.

"Anthony, honey, is there something wrong?"

"No."

"Why aren't you in bed, then?"

"I don't know." His words were like the efforts of someone seeking handholds in mud. "Go back to sleep, Mommy," he said.

"Come over here."

"You need your rest, Mommy."

Roger heaved from his back to his side, shoving with his knees against her as he flapped around. "What's going on?"

"Ohhhh, noooo," said Anthony. "Now I woke Daddy."

"What's wrong? Is something wrong?"

"Anthony was in the corner."

"What corner? That corner? He's still there. What's he doing there?" He sat up blinking.

"Come here, Anthony," said Mary. "Please."

"What time is it?" said Roger.

Anthony, with a despairing wheeze, broke from his refuge, heading to the center of the room where the moonlight was strong. The shadows thinned, yet he remained concealed. Then with one last step, he brought his flushed, stained face into view. He stood there in his pajamas decorated with bears eating soup.

"I need some medicine," he said.

Mary was already on her way to complete their rendezvous. "You have a fever, Little Man," she said, her palm pressing his face.

"I was dreaming of falling down buildings."

"Oh, no," she said.

"Yes." She was chaperoning him directly across to the bed, as he tendered his perturbed report. "Boom, boom, boom."

"What kind of buildings?" said Roger.

"Big ones. One after the other."

Mary slipped into the bathroom, as Roger assisted Anthony up onto the bed. When she emerged with a damp cloth, a tumbler of water, and a bottle of children's aspirin, Anthony was sitting cross-legged on her pillow gazing off.

She climbed in beside him, and smiled, as he turned his trusting face to her, his mouth opening to take the aspirin she was tapping into her palm. His tongue, a pink soft offering of his interior to her, took the pills and then hovered, awaiting instruction. "Swallow," she said, tipping the water to his lips.

He drank dutifully, and then said, "They were all buildings I didn't ever see before but I didn't like them falling."

"No," she said. "I would think not."

"It wasn't nice."

He lay back and she placed the cool wash cloth over the tiny curve of his forehead. Touching Roger, she said, "He should sleep with us, Roger, don't you think?"

"Sure."

Anthony looked at her and said, "Do you know that Andrew snores?"

"No."

"He does."

That was the last of his concerns. In seconds, his breathing evened out. Minutes later, Roger was gone, too. The washcloth had warmed up, so she removed it. As she lay there she felt that her alert and wakeful state separated her from the man and boy sleeping beside her. Her palm on Anthony's brow sought to measure his temperature. And it seemed he had cooled. Turning on her side, she let her hand fall to the pillow beneath his head. She scooped herself around him, a shell to the shape of his tiny body. She pressed her nose to his shoulder, sniffing the skin, and then she inhaled. Breathing him in.